"PUT THE KNIFE DOWN, MORGAN."

Tremayne skirted the desk, all dark and sleek and ominous. He made an awesome sight of towering, primal man. Resolve and purpose honed every muscle in every limb as he eased closer to her, stealing her space. Had the time and place been different, Morgan would have welcomed the chance to meet a man like him.

His smoky blue eyes narrowed fractionally, pinning her with his intent.

"I'll admit you aren't the pirate I expected to find onboard this ship, but you're still a pirate who has a price on her head for murder. Drop the knife. I don't want to hurt you."

A pensive shadow passed over his face as his gaze skimmed down her body, then up again. Evidently her fear showed on her face, because Tremayne used a tone gentler than she'd thought him capable of. A softness she didn't dare trust. "Drop the knife, Morgan."

He took another step. She sucked in a breath. In a blinding move, he caught the wrist of the hand that held the knife and bent her arm behind her, clamping it against her back. Then he caught her other wrist.

"Drop it," he ordered, his breath hot against her face.

Seconds passed. She felt the strong, responding thud of Tremayne's heart against her chest, felt the tension in the solid arm that crushed her body to his.

"Are you going to kill me now?" Morgan taunted through gritted teeth.

To her alarm, he didn't answer, but went still. Heat purled off him, soaking through her clothes, warming her chilled skin when it should have left her prickly with abhorrence. With his free hand, he grazed his thumb across her cheekbone.

"A woman like you has no place at sea," he said, his voice so low and rough and puzzled, she thought he must have been speaking to himself. "You obviously need a man to take care of you."

"Is that an offer, Tremayne?"

Dear Romance Reader,

In July, we launched the Ballad line with four new series, and each month we'll present both new and continuing stories set everywhere from medieval England to the American West—the kind of passionate, romantic stories you love best, written by the most gifted authors. At the back of each book, we'll tell you when you can find subsequent books in the series that has captured your heart.

Beloved author Jo Ann Ferguson continues her *Shadow of the Bastille* series with **A Brother's Honor,** as a French privateer and the spirited daughter of an American ship captain brave Napoleon's blockade and discover the legacy that will shape their passionate destiny. Next, rising star Cynthia Sterling invites us back to the dusty Texas Panhandle as the second of her *Titled Texans* learns the ropes of ranching from an independent—and irresistibly attractive—woman who wants to become a lady in **Last Chance Ranch**.

Beginning this month is newcomer Tammy Hilz's breathtaking *Jewels of the Sea* series, a trilogy of three sisters who take their futures in their own hands—as pirates! In the first installment, a stubborn earl wonders if the fearless woman who was **Once A Pirate** will decide to become his bride. Finally, fresh talent Kelly McClymer introduces the unconquerably romantic Fenster family in her *Once Upon A Wedding* series, starting with a woman whose faith in happy endings is challenged as a man who refuses to believe in love asks her to become **The Fairy Tale Bride**. Enjoy!

Kate Duffy
Editorial Director

Jewels of the Sea:
ONCE A PIRATE

Tammy Hilz

ZEBRA BOOKS
KENSINGTON PUBLISHING CORP.

http://www.zebrabooks.com

ZEBRA BOOKS are published by

Kensington Publishing Corp.
850 Third Avenue
New York, NY 10022

First Printing: October, 2000
10 9 8 7 6 5 4 3 2 1

Printed in the United States of America

For my agent, Roberta Brown
Thanks for believing.

Prologue

England, 1760

" 'Tis an omen, I tell you." Joanna, the middle of the three sisters, scowled at the barrier of swirling fog, daring it to creep closer. Red curls clung like fresh wounds to her sharp cheekbones and stubborn chin. She brushed them back with an impatient swipe of her hand. "Nothing good ever comes from a storm such as this. And after everything else we've suffered. . ."

Wind howled through the deserted cove, churning brackish water over a beach littered with rocks and tangled seaweed. Salty mist sprayed a cluster of battered dwellings, all dark and quiet and crumbling from neglect. Bruised clouds surged beyond the mouth of the lagoon, isolating the small village as if the vast ocean beyond no longer existed.

"Jo, you think everything's an omen," Grace said, her young voice barely audible over the rustle of trees fighting the chaotic gusts. "We have to make sure everyone is safe. Isn't that so, Morgan?"

"Aye, angel. The elders will surely need our help." Morgan Fisk, the eldest of the Fisk daughters, drew the nine-year-old, tallow-haired girl close to her side as they skirted the small fishing boats half buried in sand. Barrels once filled with cheap ale meant for market were split open as if cleaved by a fine-honed ax. Fish had been washed ashore, hundreds of them, all struggling to breathe the thin, damp air, and all without any means of returning to the sea.

They'd had storms before, but Morgan couldn't remember one so wicked or lasting so long. They'd endured three days of brutal, slashing rain. Fist-sized hail had punched holes through the roof of their small cottage. They'd scurried for safety beneath tables and beds. The wind had screeched like a wounded animal. The unholy, terrifying sound had been endless and unnerving. Grace had shivered in her arms, certain the mythical sea monster Scylla was coming after them all.

Morgan followed Joanna's worried gaze. There were no twelve-headed monsters with razor-sharp fangs amidst the debris, but there was a heartrending amount of wreckage. It would take a fortnight to repair her home, but she couldn't begin until she knew everyone else in her village had survived unscathed.

" 'Tis a bloody, hopeless mess," her Uncle Simon grumbled, coming up beside her. Age and painful joints had caused his dismissal from the king's navy, a condition he still hadn't forgiven his body for. "Lass, I'd say our cup is empty of luck, and our slop bucket is overflowing with trouble."

"Aye," Joanna answered for her. "And there's no one to take care of this waste but us."

Morgan sighed, suddenly feeling far older than her one and twenty years, not knowing how they would survive this latest blow.

"Where's me boat?" Ian Woods, a lean, gangly fisherman, asked, his voice breaking as he joined them on the cluttered beach. " 'Tis gone. They're all gone!"

Morgan wanted to put her arm around his narrow shoulders, but the way he stood, tall and trembling, his eyes brimming with defeat, kept her from moving. "Don't worry, Ian. We'll put it to right."

"Put it to right?" Jo scoffed. "The skiffs are either sitting at the bottom of the cove or they've been tossed into the trees. How can you possibly make this right?"

"Joanna!" Morgan scolded. Emotions would be low enough; she didn't need one of her own sisters making matters worse.

"She's right, Morgan."

She turned at the sound of Henry Solley's voice. She hadn't heard him or the rest of the elders approach. They were huddled together in a circle of fear and ruin, all looking to her once again for answers. "We can build new boats, Henry," Morgan said.

"Such a feat will take months, as you well know." The stocky, barrel-chested blacksmith turned and swept a thick-muscled arm through the air, drawing their attention to the desolate village. "Our food stores have been scavenged by the king's soldiers. In their haste to join the fight in Africa they've trampled our fields. What shall we do for food while we rebuild our skiffs?" He shook his head. "It pains me to say this, girl, especially knowing how hard you've tried, but the time to move to London 'as come."

"No!" Morgan held out her hands, imploring the others to listen to her. "We can't give up now. We've faced far worse than this. We can survive, I promise you."

"Our hearts aren't in it, lass." Henry took her hand in his, tightening his callused fingers around her slender ones. " 'Twill be easier to start over in the city."

This is our home."

"Morgan, lass," the blacksmith said. "Accept our fate."

"I can't." She searched the familiar faces that were drawn and weary. They wanted to stay; she knew it.

"We can't remain in Dunmore," Henry said. "To do so means certain death. If we had our boats . . ." He shrugged. "Or if our young men were here instead of fighting that bloody war . . ."

Morgan closed her eyes, envisioning all the able men who'd left her village to fight for glory in the name of the Crown. Peter Goodson had been among them, all smiles and eagerness to do his part in subduing the French. Had he remained, she'd be his wife now. She hadn't burned with love for him, but she cared for him. Their marriage could have been a good one. And though it shamed her to admit it, she wanted someone to share her burden with. She was tired. So very tired of being strong.

She felt a smothering pressure tighten her chest, the same pressure she'd felt the day her parents died, leaving the care of her siblings to her. A fine job she'd done, too. She'd lost her young brother to a severe bout of croup shortly afterward. Now, four years later, she was in danger of losing their home. The fate of her entire village rested on her shoulders, as it had her father's shoulders before her. She had to be confident and sure of what needed to be done; they were counting on her. She pressed her fingers to her temple to relieve the ache. *Think, Morgan, think.* There had to be a way to save her village.

"He may be right, niece," Uncle Simon muttered, his expression pained as he rubbed his swollen knuckles.

"No," she whispered. She'd fought to keep her family together; she'd plowed fields until her hands bled. She couldn't give up now and move to London where they'd be working the docks for a pittance, or more likely, begging in the streets, or worse.

She felt a tug on her sleeve. Grace stared up at her, her pale brows drawn into a frown. Morgan ran her hand over the girl's tangled blond hair. "Don't worry, angel. I'll find a way for us to stay."

"Oh, I'm not worried, Morgan. You always take care of everything. But what is that?" Grace pointed toward the mouth of the bay. A bank of mist billowed and swirled as if reluctant to release its grip on the narrow inlet. Shadows loomed in the center, growing darker and taking shape as the fog slowly pulled away. A long wooden pole, two dozen feet above sea level, stabbed through the haze, revealing a torn outer jib, the sail draping toward the water like a victim slain in battle.

"Look, it's a lady!" Grace squealed.

"What the bloody hell?" Ian muttered, his voice reflecting the stunned gazes fastened on the sight. "It *is* a lady."

Carved from solid oak, the lady with flowing hair, outstretched arms and tapered body was attached to the hull of a ship. At the tip of the main mast, a black flag snapped in the wind. A painted white skeleton grinned down at her, his bony hand raised in a toast of death.

"Lord love us," Joanna whispered. "Morgan, what do we do now?"

"Run," Ian shouted. "Henry, take the children. Hide!"

Morgan stared at the pirate ship. It floated toward them like a vessel of doom. She knew she should help the elders to safety, but she couldn't move. After all they'd faced, and all they'd lost, how was she supposed to fight this?

Chapter 1

Three years later

"Captain Egham's dead."

Disbelief spread in a blinding heat through Daniel Tremayne's body. He wanted to deny the biting words that hung in the air like poison. Instead, he crushed the manifest detailing the cargo stolen from his merchant ship *Intrepid* in his fist. He looked across his desk, where his partner, Thomas Burke, trembled like a soldier who'd gone too long without food or water or victories.

Dark circles bruised the lower half of Thomas's brown eyes. His gaunt cheeks belonged to that of a starving man, not the robust, jovial peer who'd been pivotal in helping Daniel start World Quest Shipping. During the last five years, he and Thomas had been to hell and back, facing financial ruin together, the loss of their ancestral homes, public disgrace—all because both had possessed fathers wealthy in friends and short on sense.

Daniel had faced so many setbacks and challenges, he'd thought that nothing would surprise him ever again.

He'd been wrong.

Seated at his desk aboard the *Valiant,* he looked out the bay of windows lining one wall of his cabin to where the *Intrepid* was harbored. The three-mast ship had limped into London's port moments before Daniel had given the order to set sail for another run to India. *Pirates.* He strangled back a curse. Lost cargo and a damaged ship were bad enough. But the loss—no, the *murder*—of Captain Egham, a longtime friend and employee, turned him cold with outrage.

He fisted his hands on the arms of his chair. "How?"

Thomas turned away from Daniel and looked about the cabin as if unsure how he got there. "I still can't believe it happened," he said, running both his hands through wheat-colored hair that reached his shoulders. In a stunned voice, he said, "I've never seen a man murdered before."

Daniel wished he could say the same. He and Thomas might be partners, and were as close to brothers as two friends could be, but during the last two years, their lives had taken different paths. With his wealth restored, Daniel had decided to repair his family name by voluntarily joining the King's Navy, bringing two of his ships into service with him. Since then, he'd seen enough death and slaughter to last ten lifetimes.

Thomas had remained in town to manage the company. He had a way of sniffing out opportunity that amazed even Daniel, and besides, there had been no one he trusted more to leave in his stead. To see his friend beaten down and trembling with fear brought out something vicious and protective in Daniel.

"Excuse me, Capt'n," Hugh Tobitt, Daniel's first officer, interrupted as he eased his big, rough-hewn body into the cabin. "The crew's restless tae leave. Should I tell 'em tae keep their shirts on or stand down for the night?"

Daniel rose from his chair and faced the panel of diamond-shaped windowpanes framing the back wall. He stared unseeing at the sprawling city. *Murder.* The muscles along his back tensed in anticipation of Thomas's explanation. The sun still sat high over London, giving Daniel enough time to navigate the Thames River before nightfall. But leaving without knowing what had befallen his ship and friend was out of the question. "Tell the crew we'll sail at dawn."

Looking over his shoulder, he asked Thomas, "Which pirate attacked you?"

"The devil's daughter, herself," Thomas spat. "Morgan the Scylla."

"And you come away with your hair and teeth still in your head?" Tobitt gasped.

Daniel turned in time to see his first officer mouth what appeared to be a prayer. "I never thought you a religious man, Tobitt."

"Ain't had the need before. But anyone who's faced that monster and walked away is deserv'n' of a little extra protection."

Daniel stared at the crewman who'd been in his service since he'd joined the Seven Years War. Equal to Daniel's six-foot-two-inch height, he outweighed him by seven stone. No one, including Tobitt himself, knew how old he was. He'd been born in the Mediterranean, somewhere between Tangiers and Athens. His mother had disappeared soon after, leaving Tobitt to be raised as a sea rat on one sailing vessel or another. The full-grown result was a man with a pittance of coarse manners, a vast knowledge of all things belonging to the sea, and a profound hatred of the land. Once, Daniel had ordered Tobitt ashore to organize the loading of supplies, but the man had turned green at the idea of standing on solid ground and had puked his stew.

But in all their time together facing down the French and cannon fire and fallen mates, Daniel had never seen anything frighten the burly, leathery-skinned seaman. Until now.

"I don't know how ye escaped with yer life, Mr. Burke," Tobitt continued. "But you're surely among a lucky few."

"I don't believe this, Tobitt," Daniel said with reproach. "You sound as if you're afraid of a blasted woman!"

"Any man who says he ain't 'fraid of Morgan the Scylla is a man who's either lying or a fool."

"He's right, Daniel," Thomas said, filling a tumbler with a hefty shot of whiskey from the decanter on Daniel's desk.

"Tell me what happened."

Thomas downed the amber liquid. He winced, then shuddered as it landed in his gut. "We were on our way home, navigating through the Canary Islands when the *Sea Queen* came upon us during the night. I tell you, Daniel, the sky was as black as sin. Nothing could be seen. There was no wind. We sat in water as slick as a sheet of glass."

Daniel had been at sea many a night when light, the stir of air and all sound fell away, leaving his vessel trapped in a motionless void. On those nights, a man could go insane fearing the rest of the world had vanished, leaving him alone and drifting.

"Go on," Daniel said.

"Before we realized what was happening, Morgan anchored her ship to the *Intrepid* with grappling lines. Her entire crew boarded us, faceless demons who moved like ghosts."

"Bloody hell," Tobitt whispered.

"You don't know how right you are," Thomas said, his face flushing with a surge of anger. He wiped a shaking hand over his mouth. "She demanded Captain Egham relinquish his cargo. I told him to do as she ordered, but he refused."

For the first time since stepping into the cabin, Thomas met Daniel's gaze, and revealed the depth of his guilt and pain. "She murdered him. In front of everyone. I tried to stop her, but she had me bound, forced me to watch. Without another word, or any sign of feeling or remorse, she pulled a knife studded with jewels from her belt and slit him from gullet to bowel, then ordered him tossed overboard as fodder for the sharks.''

"Jesus," Daniel said.

"He was lucky, then," Tobitt stated, shaking his head.

"What in blazes do you mean by that?" Daniel demanded.

"She killed half the crew, too," Thomas whispered, swallowing as if struggling to keep the whiskey down. "I couldn't stop her. God knows I tried, but I . . ." he bent his head and stared at the floor.

"They're better off dead, Mr. Burke. Surely you've heard what she does to her captives." Tobitt threw a fearful glance toward the door. "She peels the flesh off her victims."

"Nonsense." Daniel had heard the rumors before. Morgan the Scylla; Morgan the daughter of Satan; Morgan the Bloodthirsty who stalks the seas in search of helpless male victims. "The captain of the *Sea Queen* isn't a demon. She's a pirate who must be stopped. For too long she's been allowed to pillage the seas. It's time she faced England's court for her crimes against her country."

And me, Daniel mentally added. Feeling the slow burn of revenge bleed through his veins, he vowed he'd make her pay for the death of Captain Egham and his crew.

"After skinning 'em," Tobitt continued as if he hadn't heard Daniel, "she eats their flesh while the poor buggers are alive and watch'n'. God rest poor Capt'n Egham's soul, but he died luckier than most."

"Hugh," Daniel said, tempted to either laugh at the brawny privateer or shake some sense into his sorely impressionable mind. But at the moment, the vise squeezing his spine made laughter of any sort, and for any reason, impossible. "You don't honestly believe these gruesome tales, do you?"

"There's more." Hugh's eyes widened as he warmed to his story, mindless that Thomas had collapsed in a chair and held his head in his hands. "She collects the skulls and uses 'em for soup bowls."

"Hugh, for God's sake, man—"

"But that ain't the worst, Capt'n," Tobitt warned. "Should ye be ill-fated enough to come face tae face with Scylla, and should she remove her eye patch, ye must guard your jigger-bone. One look from her hideous, distorted eye and your family jewels'll be noth'n' more than dust at your feet. You being the last male in the Tremayne line, ye better hope ye never cross her path, or ye can kiss any future heirs a sad fare-thee-well."

Tobitt sent a stricken look to Thomas as if he worried that that fate might have already befallen the other man.

Daniel stared at his first mate, unsure how, or if he should even bother trying, to respond to such utter rubbish. He couldn't imagine a man gaining such a nefarious reputation, but for a woman to possess one . . . No, Morgan the Scylla or whatever the hell name she went by was nothing more than a murdering, thieving cutthroat. She may be unique to her gender and evil as a pirate, but that's all she was—evil. And she'd made the mistake of raiding his ship and killing his captain.

"Tobitt," Daniel said, though his attention was on his best friend and partner as Thomas sloshed whiskey into a tumbler, then sat staring at the brown liquid as if he were afraid to drink. "Tell the helmsman to set a heading for the Canary Islands."

"We're chang'n' heading, sir?"

"That we are, Tobitt. We're going to find Morgan, and we're going to bring her in. Before the month is out, I'm going to watch her hang at Executioner's Dock."

"Ye can't be mean'n' tae go after her, Capt'n. It's certain death for all of us."

Thomas stirred enough to raise his head and look at Daniel. "You'll never find her. And it's not worth risking the cargo waiting in the Indies. Captain Egham's dead. It's best to cut our losses and move on."

"How can you say such a thing?" Daniel demanded, fisting his hands, barely able to contain his growing rage. "How can you ignore what she did?"

Thomas pushed himself up from his chair, his lean face contorted with grief. "I can say it because I was there. I don't want the same happening to you, Daniel. Finding her isn't worth your life!"

Daniel met his friend's determined gaze. He understood Thomas's fear, felt the power of it trembling from the other man's body. But he couldn't let it sway him.

"Don't do it, Daniel," Thomas pleaded.

"I have no choice."

"Then God be with you, but I'll not accompany you on a mission of death."

Daniel nodded, understanding his friend's decision. Thomas believed that Morgan the Scylla was a demon of the sea who preyed on the weak and ill fated. But Daniel knew differently. She was only a woman, a fact Daniel had to forcefully put from his mind. Because while she *was* a woman, she was also a monster.

One he intended to destroy.

"Mr. Tobitt," Daniel said, facing the window once more. "You have your orders."

"She's dropped her sails, Captain!" Jackson, the helmsman, called from his perch on the main topcastle.

"Aye, Jackson. Come down and take the wheel. I'll send a watchman up to keep an eye on them." Standing on the forecastle, her legs braced on the sturdy bleached deck, Morgan adjusted her telescope. The other ship had first been spotted after sunrise when it had barely been a speck on the horizon. With the sloop perched on the sea like a contented duck, the *Sea Queen* had unfurled her sails, quickly closing the gap.

"Be careful, Jackson," Grace called, then turned worried blue eyes to Morgan. "I wish you wouldn't send him up there. It's dangerous."

"Jackson is surefooted," Morgan said absently, knowing what was coming next. Her sister had designated herself as Jackson's guardian angel, but Morgan knew Grace's feelings ran far deeper. She'd once tried explaining to Grace that she was still a child, and that Jackson was almost a man who only cared about the sea and the freedom it gave him. But her sister had tilted her rounded chin and proclaimed that she and Jackson were destined for each other. Morgan decided not to argue. Who was she to question destiny?

"He could get hurt," Grace said, biting her bottom lip.

"Best not say that to his face," Jo scoffed, joining them. "You're liable to hurt his pride."

"Someone has to watch out for him."

"Since you're in love with him," Jo quipped, "we'll leave that task to you."

"Jo, you shouldn't tease her," Morgan said, watching Grace head for Jackson, no doubt with the intention of telling him to stay away from ratlines.

"There's a good north-northeast wind blowing," Joanna said drawing Morgan's attention back to the other ship. "Why would they drop sail?"

"Perhaps they're making repairs of some kind." Morgan handed her sister the "bring-me-closer" and squinted against the bright morning sun.

Jo made a scoffing sound that rivaled any sailor's. "If that's the *Valiant* the longshoremen at Goree Island told us about, she should have made repairs while in port. Now she's a goose wait'n' for slaughter. Just look how low her belly's sitting in the water. Her hull must be fair to bursting with rum and gold."

"Not for us," Morgan muttered, though her tone was more forceful than she meant it to be.

"What's the word, Morgan?" Uncle Simon said as he climbed the last step to the upper deck. "Do we hold back and move in to raid them tonight? Luck's with us. There'll hardly be a sliver of moon. Or do we let 'em go?"

"I've already told the crew." Morgan ignored her sister's restless fidgeting. "We're not taking any more ships. Now that the war is over, King George III has renewed his pledge to hunt down and hang all pirates. It's too risky. We'll be home soon. Home to stay." She smiled, more ready than she'd realized to relinquish her command. "We should consider ourselves lucky that we've survived this long and will be returning to Dunmore far richer than when we left."

"We could be richer still," Joanna insisted sullenly. "I say we take her."

Morgan brushed a strand of gleaming auburn hair from her sister's cheek. The younger woman jerked away as always, her eyes narrowing in warning.

"Joanna," Morgan said, wishing she knew how to break through the stone wall that Jo had built around her heart. She had tried to help her sister, but Jo's guilt stemmed from a loss Morgan couldn't replace. Perhaps returning to their old life would change that. Perhaps . . . "It's time to go home."

Morgan arched her back and rolled her head from side to side, easing the tension pinching her shoulders. She usually found comfort when studying her maps, but not today. After leaving Jo on watch, she'd sequestered herself in her cabin, needing time alone to consider the future. And the past.

She fingered the worn edge of the yellowing parchment that charted the Guinea Basin. The map was one of her most valued possessions, taken from a Spanish merchant ship the year before.

In quiet moments when the ocean was calm and a gentle wind pushed the *Sea Queen* toward a new destination, she often thought about the miracle that had brought her to this place and time. Three years ago her village had faced fear and starvation, the loss of their homes and a soul-shattering poverty that would have resulted in a slow and demeaning death. Then a pirate ship had grounded in their small cove, delivering salvation in a way they'd never imagined.

But save them it had. Morgan smiled as she picked up the dagger she'd found impaled in the very desk she sat at now. She angled the blade, balancing the familiar weight in her palm, feeling the metal warm against her skin as if it were waking from a long, comforting sleep. A thumb-size sapphire, ruby and emerald were embedded in the crafted gold hilt. Light winked in their depth, a teasing glimmer of secrets locked within—like what had happened to the original crew? The forged blade of Venetian steel gleamed like silver, polished bright to catch her reflection. The knife's value alone would have fed her village for a year, repaired homes, bought livestock. But she'd never been able to sell it, not after what she'd done to claim it.

Alone, she'd scaled the Jacob's ladder to the taffrail, as afraid of what she'd find as she was excited. Reflecting on her actions, she realized how insane and desperate her feat had been. The ship could have been filled with cutthroats looking for a place to hide. It could have carried victims dying of the plague. But the decks had been empty, her raspy breath an echo through deserted companionways as she searched for signs of life.

That was when she'd entered the captain's cabin and found the dagger with the ship's name engraved on its blade. *Sea Queen.* An idea had come to her then, as insane as it was daring. Once she'd shared her plan with the villagers, Joanna and Grace had readily agreed to it, as she'd known they would. Convincing the elders to become pirates had been another matter entirely.

They'd called her mad, but she'd seen the wishful gleam in the men's eyes. They were beyond their prime, but most of them were seamen. To be able to sail beyond their stretch of coast in search of something besides a day's catch would be like giving them back their youth. She'd dared them to take their chances at sea instead of moving to London with the throng of other starving souls.

She'd almost had them convinced until her uncle had claimed that it would be a calamity to have a female on board. She'd shown them the blade. "Having women on their ship wouldn't be bad luck," she'd told them. "Because the *Sea Queen* had been named for a woman and a woman would captain her."

That had been three years ago. And not once had she, or anyone else, regretted their decision. Though the path hadn't always been easy.

Having often accompanied her father on his fishing boat, she thought she'd known what to expect. She'd quickly realized she knew nothing about sailing such a massive ship. But she and her sisters had learned everything her uncle could teach them. He'd boasted that his nieces had taken to the ocean like fish to water. Morgan had to admit that learning to chart a course, understanding the currents and reading the stars had been easy. Even estimating their latitude by measuring the distance of the sun had come to her naturally, as if she'd known how all along; she'd just needed reminding.

Then she'd set out to accomplish her driving goal: save her village. By sharing the plunder she took from other ships, she rebuilt their homes, replaced the fishing boats they'd lost, bought livestock and seed for their fields.

Now it was time to give up her nomadic, dangerous life at sea. And become what?

Along the back curved wall of her cabin, small, fitted panes created a gallery of windows. She rose from her desk, opened one panel and breathed in cool, salty air. She would replant her small fields, she mused, live from season to season instead of day to day. Perhaps if Peter had survived the war, he would ask her to marry him again. That is, if he didn't mind having an ex-pirate with a bounty on her head for a wife.

Peter's wife. Where she'd once dreamed for that to happen, if only to have someone to turn to, share the weight of her responsibilities, she didn't know how she felt about marriage now. She wanted a home and children; there was no disputing that. But marriage for the sake of having a husband, a mate she wasn't in love with . . . She pushed away the doubting questions that she rarely allowed to surface. There was no point in worrying about loving her husband. Peter might not want her, or he might be dead.

She sighed and started to turn away, only to stop as the sun slanted past the deck above her and shot a rainbow of iridescent light across the room. Morgan frowned. The sun shouldn't be behind her, but to the west. Had someone changed course? She stared at the deck above her, her heart starting a slow, pounding thud in her chest as she remembered the other listing ship. Her sister wouldn't have dared. She wouldn't.

"Joanna!"

"How could you go against my orders?" Morgan demanded, pacing before her sister, who didn't bother looking contrite but stood with her shoulders squared and her glass-green eyes bright with resolve.

"We took a vote."

"I'm captain of this vessel," Morgan stated, stopping within a foot of Joanna to meet her belligerent stare. "And I gave a direct order."

"Pardon me, Capt'n." Jackson Brodie, the orphaned fifteen-year-old who'd joined her ship after his father had been killed in the war and his mother died of consumption, was one of her most valued crewmen. She'd taken him under her wing, teaching him everything Simon had taught her. Surely he wouldn't have ignored her command.

"Did you agree to this, Jackson?" Morgan asked, clenching her hands in a vain attempt to control her temper.

"Don't blame him." Grace assumed a protective stance in front of Jackson, her round face flushed with worry.

The young helmsman took Grace by the shoulders and moved her behind him. With a wink and a grin, he said, "You don't need to protect me, angel."

He then joined ranks with Joanna. "We know ye mean well by steering clear of that treasure ship, but we—all of us—talked it over, and . . .well . . . if this is to be our last voyage, we want it to be a glorious one."

"I see." Morgan scanned the deck, meeting her uncle's affirming gaze. Henry Solley, Ian and the fifty-plus others all nodded in agreement. "Someone might have mentioned their desire for one more foray before we came within spitting distance of the *Valiant*."

"There's still a dozen leagues between us," Joanna said, all traces of willful hellion vanishing as she allowed her excitement to surface. She raised the telescope and peered across the ocean. "I still can't see the crew. Unless she raises sail, we have several hours before we catch her."

"Aye, but we've lost the element of surprise," Morgan said grimly. "They know we're here, so attacking under the protection of night won't work."

"The *Valiant* is still lagging, barely cutting a decent wake. We could circle her with our cannons blazing." Joanna's voice rose with the promise of battle. "She'd be brought down—"

"No." Morgan gripped the railing and studied the other ship. Half her sails were down, cutting her speed, which didn't make sense. "When we began this, we vowed to never take another life. I won't break that pledge now."

"*You* made that vow. *I* didn't. They're probably all English cutthroats, Morgan," Joanna said coldly. "We'd be doing the world a service by killing the dogs."

"Jo," Morgan sighed, knowing it would do no good to remind her sister that *they* were English as well. Because it was the *wealthy* English that Jo despised. "You really must curb your penchant for blood." A penchant Morgan feared their perilous way of life had encouraged. But once they were home, Jo's thirst for killing would die a natural death. Everything would change. It had to.

"Do you have a plan, Capt'n?" Jackson asked, laying a protective hand on Grace's shoulder. He missed her adoring glance.

"Aye." If her family wanted one more quest, who was she to deny them? Morgan smiled at her uncle, who, realizing she meant to attack, beamed back at her. "Aye, Jackson. I do indeed have a plan."

"She's the *Sea Queen,* all right." Daniel barely contained the excited tension straining his limbs. It had taken him two months to find her, and here she was, within his reach, begging him to attack. Only one thing stopped him—he had no idea what she was doing.

The sun had risen in the piercing, cerulean blue sky, then cresting with its westerly descent. All day long the *Sea Queen* had steadily gained on the *Valiant.* Yet none of Daniel's watches had spotted a single member of her crew. They'd reported the decks were littered with ropes, tackle and crumbled riggings. But there were no signs of a recent battle. No fires or smoke, no damage to her hull or railings.

So where were the pirates? Or more to the point, where was the captain?

The *Sea Queen*'s sails were raised high to the wind, though they weren't positioned to take full advantage of the northeast breeze. If the pirate captain didn't order them adjusted soon, at their present course they'd ram the *Valiant* unless Daniel took action. All his careful planning, including the rumor he'd spread about the rich bounty stuffed in his bays, had all come down to this moment.

Having added fourteen extra guns on the lower deck, and dividing another ten between the stern and the bow on the main, the *Valiant* rode a full strake lower in the water, giving the impression that her hull was stocked to the beams with cargo destined for England. Now he only needed his prey to take the bait.

" 'Tis a ghost ship," Hugh Tobitt uttered stoically beside Daniel.

Clenching his jaw, not wanting to hear any more fantastic tales about Morgan the Scylla, Daniel ordered, "Bring the ship around and bear us alongside her."

"Capt'n, ye can't be thinking . . ." Hugh's eyes widened as the plea died in his mouth. "I told ye what would happen."

"I heard your stories, Mr. Tobitt. Now turn my ship about." Motioning for his first officer to follow, Daniel led the way to the ship's wheel on the main deck.

"Aye, sir." Tobitt shouted the new settings for the sails. "We'll be ready for the thiev'n' bastards. This time tomorrow they'll be danc'n' from a rope around their necks and hanging from the main yard."

"I want the captain taken alive," Daniel said, his eyes never leaving the other ship.

"Ye can't be meaning to bring *her* on our ship, Capt'n!"

Daniel raised his hand to silence his first officer. "That's exactly what I intend to do. Now, before we're in range, I want a volley of cannon fire released. That should bring the pirates out of hiding."

"Aye, Capt'n, a warning shot. That should scare the swindling monsters from their nest," Hugh replied with the enthusiasm of a devout seaman sentenced to live on land.

Half an hour later, Daniel paced the bow of the main deck, stopping only to send an occasional scowl at the "ghost ship," as his crew had dubbed it. The warning shots they'd fired had gone unanswered. Every available telescope on board was fastened on the pirate ship, but as yet, no one had spotted any sign of life. Had the entire crew taken ill and died? Or, as Hugh surmised, had Morgan the Scylla turned on her men and eaten them one by one? Hugh stood by his argument that the devil-woman only waited in the shadows for Daniel's crew to board; then she'd spring her snare and capture them all.

Daniel thought it unlikely that the woman had served up her crew for supper, but he wasn't discounting the possibility of a trap. Morgan had proven herself cunning in the past, but she'd attacked the *Intrepid* at night. He had no idea what she'd do during the light of day. He doubted she'd let her ship run unmanned and unprotected for nearly a full day. At his present distance of two hundred yards, he could sink the *Sea Queen* without causing his gunmen below to break a sweat. Each knew how to swab, reload, tamp and fire a cannon in well under a minute. With the other vessel advancing like a silent demon, the job would be over before it had begun.

No, something was wrong. Either the entire crew was rotting somewhere in the lower decks or the ship was abandoned. Whatever the case, he had to go aboard and see for himself. He couldn't rest until he either had Morgan at his mercy, chained to the hull of his ship, or saw her ugly face as dead as one of her victims. He honestly didn't care which.

"Mr. Tobitt," Daniel shouted to his second, "break out the grappling lines so we can draw the ships together, then prepare to board."

The larger man's shoulders drooped, but he nodded

with a muttered, "Aye, sir," then relayed the orders. Daniel's crew was quick and efficient, and unerringly silent as they went about their work. Regardless of what their duties entailed, Daniel noted that no one took their eyes off the mysterious vessel as it quietly glided alongside the *Valiant*.

Once the lines were secure, planks were laid across the railings, creating a bridge that was only secure as long as the seas were calm. With his cutlass in one hand and his pistol in the other, Daniel crossed to the pirate ship first, leaping onto the deck and sidestepping a tangled pile of ropes.

His eyes wide and panicky as he crossed the makeshift bridge, Hugh led the dozen men Daniel had chosen to aid in the search.

Daniel motioned for his men to spread out and inspect the lower decks. No one moved, except to form a tighter circle, with their backs together and their swords facing out. Cursing under his breath, Daniel swore to dismiss the entire lot of worthless, gullible cowards once this mission was over.

"Come along, Mr. Tobitt." Since the upper deck was obviously empty, Daniel grabbed Hugh's shirtsleeve in his fist, pulling him away from the circle of whimpering sailors and toward the hatchway leading to the lower levels. "Follow me."

"Welcome aboard, Captain." The hushed, throaty voice of a woman emerged from the shadows directly in front of him, bringing him to an abrupt halt.

"It's her!" Hugh Tobitt's body jerked. He released a garbled, choking scream, then crumpled at Daniel's feet in a dead faint. More gasps and hasty prayers erupted behind him.

Morgan the Scylla, the daughter of Satan, the woman who reputedly ate her victims while they watched, parted from the shadows, though only enough to reveal a slender figure clad from shoulders to boots in black. He could see nothing of her face.

Daniel raised his pistol and took aim. "Stand where you are."

Without any outward signal from her, the barrels, piles of ropes and shredded flax sails began to move, eliciting screams from Daniel's group. Men, or perhaps they *were* demons incarnate, emerged from every part of the ship to encircle the sorry, shivering crew of the *Valiant*. They were dressed, like the woman, in pitch-colored pants and shirts. Ebony masks covered their faces, leaving only the whites of their eyes visible.

A rock flew past Daniel striking his pistol, knocking it from his grasp. Instinctively, he raised his sword.

"Drop it," the woman before him ordered. "Now."

Daniel clenched the handle of his cutlass. He may have underestimated the woman's shrewdness, but this was far from over. He hadn't searched for the murdering witch for two months only to surrender without a fight. He'd vowed to make her pay for killing Captain Egham, and by God, she would.

"We boarded your vessel because we thought you were in trouble," he lied. "We have no fight with you."

"Then why did you fire on us?"

Before he could answer, two dozen young boys, several old men, and God help him, another female, all armed with pistols and gleaming-edged swords, filed out from the lower decks. They paused at the gangplank, as if awaiting the order to go across.

"Don't make the mistake of thinking you can take my ship, Morgan," Daniel warned, nearly choking on his own fury.

"I see you've heard of me," she said in a prideful voice.

Daniel sensed her smile. He wished she'd step from the shadowed doorway so he could see how truly twisted and ugly she was. Give him a target for his hate. "Aye, I've heard of you, enough to cause me to hunt you down. Order your men to drop their weapons and move aside."

"Or else?" she asked, her voice rough and taunting.

"One word from me and my cannons will fill the *Sea Queen* with enough holes to ensure a quick death."

The woman stepped from the dark, her sword raised to his throat before Daniel could react. Hot metal bit into his skin. Warmth trickled down his neck and soaked his shirt. He didn't need to look to know it was his own blood.

"Utter that word, Captain. And it will be your last."

Chapter 2

Blast the man. Morgan watched blood trickle down the captain's corded neck. Instinctively she wanted to stanch his wound. Instead, she tightened her grip on the hilt of her sword and willed herself not to tremble. An easterly wind whistled across the deck, shifting the seas and setting the ship to rocking.

She felt certain the man glaring at her from the lethal point of her blade would rather die, his cutlass dripping with blood, before yielding to anyone, especially a woman. Murderous rage chiseled his broad cheekbones; supreme arrogance pulsed in the solid line of his jaw. He was tanned, rough-hewn and disconcerting in his brown leggings, capped boots and loose-fitting white shirt. The fabric ties, meant to stay the deep V of his shirt, hung loose and neglected, revealing a wide expanse of muscled chest dusted with curls as pitch black as the shoulder-length hair tied in a queue at the nape of his neck. A man of strength and stamina. She had to tread carefully or he might easily turn the tide and she'd be the one staring down the length of her own blade.

She'd faced countless captains in countless situations

such as this. She'd learned to deal with men who challenged her with mocking surprise, roaring outrage or even stunned disbelief. But this man was different. Never had she seen such cold hatred. Hatred that had leached from his eyes since the moment he'd stepped foot on her ship.

He knew who she was, which meant he knew of her vile reputation, though it didn't seem to affect him as it had the burley crewmate lying unconscious at his feet. If she couldn't instill terror in his heart, she'd have to find another way to assuage his temper.

"May I have your name, sir?" Comfortable in her disguise of fitted black trousers and matching coat, she wore a bandanna to cover her hair. She'd added an eye patch to her costume when she'd heard the spectacular rumors about her ability to wither certain parts of the cherished male anatomy.

A threatening pause weighted the air before he supplied an answer. "Captain Daniel Tremayne, Earl of Leighton."

Tremayne. Morgan felt her jaw drop despite her effort to remain emotionless now that he could see most of her face.

"Lord love us," one of her crew whispered somewhere behind her.

A wolfish grin lifted the corner of Tremayne's stern mouth. "I see you've heard of me as well."

A tremor slid through her body. Morgan tensed her arm. Heaven help her, she had the serpent of the King's Navy stuck like a fatted pig on the point of her sword. The one man all pirates from England to the Caribbean took great care to avoid, knowing that crossing paths with the famed Captain Tremayne meant an inevitable end of their freedom *and* their life.

It was whispered that he scoured the seas like a hungry beast, sniffing out his prey with unfailing ability. For the past few years, he'd hunted the French. But since the treaty had been signed and a tenuous peace was at hand, she surmised he was in search of new game. It was because of men like him, men who had a thirst for war, that her village had nearly died a painful, needless death.

"Who hasn't heard about your legendary escapades in the West Indies?" she said, sweetening her voice so he couldn't mistake the insult. "To hear the tale, you conquered the island of Guadeloupe single-handedly with a surprise attack. After which you executed French soldiers and burned the homes of helpless villagers to the ground. I've often wondered why King George II bothered wasting his fleet of ships and the countless men to sustain them when he had you to guard his vast claim on the seas."

Tremayne quirked a dark brow as if amused, but she knew otherwise. His steel blue gaze, focused tightly on her, turned crystal and cold and caused another tremor to slip down her spine.

"You don't sound as if you approve of my or the king's exploits."

"I don't."

"A strange opinion coming from a thief and murderer who reportedly eats her prisoners alive."

Morgan shrugged, unable to tell if his taunting words were his way of teasing or if he truly believed the gruesome stories that had spread from one continent to another. "The past and my opinion of it hardly matter at this point, Captain Tremayne. Only the present and the cargo stored in your bays concern me. But first, tell your men to drop their weapons."

"No."

To her disbelief, he took a step toward her, forcing the tip of the blade deeper into his skin. Blood streamed from the gash and coursed down his neck. The streak of bright red soaked his shirt, staining the cloth that had been as white and crisp as the snap of a freshly cut sail.

"Either slit my throat and end this now, Morgan, or prepare to fight and die." The wild flare in his eyes warned her that he preferred the latter. "I'll not lay down my weapon. If you want it, you'll have to take it."

"So be it." She sighed, not wanting their confrontation to end this way. It was so much easier to relieve a vessel of its burden when she had the captain's cooperation, however reluctant it might be.

She stepped back, gaining the added space she needed as well as providing a target for him to focus on. The blow came swift and hard, the surprise evident as stunned disbelief darkened his eyes seconds before they closed and he fell into a heap beside his fallen mate.

"You didn't have to hit him so hard, Uncle Simon," Morgan commented, lowering her sword and easing her stance.

"Ye see the size of this one, don't ye? A smack any less wouldn't have fazed him." Simon tossed the spare piece of strake aside, then glanced over his shoulder. " 'Sides, Jo was itch'n' tae shoot the bugger."

"She's determined to kill someone before we reach Dunmore, isn't she?"

"That she is."

For the first time since Tremayne had boarded her ship, Morgan allowed her gaze to roam over the *Valiant*. Huddled in a ragged circle, the crew looked equally disgusted and frightened that a woman had beaten their almighty captain. She'd seen it before and knew she had little time before anger would override their shock and fear and they'd fight back. She intended to be gone long before then.

She called out to Jo and Jackson, who had removed their disguises and were waiting beside the gangplank. She sighed, relieved that for once Grace wasn't shadowing the young helmsman. "You know what to do. Take some men and be quick about it. I want to leave before the sun sets."

"Henry," she motioned for the blacksmith to join her. "Can I bother you to take a look at the *Valiant*'s cannons?

I do believe their weight has become a burden for that ship."

"Aye, Morgan," Henry chuckled from behind his mask. "I'm think'n' something has to be done about their sails, as well."

As her crew set about their assigned duties, Morgan knelt beside Tremayne. "Uncle Simon, please stay with me. I'm going to need help with this one."

She ran her fingers through strands of black silk that had escaped the leather twine holding the captain's hair. Soft. The texture surprised her. She wouldn't have thought that anything regarding the legendary sea captain would be smooth and yielding.

"Now that he ain't scowling, he doesn't seem near so intimidating, does he, Morgan?" Simon commented. "Maybe he won't put up much of a fuss when he comes around, seeing how futile it'll be for him to fight us."

"Hmmm." Morgan didn't agree with her uncle on either point. Even unconscious and sprawled across her deck, with his angry, disturbing eyes closed and his rugged features somewhat relaxed, the man put a shiver in her limbs. It would take more than his being momentarily senseless before she'd let her guard down. Because she knew that once he awoke, he wouldn't behave like a hungry beast, but like a wounded one intent on revenge.

Pain shot through Daniel's head in fierce, constant spikes. He sucked in a sharp breath, causing an echo with the force of cannon fire to pound behind his eyes, hammer against his skull. He didn't know where he was, and for the moment didn't care to open his eyes and find out. What the hell had happened? Then he remembered. An oath hissed between his clenched teeth.

The *Sea Queen* and her cunning captain.

God's breath, he should have blasted Morgan's ship out

of the water when he'd had the chance instead of falling victim to a distorted version of the Trojan Horse. Daniel cursed, then cursed again for being such a fool.

"We don't allow such language on our ship, sir."

Daniel snapped his head around, then winced and would have blasted another expletive had he been able to manage it. Once his brain stopped spinning, he opened his eyes a slit and focused on the blurry image hovering much too close.

"Does it hurt?" the polite voice asked.

"W-what?"

"Your head? Does it hurt much?"

He blinked against the sunlight, and a vision of round, velvet blue eyes in a heart-shaped and dirt-smudged face came into view. A frazzled braid of blond hair draped over a narrow shoulder. More buttery-soft tuffs clouded around the girl's head. He stared at her, confused. What in God's name was a child doing on a pirate ship, where her very life and soul would be in danger? She couldn't be more than eleven or twelve. Perhaps this chit was Morgan's? Daniel deduced, feeling a new well of loathing open up. From the arrogance he'd witnessed earlier, it wouldn't surprise him if Morgan were trying to breed an entire crew of female pirates.

"Oh, I knew it," the urchin said, her soulful eyes brimming with worry. "Uncle Simon hit you too hard. You've gone daft."

"Who are you?" Daniel snapped, then gritted his teeth as lightning fired through his skull.

Her eyes widened, then softened as a smile stole over her face and produced twin dimples in her sun-pinkened cheeks. "I'm Grace, third in command of this excellent ship you find yourself on. I'm so glad you can speak. Morgan would be upset if Uncle had made you rattlebrained."

"Yes," he muttered dryly, "I'm sure your captain wants me in control of my wits when she slits my throat."

"Oh, Morgan doesn't care for slitting men's throats. It's too messy," Grace confided with a smirk that said he should have known better.

"I suppose she'd prefer to fillet me like a fish." Daniel tilted his head back and realized they'd propped him up against the fore mast. A thick rope crisscrossed his chest and waist, trapping him like a calf in a pen. He jerked on the ropes, and felt prickly hemp bite into his wrists. "Bloody hell!"

"I told you, we don't curse. Well, except for Jo. She never follows the rules."

Daniel didn't know who Jo was or why she was fortunate enough to escape their rules, and he didn't care. He forced the anger boiling in his veins to cool. He needed to think with a clear head, even if it hurt like hellfire. There had to be a way out of this intolerable mess, and he intended to find it.

He considered the little minx, who scooted closer to him as if she'd found a new best friend. "I don't suppose you'd cut me loose?" he asked.

"I couldn't do that." With a long-suffering sigh, she poked at his neck, making his wound sting. "The bleeding's stopped. I bandaged it myself. Morgan says I'll make a fine ship's surgeon one day. The Angel Doctor, she calls me."

"Why would your captain bother to tend my wounds at all, if she plans to kill me?"

Grace chewed on her bottom lip. "What day is it?"

"Excuse me?" Daniel said, barely listening to her. He'd spotted a pair of elderly, grizzly-haired men waddling across the gangplank, struggling to carry a small cask of wine as if their load were a burdensome cannon. The men Daniel had brought on board the *Sea Queen* were nowhere in sight, nor was Mr. Tobitt. Had Morgan chained them below? Or had she already slit them from ear to ear and dropped them over the railings?

"The day?" Grace repeated, interrupting his dark musings. "Which is it?"

"Sunday, I believe," he answered, wanting to growl at the girl if only to vent his anger. Somehow he refrained. She might be his only ally. "Why do you ask?"

"It's your lucky day, then. Morgan doesn't fillet her prisoners on Sundays. Only Wednesdays."

"Lucky me." He spotted his crew huddled against the poop rail as pirates scurried over the *Valiant* like mongrel rats pilfering his food stores. Another curse formed on Daniel's lips, and hung there unable to escape because of the fury squeezing his throat. He jerked the coarse rope that bound him like an invalid, mindless of the painful scrapes. Anger burned through his veins, making him want to bellow, strike out, fight, but he couldn't move!

Morgan wouldn't get away with this atrocity, he vowed. No sooner had the thought seared through his mind than he spotted a slender figure standing in the center of the quarterdeck. It could be none other than the pirate captain. As if sensing his heated stare, she turned and faced him. Since she was still garbed in loose-fitting black trousers and an oversize coat, he could tell little of her body. Given her medium height, though, and her brazen stance, he imagined she'd have the stout build of a blacksmith.

With a bandanna covering her head, he couldn't guess what color her hair was, or even if she had any. At least she had only one head, unlike the myth that reputed her to have twelve, and each one full of razor-sharp teeth. But he did remember her mouth, full and tempting, even as she'd warned him against firing his cannons. There were other things he recalled now which he hadn't had time to consider before. Her tanned skin was smooth, easing over high cheekbones, making her single visible eye that much more startling to view. The core had been gray, like forged steel, ready to strike.

Daniel wondered what lay beneath the patch. If it was

a replica of the eye in plain view, he could well imagine a man becoming trapped in her gaze, staring at her like an imbecile while she cursed his ballocks. Perhaps that was the reason he hadn't seen the blow coming. Or perhaps, he thought, his anger rebuilding until his limbs sizzled with trapped fury, he'd overestimated his strategy in his quest for revenge and had underestimated hers. The thought brought a growl of frustration deep in his throat. Obviously, she wasn't the repugnant eyesore Tobitt had claimed her to be. But she was still a murderer who deserved to hang from the gallows at Executioner's Dock for killing Captain Egham.

A tall, elderly man stopped beside her. From the wild gyrations of his arms and the crimson color darkening his weathered face, Daniel assumed the man had discovered that the *Valiant's* bays were empty of silks and gold. Daniel's scowl curved into a vicious grin.

Morgan nodded, then raised her hand to halt the man's ranting. Without breaking her gaze with Daniel, she crossed the scaffold with the grace of a cat. From her calculated steps to the lethal energy spiking from her stiff shoulders, he imagined she intended to sharpen her claws—on him.

He watched her slow approach, welcoming the chance to spar with her again. He tensed against the ropes. He'd find her weakness. And he'd escape to see her hang.

It wasn't Daniel she spoke to when she reached him, but to the young chit who had wedged herself against his side.

"Grace, you shouldn't be here," Morgan said in a smoky, carnal voice that was totally at odds with her masculine dress. An image Daniel found as appalling as he did startling filled his mind: hazy darkness, a struggle of wills, tangled sheets, sweat and sin.

Hell's teeth! Perhaps that blow to his head *had* left him rattlebrained.

"He needs tending, Morgan," Grace said. "Uncle Simon bashed his head something awful."

"If he needs tending, he will be, but not by you."

"But I'm the Angel Doctor."

"Aye." Morgan sliced a glance at Daniel before addressing the girl again. "But only for our crew."

"He should be in a cabin," Grace insisted. "He's a captain, after all."

"Grace—"

"Jackson and I could guard him."

"Leave Jackson be. He has duties to see to."

"It's going to rain," Grace insisted. "You can't leave the captain in the rain."

Daniel scanned the brilliant stretch of cloudless blue sky. Morgan turned, and slashes of afternoon sun flooded his face. Light blistered the backs of his eyeballs like a burst of fire, amplifying the pounding at his temples. Blinking away the leaping spots, he saw Morgan shield her eyes with her hand and study the clear horizon.

"How long?" she asked.

The girl shrugged. "Midnight perhaps."

"Weather predictions from a child?" Daniel chided. "I suppose I shouldn't be surprised, considering this ship is captained by a woman."

"Everyone has a talent, Captain Tremayne," she said in that rough, throaty tone of hers as she faced him. "Or should I call you *Lord* Leighton?"

Ignoring her question, he raked his gaze over her body, smiling when she visibly tensed. "And what are your talents, Morgan, besides thieving?"

"That's the only thing you need to be concerned about."

"Perhaps your skills lie more toward murdering innocent men?"

Her brow dipped into a frown. "I'm a pirate, Captain Tremayne. Not by trade, but because I had no other choice."

"There's always a choice. You obviously decided on the easiest and the worst one."

"I wouldn't be so quick to judge if I were you. Things aren't always as they seem."

He didn't bother replying to her cryptic response. "What do you plan to do with my men and ship?"

She motioned to the girl, and without another word of protest, Grace took herself off. Morgan knelt before him, her arms braced on her thighs. Her gray eye narrowed with inherent command. "Nothing seems to be wrong with the *Valiant*. Why were you drifting?"

Daniel mocked her with a smile. If she planned to kill him, he wasn't going to make it easy for her. "Surely you've already figured that out."

Considering her reputation, he expected her to lash out, maybe strike him or order him whipped with a cat-o'-nine until the deck became a river of his blood. At the very least, curse him to damnation and back. She merely held his gaze for a moment longer, then sighed. A muscle clenched in her jaw as she scanned the two ships, her expression one of concern. "Your attempt to trap us didn't work."

"Obviously," he admitted with a futile jerk on the ropes.

"You understand I can't release you," she said. "Which leaves me with quite a dilemma."

"I imagine it's difficult to decide the best way to kill me."

When she tilted her head back to him, amusement replaced some of her earlier disquiet. A coy smile curved her full mouth. "Yes, the options are endless."

"What about my ship and crew? Do you plan to murder them, as well?" He couldn't allow the fate of the *Intrepid*'s crew to befall his.

Before she could respond, a suspicious thud echoed in the air. "What's happening?" he demanded.

"I've ordered some alterations made to your ship."

Daniel spotted a barrel-shaped man standing on the ledge of the chain wale on the outer hull of his ship. With a look of pure glee on his crusty face, he swung an ax, landing a solid blow to the taut ratlines that served as ladders to the topcastles. He moved down the channel, clinging to the ship's side with the dexterity of a crab. He swung his weapon again and again, slicing the riggings one by one. Another man stationed above on the main lookout mimicked the act, calling for everyone below to retreat as his hatchet severed rope after rope, sending countless yards of shrouds collapsing to the deck with a thunderous roar.

Along the quarterdeck, the *Valiant's* crew was herded around a demicannon. With the aid of a hoist, they lifted the three-ton iron monster and heaved it overboard. A sullen splash followed seconds later. With encouragement from the pirates, his men moved down to the next cannon.

"Damn you, woman." Blinding anger exploded in Daniel's chest. His skin sizzled with scalding contempt. Never had he been so helpless, so utterly defenseless against an enemy. A blasted *woman*. A simpleminded creature God had created to better the life of man. How God must be laughing at him now.

"I've been damned by men like you before, Captain Tremayne." Morgan caught his face in her hand, startling his attention back to her. Cold, unexpected bitterness hardened her features. "It's because of men like you, men who willingly bleed one country to death in order to conquer another, that I've become what I am."

"A murdering thief? You cannot blame your actions on me or men like me."

"I already have." She released her grip on his jaw. The tips of her callused fingers scraped the growth of his beard, leaving a trail of prickly sensations behind. "Once your ship is disabled and your cannons are sitting on the ocean floor, I'll leave your men *alive,* and on the *Valiant,* to make their own way home. *You* will remain on the *Sea Queen* until I decide your fate.''

''You won't get away with this,'' Daniel vowed. If only he had one hand free, if only she would remove that bloody eye patch, if only he had listened to Tobitt and blown her ship to hell. Daniel forced himself to relax. This wasn't over, he reminded himself. She was taking him with her, which meant he had time to think of a plan, such as convincing Grace to release him.

''Haven't you heard, Tremayne?'' she said in a deceivingly female purr. ''It's impossible to defeat Morgan the Scylla.''

Meeting her direct gaze with a venomous grin, he said, ''I promise you, Morgan, before I draw my last breath, I *will* see you hang.''

Chapter 3

The *Seu Queen* keeled leeward as another wave crested, striking the hull and spewing a current of water across the deck, sweeping buckets, loose ropes and anything else not battened down over the sides. Wind-driven rain slashed from all angles, so violent and chaotic Morgan couldn't tell what came from the sea and what fell from the sky.

Tied by a thick rope to the binnacle box behind the wheel, fighting to keep the ship's bow in the mouth of the wind, she kept watch over Simon, Jo and Jackson, the only ones left topside. Simon remained, determined not to give in to his body's frailties. Jo simply loved a good fight, and Jackson had stayed because the sea had given him a purpose in life.

Having learned to heed Grace's weather predictions, Morgan had ordered the ship secured in anticipation of a squall. Shortly before midnight the gentle swells had turned sharp and biting; then the gale hit. For the past two hours the *Seu Queen* had rolled and pitched and surged as if she were lashed to the back of a wild beast—battling, fighting, wrestling to stay on the surface, when the ocean seemed determined to drag her under to a watery grave.

Morgan had faced countless storms such as this. Each time, fear and excitement had swept through her, burning her lungs like spiced wine. This time wasn't any different. With her hands aching and blistered, she gripped the wheel and faced the challenge, determined to win against insurmountable odds.

"Morgan!"

Hearing the faint call carried on the howling wind, Morgan scanned the deck. Jo and Jackson, both secured by flax ropes, were wrestling with a bowline that had come loose near the head of the ship. Simon was somewhere behind her checking to make sure the same didn't happen to the clewline.

"Morgan! You must—"

A roar heaved up from the ocean, swallowing the rest of the words. She searched the deck. Who had called out? Or had it been the sea, telling her that this time she wouldn't escape? That this time the odds were impossible to beat? The thought, the fear buried in the corner of her mind that she might fail everyone sent her gaze to the prisoner still tied to the mast midship. Lightning splintered the horizon, ghosting his face and hollowing his eyes. Black hair clung to forged, unforgiving cheeks and a jaw that threatened to snap her in half if she dared come too close. But it was his eyes, eyes she couldn't see but had felt since the moment he'd regained consciousness, that renewed the doubts, the awful, foreboding doubts that she might survive the storm but she'd never escape him.

Had he called out to her? She didn't think so. Then who had?

She saw Captain Tremayne tense, his attention veering to the hatchway leading to the cabins in the stern of the ship. He lunged against the ropes in a futile attempt to break free. His expression turned thunderous as he bellowed something that died on the wind. Morgan followed his gaze. Her throat squeezed shut around a scream. *Grace!*

She turned and shouted, "Simon, take the wheel!"

"Aye, Morgan."

Spitting out a mouthful of rain, she jerked on the end of the rope, releasing the slipknot from her waist. Without the restraint, wind buffeted her back, shoving her to the side. She slammed onto the deck, gasping when pain exploded in her shoulder.

Panting for breath, she grasped the slippery iron hull of a cannon and righted herself. Screeching, chaotic gusts whipped at her hair, the yoke of her shirt. Rain pierced her skin like stinging needles. Hand over hand, she pulled herself along the rail toward the stairs leading down to the quarterdeck where Grace clung to the portal, her nightshirt plastered to her thin body.

The ship jerked starboard, pitching the deck sideways. Without a safety rope, Morgan's feet slipped out from under her. She landed on her side and reached out, her hand closing around a breeching rope that secured a cannon.

"Grace!" Morgan screamed. On her feet again, she reached the stairs and leapt to the lower deck, stumbling when the hull groaned and pitched as another wave broadsided the ship. Somewhere above her, riggings snapped. Water gushed over the floor. Morgan heard someone shout. She didn't know who it was, or what they said. It didn't matter. She had to reach Grace.

Lightning cut the sky with bolts of erratic light, illuminating the same fear in Grace's face that pounded in Morgan's heart. Running in tune to the rocking ship, she crossed the deck, diving for her sister, catching her around the waist the same instant a wall of water crested the bow and knocked them both to their knees.

Blinded by rain, choking on a lungful of salty brine, Morgan clenched Grace to her as they rolled and slid across the planking. Grace screamed, the sound high pitched and terrified. Morgan held tight with one hand while reaching out with the other, hoping, praying she'd find something solid to cling to. Nothing but water and air. God help them. There was nothing!

Waves bowled over them, spinning them around and around like dolls, bringing them closer to the edge. *We're going over!* Morgan knew it, and knew there was nothing she could do to stop it—not without releasing her grip on Grace, and that she couldn't do.

"Morgan!" Grace cried.

Morgan clenched her jaw against the scream pushing up her throat. She wrapped her body around her sister's as they were flipped again. Something solid rammed into Morgan's back, knocking air and water from her lungs.

"Grab hold of me!"

The masculine shout brought her head around. Tangled wet hair clung to her face and eyes, but she could see the captain's wide shoulders, the ropes binding his chest to the mast. They had plowed into him, stopping them from going over the side of the ship.

Looking beyond her, Tremayne's eyes widened a split second before he bellowed, "Now, Morgan!"

She obeyed, scooting in front of him, sandwiching her sister's small body between theirs. She wrapped her arms around Tremayne's waist, and tucked her head down against his chest as what seemed like half the ocean crashed into her back. Boards moaned as the ship pitched beneath them. The squall pelted and pushed until she thought she would drown. She clung tighter, feeling another weight squeeze her body. But as the water receded, the weight remained. The ship righted itself. Grace coughed and choked as she cleared her lungs. Morgan looked over her shoulder to see Simon at the wheel, a murderous grin on his face as he shouted at the blustering wind. Relieved to know he was at the helm, she glanced down, only to see the captain's legs wrapped around her waist, holding her as tight as the ropes cinching him to the mast.

"Morgan!" Grace squealed from between them.

"Hold on, Grace. I'll get you below," Morgan said, though she had no idea how she'd manage it.

"I won't go without Captain Tremayne," her sister insisted as she transferred her grip from Morgan to their prisoner.

"Now isn't the time—"

"If he stays, I stay!"

Grace's willfulness left Morgan gaping for a stunned second. "You're going below."

"I won't!"

"Grace, listen to your captain," Tremayne said.

Morgan met Tremayne's shadowed gaze. Considering his promise to see her hang, she never would have believed he'd trouble himself to help. But he'd saved her and Grace from being swept overboard, and was now siding with her to convince the headstrong girl to find shelter.

"Cut him loose, Morgan," Grace demanded. "I'll go below if you cut him loose."

"I can't do that."

"He'll drown," Grace pleaded, tears evident in her voice if not on her face.

Morgan stared at her sister, indecision wrenching her. She knew the consequences of releasing Tremayne, but she decided to ignore them. Grace's safety came first. She slipped the *Sea Queen* knife from her boot. Reaching behind the captain, she sawed through the thick, wet rope.

Warning flashed in the captain's eyes a split second before his hand closed around Morgan's wrist. She expected him to wrest the blade from her, slit her throat or maybe bury the cold steel between her ribs. It would serve her right. Morgan cursed herself a fool for releasing another tempest. The storm she could fight, but this man with his violent eyes and pent-up fury challenged her as no other ever had.

She tensed, ready to whip out the stiletto she kept

sheathed at her back. Pushing himself to his feet, he pulled her and Grace with him. Leaning into the wind, he staggered to the hatchway. Grace fell to her knees; Tremayne lifted her in his arms, pinning her to his chest. He pushed through the onslaught as if it were a bothersome breeze and not a near hurricane-force gale.

At the portal, he forced Morgan through first, then followed, sealing the door behind him. Hurrying down the dark, narrow corridor, still clenching the blade in her fist, she bounced against walls. She stumbled into her cabin, closing the three of them inside the gloomy interior.

Moving through the familiar space, she lit the whale oil lantern bolted to the wall, then motioned for him to place Grace on the bed. Morgan sat on the thick mattress beside her sister, brushed wet, tangled hair from the girl's brow while she kept an eye on the captain. Tremayne collapsed in the chair behind her desk, its stout wooden legs nailed to the floor for times exactly like these.

Sounds of their labored breathing, pounding rain and the churn of the ocean filled the small room.

Finally, Grace whispered, "Thank you, Morgan."

Morgan stared at her sister, torn between hugging her with a whispered thanks to God that she was still alive and grasping her girlish shoulders to shake the life out of her. Though Morgan tried, she couldn't keep the anger from her voice. "What were you thinking? Venturing into the storm? You know better, Grace!"

Her sister's bottom lip trembled, announcing the arrival of tears. "I told you it would rain. Captain Tremayne, he . . . he shouldn't have been left outside." Fat, round tears slipped down her already soaked face. "He . . . he could have been hurt. What if a cannon had come loose, or a yard had broken free? He . . . he . . . would have been k-killed."

* * *

"Shhh." Morgan kissed her sister's brow and briefly closed her eyes, sighing as the panic drained out of her, leaving her sore and tired. So very, very tired. "What am I going to do with you, angel? You're too softhearted for this life."

"And too young," her prisoner, her *unbound* prisoner, interjected with clear disapproval.

Morgan met his shrewd gaze that only seemed more menacing in the dim glow of the lantern. She stood, suddenly aware of their confined space and the fact that she would be at his mercy if he chose to fight. She might be the one with the knife, but he outweighed her by ten stone. Regardless, she angled the blade in front of her.

"Grace, go get Henry. He's below, minding the pumps."

"You're not going to make Captain Tremayne go topside, are you, Morgan?" her sister whispered.

"And chase you down again? Not likely, but neither is he staying here."

Apparently satisfied, Grace slipped off the bed and hurried from the room.

Morgan held the captain's stare, refusing to look away for fear she'd miss a flash in his eyes, or a muscle leap in his jaw, some signal that would alert her to his attack. He held still, though instinctively she knew that every muscle in his long, powerful body was coiled like a wolf's, ready to pounce.

"I could wrest that sorry blade from you before you could move or scream for help," he said as if reading her mind.

"You could try," she said, forcing herself to smile. "And then bleed to death."

He returned her mocking grin, and a flash of warning lit his eyes.

"You could have let the storm wash me overboard, too. But you didn't," she said. "Why?"

"A lapse in judgment, I assure you." He rose from the chair with slow, bestial grace. "Put the knife down, Morgan."

She fought the urge to take a step in retreat. "Stay where you are."

He skirted the desk like the stalking wolf he appeared, all dark and sleek and ominous. He made an awesome sight of towering, primal man, with his sable hair slicked back against his head and shoulders, his irascible jaw studded with blue-black shadows. Resolve and purpose honed every muscle in every limb as he eased closer to her, stealing her space and strength of will. Had the time and place been different, she would have welcomed the chance to meet a man like him. But had there been no war or starvation or death, she would still be a fisherman's daughter and he would be the Earl of Leighton and he wouldn't have taken notice of her had they chanced to meet.

But he noticed her now. His smoky blue eyes narrowed fractionally, pinning her with his intent. She shivered, her skin tightening over her chest.

"You can't expect me to let an opportunity such as this pass, can you? I'll admit, you aren't the pirate I expected to find on board this ship, but you're still a pirate who has a price on her head for murder."

"So it's money you want. How much?"

"The only reward I want is justice."

Hearing the hostility in his tone, Morgan's heart lurched against her ribs.

"Drop the knife. I don't want to hurt you."

"No, you only want me dead."

"If you turn yourself in, the king might consider commuting your sentence."

"Or he might decide to hang me in chains at Sea Reach until I'm nothing but bleached bones."

A pensive shadow passed over his face as his gaze skimmed down her body, then up again. "That fate might be yours, but not your crew's. Have you thought about them? Or Grace? Do you want your daughter to hang from a noose?"

She didn't bother to correct his error about Grace. With unerring ability, he'd managed to strike her one fear. Each day they explored the sea in search of food and gold to share with their village, she gambled with her sisters' lives. They'd been lucky, so lucky, until now. Drowning at sea was preferable to what they'd face if he took them back to England.

Occasionally, pirate crewmen were granted amnesty, but as a rule they were hanged. The captains, however, received special treatment. If Tremayne took her to London to stand trial for whatever murder he accused her of committing, she'd be found guilty and hanged by the neck until dead. They'd cover her with tar, which would keep the carrion crows from eating her flesh and ensure that her bones would remain intact for as long as possible. Then she'd be fitted into a harness of iron hoops and chains and strung up along the Thames River as a gruesome example of piracy and its consequences.

But it wasn't her life or death that concerned her. If Joanna ever stood trial, she'd likely spit in the court's face for the crimes she believed *they'd* committed against her. Grace might be released, but what would become of her with no family or home to return to? And what about her uncle and the rest of the crew? They were all old enough to know what they were doing. They'd surely be sentenced to death.

Evidently, her fear showed on her face, because Tremayne used a tone gentler than she'd thought him capable of. A softness she didn't dare trust. "Drop the knife, Morgan."

She glanced down at the blade as it flashed a streak of

amber in the flickering light. It was the blade she'd found impaled in the desk, the same blade that had given her the beginnings of an idea that had saved her village. She could no more turn loose of it than she could stop loving her wayward family.

Tremayne took another step. Morgan instinctively sliced through the air to warn him away. In a blinding move, he caught her wrist, twisting it until she felt the joint crack. She sucked in a breath. He bent her arm behind her, clamping it against her back. The tip of the knife punctured her shirt and kissed the skin between her shoulders.

"Drop it," he ordered, his breath hot against her face. He found the stiletto at her waist and sent it clattering against the wall above her bed.

"No."

"I can take it from you, Morgan."

"Then take it, because I'll never let it go."

Seconds passed with her pulse pounding in her ears, the base of her throat. She felt the strong, responding thud of Tremayne's heart against her chest, felt the tension in the solid arm that crushed her body to his. She pulled back to strike him with her free hand. He caught that wrist, too.

Trapped, angry and frightened, she stared up at his imposing height and into eyes that were darker than any ocean she'd sailed, and far more treacherous. It would take a mere twist of his powerful hands to snap her in half, or break her neck to prevent her from screaming. But even if she called out, who on board could stop him? No one, and from the arrogant lift of his mouth, he knew it.

Bending her left arm behind her, he held both her wrists in one of his hands. Totally helpless and furious about it, she jerked against his hold, but he only flexed his arm. Pain burned through her shoulders. She couldn't breathe.

He pried the knife from her numb fingers and dropped

it on the bed. "Now, when your sister returns with your crewman, you're going to tell him to enter."

"You won't get away with this," she said. "You can't fight my entire crew."

"With you as *my* prisoner, I won't have to."

Morgan glared at him, knowing he was right. Even Joanna, who possessed an unquenchable thirst for battle and blood, would withdraw and do whatever he asked.

"Are you going to kill me now?" she taunted through gritted teeth. "Or try to sail this ship to England by yourself so you can fulfill your promise and watch me dangle from Executioner's Dock?"

To her alarm, he didn't answer, but went still. His brows pulled into a frown. His gaze narrowed, intensifying as it touched her tangled hair, then moved over her face. He hovered so close she could see a razor-thin scar run from his right temple to his hairline, where it disappeared in the dark waves of his hair. Heat purled off of him, soaking through her clothes, warming her chilled skin when it should have left her prickly with abhorrence. With his free hand, he grazed his thumb across her cheekbone. The touch jolted her with a tremor that tightened her stomach and stole her breath. His mouth thinned with annoyance as if he'd experienced the same bizarre sensation.

"A woman like you has no place at sea," he said, his voice so low and rough and puzzled she thought he must have been speaking to himself. "You obviously need a man to take care of you."

"Is that an offer, Tremayne?" she snapped, then wished she hadn't. His eyes turned dark and feral. She realized then that he hadn't before seen her up close without her eye patch and bandanna. Was he shocked by her plain appearance or disappointed that she wasn't the gruesome opponent he'd expected? He was obviously stunned to find her an ordinary woman. A *defenseless* and ordinary woman who was locked in his arms and without enough sense to call for help.

She parted her lips, intending to do just that when Tremayne did the unthinkable. He covered her mouth with his, startling the air from her lungs. Thoughts of survival fled her mind. His kiss was quick and hard, smothering her gasp. She struggled, but the ship lurched to the side, throwing her off balance. He locked her to him and kept them upright.

An oath tore from his chest. He buried his free hand in her hair, holding her still so she couldn't avoid the demanding rake of his tongue. The act couldn't be called a kiss; it was too hot and urgent and angry. She didn't know how to respond. Or fight.

She could ambush ships, battle storms, lead her crew, but she had no idea how to battle a man, a single, lone man who tasted of rage and fire, heat and anger. A taste that scorched her to her core.

He jerked back, releasing her so abruptly she stumbled against the trunk of the bed, her hand grazing the hilt of her knife. Only then did she realize they weren't alone and he hadn't released her at all. Simon and Henry held his arms pinned behind him while Ian hastily tied his hands using the rope belt from his own pants. All three men were dripping wet, but it didn't dampen the silent fury in their eyes.

Joanna stepped all the way into the cabin, the lift of her mouth matching the amusement in her green eyes. "Good thinking, Morgan," Jo mused. "I would have tried slitting his gut, but that probably would have killed him right off. Kissing him was undoubtedly a better idea. Tomorrow we'll come up with a slower and more painful way for him to die."

Shivering, fighting to catch her breath, Morgan wiped

the back of her hand across her mouth to remove the heated texture of Daniel's lips. Only it didn't work.

She motioned to Simon and rasped, "Take him out of here."

Grace bounced into the cramped cabin, as oblivious to the tension riveting the room as she'd been to the storm. "He goes below," she proclaimed as if she were announcing seating arrangements for a formal dinner. "Morgan said he can stay below."

When her uncle and Henry paused for confirmation, Morgan nodded. "Only until the storm passes."

The two older men started forward, but their prisoner didn't budge. She suspected the captain could fling them against the hull with little more than a shrug of his wide shoulders. But his attention was focused solely on her, as if he didn't care that his hands were tied and there were three burly men waiting to cart him to the hold on the lower deck.

His eyes, which had been turbulent swirls of dark blue moments before, were now iced and . . . and filled with something she didn't understand.

"This isn't over," he said in a deceptively soft voice.

A shudder snaked up her spine. Morgan didn't respond. She couldn't. She motioned for everyone to leave, then closed the door behind them.

Alone, with no one to witness her trembling, she rested her forehead against the solid oak panel. The ship pitched upward as it lunged over a swell, then eased down in a normal glide. She heard the tapping of rain against the upper deck and against the gallery of windows in her room. There were sounds of men moving about, some talking, some grumbling, and even some laughing.

The worst of the storm had passed, she realized, and Tremayne was once again locked away. But she wasn't foolish enough to think she was safe.

* * *

Daniel thought he might slit his own throat if he was ever free and of sound mind long enough to complete the task. Once again he was tied to a support beam. Only now he was in the wretched, stinking hull of the ship with nothing but a black, endless vacuum spread out before him. He felt the ship crest a swell, then dip unsteadily into the surf. The *Sea Queen* moaned as her wooden body bested the last of the storm.

What in God's name had come over him? He'd been unbound and alone with the pirate he'd hunted for the past two months. He'd even held her knife in the palm of his hand, only to throw it aside. And for what? So he could touch her? Shake some sense into her? Find the reason why a beautiful, spirited woman would resort to murder and thievery instead of living an honest life?

He'd wanted answers, that much he remembered. Why had she killed Captain Egham and his crew when she could have just as easily let them go? But he hadn't asked the question. And all because he'd looked into her eyes.

He'd expected the dead, merciless eyes of a pirate. Of a person who killed without thought or conscience. Instead he'd seen strength he hadn't thought a woman capable of. Buried deep in the misty gray depths there had been desperation and pain.

It would have been better if she'd never removed her damnable patch, he thought, tugging at the new set of ropes that bound him. In fact, the next time he saw her, he'd demand she wear the mask her crew had donned when he'd first boarded. Or a sack over her head; that would do the trick. Then he'd never have to look into her eyes again. Hugh Tobitt had been more right than he'd known. Morgan the Scylla did possess powers that could render a man useless. Daniel might still possess his manhood, but one look at her face and he'd lost all sense of judgment.

But covering her face wouldn't be enough. She'd need a sack large enough to hide her entire body and the soft curves he now knew she possessed. To his ire, she wasn't built like a blacksmith in the least. He could still feel her breasts, full and firm, crushed to his chest; her slender waist; the line of her thighs pressed against his.

Their kiss, if he could call the brutal taste he'd had of her a kiss, proved just how impaired he'd become. He rested his head against the wooden post. She'd been shocked, but no more than he when his mind had cleared and he'd realized what he'd done.

It had been hours since their encounter, but instead of sleeping or planning an escape, he continually replayed those few moments in his mind. He could have knocked her unconscious or, worse, snapped her neck, slit her throat. Instead he'd done the unbelievable. Why? He knew the answer, and it grated a raw nerve. She was a woman, an incredibly stunning female, and everything in him revolted against harming her. Regardless that she had committed murder.

It went against all logic. Women were simpleminded. His mother and meek aunts, who still lived at Leighton Castle and had no idea how close they'd come to losing it, had taught him that. They needed to be cared for, pampered, shielded from the ugliness of life. Obviously, he had to rethink his opinions where Morgan Fisk was concerned.

Next time, he vowed, he wouldn't let the sadness in her dove gray eyes affect him. Should he ever have another opportunity . . . Daniel closed his eyes and clenched his jaw. Should he ever have another chance, he wouldn't let Morgan trick him again.

Hearing footsteps on the stairs, he brought his head up. The flicker of light preceded a pair of leather boots and slender legs encased in dark leggings. Daniel blinked and turned his head aside as the glow of lantern light flooded the hold and pierced his eyes.

After a moment he faced his visitor. Though exhausted, he managed to keep his surprise and curiosity from his face.

"I hope you're comfortable, Captain." The redheaded female who had sheer devilment in her green eyes hooked the lamp on a nail, then knelt before him.

"If I said I wasn't, would you cut me loose?"

"Afraid not." She grinned, though the effort only hardened her eyes to shards of stone. "I'm not the compassionate one in our family. Grace is the one who saves wounded birds."

"And what do you do with wounded birds?"

"Pluck them and eat them, of course." Her gaze drifted from his face to his chest, then down the length of his legs before she met his gaze once more with a shrewdness that didn't belong on one so young—or so female.

What was it about the women on board this ship? Daniel thought with a scowl. Didn't they know how they should behave?

"Is there something I can do for you, Miss . . . ?" Daniel asked.

"Jo."

"You don't sound as if you approve of Grace's sweet manner."

"My sister is . . . innocent. Too much so to survive in this world."

"And you're not? Innocent, that is," Daniel added.

Jo bestowed a devilish grin that he decided would be dangerously enticing to another man, were she older and in a different setting.

Daniel mentally compared the two females, finding it hard to believe the two were related. Grace, with her feathery blond hair and sky blue eyes, reminded him of a pixie, all curiosity and goodness. Jo's cinnamon red hair curled about her face as if it had a life of its own. The vibrant color matched the volatile temper he sensed boiling beneath her gruff surface.

"And Morgan?" he asked, thinking how unlikely it would be for the woman with the dark, nearly black mane and troubled gray eyes to be related to the other females. From their looks to their disposition, each were as different as snakes from snails.

"Morgan's our sister," Jo answered. "The oldest. She's why I'm here."

"Did she send you?"

Jo made a scoffing sound that hinted she didn't do others' bidding. "I've come to give you fair warning, Captain Tremayne."

Daniel raised a brow, anticipating the coming threat.

"Stay away from her."

"Or you'll do what?" he taunted, too tired and angry with himself to take her seriously. "Kill me?"

"As happy as that would make me, I'm duty bound to leave that pleasant task to Morgan."

"Just what are her plans for me?"

The girl sighed as if disgruntled. "It hasn't been decided yet. But there's been mention of simply tossing you overboard."

"And letting me swim for shore?" From the gleam in her eyes, he knew she'd love to send him headfirst to the ocean's bottom.

"You might be lucky. Another ship could pick you up. But the waters are cold and infested with sharks—"

"Say no more. But tell me, are you concerned for your sister's welfare, or is there another reason you'd like to see me dead?"

"You're an *aristocrat* who helped the king rip our country apart. That's reason enough to slit your throat."

"You mean the Seven Years War?"

She didn't respond, but her mouth tensed and her cheeks flushed crimson as she pushed to her feet. Her hand flexed on the stiletto sheathed at her waist.

Seeing her aggressive stance, he reacted instinctively and pulled against the ropes. Then he stopped. What was he doing? Why was he letting a mere woman—nay, a child—prick his ire? Daniel shook his head, wondering if the entire world had gone insane. Or was it just the women? "Our victories against France brought valuable ports under our control. The money pouring into England's coffers—"

"Money for whom?" she demanded. "The king? Rich men like yourself so you can become all the richer? Tell me, Captain, will any of that money be given to the poor English subjects who were taxed into starvation in order to fund your precious war?"

Daniel stared at the young woman seething before him, realizing he'd tapped into the source of her rancor. He knew the war King George II had begun had drained England's populace. But now that the fighting had ended, the new wealth would certainly trickle down. Or would it? He knew too well how empty the royal coffers were. The new sovereign, King George III, would undoubtedly fill his own purse before bestowing help on the poor.

"I thought not," she spat, taking the lantern she'd hooked on the opposite pillar.

"Is the war your excuse for becoming a pirate, for murdering and thieving at will?"

"It's no excuse, Captain," Jo corrected him. "It was our only choice."

Our only choice. Jo was the second pirate who'd answered him with that phrase, and Daniel didn't believe her any more than he'd believed Morgan when she'd uttered those exact words. There was always a choice.

A choice to steal.

A choice to murder.

Or a choice not to.

Daniel watched Jo stalk up the stairs, taking the light with her, throwing him back into the dark, echoing dungeon of the ship's belly. Unease prickled his conscience as he recalled Jo's accusations. World Quest Shipping had profited handsomely because of the war, enough to enable him to restore Leighton Castle to its former glory. Which meant his crofters and local tradesmen would profit as well.

He'd helped them, not hurt them. He'd also erased the slur his father had brought to the family name with his gambling and reckless investments. Daniel had never hated his father for what he'd done, knowing the Earl of Leighton's greatest fault had been his gullibility. A trait Daniel didn't possess . . . or at least he hadn't until meeting Morgan the Scylla.

He turned his thoughts to the woman he'd felt compelled to hold and kiss into submission. Even now, he couldn't forget the feel of her body pinned against his, or clear his mind of the salty clean scent of her skin. The heated taste of her lips lingered on his like the remnant of a dream. Or a nightmare, he decided.

Regardless that he was bound, *again*, his duty to his country and his dead captain and crew hadn't changed. He knew what he had to do, regardless that his vow to watch Morgan hang had begun to lose its appeal.

"Damn you, Morgan," he whispered. "Why in hell's name couldn't you have made a different choice?"

Chapter 4

"We've a healthy wind in our sheets, Capt'n." Jackson shielded the sun's glare with his hand as he checked the sails. "I'd say we're making fifteen knots, maybe more, despite our damage."

Unable to match Jackson's enthusiasm, Morgan nodded sullenly as she tied off a mooring rope that had come apart during the storm. All around her, the sounds of hammers blended with jovial bickering as the crew worked to repair lines and cart buckets to the lower deck to bail water. Sections of railing that had splintered under the weight of waves needed replacing, and a downed topsail yard had been deemed damaged beyond hope. The storm had been vicious, but the *Sea Queen* had survived with only a few cuts and bruises, proving just how sturdy she was. If this had been a normal day, and they'd survived an ordinary storm, Morgan would have been thrilled, eager for the adventure of sailing home.

But this storm had possessed a unique element, appearing in the form of a man, and the resulting tremor in her limbs might prove to be her undoing.

And besides, they weren't headed for home . . . yet.

"What's to be done with him, Capt'n?" Jackson asked.

Morgan blinked, realizing she'd stopped working to search for the source of her dilemma. Daniel stood at the bow of the ship facing the wind, his solid legs braced to accept the rhythm of the ship, his arms tied to a strip of board behind his back. Henry had fashioned the knots that bound him so thick and tight the ropes would have to be cut when it came time to release the captain. She shuddered at the thought.

Grace hadn't left Daniel's side since he'd been brought up from the hold that morning. She was speaking to him now, her arms flinging high and wide as she entertained him with some tale. Morgan knew she should forbid her sister from associating with the man, but since a guard was never more than a few feet away, Morgan decided the danger was minimal.

"Are you plann'n' to take him to England with us?"

She faced Jackson, welcomed the understanding in his whiskey brown eyes. The sun had bleached streaks of gold in his wild, wind-tossed hair. She remembered how lifeless it had once been, the color of mud. The hopelessness in his eyes had been just as dull, lacking even desperation after the loss of his family. How he'd changed since joining the *Sea Queen*. How they'd all changed.

And now one man threatened to bring them all down.

"I'm afraid Captain Tremayne isn't making the complete journey with us."

"And just where will he be stopping?" Jackson asked, rubbing his hand over his jaw to disguise a mischievous grin. "At the end of a gangplank perhaps?"

Heavens, Morgan thought, *he was becoming more like Jo by the day, devilish and shrewd.*

"There's a cluster of deserted islands in the Canaries." Her stomach lurched as she said, "We'll leave him there."

"Stranded, aye, that should keep him out of our hair for a time. Maybe forever if luck stays with us."

As if he'd overheard their conversation, Daniel turned, his gaze finding Morgan instantly. His eyes were shuttered, unreadable, but she sensed anger churning in their hard depths. Given the distance between them, combined with the noise from her crew and the slap of the wind, he couldn't have possibly known they'd been discussing him. Regardless, a shiver of warning ran over her scalp and down her spine.

"Have I mentioned that you have too soft a heart, Morgan?" Jackson regarded her with a teasing smile.

"I suppose you feel as Jo does, that I should kill the captain."

"Nothing so dramatic, but I don't know why you gave him the run of the ship."

She shifted uncomfortably. Perhaps he was right and she was too lenient. But she hadn't been able to deny her sister's tearful plea. "It was Grace's idea."

"Ah, that explains it, then." His gaze shifted to the young girl, and his smile turned thoughtful. "It's impossible to refuse our Angel anything."

"At least you understand," Morgan said, searching the deck to make sure Jo wasn't anywhere near the captain.

"Still, the sooner that one's gone, the happier I'll be," Jackson muttered as he returned to his chore of coiling ropes.

Morgan silently agreed, though "happy" didn't accurately describe how she felt about Captain Tremayne leaving her ship. She'd feel relieved, that much was for certain. But happy? There was something about the man, something that had captured her attention and wouldn't let it go, tempting her to delve deeper until she learned everything about him.

Like why he kissed me. She could still taste the salty sweetness of his mouth, feel the shocking heat of his skin.

Startled by the sudden tingling in her lips, she ran her hands through her hair and turned away, searching for any menial task to occupy her mind. She snapped up her quadrant, used to measure the altitude of the sun, thereby determining their latitude. She'd performed the task barely a half hour before, but the procedure required her complete concentration, leaving no time for wondering about Captain Tremayne and his damnable kiss.

Adjusting the settings, she knew they were still on course. Another day, two at most, and Tremayne would be out of her life forever. A ripple of awareness moved over her neck.

"You're doing that wrong."

Gasping, she jerked upright, stunned to find Tremayne behind her. He'd overwhelmed her in her cabin, but on the open deck he still towered above her, blocking the glare of sun with his wide shoulders and imposing air. She thanked God his arms were bound, but wondered if that precaution was enough. She sensed that if he truly set his mind to breaking free, he could with little effort. Wilson, the elderly crewman assigned as the midday watch, stood ten feet away, his gnarled hand resting on the pistol tucked in the waist of his pants.

"What are you doing here?" she demanded.

"I believe that should be obvious," he said, glancing back toward the board pinning his arms behind him. His mouth quirked with a semblance of a grin, drawing her attention, making her recall just how firm and demanding his lips could be. "I'm your prisoner, remember?"

"I'm busy, Captain." To prove it, and to hide the sudden quivering in her stomach, she faced the binnacle where a compass was mounted and read their heading. "I suggest you stay out of my way or I'll have you locked below. And for your information, I know exactly what I'm doing."

"*You* can read a quadrant?"

She gave him a tolerant look. "Of course."

He smirked. "Who does the calculations?"

"I do."

"Then we'll never arrive at wherever you're heading."

Irritated, she faced him. "Why would you assume that?"

His gaze skimmed down her body, slowly, as if he were stripping her of pants and shirt. A strange tingling fanned out from her stomach to her breasts like an invading smoke, unfurling tendrils of pure heat. Her skin tightened over her chest; her breathing turned shallow. Why did he affect her like this? Of all men, why the dreaded Captain Tremayne, with his hypnotic eyes and formidable bearing? Without thinking, she took a step closer. His brow lifted with a cynical tilt, making it clear that he found her lacking.

Suddenly it dawned on her why he caused her blood to heat and her temper to soar. It had nothing to do with his eyes or his lips, or any form of attraction, for that matter. It was his arrogance, his insufferable confidence. He effortlessly pricked her ire and threatened her control. But no more. She understood him now. Remembering their discussion, she asked incredulously, "You don't think I can read the charts because I'm a woman?"

"It's a known fact. Women aren't capable of grasping the concept of math. It's too complicated."

"Oh, really?" she said through gritted teeth, welcoming the return of her senses. She propped her hands on her hips, torn between setting him straight or laughing at his misguided beliefs. Evidently, Tremayne thought that "Captain" was merely an honorary title for her and not a working one. She looked forward to enlightening him.

"You can blame your inadequacy on your gender," he added smoothly, but she recognized the bait he tossed out.

"My inadequacy," she mused, pasting a smile on her face.

"I'll check your readings if you'd like."

"By all means." She held out her hand, inviting him closer.

Stepping beside her so his arm brushed hers, sending an infuriating sizzle of awareness beneath her skin and to her chest, he studied the notes she'd made on a scrap of paper. He frowned and shook his head. "You'll not make England with this heading."

"What makes you think I'm sailing to England?"

He didn't answer, but just then Morgan caught sight of Grace sitting on the steps leading to the forward deck. Swinging her legs, whistling a tune as she watched the freshly scrubbed sky, she presented a picture of innocence . . . and suspicious guilt. Morgan narrowed her gaze and frowned. Just what had her little sister said to Tremayne?

She faced her captive, and realized he no longer appeared the valiant lord. Stress creased the corners of his dark eyes. The full shadow of his beard and his wrinkled shirt, stained with his blood, made him look more like one of her crew, a pirate long at sea looking for spoils and glory. The wound on his neck had scabbed over—a grim reminder of their first meeting. "Eventually, I'll be heading to England. But you won't be making that voyage with us."

His attention snapped to her. With a rippling effect, the muscles in his chest and arms tensed. Wariness and distrust uncoiled around him like invisible hands, giving her the impression he'd like nothing better than to be able to reach for her throat.

With deadly calm, he asked, "What do you intend? Given your reputation, I'm surprised I'm still alive."

The malice chilling his eyes sent a shiver sliding down her back. Before she could respond, Jo scaled down a rope and landed beside them.

Evidently, she'd overheard Daniel's statement because she said, "Consider yourself lucky to have made it this far, Captain. Because you won't have your head for long."

"So I'm to be beheaded, then?" he asked, a sardonic smile curving the mouth that plagued Morgan's dreams.

"I haven't decided." Aware of several crewmen gathering close, Morgan knew she should stop while she could, but more than anything, she wanted to wipe that confident smirk from his face. "I've been anxious to try something new."

Daniel's smile hardened.

"I thought to hang you from the riggings for a few hours," Morgan said. "By your arms. We haven't had a flogging in some time. Have you ever heard a man scream when the skin has been flayed from his back?"

Daniel's expression turned dark; his eyelids lowered to slits. Though he hadn't moved, she knew that fury tightened every muscle bunched beneath his shirt.

"It's worse after brine is poured over the open wounds, and we have plenty of salt to rub in, which will add to the pain."

"Jesus, Morgan," Jackson swore from behind her.

Morgan wanted to stop, but the insolent fire in Daniel's eyes dared her on. "But that's as common as walking the plank. I'd like to try something different."

"I don't know about Captain Tremayne," Jo said, walking casually around their prisoner. "But I'm all ears. What do you have in mind?"

"We could tie his arms and legs to four posts, then put lit matches between his fingers."

Jo glanced at her sister in surprise. A frown pinched her brow. "He'd be burned alive. Slowly."

Morgan suppressed a shudder of revulsion. "Yes."

"Morgan, what are you doing?" Grace whispered as she eased around Daniel, her face upturned with confusion. "I don't like that idea. Maybe we could think of something else."

"Go below, Grace. This isn't for you to decide." Morgan wanted to curse for even starting this game. Her crewmen, Grace, Jo and Jackson were watching her wide-eyed, as if afraid she might sprout fangs and attack them all. Tormenting a captive wasn't in her nature. But she wasn't doing this for their benefit. She was trying to . . . trying to what, she asked herself? Remove the smirk from Daniel's too handsome face, instill fear into his cobalt blue eyes? That and more, she admitted. She wanted him to realize that he might be a man, but he was at *her* mercy.

"Jackson, you make up good stories," Grace said, clasping his hand. "Help Morgan think of something else."

"You're frightening the child," Daniel said stoically, pinning her with his disapproving gaze. "Maybe you should continue this another time."

"We can tie him to the mizzenmast again." Grace pulled Jackson forward, as if she expected him to act on her suggestion. "I promise not to fuss. Even if it rains."

"Jackson, take her below," Morgan ordered.

Despite her sister's cries of protest, Jackson lifted her in his arms and carried her to midship.

Jo brushed up beside Morgan and searched her face. "Perhaps the captain's right. We can discuss this later."

"No," Morgan declared, squaring her shoulders against the tremors gripping her back. "I've made my decision."

"Then why don't we get on with it?" he said, his scowl revealing a gleam of white teeth.

"I'm not in the mood to rush things, Captain." Gathering her supplies, she pushed through the crowd, but stopped at the ladder. "But I promise you this. When I decide it's time to kill you, you'll be the first to know."

Damn the woman and her wretched, bloodthirsty control! Daniel clenched his hands and strained against the ropes. The thick hemp tightened, biting deeper into his skin, adding a burning sting to the humiliation and anger already assaulting his mind and body. He moved to the railing to observe Morgan's descent, his elderly watchdog never far behind. The rest of the crew dispersed now that they knew the killing would be postponed.

She'd changed from the baggy pants and coat that had camouflaged her body the day before, making her appear bulky, nearly twice her size. Now his eyes studied what his body already knew. She was a mere slip of a woman, delicately boned with curves that made his gut tighten. *She's a murderer,* he willfully reminded himself, *who has chosen me as her next victim.*

He cursed under his breath, willing his body and temper to cool. The woman was a living, breathing contradiction. The sight of her in slim-fitting pants of faded linen and a snug, sleeveless shirt should be appalling to him, not appealing. He tried to imagine her in silks and lace, her hair arranged in an elegant coif. He couldn't combine the two. There was nothing refined about Morgan. She was baseborn, inferior, and more tempting than his logical mind could ignore. Yet beneath that sensual veil lived an unmerciful killer.

She stopped to speak with Grace, whose arms were crossed over her narrow chest, her bottom lip in a decided pout. Morgan knelt so they were face to face, then tilted the girl's head back, revealing wide and worried eyes. Grace caught her lip between her teeth and heaved a breath as if she were on the verge of tears. Whatever Morgan said made the girl nod, then hug her big sister. Turning away, Grace skipped across the deck and disappeared through a hatchway.

What had Morgan said to her sister that had eased her mind so quickly? That his death would be quick and painless? That Grace wouldn't have to watch? An oath hissed through his teeth. He needed more time. Grace had innocently told him they were heading home for England. Precisely where in England he hadn't managed to learn, but he felt certain the girl would tell him everything he wanted to know about Morgan the Scylla. Now if only he could devise a plan to stay alive long enough to use it.

"The lot of 'em are enough to fool a man into think'n' he can live forever," said a voice as rough as broken glass.

Daniel glanced at Simon Fisk. He'd learned from Grace

that he was their uncle. He was also a man well past his prime, who should be enjoying the last years of his life in quiet safety instead of challenging death head on. Daniel had watched him the night before, battling the storm, swearing at the sky as it unleashed its might. His gangly body, the sun-spotted, weathered skin and eagle-sharp eyes all spoke of a seasoned sailor. If that was the case, then why was he taking orders from a woman? His own niece? Surely he detested the situation.

"Living forever doesn't seem to be an option for me," Daniel said.

Holding a wooden mallet, Simon tapped it thoughtfully against his palm. His outstretched fingers were bent with age, the skin scarred from years of hard labor. "The capt'n knows what she's doing."

"I'm sure she thinks she does." Never afraid to gamble, Daniel wondered if now was the time to try. He needed another ally. He would have preferred to approach a crewman not related to Morgan, but so far everyone except Grace had avoided him as if he carried the plague. "She's not the only one who puzzles me."

"Ah," the old man chuckled. "So you're curious about our little group, are ye?"

"It's obvious you've spent your life at sea. You know the rules. Women aren't welcomed on board ship, even a pirate ship." Daniel paused to gauge the man's reaction. When Simon didn't swing the mallet at his head, he decided it was safe to proceed. "If you and your men want to be sailors, I have more than enough ships—"

"Are ye offering us jobs, Capt'n Tremayne?"

"I could be, if you were interested."

"Can ye guarantee us amnesty, then?" Simon asked, stepping closer so as not to be overheard by Wilson. "We're wanted men, ye know."

"If you help me escape, I promise you'll go free."

"And we'll have work on one of your fine ships?"

"If you want, yes." Anticipation threaded through Daniel's veins, making him strain against his bindings.

"Ah, that would be something. That it would." Simon shook his head, grinning like a fool who'd been given a chest of gold and the secret to immortality. "I suppose Morgan wouldn't be captain."

"Of course not." When a laugh wheezed out of Simon's thin chest, Daniel chuckled with him. "What sailor worth his weight would want a female ordering him about?"

Simon tapped the mallet against his palm again, his laughter quieting. He glanced across the faded wooden deck to the woman surveying the repairs to her ship, not like a queen regarding her subjects but like a mother worrying over her young. *'I'd* want a female captain giving the orders, Captain Tremayne. I wouldn't 'ave it any other way. Nor would anyone else on this ship."

Anger scalded the blood racing beneath Daniel's skin. "Think about what you're giving up before you turn me down."

Simon regarded him for an instant. "If you're of a mind to gain help from someone else on this ship, you can put the thought out of yer head. No one will come to your aid."

"She's leading you to your death," Daniel said through clenched teeth. "Do you understand? You and every other man, woman and child on this ship will be hanged when you're caught."

"Morgan saved us all, that's what I understand." Simon straightened, shedding his relaxed pose to stare Daniel down with eyes so pale a blue they were almost colorless. "There's not a soul on board that wouldn't willingly give their life for her. That's something I'd not be forgetting if I were you, *Captain.*"

He turned away and made for the stairs. Daniel stared after the surly old man. He clenched his jaw as trapped frustration boiled up inside him.

No, he wouldn't forget Simon's warning. He'd handed them all a way out. When they were caught, and they would be—Daniel renewed his vow to survive to make sure that happened—he'd be standing in the crowd to watch them all hang.

And he'd be damned if he'd feel a moment's regret for their deaths.

The nameless islands were clustered together as tightly as a group of friends, small, quaint, inviting. And uninhabited, as far as Morgan knew. The crystalline warm waters teamed with fish, so she knew Daniel wouldn't starve. Still, she worried about leaving him without means of protection. She couldn't risk giving him a gun, certain he'd use it on her. She could, however, have her men hide a pistol and a knife on the island. He'd have to search for them, giving her and the crew time to row back to the *Sea Queen*.

"Which one is it to be?" Jo asked from beside her.

"The island in the middle." Morgan pointed to a small curve of land covered with sandy beach and leaning palms. "It'll be the hardest one to navigate, making it less likely for another ship to land anytime soon and find him."

"You're making a mistake letting him go," Jo argued, not bothering to keep her voice down. "I was warming to the idea of burning him alive." Chuckling, she added, "I didn't know you could be so vicious, Morgan. You had the entire crew believing you meant to set him aflame. I must be rubbing off on you. Maybe I can still change your mind. It's not too late, you know."

"We aren't killing him, Jo, and that's final."

"He'll find a way off the island and come after us," Jo complained. "The way that storm hit after he came on board. I tell you 'tis a bad omen. We'll all be doomed if we set him free."

"You and your superstitions. We've been through storms

before." Morgan cupped her hands around her mouth and shouted, "Ready about, Uncle Simon."

Her uncle spun the wheel, taking the ship in. Jackson scaled the main rail to watch for coral reefs.

"And really, Jo, how can you believe Captain Tremayne caused that last gale? He might have a ruthless reputation, but not even he can control the weather."

"He'll escape," Jo said, clearly unwilling to relent.

"He might," Morgan agreed more calmly than she felt. If Daniel did escape, she had no doubt he'd spend the rest of his life hunting her down. To reassure herself more than Jo, she added, "But escape is unlikely. Ships avoid these islands because of the currents and rocky bottom."

"If he has to build a raft from palm trees and dried fronds, the man will do it." Jo paced in a circle, hands on her hips, clearly exasperated. "He isn't one to sit by and let you get away with besting him. You claimed his ship, then dismantled it. Hell, you kidnapped him!"

"You're sounding hysterical, Jo. It's not like you."

Her hot-tempered sister threw her hands into the air. "Fine. I've said my piece. If you want to let him live so he can come after us, who am I to argue? Especially after Morgan the Great has given an order."

Morgan drew a steadying breath and kept her gaze focused on the island. Was she making a mistake by marooning Daniel? She honestly didn't know. But what choice did she have? Killing him, as Jo insisted, and as she herself had threatened, was out of the question. So was taking him to England.

That left leaving him to his own devices on a deserted stretch of land.

"I think there's another reason you want him alive."

Morgan sighed, tired of the conversation and the internal battle she fought whenever she thought about Daniel Tremayne. "What do you not understand about the words 'We do not kill people'?"

Ignoring the question, Jo asked in a hushed voice, "He got to you, didn't he?"

"Order the skiff readied." Morgan refused to address the question that had worried her for the past two days. She hadn't been able to forget the way his intense, sensual gaze had raked her body, leaving her tingling and hot and confused. "While we're anchored we'll gather what supplies we can from the island."

The green of Jo's eyes darkened with worry. "Who's taking him ashore?"

"I will, with a half-dozen men."

"You should let me take him."

"No."

Jo's gaze narrowed, a sure sign she was preparing to bargain. "What if I promise to leave him whole and healthy?"

"I'll take him," Morgan insisted. She knew Jo wouldn't harm Daniel if she gave her word, but leaving him to his fate was her responsibility. He'd want revenge. If he had to hate someone, she wanted it to be her, and not her family.

"I don't think you being alone with him is a good idea. Not after the way he kissed you."

Mockery underlined Jo's words, and Morgan knew she should ignore them, but she couldn't help asking, "What do you mean by that?"

Stepping past her, Jo whispered in her ear, "Because you didn't fight him."

Chapter 5

"It's time to go," Grace said, her young voice thready.

If Daniel didn't know better, he'd think the girl was on the verge of bursting into tears. He took little comfort in knowing that at least one person might cry over his death. He thought briefly of his mother, Lady Leighton, in her silks and powders and easy smiles. How would she react to hearing about his capture? She'd worry and fret, of course. Perhaps swoon.

At least his two aunts would be there to console her, especially after time passed and he didn't return. She wouldn't want for money. Before he'd left to fight in the war, he'd made sure she would receive his profits from World Quest Shipping. His estates were once again healthy, as well, ensuring she'd always be cared for. Thomas would be there as executor of his will. No, he wouldn't have to worry about his mother.

Regret opened up inside him. His mother was all he'd leave behind. No wife, no children. The Tremayne line would end with him. Once his mother died, his estate would pass to a distant cousin. Why hadn't he seen to getting an heir? *Because I couldn't take a wife until I'd restored my family name.* Then England and the war had needed him, causing him to set his personal needs aside once again. Now might be too late.

He stood near the bow of the ship, the morning sun still cool on his back, so he could observe the crew drop sails. Despite their age, the men were efficient, even enthusiastic about performing their duties. They'd already lowered the anchor and were preparing to disembark, he assumed for the small island they'd risked navigating a treacherous shoal bank to reach.

He didn't move from his spot, despite Grace's announcement. Rope burns laced his arms. His shoulders and chest ached from the tight, awkward restraint, and his eyes stung from lack of sleep. For two days and nights the pirates had embellished on Morgan's idea on how to carry out his demise. One option was to shoot him at close range and heave his body overboard, but that had been deemed too quick. Another alternative, one he didn't care for whatsoever, was to cut off his ears, slice out his tongue and leave him at the next port.

Whatever his fate, Daniel vowed to take as many pirates with him as possible. A part of him welcomed the coming conflict. Anything, even knowing what kind of death her sinister mind had decided on, was better than living with the frustration of being helpless, and the humiliation that his unacceptable downfall had been caused by a blasted woman.

And my own stupidity.

"Morgan's waiting for you, Captain." Grace shook his upper arm to gain his attention.

He looked into the girl's trusting blue eyes and wondered if Thomas or any of his other friends would seek vengeance for his murder, as he had Captain Egham's. Somehow Daniel doubted it. Besides his mother and his aunts, the only other family he had was a distant cousin. Rodney Wentworth would love nothing better than to claim the familial title, Earl of Leighton, and the estates that honor entailed.

The knowledge that his death would pass unnoticed and unchallenged brought a knot to his throat and a desolate twist to his stomach. But he wouldn't go easily, he vowed. If God would only grant him one blasted wish, he'd let Daniel take Morgan with him.

"Tell me, Grace," he said, following her to midship. "Do you know how your captain plans to do away with me? Will she kill me herself, or let the bloodthirsty Jo have the honor?"

"I can't tell you of her plan, but I know it'll go quickly. You won't feel a thing. Morgan always makes sure her prisoners suffer as little as possible."

"I suppose that means she's decided not to burn me alive."

Grace sighed, a weary, trembling sound that caught Daniel off guard, tempting him to reassure her that everything would turn out well. An absurd feeling to have at a time like this, he growled to himself. But she was a child who shouldn't have to live the life forced upon her.

"I'll be so glad when all of this is over and we can return to Dunmore. I'm so weary of living at sea. Morgan says we're quitting pirating for good. Oh, look, there's Jackson. Doesn't he make a fine picture standing at the helm?"

Daniel stopped and stared after Grace as her words slowly sank in. He grinned, but resisted the urge to throw his head back and laugh. They lived in Dunmore! He'd be able to track them down, arrest Morgan, haul her to London for trial. His grin faded. Knowing where they lived was valuable information indeed, to anyone except a dead man.

He halted beside the ladder that had been lowered to the waiting dinghy. Jo shoved him closer to the edge. "Down you go, Captain."

He considered the thirty-foot drop, and the sway of the

ladder as the ship rocked with the swells. "Unless you want me to jump, you'll have to cut me loose."

Though Jo's hair was twisted in a braid down her back, crimson curls made a wild dance about her face in the breeze. She would have looked impish if not for the calculating gleam in her green eyes. "I wouldn't want you damaging the dinghy. Simon, cut him free, then tie his hands in front of him."

She stepped back to give the old sailor room. Daniel held still, waiting for the moment the ropes fell away. He could easily take Simon, and any of the other feeble sailors who dared try to subdue him. He had yet to see Morgan that morning, and despite Jo's irascible nature, he could capture her. Morgan might be cold-blooded enough to kill him, but after she'd nearly drowned saving Grace, he knew she wouldn't allow any harm to befall Jo. Then he'd have the pirates sail their own ship up the Thames River to London . . . where they'd all stand trial.

Just as the rough hemp gave way, he felt something solid and round stab the center of his back.

"I've a pistol aimed at your heart, Captain," Jo said, her voice a challenging purr. "Should you move, I'll be forced to shoot you, and that would irritate Morgan."

"She wants the pleasure of shooting me herself, does she?" Daniel managed, furious that he'd lost his opportunity to escape.

"There is that," Jo mused. "But Morgan hates it when people bleed on her clean deck."

"Heaven forbid." Daniel hissed out a breath as Simon brought his arms forward. Pain burned a path down his shoulders and chest, heating his numb muscles. "We wouldn't want to upset Morgan, would we?"

"I knew you'd understand."

Once Simon retied his hands in front of him, Daniel ignored the ache in his limbs and scaled down the ladder. He thought to turn and dive into the ocean, but where would he go? To the island? With his hands bound, the pirates would easily catch him. Besides, he thought looking up, Jo had the pistol trained on his face. The little witch was undoubtedly an excellent shot. Grace appeared at the rail to wave good-bye. Christ, did the child think he was going on a holiday?

Once seated on the wooden bench, he traded glares with the six waiting men. Hearing a commotion above, he glanced up to a sight that made him clench his jaw. Morgan was descending the ladder. Black leggings stretched against her thighs and bottom, defining every slender line and lush curve that no man except a husband should see.

Beads of sweat dampened his brow. Anger and desire clamped like fists in his gut. Damn the woman, she should be wearing a gown. If she were his, he'd burn every pair of britches she owned. *If she were his* . . . What in God's name was he thinking? She was the last woman on earth he'd want to claim.

Unbidden, the memory of holding her resurfaced. He could feel her legs pressed against his, firm muscles women weren't supposed to possess. Females were meant to be soft, supple, and in need of a man's care. Everything about Morgan should repel him, yet for some perverse reason, she fascinated him.

Brown leather boots reached the top of her calves. Her cream shirt shifted with the variable wind, flattening the gauzy material against her back one second, then lifting it off her skin the next. She might be tempting, he reminded himself, but Morgan wasn't an ordinary woman, certainly not one who needed to be cared for. Beneath her lithe body and mesmerizing eyes lived a woman who brutally murdered her victims.

And he was next.

She gained the boat, then nodded to the men to push off.

"May I ask where we're headed?" Daniel asked.

"The island."

Wanting more than the obvious, he asked, "Why take me along? Or is that where you plan to dispose of me?"

"It seemed a good place." A pulse throbbed at her temple, and she avoided meeting his gaze.

Did she regret having to kill him? he wondered. Feel guilty, perhaps? He found it hard to believe that the woman he'd kissed didn't possess some trace of conscience. But then, she'd tricked him before. This show of reluctance could be another one of her ploys, or he could be wishing for some redeeming quality in her that didn't exist.

"I'm curious," he said, resolved to forcing a response from her. "Once I'm dead, will you take the time to bury me or will you leave me for the land crabs?"

With a glitter in her smoky gray eyes that struck a raw nerve at the base of his neck, she asked, "Once you're dead, will you care?"

A wave struck the side of the dinghy, throwing them off balance. Scowling, he made the rest of the trip in silence. Reaching shore, four men leapt out and beached the boat. Then everyone, Morgan included, grabbed up empty barrels, buckets and sacks before making their way to shore.

Morgan paused. "Are you coming, Captain?"

"You expect me to voluntarily follow you?"

"I hadn't thought you the cowardly type. But if it'll help soothe your male pride, I can encourage you with the point of my knife."

The wind caught her hair, pulling the toffee-colored mass loose from the scarf she'd used to tie it back. Long curls fell over her chest, soft and alluring, like a mythical goddess . . . or, he amended, an avenging Medusa.

He climbed from the skiff and followed her to the line of trees and brush where the crew had begun setting up a makeshift camp. He raised a brow. What were they up to? Why didn't they just shoot him and be done with it?

"I assume all this effort isn't for my benefit. Are you staying awhile?"

Morgan dropped her empty buckets with the others. "We need to gather supplies while we're here."

"How convenient. You'll kill two birds with one stone." Her mouth thinned with a tight smile. "I do like efficiency."

"Then why haven't you killed me yet?"

"Have a seat, Tremayne," she said, dropping to the sandy ground. "I wouldn't be in such a rush to die if I were you."

Sitting just out of arm's reach of her, he said, "I'm simply tiring of this little game of yours."

"Oh, it's no game, I assure you." She considered him through lowered lashes. "Running across your ship was a stroke of bad luck . . . for all of us. I'm just making sure my family doesn't suffer because of it."

Daniel jerked his feet back an instant before one of the men could dump a pile of firewood on them. Bending his legs, he propped his forearms on his knees. He didn't understand her reason for keeping him alive. Considering her reputation, he never should have seen the sun rise the morning after his capture.

Perhaps he'd made a mistake in the way he was dealing with her. She was a pirate, after all, and what pirate couldn't be persuaded by the lure of a pocketful of gold?

"You know, I'm a wealthy man."

Arranging the wood into neat piles so it could be bound and carried to the ship for later use, she glanced at him. "So I understand."

"If you release me, I'd be willing to pay you."

She angled her head; an enticing smile spread across her lips. "How much?"

"A thousand pounds."

She tossed her head back and laughed, a rich, velvety sound that wound through his body, reaching for a part of him he didn't want to acknowledge. He found her frustratingly beautiful, alluring, bewitching in her feminine strength. And totally at odds with the qualities he valued in a woman—which were innocence, modesty, and most importantly of all, a docile nature.

Everything Morgan wasn't.

"You don't value yourself overmuch, Daniel."

His chest tightened at the sound of his name. He forced himself to draw a breath. "State your price, then."

She shook her head. "Your offer is tempting, but I can't accept it at any price."

"Damn it, woman. Have you no sense? With my money you could take the whole blasted lot of you and sail anywhere in the world."

"With you always close behind." She scooted back and leaned against the tree, the contours of her face too damned serene given the fact that they were discussing his life.

"What if I give my word to leave you alone?"

"You'd be lying." She lifted her arms to run her fingers through her hair. Her blouse drew tight over her breasts. He stifled a groan, suddenly aware that she wore nothing beneath. "No. My way is better. For everyone."

Forcing himself to meet her gaze, he drawled, "You won't be offended if I don't agree with you."

She shook the ends of her hair loose, creating a vision of a willful temptress. "You'll just have to trust me on this one."

Trust her? He'd rather stick his head between the jaws of a shark.

Morgan fingered the knife sheathed at her waist. The gemstones were warm to the touch, the filigree hilt smooth, offering confidence she sorely needed. Two days of enduring her body's confusing response to Daniel, of pretending she meant to murder him, had taken its toll on her nerves. Not that she didn't enjoy watching him worry. She simply wanted this insanity over with so she could put him and his dark, distrustful eyes out of her life forever.

She pushed herself to her feet and paced the camp, ever mindful of Daniel's gaze following her. He considered her the lowest form of life—a pirating thief who thought nothing of bloodshed. He wasn't the first. She'd encountered dozens of sailors, even other pirates, who'd believed the vile rumors about her. She hadn't cared before, had, in fact, welcomed people's gullibility. It had helped her cause. So why was Daniel different? Why did she want to wipe the disdain from his face? Tell him the truth?

"You look nervous," he said, methodically twisting his wrists. "Is something amiss?"

She glimpsed the red welts where the hemp had rubbed his skin raw. "No."

"Your crewmen have been gone for some time. Perhaps they're lost."

"They've barely been gone an hour." In addition to finding fresh water, fruit and game, they had to hide a pistol, shot, a knife and a few utensils that would help Daniel survive. The location had to be easy enough for him to find . . . after Morgan and her men had left.

"Has being alone with me made you uneasy?"

"We aren't alone. Wilson is here, and he won't hesitate to shoot you if you give him cause."

"Seems he's preoccupied with something else."

She glanced at the sailor, who scanned the horizon with the bring-me-closer, a habit born from a lifetime at sea. Wilson had served in the Royal Navy with her uncle. "He's cautious, as am I."

A caustic laugh erupted from Daniel's chest. "Which is why I find myself at your mercy."

Morgan clenched her jaw shut. Only a little while longer and he'd know she'd never planned to hurt him. Although, she amended, considering the line of trees along the deserted beach, the thick brush that shadowed the island's interior, the distant cry of seagulls as they circled the cove, marooning him could mean his death. The lack of fresh water or food, poisonous snakes and deadly beasts could all prove disastrous. If he died, she would inadvertently be the cause. How would she live with that knowledge? It was either him or her crew, she reminded herself. The crew was her family, and they would always come first. Daniel Tremayne, on the other hand, meant nothing to her.

"Capt'n! Ye better come take a look at this."

With a glance at Tremayne, she ran to Wilson's side and took the telescope, aiming it where he pointed. She scanned the ocean, seeing nothing but dark blue water where it met cloudless sky. Then she sucked in her breath.

"Aye, 'tis a British warship. The *Pearl,* if my years in the King's Navy serves me right."

"And heading in our direction."

"They can't reach us 'ere, Capt'n. Her hull is too deep to navigate the islands."

She heard Daniel push to his feet. One enemy at her back, another at her front. Heaven help her. "Stay where you are, Captain."

To Wilson she said, "The *Pearl* might not reach us, but she can get close enough to fire, or worse, trap us here indefinitely."

"If that's Captain Andrew's ship," Daniel said, "you won't like what he does to the pirates he captures."

Morgan glared at him over her shoulder, willing him to be silent.

His mouth hardened with distaste. "Andrew's known for hanging the severed heads of his captives from the bowsprit of his ship."

She focused the telescope on the *Sea Queen.* Her chest squeezed her heart. "There's no lookout. Blast it, Jo."

She gripped Wilson by the arm and pulled him toward

the skiff. "Return to the ship. Tell Jo my orders are to leave the cove. She can use the islands as a shield to hide behind. The *Pearl* should be gone within a few hours."

"Capt'n, I can't leave ye with 'im."

She jerked the pistol from Wilson's waistband. "I'll be fine. The other men should return soon." She gripped one side of the skiff and helped push the boat into the surf.

"May God watch out for ye, Capt'n!" Wilson called as he rowed to their ship anchored in the cove.

"And you."

She used the looking glass to check the *Pearl*'s location again. The ship's distance and an ounce of luck might keep her from spotting the *Sea Queen*.

"He'll never make it."

Morgan whipped around. She dropped the telescope and extended her arm, leveling the pistol at Daniel's heart. A shiver of fear tore down her spine. Fear for her family, and for the man facing her with calm calculation. She took her finger off the trigger, afraid the tremor running through her body would cause her to shoot him by mistake.

"I have every confidence in my crew. Have a seat, Daniel. We're going to have to suffer each other's company a little while longer."

He didn't sit as she'd ordered but moved around the stack of wood, keeping wide of her, his shrewd gaze fastened on hers.

"I said sit!"

"Or you'll do what, Morgan? Shoot me?"

"If I must."

"You only have one shot," he said, boldly walking toward her. "You'd better not miss."

Chapter 6

She'd made a mistake, and she knew it. Daniel could see the panic flooding her eyes, the realization that her advantage was lost.

She was his now.

He didn't concern himself about the gun she trained on his chest. Any true pirate would have shot him long before now. Her hesitation had cost her dearly.

"Put down the pistol, Morgan," he said, cautiously narrowing the space between them. "I don't want to hurt you."

"I won't warn you again, Daniel. Don't come any closer."

He started to take another step, but stopped. She'd slipped her index finger back onto the trigger. He expected her to retreat, gain safety with distance, but she angled her body, lifted her arm further, taking aim down the barrel of the gun. If she fired now, she'd shoot him square in the head. Daniel swallowed; sweat dripped down his temples.

He raised his bound hands as a show of compliance, then leaned his weight on one leg, trying to feign a relaxed pose when he really wanted to leap at her and wrestle the weapon from her grip.

"All right," he said. "You win."

She stared at him, her eyes stony with intent.

"You can't blame me for trying." He managed a smile. "Wouldn't you try to escape if the situation was reversed?"

"I wouldn't have been caught as you were, Captain. Now return to the camp and take a seat."

He pivoted and started back, taking his time. From the corner of his eye he saw that ten feet still separated them, too much distance for him to reach her. He had to do something. He refused to be held captive by a lone woman who, he was beginning to suspect, didn't have the nerve to shoot him.

Could it be possible that she wasn't as ruthless as her reputation claimed? Or was there another reason she'd kept him alive? Did the unwanted attraction he felt for her run both ways?

Why hadn't he considered that possibility before? If this were another time, he might put that theory to a test, but as things stood, being the one in control held much more appeal.

Nearing the camp, Daniel pretended to trip. Stumbling, he went down on one knee and scooped up a handful of sand. Twisting, he threw it in Morgan's face. She leapt sideways, but not quickly enough. Sand hit her cheek and mouth. She ducked her head and swiped at her eyes. The pistol swung wide, and he knew it was now or never.

He lunged for her, grabbing her wrist with his bound hands. His shoulder slammed into her chest, cutting off her cry of surprise. They went down on their sides, the soft ground cushioning the impact. He rolled her onto her back, her body struggling against his, and struck her arm against the sand.

"No!" she screamed, holding tight to the handle.

He tightened his grip on her wrist, certain he'd crush

the bone, and banged her arm against the ground again. Her fingers fell open, the pistol slipped free. He reached for the weapon just as a flash of light and steel caught his eye. Rolling away, hearing the knife rip through air, he caught the gun and came to his feet.

Morgan struggled to stand, her hair a crazed tangle about her face. She hugged her injured arm to her hip. Good God, had he broken the bone? With her legs bent, her body loose and ready to strike, she gripped the slender blade waist high. She couldn't possibly mean to fight him. But hers wasn't the stance of a woman prepared to surrender.

"It seems the odds are evening out, Morgan," Daniel said, breathing hard. "Only this time they're in my favor. Put the knife down. Unlike you, I won't hesitate to shoot you if I must."

She jerked her head, shaking hair out of her eyes. "That's very chivalrous of you, but I'll keep my knife and take my chances."

"You've lost; admit it."

Her gaze narrowed, sending a warning tingle down his back. "The air's damp, Captain. Combine that with the way you pounded the gun against the ground, I doubt there's any powder left in the primer. Go ahead and pull the trigger. The most you'll get is a disappointing flash in the pan."

Daniel clenched his jaw. Damn the woman. The only way to prove she was wrong was to fire the blasted gun. He might have boasted that he had no qualms about shooting her, but call him a fool, he couldn't actually do it. Facing the ocean, he heaved the pistol into the cove.

"I guess the odds are back in my favor," she mused.

Giving her a shrewd glance over his shoulder, he said, "As I see it, there are two weapons left. The blade you're holding and the stiletto you keep. Where is it today? Since I didn't see it in your waistband, it must be in your boot."

"It might be."

"Well, it's not tucked in your pants." His gaze slid appraisingly over her hips and legs. "That much I know for certain."

Her cheeks, already pink from exertion, flushed deep rose. "The point, Captain, is that the weapons are with me, and that's where they'll stay."

"No," he said, approaching her. "They won't."

She tucked her injured wrist at her side and rocked on the balls of her feet, as if she knew how to fight hand to hand. Daniel swore under his breath. He didn't want to hurt her any more than he already had, but he'd be damned if he wasn't going to wrest the sorry blade from her. He meant to be free of the rope bindings ... *before* her crewmen returned.

He hurled forward like a charging bull, giving her no time to think and less to react. He reached for her, intending to knock her down as before. She sidestepped him, spinning away and using her boot to trip him up. Daniel stumbled, but recovered, spinning and leaping back just as she slashed the blade toward him, the tip so close he felt the brush of air against his cheek.

She thrust again and again. Each time, Daniel veered to the side. He tried to catch her wrist, but she was too fast, anticipating his moves. Whoever had taught her to fight had taught her well.

Circling him, she said in a voice thready with strain, "We can stop this."

"It's too late for that, Morgan, and you know it. If I'm going to die, I'd rather do it fighting you than waiting for your whim."

"I can't let you leave here, Daniel."

"You have to protect your family," he said, meaning to sound mocking but somehow failing.

"That's right."

He feigned an attack; she flinched in response but didn't

strike. Sweet bleeding Jesus, he had to catch her wrist. Cursing again, tiring of the cat-and-mouse game, he ignored the knife and lunged. He caught her forearm, jerking it above her head. They fell to the ground, landing with a thud with him on top of her. She grunted and didn't move, didn't struggle; God help him, she didn't even breathe.

Daniel lifted his weight. Alert to her closed eyes and the possibility that this might be another one of her tricks, he took the knife from her limp fingers. Gripping the hilt in his palm with the blade facing himself, he sawed the rope that bound his wrists, wanting to laugh when the blade sliced through.

Reaching inside her boot, he found the stiletto, then stuck both weapons in the sand. He spread his arms to his sides, stretching his muscles, bringing life into his sore limbs. Feelings of relief swept up through his body, but the woman lying as still as death snapped the joyous feelings in half. He shifted his weight so the length of his body hugged the side of hers. His leg draped over her thighs, a position as forbidden as it was erotic. Her sweat-damp shirt clung to the upper slope of her breasts, tempting him . . . God, tempting him to touch her. In spite of everything, who and what she was, he wanted to touch her.

Her chest shuddered as she dragged in a deep breath. Before she regained consciousness, Daniel caught both her hands over her head and gripped them in his. A groan rose in the back of his throat. The linen fabric stretched tight, outlining her full curves, her nipples pebbling from the friction.

Sweet Jesus, the woman drove him to distraction. He should be tying her up and preparing to subdue the other men. Instead, he ogled Morgan as if he were a starving man eyeing the last crumb of bread on the serving platter.

She stirred, turning her head, a frown pinching her brow as if she were in pain.

The hell with it, he thought. He wanted to touch her, and this would undoubtedly be his last opportunity. He brushed her hair from her face, the wild strands as dark as midnight against the pale sand. Long lashes brushed tanned cheeks. Her jaw was like the rest of her—strong, willful, stubborn.

But it was her mouth that drew him.

He never should have kissed her. If he hadn't, he wouldn't know she tasted fresh, like rainwater falling through sunshine. Or how soft she could be. She'd yielded to him in that final moment before he'd been pulled away. What would have happened if they hadn't been interrupted? How far would the kiss have gone? He would have come to his senses eventually. Or she would have. But when? Before he'd made love to her, or after?

He grazed his fingers down the side of her face to her lips. Lush, pink, they were slightly parted. Desire pushed through him like a stream of hot wine. His manhood hardened against his pants. He clenched his teeth, wanting her like a gambler wants a gaming table. She was bad for him. He had no business feeling the way he did, as if he were in an intoxicated trance and would willingly give up his wealth, his life, just to bury himself inside her. Feel her fire and spirit just once.

Her eyes fluttered open. Daniel took it as a sign and caught her lips with his. She was warm and supple and richer than he remembered. He watched her eyes focus on him; a frown marred her brow as he angled his head, taking her lips fully, urging her to respond.

A breath hitched in the back of her throat. She twisted her head to the side. Arching her back, crushing her breasts against his chest, she tried to push him off. "No!"

He threaded his fingers through her hair and held her still. Kissing her again, he watched her, saw the battle in her eyes, the will to fight clashing with the temptation to give in.

"Don't do this to me." Her voice broke with the plea. "Do you think I like this?"

Her eyes darkened with confusion, but he didn't stop to consider the reason. He claimed her mouth again, savagely, relentlessly, like the first kiss they'd shared. There was possessiveness in the kiss, anger and need. He forced her mouth open, mated his tongue with hers. Tremors pulsed through his body, pouring desire through his veins.

Her fingers curled over his, holding on tight. He ran his palm down the side of her neck to the swell of her chest. He smoothed his palm over her breast, closing his eyes, sighing into her mouth with satisfaction. Gasping, she arched her back and pushed her fullness into his hand, filling it, urging him to lift and shape and hold.

He had to get rid of her clothes, had to feel her hot skin. She'd be slick and quivering, ready for him to take.

He heard the click of metal, but it wasn't until he felt the cold barrel of a gun at his nape that he froze. His vision blurred, going red with anger. Not again. Not bloody *again*.

"You'll be letting her go, Captain," a voice snarled from behind him. "Or ye'll not be drawing another breath."

Daniel's body burned, with rage, with desire. Every muscle strained, needing to strike out, find some means to rid himself of the loathsome need tearing beneath his skin. And fury, staggering, smothering waves of fury exploded in his mind.

He stared into the icy bearing of her pewter gray eyes and called himself every kind of fool. A breath shuddered out of her, and she tilted her chin in defiance. He saw the truth in her challenging gaze then. She'd yielded to his kiss, hoping her men would return. Unarmed, she'd had no way to fight him. Or so he'd thought.

In truth, she had a weapon Daniel had never encountered before—the power to numb his senses, blind him to everything except her. She'd employed that deadly tactic on him twice now. This time he knew it would mean his end.

Two sets of hands gripped his upper arms and hauled him upright. They twisted his arms behind his back with a force meant to hurt. He clenched his jaw to keep from grunting in pain. Morgan scrambled to her feet, refusing the aid from her men.

"We've no whip, Capt'n," the largest man in the group said. "But we can teach 'im a lesson with our fists."

Straightening her shirt, Morgan said, "That won't be necessary, Henry. Our time with Captain Tremayne is almost up."

"He can't get away with mauling ye the way he did."

"He won't."

"But, Morgan . . ." The sailor sputtered to a stop beneath her warning stare. Henry had to be nearly three times Morgan's age and as solid as a demicannon, yet he deferred to her decision. Daniel wondered if the intoxicating force that affected him was what caused these men to follow her.

Since they wanted to beat his skull to dust, he was grateful for her interference. She wanted him whole and healthy. Why? Considering their recent struggle, he hadn't thought her capable of killing. But she obviously had something planned. Something that would undoubtedly be worse than the punishment her men could mete out.

"Tie him up," she ordered. "And this time, I don't want him to be able to move."

"Aye, Capt'n."

Dragging him back to camp, the two men slammed him against the trunk of a tree. Morgan stayed a safe distance away. He thought she shivered, but decided he'd imagined it. She watched him with her dark, disturbing eyes, probing as if searching for an answer to a riddle. Holding her injured arm against her waist, she seemed small, vulnerable, revealing something he'd never seen in her before:

insecurity. As if to wipe away the weakness, she rubbed the back of her hand across her lips, then turned and left him to her men.

Henry looped a rope around his chest, fastening the bindings so tight Daniel could scarcely breathe. Moving wasn't possible. He wished thinking . . . remembering . . . wasn't either.

By the time the *Sea Queen* had finished its game of hide-and-seek, the blistering sun had nearly completed its descent. The dinghy had been launched, carrying half a score of men to shore. By torchlight they created an assembly line, loading the boat with supplies, then rowing back to the ship when full. Daniel estimated they had one more trip before they were finished. Then their attention would turn to him.

As word about his violating their captain had passed from one man to another, tension had unfurled like a dying breath. No one spoke to him, or came near where he stood lashed to a tree. The accusing silence sent a warning chill down his spine. He didn't know which reaction was worse, their intimidating, closed-mouth glares or their earlier threats to mutilate him, one body part at a time.

A sudden stillness drew his attention to the shore. The final barrels of water, fresh game and fruit had been loaded. A half-dozen men stood knee deep in the water by the skiff, waiting to leave. The last remaining rays of sun fanned out over the sea, spreading a breathtaking blanket of amber across the rippling surface. The chattering birds had settled for the night; even the brush of wind seemed to be resting. Or perhaps the world around him knew what lay ahead, when he still wasn't sure himself.

He rejected the idea that this would be his last sunset,

his last lungful of fresh air. But for him to survive another day, he would need a miracle.

Along the isolated stretch of beach, he saw a lone person part from the shadows and approach. He knew the slender figure, could still feel her lithe curves meshed with his own. The silky strands of hair, ink black in the growing dusk, cascaded down her body like a protective shield.

She didn't hesitate as she drew closer but advanced with the resolve of a person determined to accomplish her task. She stopped before him, well within reach . . . if one of his hands were free. The flickering light of the torch highlighted her tangle of hair but failed to reach the depth of her eyes. They were soulful, dark, swirling with hidden emotions.

Or was it resignation he saw? She knew she had to complete the task she'd postponed. She certainly didn't appear the gleeful pirate, eager to make a kill.

"Well, Morgan," he said, not understanding why he spoke first, only knowing that the quiet listlessness of her gaze unnerved him. "I suppose it's time to part company."

She managed a half smile. "Yes."

"Then get this the bloody hell over with," he snapped.

She stepped close enough for him to catch the scent of her sun-warmed skin, feel the heat of her through their clothes. She drew her jewel-studded knife from the sheath at her waist.

"I wish I'd never met you," she whispered, her gaze frustrated, angry.

"Had you not taken up arms and become a pirate, we wouldn't have."

"Would you believe me if I said I was sorry about this?"

"Why should I?"

Her gaze slipped down his face, focusing on his mouth. He bit back a curse as his body responded with a will of its own. He'd been caught like a fool; evidently he was going to die like one, too.

"Because it's the truth. I regret what I have to do, but"— she glanced behind her at the waiting men—"it has to be done."

"Then do it, Morgan. Kill me the way you butchered Captain Egham!"

Willful determination flashed silver in her eyes. He saw her raise the knife. She stepped closer still, pressing her body to his. He sucked in a breath at the unexpected shock. She gripped the back of his neck with her free hand and pulled him to her. Reaching up, she closed her mouth over his, stunning him with a riot of sensations: lust, fury, desire. With his blood burning beneath his skin, he thought he might not feel the cold blade when she sliced his throat. Perhaps he should thank her for the kiss.

She slanted her head, forcefully taking what she wanted. Her tongue swept inside his mouth, deep, possessive, with an urgency that screamed of turmoil and need. And hunger for more.

He opened his mouth to accept her, anticipating the bite of steel in his belly. Vaguely, he admitted there were worse ways to die. With a frustrated oath, she jerked away. Confused, he fought for breath. She took another step back, further into the shadows.

"There's an animal trail to the left of here," she said, her breathing labored. "Follow it a mile until you reach a stream."

"What?"

"There you'll find everything you need to survive."

He clenched his jaw, his gaze narrowing as the meaning of her words sank in. "You little witch. You never planned to kill me."

A teasing smile softened her eyes before she disappeared into the dark. "Don't try to reach the ship, Daniel. We won't let you board."

Reach the ship? How the hell could he do that tied to a tree? Furious, he jerked against the ropes. The bindings gave way an inch. He glanced down and saw that one strip of rope had been sliced through. He snapped his head up, straining to see into the gloom. She'd cut him free when she'd kissed him. And he'd stood there, his mind in a haze of angry lust.

Tearing the ropes away, he stalked to the water's edge. A crescent moon hung low in the horizon, edging upward, shedding an illusion of light over a sin black sea. Thready beams ghosted the *Sea Queen*. He heard the hush of voices, the click of a chain as the anchor was raised, the gentle lap of waves against his feet.

"This isn't over, Morgan," Daniel vowed, rubbing his hand across his lips, sealing the taste of her in his mouth. "I'll find you, so help me God. I will."

Somehow he'd get off this accursed island. Then he'd hunt her down. A task that would be made easy, since he knew where to look.

Chapter 7

Morgun cupped a handful of fertile soil in her hand, rich black earth that had rested during her absence. The field had recently been churned and plowed, creating orderly rows. Seeds nestled within the mounds of warmth, promising crops of wheat and corn. And hope. She'd been home almost four months, and still the sight took her breath away. Not until she'd returned, vowing to stay home for good, had she realized how much she'd missed the sloping, moss green hills dotted with grazing cattle, the cluster of homes that were as familiar as her own.

It was hard to imagine that they'd come so close to losing it all. Four years ago, the *Sea Queen* had sailed from their cove, leaving death and destruction behind, to search for a miracle. They'd found one and more.

Gradually the streets of her village had begun to bustle with activity. With the money Morgan and her crew had thieved, homes had been repaired and painted. Roofs had been replaced or strengthened. Livestock now crowded pens and pasture alike. There was laughter in the streets instead of the haunting cry of tears. Life instead of starvation and death.

She wished there had been another way to gain the coin she'd needed to save her village, but there hadn't been. Turning to piracy had been her only option.

"Had you not taken up arms and become a pirate we wouldn't have met."

She shut out the voice that continually echoed in her mind. The looting of ships, the disguises, the tricks she'd used to terrify men had all been necessary. Her village was alive today because of the choice she'd made. She'd do it again, regardless that it would force her to cross paths with Daniel Tremayne.

"Daniel," she whispered, not seeing the newly turned earth any longer but enigmatic blue eyes that smoldered and damned. Eyes that invaded her dreams. "Where are you now? Are you alive? Do you hate me as I know you must?"

She opened her fist, letting the soil drain back to the earth, where it belonged. Where she belonged. She barely had her land legs back, yet she knew she'd never return to the sea. To do so would be folly. Even if she evaded capture from the British Navy who swarmed the oceans in search of sea robbers, the temptation to return to an unnamed island would be too great.

"For a woman who's about to become a bride in a day's time, you look awfully glum, sister," Jo said as she knelt in the field beside Morgan.

Peter. Morgan closed her eyes, not ready to think about him and the change *he'd* brought to her life.

"Now, me," Jo said; "I know why I feel like a fish stranded on shore."

"We've been over this." Morgan wiped her hand on her skirt. "We had to come home."

"I don't belong here anymore."

"Yes, you do, Jo." Morgan sighed, feeling her responsibilities pressing in. Somehow the weight never seemed to lift.

"You're wrong. I have no place here. Not after—"

"It's time to let go of the past." Morgan wanted to reach out and smooth the red curls from Jo's brow, but she didn't, knowing her sister would pull away. "It wasn't your fault Robby died."

"It was my job to take care of our brother." Jo swallowed and turned her face away. When she turned back, Morgan expected to see tears, but this was Jo, she reminded herself when she saw her sister's dry eyes and jaw clenched with suffocating pain.

Jo pulled out the small toy soldier she kept tied to a string and wore around her neck. The toy had been Robby's favorite, one of an entire troop their father had carved for him. Jo had painted each of the little men herself with crushed berries, creating different faces, beards and hair She'd kept the one soldier after Robby's death. As a tie to the past, Morgan wondered? Or a token of her guilt?

"You were little more than a child, yourself," she told Jo for the hundredth time. "He was sick."

Jo closed her eyes and held up her hand, a clear sign she refused to listen to Morgan's reasoning. "I didn't traipse out here to talk about me. I want to know why you've been sulking. It's not like you." A shrewd gleam replaced the disquiet in her eyes. "Becoming Peter's wife is what you wanted before he left to fight in the war."

Anxiety tightened like a claw around Morgan's spine. "It's what we planned."

"And now?"

"Am I doing the right thing?" she wondered aloud. "Marrying Peter?"

Jo scoffed. She picked up a pebble and tossed it into the field. "Am I hearing this right? Captain Morgan is asking for my advice?"

"Yes. Why do you find that so hard to believe?"

"Well, you've never asked before. You charge through

the day, making all the decisions, thinking you know what's best for everyone.''

"I do what I think is right . . ." Morgan stopped herself. She didn't want to lecture. She wanted to shed her role as captain and be a normal woman with a normal life. Something trembled inside her, a fear that what she wanted would be impossible to gain. "Tell me what you think."

Jo pursed her lips, not saying a word. She pulled a frayed scarf from the waistband of her pants and tied her unruly red curls back. Unlike Morgan, who wore a green homespun skirt and a linen blouse, Jo refused to relinquish her britches and boots, insisting she'd reclaim her life as a pirate or die trying.

But was it the sea her sister craved, or escape from the memories and guilt of losing their baby brother?

"Do you love him?"

"Excuse me?" Morgan blinked, startled by the question.

"Peter. Do you love him? You know, the man you're preparing to spend the rest of your life with?"

"I . . . I . . ." Morgan tried to force more, but an answer wouldn't come. "It's not that simple."

"Really?"

"He's a good man, Jo. Or at least he was." Morgan ran her hand through her hair as her stomach tightened with unease. "We've been apart for over four years. He was at war. I was at sea."

Jo rolled her eyes. "I know where everyone was, Morgan."

"It's just that we don't know each other any longer."

"He's considered the two of you engaged all these years. He still wants to marry you, despite the fact that you have a bounty on your head."

"But it's all happening so fast. I didn't agree to marry him this time. Everyone just assumed I would."

"Well," Jo smirked. "You have your answer then."

* * *

"I have my answer, indeed." Morgan stormed into her cottage, slamming the door behind her, and paced to the cold hearth. Grumbling to the empty room, she said, "Do I marry Peter, or not? A simple yes or no would have been nice."

Wrapping her arms about her waist, she circled the sparsely furnished room. The woven rug before the hearth had been her mother's creation, a blend of specially dyed wool her father had brought home from a rare trip to London. A rocking chair of untold years sat beside it, waiting for one of the Fisk sisters to take a seat and do their mending. A sturdy table with two benches occupied most of the space. Dishes from the morning meal still crowded the scarred surface. A shelf held their few plates, pots and pans and the rest of Robby's toy soldiers. Her father had always meant to build a hutch, but he hadn't had time. And truth be known, her mother hadn't cared.

Belongings had meant little to Miriam Fisk. She'd loved her husband and children, valuing her time with them more than what she owned. Love had adorned this house. Remnants remained everywhere Morgan looked.

She tightened her grip on her waist to keep the loss from taking over. She missed them so much. She wanted what her parents had built between them—companionship, commitment, passion. Would she find those with Peter? Companionship, yes. And the fact that he still wanted her as his wife proved he was committed to her.

But passion? They'd grown up together; she'd always liked Peter. But would her skin burn from his touch? Would his kisses taste like sin, pleasuring her beyond her wildest dreams, leaving her trembling for more?

Like Dan . . .

Morgan gasped and clamped her hand over her mouth. "No, no, not like Daniel's."

She clenched her jaw and closed her eyes, but couldn't stop the rush of memory, couldn't block the fire of his eyes, the heat of his skin, the possessiveness of his kiss. A moan rose from the back of her throat. She sat on a bench and doubled over. "I have to forget him."

"Morgan!"

Grace's frightened cry as she came through the front door brought Morgan erect.

"What's wrong?" her youngest sister demanded, rushing across the room and kneeling before her.

"Is something ailing ye?" Simon asked, following Grace inside.

"I'm fine." She drew a steadying breath and pushed to her feet.

"Are you angry, then? Is that why you look like you want to cry?" Grace asked, chewing on her bottom lip. "I know I was supposed to clean the dishes, but Uncle Simon told me about a new calf being born. And I so wanted to see him."

"I'm not angry, angel." Morgan smoothed her hand over her sister's blond curls.

"Then what's wrong?" Grace rose and slowly began collecting the bowls to put in a bucket of water to soak.

"Nothing. And everything," Morgan murmured as she helped her sister.

Simon settled in the rocker and busied himself with refilling his pipe. "Why don't ye leave out nothing and tell us everything. It'll make ye feel better."

Adding bowls to the water, she grabbed a cloth to wipe down the table. "It's just . . . oh, I don't know. Things are happening too fast."

"If we'd waited any longer tae plant the fields, we would've missed the growing season," Simon said, tapping down his tobacco.

"It's not the crop, Uncle."

"It's the wedding, isn't it?" The understanding in Grace's eyes ripped something open inside Morgan.

Sinking onto the bench, she whispered, "Yes."

"Feeling nervous, are ye, lass?" Simon chuckled. " 'Tis to be expected."

"Do you think it's just nerves, Uncle?"

"Of course. You're a score and four now. Long past the age of settling down, starting a family. You're afraid something will stop ye from marrying Peter this time."

Could that be it? she thought. Was she afraid of never having the one thing she'd always wanted? The possibility had never occurred to her. She did want to marry; have her own children to love and teach, and a husband to share her life with. Even before the war and the loss of her parents, she'd dreamed of a man coming home to her each day, wrapping her in his arms, holding her through the night. Someone who would share the joys and the burdens.

He'd always been a faceless ghost in her dreams, yet the qualities she'd sought were as real as any man could be— loyal, caring, protective of those he loved. She simply needed to imagine Peter as the one who held her, the one who would father her children. She closed her eyes and tried to envision him, his wheat-colored hair and soft brown eyes.

"Give it time, Morgan," Simon said thoughtfully. "Once you're married, the two of ye will come together. You'll see."

The vision hovered, struggling to take shape in her mind. She saw hair the color of wheat and a ready smile, a body lanky and tall. She focused on his eyes, and frowned. They weren't the soft brown she'd expected but dark, brooding and *blue!* The short-cropped hair became black, shoulder-length waves, the smile menacing and sensual. The towering body honed with awesome strength.

She snapped her eyes open and shuddered. With a

quiver in her voice, she said, "Perhaps you're right. We just need some time together."

"Come tomorrow, you'll have time aplenty," Simon chuckled.

Grace crossed her arms over her small chest and pursed her lips. "I don't think you should marry Peter at all."

Taken aback, Morgan asked, "Why would you say such a thing?"

"He's the wrong one."

"Now, who else would she be marrying, Grace?" Simon quipped, striking a match on flint and setting it to his pipe. "Peter's the only one who's shown interest, and he's the only one near Morgan's age."

"Thank you so much, Uncle," Morgan retorted. "But I've done just fine without a husband so far."

"Aye, that ye have. But you're still need'n' a man."

"Morgan, you're not listening to me!" Grace's cornflower blue eyes narrowing with annoyance, she tapped her leather-booted foot on the dirt floor. "I said he's the wrong one."

Turning her full attention to her sister, Morgan asked, "And who would the right one be, angel?"

"Captain Tremayne."

Morgan felt her spine stiffen. A tingle rippled across her skin as if she'd been touched by an invisible hand.

Simon growled. "The man's lucky we left him alive, after the way he treated our Morgan."

"Well, I liked him." Grace pursed her lips as if daring anyone to object.

"I know you did, sweetheart." Morgan swallowed past the tightness in her throat. "But even if things hadn't happened the way they did, the captain never would have married a woman like me."

"He might have, if you hadn't been so mean to him."

"He wanted to arrest us, Grace." Morgan didn't want to frighten her sister, but she had to understand that their lives, hers included, had been in danger. "He would have taken us to London to stand trial as pirates. You know what would have happened then, don't you?"

Grace dipped her chin and regarded Morgan through lowered lashes. In a reluctant whisper, she said, "You shouldn't have left him on that island, Morgan. It wasn't right."

"You know we had to."

"He might be dead now, or close to dying." Her bottom lip quivered. "What if there were wild savages on the island? They'll cook and eat him. Or there could be horrible animals. With claws and sharp teeth."

Morgan reached out and drew her sister into her arms, needing to ease both of their tremors. Grace had no idea how closely her fear matched her own. If Daniel died . . . She rocked her sister back and forth, refusing to finish the thought. "Captain Tremayne is a smart man. There isn't an animal or wild savage alive that will get the best of him."

Morgan pulled back and smiled reassuringly. She tickled her sister beneath her chin until Grace relinquished a laugh.

"A barbarian doesn't stand a chance at bring'n' down the great Captain Daniel Tremayne," Simon boasted. "Listen to your sister, Grace. It took a woman pirate to accomplish that."

Morgan welcomed the hesitant knock at the front door, anything to distract her from her present task of arranging her hair. Her shaking hands had made pinning it up impossible, so she'd brushed it straight down her back, clipping two strands at the crown of her head with a hammered gold clasp she'd bought from a street vendor in Madagascar.

Leaving her room, she touched the weight strapped to her thigh beneath her gown—the *Sea Queen* blade. The women in the village would grumble and shake their heads if they knew she planned to wear a knife on her wedding day. But after carrying it for so long, she felt defenseless without it.

Reaching the door, she opened it and felt her stomach flip. "Peter."

Peter Goodson stood on the threshold, a wavering grin on his familiar face. "I know it's not proper for me to be here, Morgan, but . . . I wanted to speak with ye before the ceremony."

"Of course." With an awkward smile, she said, "Come in."

Wearing a freshly brushed wool coat and pants, he stepped inside and removed his hat.

"Please, sit down," she offered nervously, extending a hand toward the kitchen table.

"I think I'd rather stand." He watched her with brown eyes that were kind, nonthreatening, certainly not challenging. His features were honed thin by hard work and years of worry. And war, she added. She knew some of what he'd been through, but not everything. Likewise, he knew what she'd accomplished during her time as a pirate and that she was a wanted woman. He'd never asked her for details, and she hadn't offered any, wanting to put that part of her life behind her.

Once they married, they'd have years to fill in the gaps. She pressed her hands to her waist to ease the trembling that never seemed to disappear entirely.

Peter would be her husband within the hour. The reminder sent her nerves cresting like a wave.

"You're beautiful," he said, sounding stunned.

She glanced down at the burgundy gown she'd purchased at the same market as the hair clasp. After all the ports she'd visited, it had been the only time she'd splurged on herself, unable to resist the simple design with its scooped neckline and tight-fitting sleeves. Silver vines and roses were threaded across the bodice and around the cuffs. When she'd paid for the dress, she'd never thought it would become her wedding gown.

"Thank you."

He bent his head and studied his boots, as if there he'd find the courage to continue. "There's things I've been want'n' tae say tae ye. I thought it best I do it now, before we meet with the priest."

She stepped forward and caught the back of the rocker. Was he calling off the wedding? Had he sensed her hesitancy and realized he didn't want a reluctant wife? She wouldn't blame him. Peter deserved someone who cherished him. And she would, she was certain of it, but only if they were given a chance. *And only if I can forget Daniel Tremayne.*

She closed her eyes and forced the thought away. Peter was the man she'd decided to marry, she reminded herself adamantly. He's the one she could build her hopes and dreams with. Daniel would only tear her world apart. He was dangerous, destructive. From this moment forward, she vowed to think of him as dead. Dead and out of her life forever. She refused to ruin her one chance at a normal life. She wanted this marriage. She needed it.

"I'll make ye a good husband, Morgan."

Opening her eyes, she blinked back sudden tears. "I know you will, Peter."

"We aren't the people we were four years ago. We've changed."

In more ways than you know, she thought, wishing it weren't so.

"My parents—their marriage was arranged." He looked past her to the front door. "The entire village is ready to celebrate our wedding. They've waited a long time for us to say our vows."

She nodded, because he spoke the truth. For as long as she could remember, she'd heard the elders speak about the two of them marrying. Her parents hadn't objected, and Morgan hadn't thought to.

"I've done things I'm not proud of," he said, swallowing as if he, too, were struggling with memories that wouldn't fade.

"So have I." She crossed to him and took hold of his hand, feeling the scrape of calluses across his palm. "This is going to be a new beginning for us, Peter. We've both been through so much. Our lives have been on hold. It's time to change that."

Saying the words out loud, she knew she meant them. Holding his hand, feeling the roughness of his skin, looking into his compassionate eyes, she knew she'd never burn for his touch. It didn't matter, she told herself. She cared for him, and given time, her feelings would deepen. There was hope and promise between them; she could build their lives on that.

She reached up and kissed him on the lips. Stepping back, she smiled as a flush darkened his face. Feeling more determined than ever, she said, "We've both done things we regret, Peter. But we did them in order to survive. Those days are in the past. Our future begins now."

"You're going tae make a fine wife, Morgan Fisk." With a timid smile, he lifted her hand, kissing the back. "I suppose the next time I see you, we'll be man and wife."

She nodded, ignoring the way her breath shuddered from her lungs after he left. *Man and wife, man and wife.* This was what she wanted. She refused to give in to a case of bad nerves now.

Returning to her room, she closed the door and leaned against the frame. She only needed another moment, then she'd be ready to face the priest and begin her new life. She took a steadying breath, then another. Her quivering stomach eased, almost returning to normal.

"Hello, Morgan."

It was the voice in her dreams, belonging to a man she

couldn't forget. Morgan snapped her eyes open to see him standing beside the open window. A scream lodged in her throat. She reached for her knife but couldn't grasp it through her skirts. Spinning, she jerked on the handle. Daniel closed the distance and slammed his hand against the door.

She turned, pressed her back against the panel. Her heart pushed against her chest, pounding with sudden fear. He was here, alive . . . God, no . . .

Burying his other hand into her hair, Daniel cupped her head, forcing her to look at him. He leaned so close she could see nothing but a mad kind of fury boiling deep in his blue eyes. The scar at his temple bled white with his anger. In a voice that was hoarse, grinding with rage, he said, "I'm sorry to disappoint that fine young man, but you'll not be marrying him today."

Chapter 8

Daniel fisted his hand against the door until his knuckles turned white. He shook with the temptation to slide his fingers around Morgan's neck and squeeze until the disbelief in her eyes turned to blind, undeniable fear. She jerked free and tried to spin away. He slapped his other palm against the wall, trapping her between his outstretched arms.

Facing him, she opened her mouth to scream. He clamped his hand over her lips, cutting it off. The rebellious thought of quieting her with a kiss leapt to the forefront of his brain. She'd been a reckless beauty in her pirate garb of fitted pants and wind-blown shirt. But dressed as a lady in a blood red gown, she was all the more tempting, she was a vixen who stirred his most basic, carnal needs.

But he wouldn't be making that mistake again. He'd learned his lesson, having been snared twice before like a witless rabbit. He wouldn't be kissing her now. But the moment he had her away from her village, she would be his, to do with as he pleased.

Afterward he'd turn her over to the king, where she'd stand trial for her crimes.

Her surprise wearing off, she kicked him in the shin, then pushed against his chest. He'd forgotten how strong she was. Daniel stumbled back, but not before locking his arms around her waist, bringing her with him. They landed across the bed, with her on top of him. Morgan reached back, her hand clenched. He caught her wrist an instant before her fist could smash his face. He flipped her on her back. The ropes supporting the straw mattress groaned with their combined weight.

Breathing hard, he stared into eyes bright with fear and desperation. She lay beneath him, her body stretched out against his. The feel of her brought unwanted memories of another time they'd lain just so, all hot and eager, with passion roaring through their limbs. Or so he'd thought.

She'd pretended to want his touch, he was certain of it. During the past months he'd convinced himself his reaction hadn't been caused by her allure, the seductive cast to her eyes, the scent of her skin. He'd been at sea for months with vengeance hot in his veins. *That* had been the reason he'd wanted her.

Only now, he wondered if he'd been lying to himself. The boiling lust hardening his shaft was unlike anything he'd ever known . . . except with her. A fact that infuriated him.

"Let me go."

"I think not." He scowled, letting her struggle against him. She wouldn't escape him this time. She was his. Lifting her skirt, he found her knife tucked into a leather band around her thigh. Slipping it free, he secured it behind him in the waistband of his pants.

"How did you find me?" she demanded. "I left you on an island."

"A fact I will never forget," he said with such bitterness a tremor ripped beneath her skin. "Or forgive."

"I treated you fairly, Daniel."

"You call marooning fair treatment? I was trapped on that island for three bloody months."

Her chin tilted in a stubborn angle. "I could have ordered your execution."

"Then why didn't you?" That question, among others, had compelled him to find a way to escape his prison. He'd become obsessed with finding her again, confronting her, seeing her punished for every injustice she'd done.

"Perhaps I didn't want you to die a quick death," she said with mocking derision. She gave a futile tug of her arms, glaring at him when he easily held her. Cursing under her breath, she added, "I made sure you had enough food and supplies to survive. You should be grateful for that."

"Oh, I am grateful—to the merchant ship who investigated the signal fire I'd set. If not for that captain's curiosity, I wouldn't be here now."

"What do you want, Daniel?" she demanded, but he could see it in her eyes. She already knew.

Holding both her hands in one of his, he slid his fingers around her neck, resting his palm against the frantic rise and fall of her chest. "I always finish what I start."

"I thought rape was beneath even you," she spat.

Her nipples pearled against the tight fabric. Daniel wondered if he'd have to force her. If he stoked the fire that simmered between them, would she surrender to him willingly? She possessed an untapped passion, a hidden sensuality she kept buried beneath cool control. He sensed it as surely as he could see the frantic pulse beating at the base of her throat.

"While the thought of taking you right now has its appeal, rape isn't in my plans for you, Morgan."

She shook her head and started to speak, but stopped.

"I'm taking you to London."

She bucked against him. "No!"

Throwing his leg across her bared thigh, he pressed her

further into the mattress. "It's no use to struggle. This time, none of your tricks will work."

"You can't, Daniel." Tears pooled and dripped a shimmering path down her temples. Her pleading eyes expressed the words she was too proud to say. *I don't want to die.*

He willed himself to ignore her tears, just as he ignored the tremor in her limbs. He jerked her off the bed. "Save your begging, Morgan. I didn't come this far only to leave empty-handed."

"Please, no, God, no, you can't take everyone. They're old men. They never would have turned to pirating if not for me. Please, Daniel, you know what they do to pirates." A sob broke from her chest. She gripped the lapels of his coat. "It's me the king wants."

Daniel glanced at the closed door. His obsession had been to find Morgan. He'd given her crew little thought. He knew they all lived in the village. He'd hidden for the past week on the outskirts of town, watching the men, who'd once goaded him with grizzly accounts of his impending death, go about their lives, feeding farm animals, working their fields. They were unlike any pirates he'd run across before, who drank and whored and fought, spending their plunder at the first port they reached.

Morgan's crew were family men, farmers and fishermen. His orders had been to bring in all the pirates, but King George would be satisfied with their captain. But she didn't know that.

"I'll make a bargain with you," he said.

She drew a shuddering breath.

"I'll take only you, but only if you come without a fight."

She clenched her jaw, her body going rigid with a courage he'd witnessed in her before. "I'll go with you."

Daniel stared into her reflective eyes. He saw her resignation and fear. Something inside him rejected what he was about to do. She was a woman. *But not one that needs my care,* he reminded himself. She'd proved that time and again.

But he knew that a deeper reason caused his hesitation. Receiving Morgan's acceptance meant sealing her death.

Grace crushed the bouquet of wildflowers to her chest. She leaned back against an inside corner of the oak armoire and stared, wide-eyed, into the dark. She'd spent half the morning searching for just the right flowers. Yellow dahlias mixed with daffodils and bluebells. She'd used her last hair ribbon to tie the bundle together. They were to be a surprise for Morgan, her gift for her sister's wedding day. Now they were ruined, their sweet scent overwhelming the tight space.

But that hardly mattered. Captain Tremayne was alive! She could hardly believe it. Hiding inside the wardrobe, she listened to her sister and the captain crawl through Morgan's bedroom window.

When Peter had arrived to visit, Grace had crept into Morgan's room and into the wardrobe, not wanting to interrupt the couple. When she'd heard Peter leave, she'd been about to emerge from her hidey-hole when she'd heard the captain's ominous voice. Her heart thudded against her ribs, the heat inside the armoire making her dizzy.

The captain was here! He wasn't dead. She'd been so afraid that bloodthirsty savages had scalped him. She should have believed Morgan. The captain knew how to take care of himself.

When all the muffled scrapes and urgent whispers ceased, she pushed open the armoire door. Biting down on her bottom lip, she peeked into the room. Empty. No one would have seen them leave, Grace realized. The entire village waited at the church for Morgan to arrive so the wedding could begin.

With her blood rushing through her ears, she climbed out of her hiding place and raced to the door. She had to find Jo and Uncle Simon. They would know what to do. She grabbed the door handle, but stopped and stared at the flowers that had begun to wilt. If Jo left now, she'd find Morgan; then she'd kill the captain for sure. Grace's heart skipped erratically with the thought. Once safe, Morgan would come home and marry Peter.

"I might only be twelve," Grace muttered, "but I know *that* marriage is one that shouldn't take place."

Morgan belonged with Captain Tremayne. Why didn't everyone see that as easily as she did? She'd seen the two of them watching each other when they thought no one was looking. She knew about the kiss they'd shared in Morgan's cabin, regardless that everyone tried to keep it from her. To protect her, she thought, smiling with annoyance. She'd also been aware that neither Morgan nor the captain had been the same after their kiss.

And they'd been alone on the island . . .

Her sister and the English lord were destined for each other, Grace knew it as surely as she knew it wouldn't rain for another two days. Which meant their escape would be all the easier. But to where? she mused.

To London, as Daniel had said? To stand trial?

She couldn't believe he'd be so spiteful, regardless that Morgan had duped him more than once. If he had come to Dunmore to arrest all the pirates, why had he settled for only one? And where were his men? Why hadn't they raided the village, burnt the homes, trussed everyone up in chains?

She crossed to the window. Her sister was nowhere in sight, but Grace thought she heard the pounding of horses' hooves fading beyond the distant hill.

Daniel wouldn't bring Morgan to harm, Grace reaffirmed silently. He loved her; he just didn't know it yet.

But still, she better tell someone what had happened, just to be safe.

Tossing the flowers out the window, she turned away and slowly headed for the church and her waiting kinsmen. And Peter. Yes, she had to tell Peter his bride wouldn't be able to make the wedding.

—

Wind buffeted Morgan's face, drying her tears before they could fall down her cheeks. Seated sideways on the roan stallion with her skirts hiked around her knees, she gripped the horse's mane as he raced over ground rough with rocks and brush. She had no fear of falling, though a broken neck would be preferable to what she faced. With Daniel behind her, his arm locked around her waist, she knew he'd never let her go.

Not after he'd accomplished the unthinkable—escaping from a barren island and hunting her down—to fulfill his vow of revenge.

She wanted to turn around, glimpse her home one last time. But it was too late. They'd ridden too far, too deep into the sweeping foothills that surrounded her small village, isolating it from the harsh world. But this was land she knew, which meant she had hope. They would have to stop somewhere along the road to London, rest the horse, camp for the night. Even if he chose to stay at an inn, he'd have to sleep eventually. Then she'd find a way to escape. She had to. She had to warn her people.

By freely leaving with Daniel, she'd bargained with the devil. She had no doubts that once she faced the hangman's noose, Daniel would change his mind and return for the rest of her crew. But what if she couldn't find a way to escape? She'd have to find a way to send word for her family to run. Soon everyone would realize she was missing. Hopefully, Jo would know to abandon Dunmore, their homes and fields, and escape to safety. The thought of losing what they'd fought so hard to rebuild infuriated Morgan. But starting over in another village was a far better fate than what she now faced.

Morgan resisted leaning back, not wanting to touch Daniel any more than she had to, but the muscles in her back burned, her thighs ached, unaccustomed to clinging to a racing horse. Since leaving her room, Daniel hadn't spoken another word to her, and his silence was as chilling as his threats.

She gripped his hand holding the reins and urged him to ease the horse into a lope. Amazed that he complied, she said over her shoulder, "I need to rest."

A discerning grin spread over his mouth and hardened his eyes. "They won't catch us, Morgan. So don't bother trying to slow me down."

"I'm not trying . . ." She clamped her jaw shut. She *did* want to slow him down, better her chances of finding help. "Where are the rest of your men?"

"I came alone."

"You . . ." Her mouth gaped as realization dawned. "You never planned to take my crew to London?"

"They're safe, for now. I imagine they're still waiting in your chapel, wondering why the bride hasn't arrived."

The bitterness in his tone caught her off guard, but she ignored it. Anger squeezed her throat so tight she could barely get the next words out. "Do you intend to go back on your word and arrest them?"

"Not as long as you behave and don't try to escape."

She swallowed, wanting to believe that sacrificing herself hadn't been for nothing. "By now they know I'm missing."

"A lot of good it'll do them," he scoffed. He glanced at the surrounding landscape, however, as if expecting outraged pirates to charge over the hill after him. Wariness sharpened his eyes when he met her gaze. "Tell me, does your fiancé know about the kisses we shared?"

"Don't be ridiculous."

"I only ask because if you were my woman, I'd take offense at you lusting after another man."

Morgan swung her arm around to strike him, but Daniel caught her wrist, something he seemed disgustingly proficient at doing. Twisting her hand behind her back, he held her prisoner in his arms. The horse slowed to a walk, giving Morgan a chance to catch her breath and realize the intimacy of their position. Her bottom fit snug in his lap; her left side and breast were trapped against his torso. The situation was erotic and maddening, making her feel more than she wanted to feel.

"Let me go."

"No," he said, his pensive eyes studying her face. "I don't think so."

She wedged her free hand between them, pressing her palm against his chest. His heart beat with violent thumps. She felt an answering pulse in her fingers. A birth of tingles made her breath hitch in her throat. Heat poured off his skin, soaking through her skirts, warming her legs, her back, moving up her arms and down to her center, where it felt she would erupt into a flame and burn to ash.

No, not again. She wanted to whimper and bow her head in shame. But that would be giving in, surrendering to her attraction to him. Furious with her betraying body, she tilted her chin in defiance, refusing to feel anything for him but loathing. Hatred! Daniel Tremayne wanted to see her dead. And she would despise him until her dying breath.

Wanting Daniel would only lead her to a wicked trap and end with a hangman's noose. Defying her mental vow, her body tightened, straining toward futile desire.

"Do you think it's safe to kiss you now?" he taunted. "Without fear of having your men interrupt us?" His breath teased her lips with an imagined touch. Lines of stress creased the corners of his mouth.

"Do so and I'll bite off your tongue."

"Ah," he chuckled and leaned so close her head filled with his scent of leather and sun-warmed skin. "Morgan the Scylla until the end."

She tensed, preparing herself for his assault, the force of his lips, the staggering power of his taste.

He straightened, his eyes narrowing as if he didn't like what he saw. "Another time, perhaps."

Quickly scanning the horizon, he released her arm and spurred the horse into a steady lope. Morgan faced front. She'd escaped the threat of his kiss . . . this time. She had to be stronger the next, better prepared to defy him if she intended to keep her wits about her. And her neck intact.

Daniel maintained their rigid pace throughout the day, stopping only twice to rest and water the horse. To her frustration, he didn't let her out of his sight either time. Morgan had thought she'd seen his relentless, driven nature before, but today she'd discovered a new depth. Sweat lathered the horse's neck. Morgan's muscles were beyond aching; they were numb with pain. She'd given up her vow to touch him as little as possible. Now she leaned against his chest, letting him support her tired body.

With each turn they made, she tried to keep her bearing. She knew the seas, but she'd rarely traveled so far from home by land. The sun had increased its westerly descent, allowing night to push closer in. The breeze skirting the hills had lost its heat; the chill taking its place bit her to the bone.

They'd have to stop soon, make a camp or find a barn in which to sleep. Her stomach rumbled, reminding her she hadn't eaten all day. She'd been too nervous before the wedding, and Daniel hadn't offered anything since kidnapping her.

The wedding. She closed her eyes, imagining the frantic

state her family was in. If Daniel had never found her, she'd be a married woman right now.

If you were my woman, I'd take offense at you lusting after another man. She closed off Daniel's taunt. He'd ruined everything—her chance for a normal life, a companion to share a future with. She'd never experience the celebration the women in her village had planned. If she'd exchanged her vows, the festivities would be at their peak with kegs of ale, a feast of fresh vegetables and beef. Ian would be playing his prized violin, encouraging everyone to dance. And Peter . . .

Sweet Peter would soon be leading her to their bedchamber for their first night together as man and wife. She didn't feel the pang of regret she should have at missing their night together, which only brought tears to her eyes once again. Life would have been good with Peter, she reaffirmed. She would have *made* it work.

She drew in a sharp breath and pushed the thoughts away. It wouldn't do her any good to think about something she couldn't have. Was never meant to have, she realized with an ache in her chest.

The hesitancy she'd felt clear to her soul had been there for a reason. She didn't love Peter. Marrying him would have been wrong. She wondered if he'd felt that, too, if that was the reason he'd come to see her. Perhaps Daniel had done him a favor by stopping the wedding. Perhaps Peter would someday find a woman worthy of him. No matter what happened from this moment on, she knew that woman wouldn't be her.

Shivering, not caring if Daniel objected, she pulled the sides of his coat around her arms. The man emitted more heat than a hearth full of embers. He had to be exhausted, yet he showed no signs of slowing.

Though she didn't want to speak to him, she had to ask, "When are we going to stop?"

He didn't answer, but continued riding for another few

minutes. She sighed in disgust, hating the fact that he'd gotten the better of her. If only she'd known he'd come to Dunmore alone . . . But she'd fallen for his trick, just as he'd fallen for hers on board the *Sea Queen*. She hadn't tricked him on the island, though. If Henry hadn't returned . . . She pressed her lips together, not wanting to think about what she'd have let Daniel do to her.

As they crested a hill, icy wind slapped their bodies and pulled at her hair, bringing her out of her ponderings. Below, situated in the growing dusk, a village twice the size of her own was nestled against the shore. She breathed a sigh of relief. They'd soon find a warm place to stay, food to eat. And hopefully, someone who would carry a message to Dunmore for her. She sat up straight, eager to be on their way.

Daniel nudged the horse and sent it galloping down the slope. He slowed to a walk when they reached the main street. Few people were out, and those who were didn't pay them much attention. On her right, Morgan spotted a sign with two bulls charging each other. Butting Heads Inn, a two-story building in sore need of repair and paint. She bit her lip to keep from asking Daniel any questions, such as would she be allowed her own room, would they stay the night, would he consider releasing her? She'd decided that the less they spoke, the better off they'd both be. Besides, she probably wouldn't like any of his answers anyway.

When he continued past the inn, however, she couldn't keep quiet. Pointing at the building where lantern light glowed through the open windows, revealing people sitting down to a supper of stew and baked bread, she asked, "Aren't we stopping here?"

"No."

She twisted to face him. "If you aren't going to think of yourself, or me, then consider your horse. He's exhausted."

Daniel tightened the arm he'd kept pinned at her waist all day, forcing her to face front. "We'll be there soon enough."

"Be where?" she demanded. As soon as the words left her mouth, she wished them back. She spotted a schooner, five decks tall, waiting for them at the end of town. How had she missed seeing the monster ship before? Three masts, their sails rolled and bound for the night, towered over the plank deck. A man on board spotted them. He called out orders, sending a dozen sailors scurrying about.

A red flag snapped in the changing wind, revealing a golden lion, his single, outstretched paw raised to ward off an attack. She knew the flag, had learned to avoid it during her life as a pirate. It belonged to the Earl of Leighton, the equally renowned and feared Captain Daniel Tremayne.

The horse walked down the pier and up the gangplank, his hooves echoing like nails being hammered into her coffin. Arriving on deck, Daniel reined to a stop. He leapt from the animal's back and reached for her. When his hands closed around her waist, she knew she'd lost any chance to warn her people. Tears burned her eyes. She'd failed them. After all they'd been through, *she'd failed them.*

"Come, Morgan," Daniel said. "It's time for your last trip at sea."

Chapter 9

Daniel opened the door to his cabin and ushered his prisoner inside. It was dark as coal in the room, but having spent several days sailing for the port nearest to Dunmore, he knew the ship well enough to find the brass lanterns hanging from the overhead beams. Lighting one, he closed the door, bolting it more for effect than for his fear that Morgan would somehow escape.

She stood in the center of the spacious chamber, scanning the teak desk, the wired cabinets filled with books, ledgers and charts. A gallery of paned windows splayed across the rear wall, a luxury on any ship, but after spending months at sea in a confined cabin during the war, Daniel had added the extravagance to his newest vessel.

"It seems I'll be traveling to London in style," she said with little enthusiasm, tossing a length of sable dark hair over her shoulder.

"I added the *Pursuit* to my fleet last year."

"The *Pursuit*," she mused. "How appropriate."

"It was meant as a metaphor in my quest to secure my family estate," he explained, not sure why he bothered.

Instead, he realized it had become a tool to track down a woman.

That woman stood before him, rigid with stubborn strength. And pride that compared to his own. The light softening her tanned complexion also darkened her gown to blood red. She held her shoulders back and tilted her chin. The fire that he knew burned at the core of her spirit also flushed her cheeks. Only her eyes hinted at the fear he knew she had to be fighting. The gray orbs were dark, alert, prepared for battle. Seeing her this way, with her hair loose and untamed from their ride, her simple dress— *her wedding gown*—a feminine contradiction to the pirate he knew her to be, called to his chivalrous nature.

It wasn't in him to harm a woman. It had taken weeks of being marooned on that blasted island to come to terms with what he now recognized as his one principal fault: he'd believed *all* women were weak.

He'd accepted that he couldn't pigeonhole Morgan as a typical female. She wasn't a lady who needed protection. She didn't care if she dirtied her hands or if her clothes were mussed. She didn't need him to take care of her.

So why was he tempted to do just that?

Was this another one of her tricks? he wondered. Was she using the very strengths he'd first found repulsive to her advantage?

Or was he finally seeing a glimpse of the real Morgan, the woman she could have become if she'd taken the path of respectability instead of piracy? Whatever the case, she was beautiful. He couldn't deny that. Nor could he deny wanting her. The thought of taking her in his arms now, kissing her, tasting all of her, driving inside her, left him shaking. He should do it, he thought, and finally rid himself of this destructive obsession.

But seduction, maybe even rape, was what she expected from him. He didn't plan to end her torment so soon. No, he planned to prolong her apprehension as she had his.

A knock at the door drew his attention. He threw the bolt and said, "Come in."

Mr. Tobitt, his first officer who'd fainted like a virgin maid at the sight of Morgan, eased partway into the cabin, careful to keep his gaze fixed on the floor. "Excuse me, Capt'n. We're ready to get under way."

"Excellent, Mr. Tobitt." Daniel resisted shaking his head. He'd explained what had happened aboard the *Sea Queen,* but Tobitt and the rest of his crew still thought it a miracle he'd escaped with his life and all his body parts intact. Stepping around Morgan, he took his seat behind his desk. "You have the helm."

"Ah, sir," Tobitt said, still averting his gaze. "I brought ye some things I thought ye might be need'n'."

"And what's that?"

"A pair of chains, the strongest we 'ave."

Morgan visibly stiffened; her worried gaze snapped to Daniel. He watched his crewman, not wanting to see the silent accusations in her eyes.

Tobitt held up a pair of slave chains with thick ankle and wrist cuffs. Next he produced a black scarf. "Ye should blindfold her before it's too late."

"Thank you, Tobitt. Bring them in."

The sailor declined, laying the items inside the doorway instead. "I still think ye should put her in the hold. There's naught down there for her to terrorize, except for the rats, that is."

"Thank you, Mr. Tobitt. If I change my mind, I'll let you know."

Daniel scowled at the closing door. He *should* put Morgan in the hold, where light never penetrated and the air smelled as dank as a tomb. So why couldn't he do it? Give the order to lock her in chains as she'd done to him?

He pushed himself up from his chair and turned away from the question ... and from Morgan, who quietly watched him.

He spun around, realizing the mistake he'd just made. A steel letter opener lay on his desk. A quill pen, the tip honed to a deadly point, rested beside it. Lanterns hung from the ceiling—all items Morgan could use as weapons against him.

But she hadn't moved. She returned his gaze, her expression steady, restrained. He eased his stance, but tensed when she turned for the door. It wasn't locked. If she tried to leave, she wouldn't get far, not with a ship full of crewmen roaming the decks above. *Who were terrified of her.*

They'd probably cower in fear or, worse, riot and throw her overboard.

She didn't reach for the handle but bent to retrieve the chains and scarf. Facing him, she said, "Should I put these on myself, or would you like the honor?"

Her somber tone set his teeth on edge. Where was the woman who'd fought him at every turn, the pirate who'd won through cunning and courage? Why didn't she try to outwit him? Argue to change his mind? Use her damnable female allure to weaken his resolve? Or was this another one of her tricks? Was she pretending to cooperate instead of using arguments and tears?

He couldn't fall for this ruse like he had her others. He'd vowed to bring her to trial for Captain Egham's death, and he would. He had to. King George had organized an expedition to find Morgan, demanding she be brought to justice. If Daniel hadn't found her, another British captain would have.

But why didn't she fight? She knew her capture meant her death. He couldn't believe she'd quietly accept that.

Crossing to her, he took the chains and blindfold and tossed them to the floor with a rattling clank. "Unlike my crew, I don't believe these are necessary. As I'm sure you're aware, escape is impossible."

"We made a bargain," she said, her low, smoky voice

rolling inside him. "You promised to leave my men and family alone if I came willingly."

The answer cut through his craving for revenge. She'd agreed to forfeit her life to save her family and village. She wouldn't fight as long as she thought he would keep his word. How many women did he know who would sacrifice their life for others? How many men? To his amazement, he admitted the answer was none.

For some insane reason, Daniel wanted to take her by the shoulders and shake her. Make her realize how dire her situation was. Didn't the woman know she faced a gruesome death? He clenched his hands at his sides, but the need for some emotion from her overwhelmed him. "When you stand trial in London, you'll be found guilty."

She nodded.

"You'll be hanged as a murderer and a thief." His stomach knotted as a grisly image of her dangling from a rope, her neck broken, flashed through his mind.

Outrage flared in her eyes. "I may be a thief, but to convict me as a murderer would be a travesty."

"I have proof otherwise."

Her gaze narrowed. "What proof?"

"You raided my ship the *Intrepid.*"

She straightened her spine and waited for him to continue.

"Do you deny it?"

"No."

Until this moment, Daniel hadn't realized how much he'd wanted her to deny the charge. She was a criminal. The fact settled over his soul with suffocating weight.

With forced calm, he said, "You stole the cargo of gold and rum. Then demanded more. When Captain Egham didn't produce what you wanted, you killed him."

"That's a lie!"

"You slit him open, Morgan."

She shook her head in denial.

He advanced on her, forcing her to retreat. He jerked her knife from his waistband. "With this blasted dagger you're so proud of, you cut him from neck to belly."

She was forced to stop when her legs butted against the bed. She lifted her chin, her unwavering gaze locking with his.

"Did you enjoy it?" he asked in a vicious whisper that trembled up from the black depths of his soul. "Did you laugh when his entrails bled across the deck?"

An erratic tremor gripped her shoulders. She clenched her jaw, her eyes widening with horror.

"You threw him into the sea."

"I didn't."

"I have a witness, Morgan." He towered over her, mere inches away from touching her. "Admit what you did. Then tell me why you killed an unarmed man who had a wife."

She closed her eyes, and he saw tears glistening at their corners. Somehow she kept them from falling. No doubt, her damnable cold heart, he thought. "Aye, he had a wife of fifteen years and three children. You murdered their father when you could have let him go."

Trembling, she opened her eyes, staring at him with a look that was bright with defiance. "I've never killed anyone."

Daniel gripped her shoulders and hauled her against him, shaking her once. "Damn you, woman, don't lie to me!"

"I'm not."

"You butchered a dozen crewmen on the *Intrepid.*"

"Daniel, no!"

Her voice broke, and so did Daniel. He crushed his mouth to hers, stopping her denials, punishing her for the lies that tempted him to listen, begged him to believe. He invaded her mouth with his tongue, absorbed her cries of protest. He ignored her fists pushing him away. Tossing the knife aside, he fisted one hand in her hair, holding her head still. He wrapped his other arm around her back, locking her to him, molding the curves that haunted his dreams against his frame. Her stomach protected his swelling shaft, forcing a groan of torment and frustration from his throat.

This was revenge, savage and base. He knew he was hurting her and condemning himself to an allure that would damn his soul. But he couldn't stop. He wanted more, wanted it deeper. She tasted hot and silky and forbidden.

Then he felt her fingers sliding through his hair, felt her body strain against his. She quivered in his arms— with desire? he wondered, running his thumb over her breast, feeling her nipple harden against his touch. Tasting salt on her lips, he realized she shook with silent tears. He broke the kiss, but only enough to allow a breath between them.

She tried to speak, swallowed, then tried again. "I didn't kill your captain, Daniel."

A part of him listened, tempted to believe her. He pulled away slightly and raked a hand through his hair. What in God's name did he think he was doing? She was a pirate! A cunning, deceitful woman who'd tricked him too many times. And she was trying to again.

"The man who witnessed the murder is my partner, Morgan. He wouldn't lie to me."

"Then someone masqueraded as me, used my name."

"There aren't many female pirates. The crewmen knew who you were. You even admit to being there."

"But I didn't kill anyone." She drew her hands down his chest and fisted them. Her eyes glittered silver with tears and the desperate need for him to trust her.

But he couldn't. If he believed her, that would mean he'd have to believe Thomas had lied. And that was unthinkable. Even now he could see the torment in his partner's face as he relived the horror he'd witnessed.

No one could have faked the agony that had weighted Thomas's words. His shoulders had been stooped with defeat and guilt for living when so many others had died. He'd pleaded with Daniel not to hunt Morgan down, worried that Daniel would meet the same fate as their captain.

She released him and crossed her arms beneath her breasts. He accepted the break, needing distance. She had the power to make him lose control. He'd kissed her when he should have done as Tobitt suggested and locked her in the hold. He couldn't touch her again; he shouldn't even attempt to go near her.

Backing away, he went to the desk, but he didn't sit. Instead he stared out the paned windows. He didn't worry that she would try to stab him in the back. In a way, he wished she would. Then he wouldn't have to watch her hang.

"You've heard the rumors about me," she said more as a statement than a question.

He nodded, angling his head to watch her from the corner of his eye.

"I supposedly have twelve heads and fanged teeth and can dissolve parts of a man's body with a single look."

Daniel almost grinned, recalling how terrified Mr. Tobitt had been the day he'd decided to track Morgan down. "It's also rumored that you eat your captives."

She wrinkled her nose with distaste. "Did you believe any of those tales?"

"No."

She considered him a moment. "Then why are you so quick to believe I'm capable of murder?"

"Because you're a pirate," he said, for lack of a better answer. He realized then that she would have made an excellent barrister . . . if she'd been a man.

"Yes, I am. But consider this, Daniel. It's true that I robbed the *Intrepid* of rum and spices." Her crystalline eyes narrowed, and he knew he wasn't going to like whatever she had to say next. "But there wasn't any gold."

Morgan gripped the railing with both hands, embracing the feel of wood beneath her palms. Pristine white sails snapped overhead, caught tight against the blustering wind. Closing her eyes, she tilted her head to the morning sun, letting warm rays dry the mist of seawater on her face. Daniel's ship, the *Pursuit*, rocked beneath her feet as it cut through rolling swells. The ocean churned beneath the hull, rumbling like the growl of a beast, she thought, a lion with his paw raised and his mouth open in a roar of victory. She opened her eyes to the Earl of Leighton's flag soaring against the brilliant sky.

Daniel's victory.

He'd tracked her down because he thought her a murderer. He wanted her to stand trial for her crimes. There would be no trial, at least not a fair one, she thought, her eyes watering from staring at the glaring blue expanse above. Blinking, she lowered her gaze to the rough sea. She was guilty in Daniel's eyes. He'd already convicted her, closing his mind to the truth.

She narrowed her gaze, envisioning, remembering the *Intrepid*. She'd attacked the sloop at night, with only a half moon to guide her. The seas had been calm, the winds steady from the south. Throwing grappling lines and gaining their ship had been easy. The night watch had fallen asleep, so the alarm hadn't sounded until it had been too late.

The captain, a stout man as round as a keg of ale, had been furious, promising retaliation, but he'd cooperated. She'd heard her name whispered among the crew as they'd hauled rum and spices and part of their food stores up through a hatch leading to the lower bulkhead. She recalled the relief she'd felt that the men knew about and feared her reputation. They'd been more than happy to unload their cargo and send her on her way.

With her own bays full, she'd sailed from the *Intrepid*, leaving every one of those men alive.

But someone had killed them and had blamed the murders on her. The tremors she'd been fighting since first seeing Daniel in her room the day before intensified. She drew in a breath and tightened her grip on the balustrade. Everything inside her screamed to prove her innocence to Daniel. But would it really matter? She would still be tried as a pirate. The end would be the same. She would be put to death; then they'd tar her body and lock her in a cage where she'd be displayed for all who traveled the Thames River to see.

Her death. She tried not to think about how her life would end. Death she didn't fear. It was the waiting, the terror she would face when she stood before a hostile crowd, a crowd that would include Daniel. It shouldn't matter what they did with her body afterwards, but it did. A helpless shudder gripped her shoulders.

"Are you cold?"

Daniel's voice startled her into turning around. No one had come near her since she'd stepped foot above deck, leaving her free to wade through her own thoughts. The crew had skirted out of her way, keeping a safe distance, but she'd felt their stares on her back, questioning, fearful. She'd surmised that Daniel's men still believed her capable of unmanning them. A few days ago, the absurd thought would have made her smile. Now she realized her reputation had caused her downfall.

"Perhaps you should go below." He leaned against the railing as if his cares were no greater than which direction he'd like to sail.

"I prefer being in the open." She faced the horizon, escaping his scrutiny. "I'll be in prison soon enough."

She sensed him stiffening beside her, his easy mood

plunging. He shifted, moving so close the sleeves of his cream shirt billowed against her arm. He wore saddle brown pants tucked into knee-high black boots. A simple outfit meant for a rogue, a reckless man destined for adventure. Not a jailer. Certainly not an earl.

Her fate would be so much easier to accept if someone else had captured her. She could hate another man, loathe him for stealing her life. Daniel she didn't understand. She saw the hunger in his eyes when he looked at her, felt it each time they kissed, yet he kept his mind closed to the truth. She understood the battle he fought; he wanted her in spite of his need to avenge the loss of his friend. If she weren't the one he was determined to see hang for the crime, she might sympathize with him.

But were his rough kisses a result of simple lust? she wondered. Or did his anger blind him to feelings that might run deeper? Those were questions she'd never know the answers to, because she was running out of time. Within a day, she'd catch her first glimpse of Executioner's Dock.

But before they reached land, there were other things she had to know. "Daniel, do I have your promise that you'll leave my family alone?"

"I told you I would. Do you doubt my word?"

"I have no reason to believe you."

"Ask my crew. I never go back on a promise."

She snorted with amusement. "Your crew would be more likely to slit my throat than answer my question."

His eyes narrowed on her, and his jaw flexed with tension. "I'm the only one who knows where your family lives. Your secret is safe with me."

Daniel's words pushed relief to the surface, bringing the need to cry. She stared harder at the pulsing water below.

"What if I'd said I intended to go back for them?"

She didn't dare look at him. "Then I'd find a way to escape you."

"I don't doubt you would," he said thoughtfully.

Hearing the awe in his voice, she faced him, and caught her breath. Longing and regret darkened his blue eyes. He didn't hide his emotions well, she thought. All he had to do was look at her, or kiss her, and she felt the depth of his anger and frustration.

On some level he wanted her, and that, she realized, seemed to make him the angriest of all.

If only things could be different, she heard a wishful voice say in the back of her mind. She fisted her hands and mentally shoved the thought away. Things weren't different. She would be dead within a week. How Daniel felt about her didn't matter. And how she felt about him . . . pressure caught in her chest, squeezing her lungs. *Don't care about him, Morgan,* she silently pleaded. *It will make things easier if you don't care about him.*

"How much longer until we reach the Thames?" she asked, not really wanting to know but needing anything to distract her.

He ignored her question and demanded, "Why in God's name did you do it?"

She sighed, feeling worn down to her last ounce of strength. "I told you, I didn't kill Captain Egham."

"I'm talking about becoming a pirate. Damn it, Morgan!" He fisted his hands against the railing. Stiffening his arms, he bent his head as if needing the ship's strength to continue. "You risked your life, Jo and Grace, the family you seem so concerned about. Why did you do it? The men aboard the *Sea Queen* are the same ones I saw in your village, farmers and fishermen. How did you convince them to leave the safety of their homes and become outlaws?"

"The safety . . ." She had to clench her jaw to keep her voice from rising to a screech. "You know nothing about what our lives were like before."

"Then explain it to me."

"Why, Daniel? What difference would it make?"

He looked at her then, his eyes shadowed with a new depth of confusion. "Tell me."

"Why?" she insisted. "You'll still take me to London, force me to stand trial for a murder I didn't commit. And you'll be there when they hang me, Daniel, to make sure they do it right. So what does it matter why I became a pirate?"

"Because I need to understand."

She bent her head in concession, then met his gaze with clear determination. "We had no other choice."

He gritted his teeth. "You said so before. As did your sister Jo. You took the easy way out, Morgan. There's always another choice."

Fury split open inside her. Morgan reached back and slapped his face before he realized her intent. She heard gasps from behind her, but could only focus on Daniel's fierce gaze.

"You're right," she said, trembling from the sudden outpouring of anger and fear, locked away for years, waiting for the moment she thought it safe to release them. Now seemed as good a time as any.

"We did have another choice. We could have abandoned our homes, leaving behind everything we loved and valued about our lives. We could have gone to London and hunted for work with the thousands of other people who'd become homeless and were starving because of the war. What kind of work do you think I would have found, Daniel? None, except perhaps selling myself for a half-penny in the nearest alley."

"Morgan—"

"You wanted to know, and you're going to listen. Or are you too much of a coward to hear the truth?"

The muscles flexed in his jaw. He gave her a brusque nod to continue.

"The Seven Years War you gloried in nearly destroyed everyone I loved. It killed my parents and my brother when the fever came and we had no money for medicine. The war took the young men away to fight. But the king still wasn't through with us. His armies arrived to pillage what was left of our crops and cattle."

Daniel reached for her, but she slapped his hand away.

"It didn't end there. A storm destroyed our boats, leaving us . . ." She swallowed back the hot tears crowding her throat. "Leaving us with no hope of survival. We were running out of food. I had sisters to feed, a village turning to me for guidance. What would you have had me do? They were starving! *Starving!* Do you know what it feels like to go hungry? To feel your stomach growl and knot and feed on itself? Have you ever gone to bed famished? No? Have you ever woken up with an ache in your belly that you'd give anything to fill? Only you hear your sister weeping in her sleep, begging for food?"

She drew a shuddering breath. She wiped the heels of her palms over her heated cheeks. They came away wet with tears, the sight adding to her fury.

"But we found a way to survive, Daniel. We became pirates. We broke your precious English laws. If the price I must pay for feeding my people is forfeiting my life, then I say it's a fair bargain."

"You're wrong," he said, his Adam's apple working as he swallowed. "The price is far too great."

"It's kind of you to think so," she said, her tone every bit as hostile as she felt. "But the decision wasn't yours to make."

"It shouldn't have been yours to make, either."

She stared at him with no idea what he meant.

"You obviously needed a man to take care of you."

"So you've said before. And I'll ask you again. Are you offering?"

His eyes narrowed, giving her the only answer she expected.

A caustic laugh bubbled up from somewhere deep inside

her, surprising her. Her shoulders shook. She pressed a hand to her mouth, afraid that if the giggles strangling her throat burst free, he'd think her hysterical. He'd be close to the truth, she thought.

Her eyes blurred with more sobering tears as she considered the folly of her situation. She'd wanted someone to help her, but who could she have asked? The elders? The children? It had been up to her to save her village.

She squelched her overpowering emotions, but she couldn't stop a remorseful smile that felt awkward, painful. "I managed fine without a man, Daniel."

"Yes, and look at you now." His scowl turned thunderous as his gaze raked over her.

Morgan knew he referred to her plight as his prisoner, but she couldn't help looking down at her wrinkled burgundy gown, now damp from the morning mist. She hadn't bothered tying up her hair, so it lay in a tangle down her shoulders and back. Compared to the women he was accustomed to, perfect women whose flawless skin would smell of lavender instead of sweat and hard work, she knew she presented a sorry sight. But she'd be damned before she'd feel shame.

"No man should have allowed you to take such risks. Why aren't you married?"

She quirked a brow at him. "You interrupted the wedding, remember?"

Daniel stepped in front of her, bracketing his arms on either side of her waist, trapping her with him at her front and the sea at her back. "Before then."

She needed to push him away. He stood too close. She couldn't escape the dark pinpoints of his eyes, the strength of his smooth-shaven jaw. She could smell his sun-warmed skin, feel the severity of his emotions. They were wild and turbulent, chaotic. And they made rational thinking impossible. He shouldn't affect her this way, but he did. Sweet Lord help her, he did. Somehow she had to stop it.

She recalled his question about her wedding. "Peter and I were supposed to be married four years ago, but he was called away to the war."

"He shouldn't have left."

"You think he should have defied the king's orders?"

"He should have married you first," he growled so forcefully the words vibrated in her chest. "I would have."

"You—"

Daniel jerked back and raked his fingers through his hair. He stared down at her, his gaze focusing with hot intensity on her mouth. Morgan resisted the urge to lick her lips, afraid of what the act might cause him to do.

"Women don't belong in a man's world," he said as if determined to make his point.

"I managed."

"There are rules, Morgan. Women are to be cared for."

Feeling her anger simmer into a low fire, she asked, "If I had married Peter, what difference would it have made? He still would have left; I still would have been faced with a starving village. Or is being married and dead of starvation better than being a pirate and dead from hanging?

"I don't know about these rules that apply to the world you're speaking of, Daniel. But I know that world isn't mine."

"It should have been."

The wind almost snatched away his whispered words. As she saw the conviction in his eyes, her breath caught, stealing her chance to respond.

A watchman stationed in the crow's nest called down, "Capt'n! Capt'n, there be a ship off starboard bow. She's one of yours, and she's listing."

Daniel ran to the right side of the deck, snatching up a telescope on his way. Morgan didn't move as orders were given to intercept the other vessel and his men leapt into action. She didn't care about the other ship, or its crew or whatever trouble they might be facing.

She watched Daniel, his legs braced as the *Pursuit* cut through waves, pitching the deck into a roll. His black satin hair whipped about his shoulders, free and untamed. He held his body rigid. She knew how tense his arms would be, the muscles tight and inflexible. Strong enough to support the world's problems. Or a woman's.

It should have been.

His words, so reluctantly given, taunted her mind, teased her with glimpses of a life different from what she'd known.

Had she taken the easy way out, as he'd accused her of doing? Had there been another option she'd overlooked? If she'd had a husband, a man like Daniel, to help guide her, would she be in her own home today, with her own children?

It should have been.

But it wasn't.

Chapter 10

The *Black Pearl* rode the waves like a dying whale, aimless, vulnerable to the pull of the sea. Swells broke against her hull, pushing her leeward, her twin masts pitching dangerously close to the surf. Ripped canvas snapped on the breeze like a flag of truce—an offering that had come too late, or had gone ignored.

"Mr. Tobitt," Daniel shouted from his position on the forecastle deck. "Have the grappling lines ready to throw across as soon as we're within reach."

"Aye, Capt'n. Just give the word."

Daniel signaled to the man at the wheel to adjust his heading, then clenched his hand around the scope and surveyed the floating wreckage. The ten-foot bowsprit had been shot off the front of the ship, and the blackened rear of the hull showed signs of a near-fatal fire. Railings had been smashed to splinters. From the way the vessel rolled with the surging sea, he supposed the wheel or perhaps the rudder had been damaged as well. He could only guess how much water she'd taken on.

The few men visible were clinging to masts, head rails, the belfry, anything solid as the *Black Pearl* drifted out of control. Whether the damage was due to a storm or a battle, Daniel couldn't tell.

A few more minutes and the ship would be within range to board, though he couldn't bring the ships too close. The choppy swells would make kindling out of both vessels. His blood flowed like a vengeful roar in his mind. Sweet bloody hell, he fumed silently. "Whoever is responsible for this will pay."

"Are you sure it's your crew on board?" Morgan asked, surprising him. He hadn't heard her join him on the deck, and in fact had forgotten all about her. It was a small comfort, but at least he knew she wasn't responsible for this new atrocity.

Noting her brazen stance, hands on her slender hips, her critical gaze on the *Black Pearl*, he said, "Why do you ask?"

Her expression turned calculating. "It could be a trick."

He stared down at her.

"It's obvious she's seen battle."

"Go below, Morgan. This is no place . . ." He stopped himself.

She lifted a brow. "For a woman?" she finished for him. "You're right. So I think I'll stay topside and watch."

Annoyed, he turned away, dismissing her. "Bring her about, Mr. Tobitt."

"If I had been the one to capture her," Morgan said in a boastful tone, "I wouldn't change her flags."

"Those are my men, Morgan," he said through gritted teeth.

"Are you sure?" She asked the question in a seductive challenge. The hairs on the back of his neck stood up in warning. "It doesn't matter to me if it's a trick," she continued. "I'm already your prisoner; how much worse could it be if I became someone else's?"

He glared at her, irritated that everything she said was true. But he was used to honorable fights, head-on confrontations, not cold-blooded sneakiness. He'd already fallen for a trick almost identical to this situation. If he fell for another one, he deserved to be hanged as an idiot. Maybe he should start thinking like a pirate . . . like Morgan.

"Bloody hell. Mr. Tobitt!" Daniel shouted, keeping his gaze focused on her satisfied grin. "See the cannons are manned."

"Capt'n, did ye say man the cannons?" Tobitt asked, leaping onto the stairs to the upper deck.

"I did."

"Excuse me for ask'n', sir, but are ye out of your bloom'n' mind? Fire on our own ship?"

"Just ready them, Tobitt. And distribute pistols."

"This makes about as much sense as tryin' tae drown a fish," Tobitt muttered as he stormed off to see to his orders. "It's gotta be that woman . . ."

Aye, everything had to do with *that woman,* Daniel realized. He was grateful he couldn't hear the rest of his first officer's mumblings, because he didn't want to consider that Morgan might be affecting him more than he thought.

He faced her and was caught by the confident gleam in her silver eyes. *Confident:* that word seemed to define her as no other could. How in bloody hell did a woman ever gain such strength? And how was he supposed to break it?

Morgan stood at the taffrail, the highest point at the rear of the ship, so she could observe the crew without getting in their way. She hadn't received a single curse or a hand signal to ward off the devil for the past half hour. Everyone was too busy preparing to help the ailing *Black Pearl* to worry about her. As they'd closed the distance, Daniel had announced with satisfaction that it was his crew on board, but from his worried expression and what she'd observed, only a sparse number of men remained.

The other vessel was without her anchors. She soared

and plummeted at the whim of the sea. The lack of stability and the rough swells made using grappling lines impossible. Daniel had ordered the dinghy sent across to retrieve the captain and high-ranking members of his crew. He paced his deck now, his focus on the crowded skiff as it bobbed across the ocean's surface.

As the crew climbed aboard the *Pursuit*, Morgan moved closer to learn what had happened. She welcomed the interruption—anything to delay her arrival in London.

A dozen men gained the rope ladder and grouped behind Daniel; some she recognized from the *Pursuit*'s crew. The men from the *Black Pearl* looked haggard, unshaven, gaunt in the face and ribs, as if they'd lacked the most important food item of all—fresh water. Their clothes were ragged, hinting that they'd drifted for endless days.

Daniel greeted each man, undoubtedly saying something reassuring, she thought. He'd feel responsible for their plight, as he had with Captain Egham and his crew. He'd searched an ocean for the person he thought responsible for their deaths. How would he take the news of this latest assault?

A final man gained the railing and climbed on deck. Daniel's eyes widened with recognition; his body tensed. From where she stood, she saw the outrage in his fisted hands, the brace of his legs, the fire in his gaze. Those closest to him scooted back, away from his fury.

Daniel stepped forward and clasped the man's outstretched hand, then pulled him into an embrace that spoke of age-old friends. The sight drew Morgan down the stairs and to the edge of the scene. She didn't want to intrude, but she had to know what had happened.

Daniel held the man at arm's length, demanding, "What the hell are you doing on the *Black Pearl*, Thomas?"

The man named Thomas answered in a shaky voice, "Until I spotted you, I'd been contemplating my death."

"Damn it, I thought you were in London."

"You know me," Thomas shrugged, looking helplessly at his disabled ship. "I couldn't resist another trip to Africa."

Releasing the man, Daniel swiped one hand through his hair. "What happened?"

"We were raided." As if a tremor had settled permanently in his arms, he repeatedly rubbed his palms against his thighs.

Morgan inched closer. Despite his dirty blond hair, the bruise darkening his cheek, the nervous, hunted look in his eyes, the man looked familiar. She searched her memory but couldn't place him.

"All that's left is myself and the few crewmen you see. And the ship, what's left of her. The cargo, Daniel—the cargo of spices and silks . . . they're gone . . . all gone. I don't know how we're going to recover from this. Not after the last attack we suffered."

A thread of suspicion wove through Morgan's mind, but she couldn't make it take shape. Who was he? Why did he look familiar? She was grasping at straws, she realized—anything to keep her occupied with something other than her own dilemma.

"Ye have the devil's own luck," Tobitt piped up, winning a scornful glare from Daniel.

"Captain Williams?" Daniel asked somberly, squaring his shoulders to prepare for the worst. "Where is he?"

"Dead. The murdering pirates butchered him first as a warning to the rest of us." A shudder racked Thomas's narrow frame. His eyes glazed as if he were reliving the moment the bloodletting had begun. "The pirates went berserk after that."

"You're lucky to be alive, then," Morgan said without meaning to.

Thomas's head snapped to where she stood. His bloodshot eyes narrowed with curiosity. "Who are you?"

"At least ye didn't 'ave tae face Morgan the Scylla again,"

Tobitt interrupted. "We've had that particular blackguard on our ship. Though not locked in the blasted hold like she should be. We've all been feel'n' sickly since she come aboard."

Morgan focused on Tobitt's words. What did he mean, Thomas hadn't had to face her *again*? Had she raided his ship before? Obviously, she had. Perhaps that was why he seemed familiar.

Thomas arched a brow at Daniel, his mouth lifting with a stunned grin. "You found her?"

"A lot has happened since I last saw you aboard the *Valiant*. But, yes, I found her."

Thomas clapped his hands together and threw his head back with a biting laugh. "I shouldn't have doubted you, Daniel. If anyone had the tenacity to find the murdering bitch, it would have been you."

His caustic laugh and chilling words flowed like ice over Morgan's skin. Her stomach quivered, the shaking spreading out to her limbs. This was only a glimpse of the hatred she'd have to face in London. Why hadn't she kept her mouth shut? She shouldn't be here. Tempers were too volatile. She had to get below to Daniel's cabin. She retreated a step, and bumped into a wall of angry sailors. They glared down at her, making it clear that they wouldn't allow her to pass.

Daniel crossed his arms over his chest and looked at her. She couldn't read the meaning behind his scowl, and the inability added to the determination building inside her.

Thomas crossed to her, staring down with gleeful hostility. "Perhaps this day will have a happy ending yet."

With her heart pounding at a frightening speed, she tilted her chin and willfully locked her gaze with his.

"There's something pirates like you seem to never learn, Morgan. Justice always prevails." Thomas ran his dirt-caked finger down her jaw. "I think it's time we had a hanging."

* * *

A cheer roared through the crew. Caps flew and men clapped each other on the back. Two seamen grabbed Morgan by her arms; another pair ran for a rope with which to hang her. Their cries of celebration became a hazy noise, distant and indiscernible in the back of Daniel's mind.

He felt the world narrow down to one moment, one pulse that beat behind his eyes as he watched sudden terror leach the color from Morgan's face. She didn't fight the men who held her, but glared at the others who wanted her dead. Standing tall, her fists clenched, she didn't say a word, didn't plead for her life. Or faint, as any sane woman would have done.

No, she faced the noose and her death with the same conviction as she had everything else. She'd do it because she had to. Because she thought she had no other choice.

The rope was strung over the mizzen yard above her head, the end coiled and knotted tight. A sailor known only as Smith looped the noose around her neck, pulling it tight against her skin. Morgan sucked in a breath and closed her eyes.

"Let her go." Daniel's order was lost in the shouts and building mayhem. Someone had thrust a tankard of ale into Thomas's hand. He held it aloft, toasting their victory.

Stepping forward, using a tone that could have drawn blood, Daniel demanded, "Let her go."

The two men holding Morgan heard him. They released her immediately, stepping out of his path.

Thomas slapped him on the back. "That's right, men. Your captain is the lucky man who caught this she-devil. It's his right to be the one to hang her."

"There'll be no hanging," Daniel said, unable to look away from the brilliance in Morgan's silver eyes, the tremors that shook her jaw.

The shouts died and everyone stood still.

"You can't be serious." Thomas gripped Daniel's shoulder, forcing him to turn around. "She's a murderer."

"She'll stand trial in London. If she's found guilty, then . . ." Daniel clenched his hands at his sides and forced himself to finish, "she'll be hanged."

"I don't believe this!" Thomas took two stumbling steps back. His mouth gaped as disbelief settled in. He looked from Daniel to Morgan, his hate-filled gaze slicing down her body. "She's gotten to you with her cat eyes and wicked looks."

"Thomas . . ."

Thomas spun around. With a shout of rage, he threw his tankard into the sea. Facing his partner, Thomas pointed a finger in Daniel's face. "You want her, don't you? You want the whoring murderer!"

"That's enough."

"Fine, Daniel. We'll do it your way. You can have her . . . first." Thomas swayed with the roll of the ship as he looked at the men gathered close. "Then it'll be our turn. We'll all have a go at her; then we'll hang her."

Daniel reacted with blind rage, swinging his fist, striking Thomas in the jaw. His partner fell back against the railing. Blood smeared his lip. Disbelief blazed from his eyes.

Not believing he'd hit his best friend, Daniel moved to help him up. Thomas held up a hand to warn him off. Struggling to stand upright, he dabbed the blood dripping down his chin with the back of his hand.

"I see you've made up your mind." Thomas spit a red stream of blood onto the deck perilously close to Daniel's boot. "But heed my warning. If she makes one wrong move, if she even looks at me in a way I don't like, I'll kill her."

Once Thomas left the deck, Daniel forced his hands to unclench. With a nod, he silently ordered his crew back to work. They still had to contend with making the *Black Pearl* seaworthy.

Once they'd dispersed, he released the noose from around Morgan's neck. Taking her by the arm, he led her to his cabin. She should go in the hold, he warned himself. Thomas's allegation still rang in his ears. *"You want her!"* The accusation tore at him—because it was true.

He didn't want her like a man wanted a whore, a woman whose body would give him a moment's relief. He didn't want to conquer or control her. God help him . . . he wanted . . . *her.*

He bypassed the stairs leading to the hold and continued down the companionway to his room, his anger at himself, at her, intensifying with each step. He thrust her inside, shutting the door before she could spin around, before he had a chance to see the relief in her eyes. Or, sweet Mary, the hope. Withdrawing a key from his pocket, he locked her in. Safe and away, separating him from a temptation that could prove to be his downfall.

Morgan stood rooted to the floor. She stared at the locked door, defying the tremors snaking through her limbs like poison.

The ship pitched with the breaking swells. The overhead lanterns swung from their hooks like flowers jostled by the wind. She sensed more than heard the pounding of feet, the bellowing shouts, the frantic hammering. The dark texture of walls surrounded her, but she didn't see them. Not really.

One thought blazed in her mind above all others.

They want me dead.

Every man on board ship not only wanted to see her hang, they wanted to have a hand in it. Daniel included.

He'd stopped the execution from happening now, but he'd only delayed the inevitable.

A sob pushed from her chest. The effort to hold it in burned her lungs. She held her breath, held it until forced to take another. She gulped in air, clenched her jaw to muffle the anguished cry that wanted to escape.

The terror she'd felt, the fear still shooting through her veins, was nothing, a mere glimpse of what she'd endure after her trial. Her body jerked with the need to cry. She covered her mouth with her hands. Pressed hard.

Soon she'd have to face an angry mob that would demand her death. A king who would insist on it. She'd have no chance then. No one would save her. No one . . .

She'd die alone. Jo and Grace would never know. They'd never see. But they'd be safe.

She sat on the bed and bent at the waist with the effort to cut off her tears. She couldn't cry. She'd made her decision, and she wouldn't regret it.

Yet she couldn't stop the small voice in the back of her mind from pleading, *Please, Daniel. Please don't let them do this to me.*

A useless thought, she argued, her shoulders shaking as fear swallowed her control. Futile tears streamed down her face.

Useless, she thought, giving in to her sobs. No one would save her. Least of all Daniel.

It took six hours of backbreaking work to make the *Black Pearl* seaworthy. Despite the rough seas, spare canvas had been sent across to repair the sails. A force of twelve men had sewn and patched like a horde of fanatical tailors, completing their task in record time. A spare anchor from the *Pursuit* had been suspended from the hawsehole at the bow, and fresh planks covered the worst of the damaged deck. Only food and water needed to be transferred so the ailing ship could continue its voyage to London.

Daniel had selected a handful of his men to accompany

the *Black Pearl's* crew. He could have towed the vessel to port, but once Thomas's anger had abated and they'd talked, he realized he couldn't return to the city just yet.

His eyes gritty with exhaustion, his body aching with a weariness that went beyond physical, Daniel unlocked the door to his cabin, dreading the coming confrontation. He pushed the panel open but remained on the threshold to get his bearings.

Moonlight streamed through the rows of square window-panes, reaching for shadows that cloaked every corner of the room. With the setting sun, the ocean had ceased its battle, settling to manageable swells. Now the only sounds he heard were the creak of wood, a few men moving about on deck and his own cautious breathing.

Where was she?

He wouldn't put it past Morgan to leap from the dark and smash him over the head with the brass hourglass from his desk, or more likely, stab him with the letter opener. *It's no more than I deserve.*

The self-recrimination struck hard and quick. He flinched, but didn't deny the censure. He could have left Morgan alone, to lead her life, marry the man of her choosing. But he'd been driven not only by duty to hunt her down, but by *revenge*. Duty he couldn't ignore, but revenge . . . The taste of it had begun to sour in his mouth.

Stepping into the cabin, he eased around the small room, alert for any movement. Hearing a rustling noise by the bed, he moved forward. There he found Morgan, curled on her side, her hair a splash of midnight across his pillow. Milky light coated the hollow of her pale cheek, her closed eyelids, the hand she fisted beside her face.

Even in sleep she didn't relax. Considering what she'd been through and what she still faced, the knowledge didn't surprise him.

He lit a lantern, turning the wick down low. Kneeling before her, he reached out to shake her awake, but stopped. Her closed eyes were puffy, her lips red—telling signs that she'd been crying. He touched the damp pillow and confirmed his suspicion.

Before he could think otherwise, he ran the back of his finger across the cool softness of her cheek and whispered, "Praise God I didn't see you break, Morgan."

Just the thought of her shedding hopeless tears, her courage shattered by fear, was more than he could stand. Daniel bowed his head and silently cursed. He mustn't think about Morgan this way, mustn't care if she trembled with panic or cried herself to sleep. It was his duty to see she stood trial for her crimes. It was his goddamned *duty!*

He lifted his head to wake her, and met her gaze. Resignation dulled her silver eyes. Her lids were red-rimmed, intensifying the eerie stillness about her.

He didn't like her this way, compliant, accepting of her fate. He wanted her to fight, battle her way out of her nightmare. But he knew she wouldn't; not if it meant jeopardizing her family.

"You look like the very devil, Daniel." She pushed to a sitting position; her gown, creased beyond repair, bunched around her bare legs.

Her hair fell in a tangled web about her shoulders. Even in the dim light, he could see ruby and amber streaks in the mink-dark color. The rich strands were a glossy lure, making him want to gather the silky waves in his hands, bury his fingers in their length, then his face. He knew how it would smell, free and natural, of salt and sea and sunshine. *And tears.*

"I'd say you've been drinking, except you don't smell of liquor," she said.

"It's been a long day." Her words would have been teasing if not for her indifferent tone, the weariness of her eyes. Inconceivable longing pushed through his veins, hardening his core, warming his blood in a way that seeking vengeance couldn't do. He wanted to hold her, he realized with startling clarity; wanted it in the same way he wanted his next breath. But he knew where the protective urge would lead. He'd make love to her, slowly, the way he did in his dreams. If he so much as dared to touch her, there would be no stopping him. Yet nothing could happen between them. Ever. He knew it, so why couldn't he accept it?

She glanced at the windows behind her, to check their position, he assumed, but he only saw the slope of her neck, the curve of her jaw. Her parted lips. "We've not set sail?"

"In another hour or so." He could barely manage the words. She needed to be held. When her villagers had relied on her for strength, who had Morgan turned to when she felt frightened or in doubt? he wondered. Who had put their arms around her, given her strength and reassurance?

Something like desire shook through him. He wanted to slide his hand across her cheek and into the hair that had snared him like a trap. He wanted to pull her to him and kiss her. Deeply and slowly, thoroughly, the way his body craved.

Would she fight him? He'd thought she'd pretended to respond to his touch when they'd been on the island. Now he wasn't so sure. The same traitorous desire that pulsed through his veins now had darkened her eyes the night before.

Did she fight the same passion, feel the same need? Did she want him when she knew she shouldn't? The questions were dangerous ones to consider, he reminded himself. They were better left alone, especially now. He might find her beautiful and strong-willed, but his feelings for her had to stop here. He couldn't risk their turning into something unimaginable . . . like caring.

He realized she was watching him. He broke the tense

moment by saying, "Before we sail, there's something I need you to do."

Standing, he cupped her elbow, helped her to her feet and led her to the door. He felt the tremor in her arm, saw her pulse leap at the base of her throat.

His gut tightened. Causing her such fear went against everything he believed in. *Her actions caused her downfall,* he admonished himself, doubting the words even as he thought them. God's teeth, but he found her guilt harder to believe than he had a few days ago. She was strong and cunning, but was she a killer? His instincts told him no. But the proof—Thomas's insistence.

He led her through a companionway crowded with barrels of salted fish, spare riggings and kegs of ale. The hallway opened to the crew's sleeping quarters. Empty hammocks hung from hooks in the ceiling. At any given time, groups of men off duty would be sleeping or gathered in corners waging a game of dice. Since all hands were needed to make repairs, everyone was above deck—except for the two men at the far end of the room. One lounged in a hammock, the other stood beside him. Hearing Daniel's approach, they turned suspicious gazes on Morgan.

"Did she agree tae help us?" Tobitt asked, his brusque tone neutralized as he edged back to a safer distance.

"I haven't asked her yet." Daniel stopped and reluctantly released Morgan's arm. "I thought I'd let Thomas do it, since it was his idea."

"The hell I will!" Thomas swung his feet to the floor and rose. "I told you, we don't need her."

"I disagree." Daniel hadn't wanted to expose Morgan to Thomas's hatred again, but once he'd learned the circumstances behind the attack on the *Black Pearl,* he'd realized he had no choice. The phrase stopped him: *no choice.* He pushed Morgan's words aside. "She knows more about this than we do. She might be of help."

"Perhaps someone should ask me the question first,"

Morgan said, surprising everyone to silence. "And argue about it later."

Daniel fought the urge to smile with relief. An ember from the fire that had once burned in her eyes sprang to life. "Do you know Halo Jones?"

She raised a brow, her attention swerving to Thomas. "Is he the pirate who attacked you?"

Thomas reluctantly muttered, "Yes."

She crossed her arms over her waist. "It isn't like him to leave survivors. You are lucky, indeed."

"So you know him?" Daniel asked.

"Of course she does, Capt'n," Tobitt put in. "Sea robbers are a tight lot. They probably meet tae decide what ocean belongs tae what pirate. I've heard it said they 'ave a code tae never steal from their own kind."

"You know an awful lot about pirates, Mr. Tobitt," Morgan murmured.

Tobitt's eyes widened at her use of his name. "I've been at sea longer than you've been alive, missy."

"Is what he says true?" Daniel asked. "Are the pirates organized?"

She shrugged. "We're careful not to step on each other's toes."

"You see?" Thomas spat. "She has an alliance with Halo Jones. She'll never betray him."

Her eyes narrowed with reproach. "What is this about?"

"Do you know how to find Halo?" Daniel wiped a hand across his jaw, not liking the way his skin prickled at the thought of involving Morgan in a dangerous situation. This was his responsibility. Yet she was a pirate, and what better way to catch a pirate than to interrogate one for information?

"I told you we don't need her help," Thomas shouted, throwing his hands out to his sides for emphasis.

"I know where his island hideout is, if that's what you're asking."

"Will you give me the location?" Daniel stepped closer to her, wanting to shut out the other two men.

"She'll send you into a trap, Daniel," Thomas asserted. "Open your eyes! You can't trust her."

"Will you?" he asked again, anticipation tightening the muscles along his spine.

Her eyes clouded as she stared into the dark corners of the room. He could only guess what cunning and unpredictable thoughts churned through her mind.

Drawing up her body and tilting her chin, she said, "No."

He clenched his jaw and hissed out a breath, wanting to shake her stubborn hide.

"I told you she wouldn't help." Thomas turned away with a caustic laugh.

"But I'll take you to him."

This time, seeing the calculating glint in her eyes, Daniel understood her ploy. He had the insane urge to smile.

"I'm afraid not, Morgan." Thomas faced her and grinned with cheerful disdain. "You'll be on the *Black Pearl*, with me, sailing to London. It's been some time since I've attended a hanging, and yours I wouldn't want to miss."

"Why not just give me the location?" Daniel crossed his arms over his chest to keep from smashing his fist into his partner's face.

"The location won't do you any good. He'll know of your arrival and sink your ship within a half league of the island."

"What do you suggest?" he asked, when what he really wanted to know was what had her devious mind created.

"I can get you in."

"No! Out of the question," Thomas declared. "You can't take her with you."

"Why not?" If Morgan had truly murdered Egham as Thomas claimed, Daniel could understand his partner's frenzied anger. But her suggestion, while not ideal, had merit. "And by the way, Thomas, you're coming to Halo's island with me."

"The hell I will. I've been attacked twice by pirates."

"And lived tae tell about it," Tobitt piped in from his corner.

"She killed Captain Egham." In a frantic gesture, Thomas swiped his hands through his hair. "Or have you forgotten?"

Daniel scowled. "Captain Egham was murdered. That I don't doubt." *But by whom?* a troubled voice asked in the back of his mind.

"She's not to be trusted. If you were thinking with your head instead of your—"

"Enough!"

"You know I speak the truth." Thomas's face darkened. He sneered so viciously his cut lip began to bleed. He stabbed his finger at Daniel. "We should hang her now. The Act for Effectual Suppression of Piracy gives us the right to try her here and carry out the sentence."

"No!" Daniel said, the word slamming with the impact of a gavel.

Thomas took a step forward, his shoulders squared, his hands fisted at his sides. Blood dripped down his chin unheeded. Daniel tensed, fearing he'd have to fight his friend again. He prayed it didn't come to that, but he would face down every man on his ship if it meant protecting Morgan.

"I'm one of them," Morgan said quietly from behind them. "I can lead you in."

Silence hummed through the room, with neither man backing down. The hairs on Daniel's arms and neck stood on end. Christ, he thought, refusing to let Thomas pass. They were best friends. How had they ever come down to this?

"She'll lead you into a trap." Thomas's voice was rough,

trembling with emotion. "Think about it: Why is she suddenly so willing to help?"

Daniel met her gaze. Hers was clear, cool, filled with a control he remembered so well. "Why are you offering?"

"I can get you into Halo Jones's lair." She braced her hands on her hips as if she'd just assumed command of the ship. "More important, I can help you capture him."

"In return for what?" Daniel asked, but he already knew.

Evidently, so did Tobitt, because he whispered from his safe nook, "Sweet Mother of Jesus, help us."

Hearing the entreaty, Morgan smiled and said, "My freedom."

Chapter 11

Quiet descended upon the room with the finality of a tomb door being sealed. All three men stared at Morgan, their expressions ranging from outrage to fear to worry. She'd anticipated the first two reactions, but the concern in Daniel's eyes surprised and confused her.

She didn't expect him to agree to her terms. Why release one pirate with a horrid reputation for another one who was equally grisly? The only difference between the two was that Halo Jones had truly earned his notoriety. But Daniel didn't know that.

Thomas broke the silence first by jeering, "When you reach hell, Morgan, you can ask the Devil for your freedom. Because you'll not be receiving it from us."

Daniel's expression hardened; a muscle in his jaw pulsed with trapped tension. "I can't release you, Morgan. You know that."

"I didn't kill Captain Egham."

"You did," Thomas declared. "I was there. I saw you."

"If you were there, then you know I didn't do it." Morgan tightened her fingers on her waist to keep from grabbing the man and shaking him until he spoke the truth.

"We'll not believe your lies, woman."

"I saw you aboard the *Intrepid*, as well," she added, piecing that night together now that Thomas had washed his hair and changed his clothes. "The ship carried rum and spices, which I took, along with a portion of the crew's food. But I left your captain and his men very much alive."

"You butchered a dozen crewmen!" he seethed. The veins at his neck throbbed and his eyes brimmed with fury.

Cold alarm raced beneath Morgan's skin. *He's lying, but why?* The cold moved around her chest, tightening, making her shiver. Men had repeatedly embellished their encounters with Morgan the Scylla, in vain attempts to overcome their humiliation at being bested by a woman. Was it humiliation that forced Thomas to keep to his lies? Would he ruthlessly send an innocent woman to her death to protect himself? Or was there another reason, a missing piece to the puzzling situation she found herself in?

She intended to find out. "I understand gold was stolen from your vessel."

His nostrils flared as he drew in a breath. "Don't attempt to play games with me, Morgan. You know well what you stole."

"I never saw any gold on your ship."

"You lying whore!" He lunged forward, his fist swinging for her face.

Morgan reached for her knife, forgetting it wasn't strapped to her waist. She raised her hands to block the blow. It never came.

Daniel had caught Thomas's arm in midair. He shoved him back against the wall. Banging his head against the planks, Thomas slid to the floor, where he stayed, glaring up at his partner.

"Do you see what she's doing?" Thomas's chest heaved with each breath he took. His face turned blood red with anger. "She's purposefully coming between us."

"Perhaps, but she knows where Halo is," Daniel said in her defense. "We don't."

"If you release her, King George will demand your head in her place."

"Listen tae 'im, Capt'n," his first officer pleaded.

"Stay out of this, Tobitt," Daniel ordered. "Do we let Halo Jones get away with murder, Thomas? Is that what you're suggesting? The king won't stand for it, and neither will I."

"Neither will he tolerate releasing one murderer for another," Thomas countered, refusing Daniel's help as he pushed himself to his feet.

"I'm not convinced Morgan's responsible for Egham's death." Daniel turned away with an oath as if he regretted what he'd just said.

Morgan held her breath. Daniel's words buzzed through her mind like whispers of hope. When had he begun to have doubts, and if so, why? The questions were on the tip of her tongue, but she kept silent.

"You believe her lies?" Thomas ripped a hammock from its hook and sent it flying across the room. Stepping forward, he pointed his finger dangerously close to Daniel's face. "You have sunk low, my friend, falling for a tramp such as her. If you do this, I won't be there to pick you up when the courts flay your back."

"I've made my decision," Daniel said with quiet conviction, belying the explosion that Morgan sensed gathering force in the taut muscles of his arms and his iron-hard fists.

"Then you do it alone." Spinning on his heel, Thomas left.

Daniel nodded to Tobitt, a wordless signal sending his first officer after his friend.

The instant they were alone, Daniel rounded on Morgan and stared at her for a long, frightening moment. Tension pulsed, expanded, suffocating the chamber like a hot breath. She stepped back, pushed by the force of his fury.

"There wasn't any gold, Daniel. None that I saw, at least."

"Your word against his. Who do I believe?" he asked, though he'd directed the question at himself. "My best friend or a self-proclaimed pirate?"

She didn't say a word, knowing he had to make the decision on his own. Besides, other than her *word*, which was virtually worthless, she had no proof of her innocence.

"If you help capture Halo Jones and I release you," he said, the words forced through his clenched jaw, "you'll never be able to set foot on English soil again."

"I'll be alive."

Alive, she silently added, *and alone,* forever separated from her family, the home she desperately wanted to return to. Could she live such a life? Where would she go? The questions and doubts gathered speed in her mind, but she willed them to stop and shut them away. She couldn't think about the future until she was sure she'd have one.

"Do you understand that you'll be an outcast wherever you go? Alone with no one to turn to?"

The reality of his words made her shudder. Light from a nearby lantern exposed the fierce emotion in his eyes. Regret? she wondered. Or anger that she'd managed to outmaneuver him again?

Holding out her hand, she nodded. Not only would she never see her family again, she'd never see Daniel. He gripped her hand, his fingers rough and warm against her skin. That sensation, too, she shut away.

Uncertainty tightened her throat. She gathered the strength that had brought her this far and said, "The only thing you need to worry about, Daniel, is capturing Halo. What happens to me once I'm free doesn't matter."

* * *

Daniel stood outside his cabin door with his hand on the handle, debating what he was about to do. This was insanity. He should go to the deck below and sleep in a hammock with the other men—as he'd done since bringing Morgan aboard his ship.

But Thomas's arrival had changed all that. Daniel cursed himself for insisting that his partner sail with them to Halo's island. Having Thomas along was like striking flint over a keg of gunpowder.

His men were still agitated, angry. Their fear of Morgan's reputation and presence had them bickering with one another, swinging fists at the slightest offense. They wanted her off their ship, now. Wariness crept down Daniel's nape. He sensed a riot in the air. His crew wasn't like the loyal seamen he'd met on the *Sea Queen*. With Thomas fueling their tempers, they might ignore Daniel's orders and finish the hanging they'd begun.

Which meant he couldn't leave Morgan alone. Until he could get her off his ship, they'd have to share his cabin.

His pulse pounded, heating his blood. He bit off a curse. He was here to protect her, nothing more. He wouldn't touch her. Hell, he wouldn't even talk to her.

Clenching his jaw, he shoved the door open, letting it bang against the wall. Morgan jumped off the window seat, her hand curling around a knife that wasn't there. Spotting him, she straightened her stance and released a deep breath. He stepped into the cabin, shutting the door behind him.

"You might have knocked," she said, reclaiming her place by the window and tucking her gown around her bent legs. Her bare toes peeked from the edge of her hem. He wondered what else she *wasn't* wearing beneath her gown. Too well he recalled that she didn't wear corsets or stays. He released a slow breath.

She relaxed her body against the wall at her back, but her eyes remained narrowed with caution. Light from the low-burning lamp barely reached the corner she'd taken, shadowing the hair falling in a thick mahogany tumble over her shoulders. She studied him with eyes as pale and disturbing as ghosts, haunted, unnerving. Questioning. His gaze slipped lower, to the steady rise and fall of her chest. Shadow and light danced over the smooth mounds above her bodice. As he watched, her breasts seemed to swell against the fabric of her gown—an illusion, he was sure. While his eyes might have been playing tricks, he knew for certain how she'd feel—soft, full, fitting perfectly against the palm of his hand. He curled his fingers into fists. He reached for a pitcher of wine, pouring himself a cup. He downed it before thinking to offer Morgan any. She declined with a brisk shake of her head.

"We should make Cape Verde soon," she said, looking out the window.

"Are you sure that's where his hideout is located?" Daniel poured another portion of wine, more because he needed something to do than because he wanted the drink. "I've been through that area countless times."

"His hideout is separated from the main islands. The coast is nothing but jagged cliffs. There are no accessible beaches or clear paths leading inland. But the cliffs are deceptive, an illusion of solid wall that conceals an inlet that leads to his cove." She leaned her head against the wall and watched the black sea rolling out behind them. Moonlight washed the slender column of her throat, the curve of her cheek, her straight nose. "You can sail within half a league and never know it's there."

Her words were soft, dreamy, as if she had fond memories of the island. Or the pirate who lived there. *"She'll lead you into a trap!"* Thomas had shouted. Daniel didn't want to believe him. But traps and Morgan seemed to go hand in hand. Christ, who was he to believe?

She'd volunteered to take him to another of her kind. Was she really going to help him, or was she leading him down a path of destruction? And just how close was she to Halo? Enemies? Friends? Lovers? Would she really help plan another pirate's capture?

Daniel tightened his hand on his cup. "Just how well do you know Halo Jones?"

His demanding tone brought her attention back to him. She shrugged. "We met a little over two years ago."

"And?"

"If you mean do I trust him, the answer is no."

That wasn't what he was asking exactly, but he couldn't voice his other question—had they been lovers?—because it didn't matter to him. He held on to the lie, letting it stick in his throat.

"We met in Jamaica. I was there gathering supplies; he was spending his recent plunder. They don't like having pirates in Port Royal any longer, so I knew to be careful. We were disguised as a merchant ship, but we couldn't fool Halo."

Daniel sat on the window seat opposite her and braced his leg on the bench, his knee mere inches from her toes. He listened to her describe their meeting and sipped his wine to hide the sudden ire blurring his mind. Emotions that bordered on fury pushed through him, tightening his skin. He clenched his jaw, trying to stop the burning rush. The emotions were unlike anything he'd known before, but he knew what they were.

Protectiveness. Fear. Jealousy.

She said she didn't trust Halo, but that didn't mean she hadn't felt something else for the man.

"He knew what I was." She laughed softly, the melodious sound surprising him out of his angry haze. "Halo thought it was *unique* that I captained my own ship, so he decided to teach me everything he knew. I took the opportunity to learn all I could."

"About what? Killing or making love?" Daniel cursed, thinking he should give Morgan her knife back so she could cut out his tongue.

She went still, her earlier wariness returning. "Neither. But then I don't expect you to believe that."

"You weren't his lover?" Daniel wanted to damn himself for asking, but he had to know.

"I've lain with no man, not that it's any of your business."

Daniel took a deep drink of his wine, letting it run down his throat like cold fire. He didn't know what to say, and he didn't dare move for fear of gathering her in his arms and kissing her to quench the heat roaring through his blood. The way she looked now, her body soft and feminine, her temper bristling for a fight, nothing would stop him from making love to her. She was a contradiction, a challenge that had invaded his mind, and he feared that nothing short of claiming her body and soul would cure him.

Instead, he forced his thoughts down a different path. "Do you have any qualms about helping me capture Halo Jones?"

She shrugged. "No."

"You know the kind of death that awaits him. It doesn't bother you that you're sacrificing him to gain your freedom?"

Guilt flickered through her eyes. "It sounds horrible when you put it that way."

"Then rephrase it so it doesn't."

Her expression grew still and troubled. "Halo enjoys raiding ships, torturing his captives. It's a game to him."

"But not to you?"

The haunted look he'd seen in her eyes the night before turned. "It wasn't a game. It was survival."

She seemed vulnerable all of a sudden, yet her shoulders were stiff, her jaw set with determination.

She broke through the building tension by saying, "I'm concerned about your plan to attack Halo."

"My ship is well gunned and manned, and we'll have surprise on our side."

"He'll see you long before you reach his cove."

"What are you suggesting, Morgan? Wait until he leaves his island and challenge him on open sea? I'm not opposed to an outright battle, in fact I'd prefer it, but it could be days or weeks before he leaves his nest."

She shook her head, frowning. "We could sail in as pirates."

He returned her frown and added a scowl.

"Don't look at me as if I'm mad," she scolded as if he were a child. "It's the perfect solution. You don't stand a chance of getting close enough to the island otherwise."

"What you're suggesting is out of the question—"

"You'll have to change your pennon," she interrupted, then quirked a brow. "I suppose it'd be too much to hope that you'd have a Jolly Roger on board."

"I'm afraid I'm without my black flag boasting a skull and bleached bones," he countered dryly.

A smile threatened the corner of her mouth. " 'Tis a pity. But any black cloth will do for now. Once we're in, we could meet with him, learn the layout of his camp."

"Won't he be suspicious of our visit?"

"Of course. We'll tell him we're making repairs." She pressed her hand to her forehead. "No, that would make us look weak. Instead, we'll say we're gathering supplies."

"It won't work, Morgan."

"Then we can attack him," she continued, refusing to listen to reason.

He frowned, feeling his reluctance slip.

"It will work if you'll only think it through," she insisted.

"I won't masquerade as a pirate. It goes against everything I believe in."

"Daniel, listen to me." She reached over and gripped his thigh. Lightning streaked up his leg to his groin. His stomach clenched. Sweet Jesus, didn't she know what she did to him? He had to get away from her—yet he couldn't leave.

"Go to bed, Morgan," he ground out suddenly.

"But—"

"It's late."

"But my plan—"

"I'll consider it. Now go to bed." Couldn't she tell he was close to losing control? Or did he need to pull her beneath him for her to understand how much he wanted her?

She looked from the bed to the door, and finally back to him. Her eyes were dark with suspicion. "Aren't you leaving?"

"No."

"I see." She released his leg and touched her waist. He wondered if her stomach was as knotted as his, or was she perhaps looking for her knife? He ought to give it to her, he thought, to give him another reason to keep his distance.

"Where will you sleep?" she asked.

"Right where you see me."

Her mouth dropped open in dismay, but she quickly shut it. She rose, and had to move past him to reach the bed. Daniel caught her hand as she passed him, knowing it was a mistake but unable to help himself.

"You're not to leave this cabin without me." He ran his fingers over her skin, cursing himself for the foolish act.

"Where would I go, Daniel?" Her puzzled tone drew his gaze to hers. "I'm at your mercy until this is over and you release me."

Feeling his hunger for her bleed through his veins, clamping his body with an unbelievable ache, Daniel knew "mercy" had nothing to do with it.

* * *

"She's as pretty as a fishmonger's wife," Tobitt said beside Daniel from their watch on the forecastle deck. The first officer adjusted the bring-me-closer and released a disgruntled sigh. "And just as deceiving. Daft is the man, I say, who wants to live on land."

They were still three leagues away from Halo's island, a safe distance for Daniel to learn what he could about the place and decide if it would be wiser to abandon Morgan's plan. She hadn't exaggerated—or lied—about the island's lack of appeal. The oval-shaped island appeared to be nothing more than towering cliffs of limestone rock, capped with dense trees and tangled brush. There were no obvious sources of fresh water or smoke from a native's camp. Signs of edible vegetation were questionable—nothing worthy of attracting the notice of a passing ship. Which was undoubtedly why Halo selected this little nest to hide in, Daniel mused.

Situated off the African coast, it was a short sail away from England and Europe, yet within easy reach of the Caribbean, too. According to Morgan, the cove hidden by a rocky inlet awaited them on the northern point. And there they'd find Halo Jones.

Daniel forced his hands to relax, but they fisted on their own accord until his knuckles bleached white. Was he making a mistake? There was more at stake than releasing Morgan—an event he couldn't think about right now. If her plan failed, the sentries guarding the cliffs would blow the *Pursuit* and every man on board to kindling. He had two alternatives: sail in firing or turn away now and head for London.

"They'll have spotted us by now," Morgan said quietly. "Though we're too far away to cause them worry. Another hour—then their interest will pick up." She gripped the railing, leaning against the edge as if anxious to reach a safe harbor and taste her freedom.

The sun rode low on the horizon behind them, softening the amber streaks in her hair. Curling strands danced with the breeze. Daniel was tempted to reach out and catch them, hold on to them, tame them. Tame *her,* but that would be impossible, he thought. Dressed as she was in her wrinkled burgundy wool gown, the silver brocade adorning the cuffs and bodice, she appeared feminine, fragile. In need of care. But he knew differently; knew she could wield a sword with the best of men, command her ship through a raging storm. A voice in his mind said to trust her, but she'd tricked him too many times, and they were lessons he couldn't forget.

They had another two hours of light remaining, enough for them to reach the cove and set their plan into action. If they succeeded, he'd have to honor his bargain and release her. Put her on a ship that would take her as far from England as possible.

A breath hissed between his clenched teeth. It would be for the best, he told himself. She'd be alive; he wouldn't be forced to watch her stand trial, knowing he'd played a vital role in sending her to her death. A death that made him ill to think about. When he'd first begun his search for her, he'd been adamant that nothing would stop him from seeing her punished. He realized now that he'd tried and sentenced her without hearing her version of the truth. But what was the truth?

Thomas had been unbending that she'd attacked the *Valiant.* But Morgan had been just as steadfast and believable in her claim that she was innocent. Who was he to believe?

Perhaps the matter would be taken out of his hands. They might never reach the cove and might all be dead before the sun fully set.

"I can't go in like this," Morgan said, looking down at

her creased and stained gown. Frowning, she turned and
scanned the men around her, as if sizing them up. She
tilted her head back and gasped. "Daniel!"

He followed her gaze to the main mast. A cold chill
gripped his neck. "Tobitt, I told you to remove our flag."

Morgan pointed at a crewman who was coiling rope
nearby. "You there, retrieve your captain's pennon."

The sailor pursed his weathered lips in a sneer. "I don't
take orders from no pirate, 'specially no female sea dog."

Daniel started to reprimand the sailor, but stopped when
he saw Morgan brace her hands on her hips and stare at
the man until he cleared his throat and went back to
work. Muttering a curse for his disobedience, she headed
midship.

"Morgan, what are you doing?" Daniel asked, following
her.

"Don't let her trifle with our ship, Capt'n," Tobitt
warned, shadowing Daniel.

"Your flag is coming down if I have to climb up there
and get it myself." She gathered her skirts in one hand
and reached for the ratline.

Daniel took her by the arm and pulled her away from
the mast. He nodded to his first officer, whose sun-tough-
ened face had gone scarlet with distress. "See to it, Tobitt."

"Aye, Capt'n."

"That's another thing we need to change, Daniel," she
interrupted. "I was going to discuss this with you before,
but I . . . well . . . you didn't seem to be in the mood."

"Look at that glint in her eyes, Capt'n," Tobitt declared.
"We aren't going tae like whatever she's gonna say next.
Not at all."

"I don't doubt you're right, Mr. Tobitt," she said. A
shrewd gleam sparked beneath the gray depth in her eyes,
firing them like lightning. "If we hope to have any chance
of success, I'm going to have to captain the *Pursuit.*"

"The bloody hell ye will," Tobitt choked.

"The crew would feed you to the sharks before taking orders from you, woman," Thomas said, coming up behind Morgan.

She spun to face him. "Halo Jones knows me. He'll expect me to be in command of my own ship."

"We aren't going to get close enough to Halo Jones for him to know the difference."

Daniel listened to the exchange, his gut tightening. He didn't like what Morgan said, but knew she spoke the truth. He should turn his ship over to her, exploit their roles as pirates to the fullest. She wouldn't truly be in command, but would his men see it that way? Though she'd been on his ship for three days now and had yet to scorch the flesh off one single soul, his crew still regarded her as a demon in disguise and made the sign of the cross whenever she was near.

He glanced at Thomas, and once again realized the extent of his mistake by insisting his partner stay on board. Thomas's animosity toward Morgan had turned the crew's fear into hatred. They'd begun to openly insult her. Daniel had ordered them to keep their mouths shut, but now he worried about what they whispered among themselves. Keeping her in his cabin and out of sight had helped alleviate the tension, but defusing the men's rancor altogether had been a losing battle.

Because they don't know her as I do, he thought. *They haven't witnessed her courage, her devotion to the ones she loves.*

He clenched his jaw as he heard her desperate plea. *"Have you ever woken up with an ache in your belly that you'd give anything to fill? Only you hear your sister weeping in her sleep for food?"*

Remorse for what she'd endured pulled at him. How could he possibly convince his crew to follow her orders, when they'd prefer to lynch her, instead? If they were forced into a hand-to-hand battle with Halo's men, what was to stop a member of Daniel's crew, or even Thomas, from sliding his blade into Morgan's back? He shuddered, feeling his heart miss a beat. He'd brought her into this situation, and he'd be damned if he'd allow his own crew to hurt her.

Daniel gripped her upper arm and pulled her toward his cabin. "I can't allow you to act as captain, Morgan. There has to be another way."

"You know I'm right." She tensed against his hold, but thankfully, she accompanied him without a fight.

"Aye, but my crew won't see it that way."

"Then convince them, or turn your ship around." At the portal leading to his cabin, she jerked out of his hold.

"Damn it, Morgan."

"If we meet Halo and he learns I'm not the captain, he'll know something's wrong." She laid her hand on his chest to make her point, but Daniel thought she might as well have singed him with an iron brand. Heat flared from her touch, as fast and devastating as a cannon blast.

He wanted to pull her closer, but he couldn't, not with his crew watching. He ran his fingers through his hair in frustration.

"Tell your men it's just for show," she said, her voice unsteady. She pulled her hand away and pressed it against her stomach. Had she felt the same fire? he wondered. Was she as confused by the same, unwanted longings that welled inside him? Or was she simply annoyed because she wasn't in charge?

"There's one more thing I need you to do," she said.

"What now?" He hadn't agreed to her acting as captain, but he knew he had to. Obviously, so did she. Suddenly he wished he could spin back time and return her to the life he'd ripped her away from. She should be in Dunmore, with her family and friends, safe and happily married to her farmer.

Meeting his gaze, she gave him an encouraging smile

that made him feel his regret all the more keenly. "I need clothes fit for a pirate."

No, you need silks and lace, he thought, wanting to hold her to him. Things she deserved, but undoubtedly would never have.

"Sweet Mary, do your men never bathe?" Morgan averted her head and held the pants and shirt at arm's length.

"Aye, when it rains."

She laughed, but the sound died in her throat when Daniel smiled in return. She'd only seen him scowl or frown. The relaxed pull of his mouth, the glimmer now lighting his eyes, made her stomach constrict and her breath lodge in her throat. God help her, the man was handsome beyond reason.

She turned her attention to her new—or rather extremely used—outfit. She inspected the seams of the faded blue and white striped shirt, then the inside of the sleeves.

"What are you doing, looking for a place to hide a weapon?" Daniel reclined in his chair, settling in as if he expected to watch her change.

"I'm checking for lice."

"And if you find any?"

She gave him a salty-sweet smile. "Then you'll have to return these to whomever you borrowed them from and loan me something of yours."

Her pretense of a grin faded, as did the teasing glint in Daniel's eyes. Her stomach contracted, her lungs tightened, slowing the beat of her heart. She had no idea what caused his change in mood, but for her, the idea of wearing something belonging to him, being wrapped completely in his scent, was too much to bear.

She turned her back to him, determined to wear the soiled clothes whether they were full of vermin or not.

"Excuse me, Daniel, but I must change."

Hearing him move to leave, she closed her eyes and waited for the door to open and close behind her. Her blood pulsed through the veins in her chest. Heat gathered at the base of her neck. It spiraled upward, making her head spin. She held her breath, willed herself to control her reactions. Her attraction for Daniel was insane. He might have agreed to set her free, but his reasons were selfish ones. They had nothing to do with his caring for her. He might have kissed her before, might have wanted to do more, but what did that mean? He desired her, but desire had nothing to do with caring or love.

She turned her thoughts to more practical matters. *"I'm not convinced Morgan's responsible for Egham's death."* What had happened to make him doubt her guilt? Was she finally breaking through his stubborn convictions? Or did he simply want Halo Jones to hang more than he wanted her to? She stifled a groan, her thoughts only confusing her more. The sooner she was alone, the sooner she could get herself back under control.

Morgan gasped, feeling Daniel's fingers run through her hair, gathering it and lifting it aside. Tingles fled over her scalp. He fumbled with the buttons at the nape of her neck, brushing her skin as he loosened one, then another and another, the tiny buttons popping free under his touch. "Wh—what are you doing."

"Helping you out of this."

"I don't need your help." She whipped around to face him, and instantly realized her mistake. A whirlpool of darkness swirled in his eyes, emotions that spoke of lust when she wanted to see longing. "Daniel, don't."

He drew his hands down her arms, igniting a firestorm of desire that heated her core. God, to feel him again, to taste him. Isn't that what she'd wished for on the day of her wedding? One last kiss? Now was her chance. All she had to do was rise up on her toes, angle her head, run her fingers through his hair. So why didn't she do it? They still had time, more than an hour before they reached the inlet and Halo's cove.

So why didn't she kiss him? But she knew the answer. She'd want more than a kiss. And if he gave her more, she wouldn't want to leave.

She stepped back. Her calves butted against the trunk of the bed, blocking her escape. Daniel let his hands fall to his sides. Releasing a sigh that matched her frustration, he turned for the door.

Halfway to the threshold, he stopped to look at her. "I've spoken with my crew. They'll pretend you're their captain when we reach Halo's camp."

"You must have bribed them handsomely to get their agreement."

Her quip didn't produce the smile she'd hoped for. "I want you at my side, Morgan, so I can keep an eye on you."

The order brought her chin up in defiance. "You still don't trust me." She didn't expect him to, but the truth hurt nonetheless. "Do you believe as Thomas does, that I'm leading you into a trap?"

Daniel glanced at the dark companionway behind him. "Halo Jones isn't the only one who's given me cause to worry. Some people have foolish ideas about meting out justice. I don't want you getting harmed because of it."

The sincerity of his voice caught her off guard. "I can take care of myself."

"Against my entire crew if they choose to disobey my orders?" He shook his head. "Not this time, Morgan. You'll stay with me when it comes time to attack Halo's camp."

"There are things we still need to discuss about this plan."

His gaze slid down her body, slowly, before burning its

way up again. Tingles sizzled over her skin, warming her blood, making her catch her breath. When his eyes met hers, they were hard and focused. He clenched his jaw. "After you've changed, we can talk. Meet me above deck."

He slammed the door closed behind him. Morgan listened to the angry tread of his footsteps. Before they faded completely, she ran to the door and jerked it open. "Daniel, wait!"

He paused on the lowest rung of the ladder and bent his head as if cursing her for stopping his escape. "What is it, Morgan?"

She walked to him, controlling her pace when she wanted to fling herself into his arms. She might never have another chance. Halo might decide to blow them out of the water. Or if her plan did succeed, Daniel would send her away, ensuring an end to whatever this was between them.

"There's something I've wanted to ask you."

"Can't it wait?" He glanced up the stairs, clearly wanting to leave. Pale streams of sunlight washed the angles of his jaw, the hollows of his cheeks. Raven black hair fell in glossy waves against his shoulders, begging her touch.

"We might not have another chance."

He swiped his fingers through the hair she longed to feel. Sweet Mary, why couldn't she stay focused on the real issues at hand instead of her fascination for a man who'd only brought her grief? "It's about Captain Egham."

He frowned. "Go on."

"You told Thomas you had doubts about my involvement with his death."

Daniel braced his hand against the hatchway. His eyes hardened as if he regretted hearing his words tossed back at him.

Her stomach roiled, but she pressed on. "Is it true, or did you say that to gain his cooperation?"

Daniel regarded her, his expression somber. "I don't

know what to believe about Captain Egham. Thomas wouldn't lie to me about something so important. Yet . . .''

Morgan felt on the edge of her nerves. She crossed her arms around her waist and waited for him to continue.

"You didn't kill me when you could have," he said. "Considering what you currently face, I'm sure you wish you hadn't been so charitable."

She waved a hand in the air to dismiss his statement. "You didn't answer my question. Do you think I killed your captain?"

"What I believe isn't important, Morgan."

"It is to me." She closed her eyes, horrified that she'd revealed a portion of what she felt for him. Would he laugh if he knew how much she cared? How desperately she wished life had taken them down different paths?

"You admitted to being on the *Intrepid.*" Daniel's cool tone jarred her back to reality. "Thomas says he witnessed you butcher the captain and half the crew. The courts will believe *him.* Not me, and certainly not you."

"Do *you* believe I murdered your captain?" Morgan fisted her hands at her sides. "Damn it, Daniel. Tell me!"

He stepped off the ladder, yet he still towered above her, his wide shoulders blocking all but the faint light slipping through the hatchway. Shadows ghosted his face, darkening his eyes, hiding his emotions.

He ran his thumb across her chin. When he spoke, his voice was grim and harsh, and rumbled in her chest. "I don't want to believe you had anything to do with Egham's death. But is that the truth, Morgan, or is it something I only want to believe? That's a question that will surely be the death of me."

He kissed her then. She should have sensed it coming. Felt the surge of frustration and need that lifted off his skin. But she was caught unprepared for the hot taste of his mouth. His scent filled her head and left her swimming, groping for solid ground. But it was slipping out from under her faster and faster.

He broke away with an angry growl. With a look torn between fury and need, he spun away, leaving her alone in the dark hallway with nothing but the sounds of the creaking hull and her own ragged breathing.

"I think, Daniel"—she touched trembling fingers to her damp lips—"you and I might be the death of each other."

Chapter 12

Cool air skimmed over the sea, creating ripples in the pale blue glass. The *Pursuit* rode the current past razor-sharp cliffs studded with willful shrubs, seagulls settling in for the night, and—Morgan knew—a string of primed cannons. They'd yet to be hailed by the guards undoubtedly stationed above. Even if Halo Jones had left his safe harbor in a quest for new treasures, a handful of men would have remained to protect their lair.

"Do you see anything, Mr. Tobitt?" She clasped her hands behind her back and assumed a casual stance.

Squinting into a spypiece, he grumbled, "Not a blasted thing. Are ye sure ye have the right island? There's nothing on those cliffs but bloom'n' birds and lizards."

"They're here," she assured him. She faced Daniel, though she needn't have turned. Once she'd stepped foot above deck, he hadn't let her be more than two feet from his side. Like her, he'd changed into wool pants—worn thin by washing—tucked into snug-fitting boots. He'd rolled up the sleeves of his black, collarless shirt, revealing forearms taut with muscle, the tanned skin dusted with dark wisps of hair.

With his hands resting on his lean hips, he searched the
island for signs of life. Though Morgan watched him, she
was aware of the tension unfurling from every man on
board, coating the ship's deck. Yet the anticipation she
sensed in Daniel was different. It possessed a life of its
own, so vivid her fingers tingled with the need for action.
Like touching him, though she didn't dare.

"Daniel," she said, and was rewarded with his cobalt
blue eyes locking on her. "Try to relax. You're a member
of the crew, remember?"

His mouth barely gave birth to a smile, but his eyes
glittered with levity. "Sorry, Captain."

Tobitt gasped out a curse and nearly dropped the spypiece over the railing.

"This plan better work," Daniel said, moving closer.

"It makes better sense than sailing in with guns blast-
ing." Morgan tilted her head back to keep his gaze, but
she found hers slipping to his mouth. The memory of
his musky taste, the warmth of his lips, sent heat trailing
through her veins just beneath her skin. Yes, her plan
had better work, because if anything happened to him . . .
Swallowing, she turned away and gripped the rail.

"Instead we're going tae just limp in with our tails tucked
between our legs," Tobitt grumbled.

"Our tails might be between our legs," Thomas Burke
voiced as he joined them, "but we'll hardly care, since our
heads will likely be blown from our shoulders. But that's
no less than we deserve for trusting a murdering whore."

"Thomas," Daniel said in a low, dangerous voice, "I'll
warn you to keep your mouth shut."

Morgan stiffened as if Thomas's venomous barb had
stabbed her in the back. "Mr. Tobitt, we're going to sail
into Halo's cove as if we have every right to."

Gathering her nerve, she turned around, and was startled to find Thomas disheveled and reeking of liquor. "For

my plan to succeed, Mr. Burke, you'll need to stay below. We wouldn't want Halo Jones recognizing you."

"Yes, that would be a pity," he jeered, lifting the whiskey bottle to his lips. Amber liquid trailed down his chin and soaked his linen shirt.

"She's right, Thomas." Daniel took his partner by the arm and led him to the hatchway, but Thomas jerked free and staggered back.

"I don't need your help, *old friend.*" With eyes bloodshot and filled with grief, Thomas pierced Daniel with an accusing glare. "They say three times's a charm. Perhaps this time those blasted pirates will kill me first so I won't have to watch the rest of you die."

Silence descended over the ship as Thomas made his way to the hatchway and down the ladder, hopefully to his cabin, Morgan prayed, where he'd stay.

She dared a glimpse at Daniel, saw the steel set of his jaw, the muscles bunched in his shoulders and arms. Without realizing it, she lifted her hand and touched his sleeve, drawing his attention. Fierce emotion darkened his eyes, their hardened centers piercing her with his anger and frustration.

She could see his doubts, the questions. He didn't know whom to trust. Thomas or her?

She tightened her fingers around his arm, but he shook her off and walked away. She wanted to go after him, but her own pride and determination held her back.

"But before this day is through, Daniel," she whispered to herself, "I will have succeeded in earning your trust. Or died trying."

Daniel stalked to the quarterdeck and relieved the helmsman at the wheel, needing something physical to occupy his mind. Gripping the knobbed handles, he felt the ship's hull vibrate, a telling pull of ocean against wood, and instinctively made a course correction. He glanced at the canvas sheets, unfurled to catch the barest breeze, then to the sun edging closer to the horizon. The inlet Morgan assured them existed had better appear soon, he scowled to himself, or they'd be forced to anchor and wait until morning to navigate the cove.

He didn't know if his men could withstand the tension of waiting through another night. The threat of more brawls hummed beneath the surface of suspicion. His crew wanted Morgan off their ship, and Daniel would be powerless to stop them if they decided to act. Especially if Thomas supported a mutiny.

But there was another reason he wanted this blasted mission over and done with. He couldn't survive another night of sleeping on the windowsill with Morgan only an arm's length away . . . in his bed.

He doubted he'd ever be able to occupy his chamber again without inhaling the sun-warmed scent of her, or feel her lingering presence. But as he'd spent the last few days with her, touching her, feeling the heat of her skin, witnessing the strength and purpose flame once again in her eyes, his resolve had steadily been stripped away, or hammered, he thought, like barnacles from a hull.

He'd walked away from her just now when he'd wanted to gather her in his arms, the only place he knew she'd be safe. Damn it! Why did a woman who lacked everything he valued tempt him to discard his career, his values, hell, even his life? Thomas hadn't been lying when he'd said King George would demand that Daniel pay for releasing Morgan. He shoved the worry aside. That was something he'd have to face when . . . and if . . . they survived.

"The devil's mouth. Leeward, Capt'n!" came the shout from the lookout stationed aloft.

Daniel scanned the island to his right. As if by magic, the rocky wall pulled away, revealing a narrow opening, just as Morgan had described. Looking deeper into the inlet, he spotted a secluded cove and glimpsed another ship roughly the same size as the *Pursuit*. Luck was with him. Halo was home, and he was about to receive a surprise visitor.

Daniel grinned and felt some of the anticipation tightening his chest loosen. He opened his mouth to order the sails lowered, but Morgan beat him to it.

"Strike the topmasts!" she called to the crewmen waiting for just such an order.

No one moved. Daniel cursed and gripped the wheel, ready to bark out an order, but Morgan surprised them all. She faced his men, her hands planted on her slender hips. A stillness gathered around her, an intensity that no female should have the will to possess. In a voice low, yet solid with strength, she pointed a finger at the loitering men and said, "Do it or die."

Every man within hearing range, and even those who weren't, leapt to do her bidding. Men scaled the shrouds to the topmasts. Ropes were pulled and tied off, sails were lowered and bound. Morgan moved among the men, giving orders, nodding with approval, and even offering encouragement when needed.

He watched her every move with a growing sense of awe.

With the curling length of her mahogany dark hair tied back with a piece of yarn, her borrowed pants and shirt hugging her waist and hips, she exuded confidence and control. And charm. The kind of which he'd never known. If a woman wearing satin and pearls, a lady who'd been groomed by social disciplines, boarded the ship right now and stood beside Morgan, the socialite would pale in comparison. He tried to imagine Morgan in a London parlor, sipping tea, gossiping about fashion or the latest scandal. He scowled, not caring for the frivolous image at all. She'd faced life and death, fought for her family and friends. She was capable of more than whiling away her days at garden parties and dances.

"Helmsman!"

Daniel glanced behind him before realizing Morgan was speaking to him. "Captain?"

"Would you care to turn the ship?" she asked, amusement arching her sculpted brow. "Or were you perhaps planning to circle the island once more?"

He should have been annoyed with her censure, but damn if he didn't want to kiss her full mouth and the smile she didn't bother trying to hide. Spinning the wheel, he put thoughts of Morgan aside and sent the ship on a heading for the cove. He gave a cursory glance at the black flag flapping from the mast overhead, praying it fooled the pirates long enough for their plan to work.

Morgan joined him at the wheel as they cleared the outer barrier. She tilted her head back and sighed. Daniel followed her gaze and spotted four swivel cannons trained on his vessel. Another dozen men with loaded guns lined the cliff.

"I take it it's a good sign they haven't fired yet."

"A very good sign." Her gaze turned to Daniel's men, who had fallen quiet and watched her with obvious distrust as they drew closer to the pirate ship anchored in the cove. "Do you suppose they feel they've stepped into the lion's den?"

"They're just wondering if the gate is going to lock behind them." Daniel signaled for the helmsman to take over. With a hand at the small of her back, he led her to midship. As they drew up beside the other vessel, Mr. Tobitt gave the order to drop anchor.

"And you?" she asked, slicing him a glance with her discerning gray eyes.

"I'm trying to keep an open mind. But I must warn you, Morgan, if you try to betray me, I'll—"

"You'll what?" she said, stopping to face him. "Kill me?"

The muscles in his gut tightened in protest. "You'd be wise not to put me in that position."

A booming explosion caught them all off guard. Daniel gripped Morgan around her waist and shielded her with his body. The cannonball struck dangerously close to the bow, spraying water over the rail.

"Damn it, Morgan!" Daniel pushed her ahead of him, prepared to lock her below. His first officer raced across the deck in front of him. "Tobitt, have the gunner ready the fuses."

Daniel cursed. Thomas had been right all along. Morgan had led them into a trap, and he'd willingly followed. He hadn't believed her capable of such trickery . . . What had he been thinking? Morgan knew only lies and deceit. How could he have expected anything else?

She twisted out of his hold and gripped his arm. "It's a warning shot, Daniel! Tell your men not to fire."

He stared at her for the split second it took for her words to sink in. "Tobitt, delay that order."

"Are ye out of your bloom'n' mind?" Tobitt called, popping back up the hatchway. Men scurrying in every direction came to a stop.

"Did you know they would do this?" Daniel demanded, gripping her upper arms.

"Yes."

"And you neglected to inform me?" he said with a growl that vibrated his chest.

"You are supposed to be following *my* orders, remember?" Morgan straightened and glanced at the men drawing near. "Trust me. For God's sake, please trust me in this."

"Trust a bleed'n' pirate," someone muttered.

"Aye," she snapped. Then, in a voice that carried to the men close by, she added, "Trust me to capture Halo Jones *and* recover the bounty he's thieved."

The crew looked from one man to another, and Daniel knew she'd finally succeeded in gaining their cooperation, reluctant though it was. It was common practice to divide the plunder retrieved from a pirate vessel among the crew. A smart sailor could become a wealthy man in the process.

"We've got company, Capt'n." Tobitt pointed to two men untying a skiff from a decaying pier. In preparation for the coming dark, one placed a metal lamp on a hook at the bow. Taking up oars, they headed for the *Pursuit*.

"You there, Roscoe," Morgan ordered. "See the lanterns are lit. It'll be full night soon." To Daniel, she said, "Since you won't return my blade . . ." She crossed to the carpenter and took his knife from his worn leather sheath. Tucking the simple blade into the waist of her pants, she gave Daniel a look that dared him to object.

To the gunner, a short, barrel-shaped man, she said, "Make sure the muskets are loaded and ready when we return."

Daniel clasped her arm. "Where do you think you're going?"

"To the island to meet Halo. That's why we're here, isn't it?"

"You're not going."

"He'll be expecting me."

"Then he can come aboard the *Pursuit*, but you're not going ashore."

She struggled, but he refused to release her. "Daniel—"

"I can't protect you out there, Morgan."

She froze and stared at him. Seconds passed before she drew a breath. "You don't have to protect me."

"Blast it, Morgan . . ." Daniel cursed himself, finally realizing what he'd risked by going after Halo. At this moment, he didn't care about the king's wrath, or seeking vengeance. All that mattered was keeping her safe. Morgan might be prepared to face a murdering outlaw, but he wasn't about to take that kind of risk with her life.

"I can take care of myself," she insisted. "I always have."

"I forbid you to leave."

"You forbid?"

At that moment, the two men climbed over the railing and headed straight for Morgan. Taking her by the arms, one said, "You're tae come with us."

Pushed to the side, Daniel had no choice but to watch her go.

Chapter 13

"Halt!" Daniel ordered.

He crossed the deck just as the first man climbed over the railing. The second pirate drew his pistol, leveling it at Daniel's chest.

Daniel slowed his gait and raised his hands out to his sides. Torches snapped and hissed in the breeze; light flickered across the black steel barrel like a dancing moth. "You aren't taking her."

Locking back the metal hammer with his thumb, the pirate grinned. "Ye don't give the orders, round 'ere, mate. This 'ere is Halo's realm. 'E sets the rules, and if ye follows 'em, 'e might let ye live."

Morgan gave Daniel a look of entreaty. "I'll be fine, Daniel. Stay with the ship."

"You're not going alone."

"There's no need tae worry," the man said, gripping her arm and drawing her up against him. "Halo won't hurt her none. 'E has a special fondness for this one." Laughing, he added, "Ain't that so, Morgan? When we realized you was on board, Halo demanded you be brought to him straight away."

Daniel willed his hands not to clench. What he wouldn't give to smash the man's teeth down his throat. But there was no way in hell Morgan was leaving this ship without him.

"Fine," he said, lowering his arms and stepping forward. "Then I'm coming with you."

"Like 'ell ye are." He straightened his arm, bringing the barrel of the pistol within inches of Daniel's chest. Glancing at Morgan, he asked, "Just who the bloody blazes is he? Your lover? Halo ain't gonna like that at all."

Color fired Morgan's cheeks. She placed her hand on the man's wrist. "I'm sure Halo won't mind if my first officer joins us."

"It's you 'e wants tae see, Morgan, not this puffed-up bloke."

She gave a caustic laugh, one he'd never heard from her before. "If Halo objects, I'll send my man back to the ship. He knows my crewmen are somewhat overprotective of me."

The sailor wavered for a moment, his hungry gaze raking every curve she possessed. The muscles along Daniel's spine knotted with strain. Breaking the man's teeth wouldn't be enough, he decided. The miscreant needed to be taught a lesson.

Nodding his consent, the sailor lowered his weapon. "Can't say I blame 'em none. But Halo ain't gonna like the competition."

Competition? Daniel glared at Morgan for an answer. Her cool gray eyes slid past him without revealing her thoughts. Her shoulders were squared, her back ramrod straight. Determination set her jaw in a rigid line. Stunned, he realized he was seeing the woman he'd first met, Morgan the Scylla, the infamous pirate who wielded determination like a shield.

The change in her shook him to the core, not with disgust, but with awe. Was there no limit to the woman's strength? *Unless this is the real Morgan,* a doubtful voice whispered in the back of his mind, *and the softer, gentler woman had been nothing more than a ruse.* Not liking the thought, he said, "Tobitt will accompany us as well."

"Now see 'ere," the man scowled. "If ye don't stop yapp'n' with demands, I'll shoot your bloody face off."

Which was exactly why Daniel wanted his first officer there to back him up. "We have crates of whiskey for Halo. They're quite heavy, and as you can see"—he nodded to Tobitt, whose bulky form contradicted his horrified expression—"he's quite capable of handling the weight."

"Whiskey, ye say?" The man released Morgan to scratch his ratty, lice-infested beard. "All right. But just the two of ye, and no more."

Exchanging a wary glance with Morgan, Daniel nodded for Tobitt to retrieve the liquor from below. Morgan climbed over the railing with ease and descended the ladder, disappearing from sight. Daniel's heart lurched against his chest. She might be strong, and he didn't trust her completely, but she was still a woman. And he was determined to protect her. Instinct told him to grab hold of her and lock her below, sail out of the blasted cove and forget he'd ever heard the name Halo Jones. Only it was too late to change his mind.

"Capt'n," Tobitt whispered frantically in his ear.

"The whiskey, Tobitt." Daniel started after her. "I don't want them leaving without us."

"But it's land, Capt'n. Yer ask'n me tae go on *land*!"

Daniel had never heard the simple word uttered with such contempt. If this had been another time, he would have grinned. "You can do it, Tobitt. And don't call me Captain."

"I'll puke me guts up."

"Let's hope not, but if you must, wait until we're in need of a diversion."

Tobitt glanced longingly over the ship that was his home.

His gaze narrowed on the hatchway leading to the cabin where Thomas was hiding. "I'll go with ye, Cap ... sir." He looked at Daniel. "I just hope this ship is here when we return."

While Tobitt gathered the whiskey, Daniel met with Roscoe, charging him with the responsibility of securing the ship and keeping Thomas below. He didn't want to think his crewmen or partner would set sail without him, stranding him on a pirate island, but considering what he'd been through during the past months, he knew anything was possible.

Five minutes later, Daniel, Tobitt, Morgan and their two escorts were rowing across the ink-black cove. The moonless night had settled around them, a black curtain the yellow glow of lantern light struggled to pierce. Lights from their ship faded to starry specks. The men's voices on deck drifted into nothing, leaving only the steady slap of oars against water and Tobitt's worried moans.

Reaching the pier, the two pirates leapt out and tied off the skiff. Tobitt heaved up the crate of whiskey, then joined them. Daniel gripped Morgan's arm as she reached for the lowest rung. "You're not to be alone with him."

He couldn't read her expression in the dark, but he felt her muscles flex with tension. She whispered, "You're going to have to trust me."

Trust her? If only he could.

"Whatever happens," she said, "let me do the talking."

He followed her up the ladder and along the pier, scanning the deserted beach for any signs of trouble. Shadows blacker than a midnight sea swallowed the land before them. He couldn't discern a trail, and the lamp one man held aloft leaked a pitiful amount of light. Yet they trudged on through the dark.

Behind him, he heard Tobitt shift the crate on his shoulder and repeat a string of prayers for his unfortunate soul and nauseous stomach. Morgan walked ahead, her hand

on the hilt of her borrowed knife. Accompanied by the
drone of crickets and the whine of mosquitoes, they pushed
through the brush in what Daniel guessed to be a southerly
course. Finally they came to a clearing. He stopped to get
his bearings and learn the layout of the camp.

Torches burned around the perimeter, throwing light
across disheveled huts and lean-tos. Half buried in dirt
and debris, discarded bottles glimmered like dying embers.
Trunks, long emptied of their treasures, were stacked
against the base of a palm tree. Scraps of paper, books
and scrolls had been trampled into the uneven ground.

Daniel continued through the center of camp to a shack
of weathered gray planks. There were no windows. A red
and green blanket woven in a tartan design had been
nailed to the beam and served as a door. Dried ferns draped
the sloped roof—the pirates' attempt at construction, Daniel supposed. As lacking as the building was, it was the best
of the lot, which meant it had to be the residence of Halo
Jones.

The man who'd wielded the pistol at Daniel ordered
them to wait. Pushing the blanket aside, he slipped into
the interior. Daniel glanced at Morgan, noted her shrewd
expression, the sensual purse to her lips. Was she enjoying
this? he wondered. Did she look forward to seeing Halo
again? She'd said she didn't trust the pirate, had never
been with him. *"I've lain with no man."* But did Daniel
believe her? When the notorious pirate arrived, would
Daniel feel the trapdoor close on him like the lid to a
coffin?

Then he noticed the frantic race of her pulse at the base
of her throat, her white-knuckled grip on the hilt of her
knife. She wasn't as calm as she appeared, which irratio-
nally made Daniel release a sigh of relief.

Like rats in an alleyway, men emerged from their huts,
from behind trees and from the shadows themselves. In
the erratic light, their faces appeared burned, weathered

to a nut brown, hardening their scowls like chipped sandstone. Most wore baggy breeches and filthy checkered shirts with red scarves knotted around their necks. They were pirates, the lot of them, Daniel brooded, who'd most likely started out as honest sailors.

He spotted several equally rough women in the background, some with naked children clinging to their legs. The toddlers watched him with dark, untrusting eyes. His stomach clenched. He'd seen enough children killed during the war; these he vowed to save.

The blanket fluttered, drawing his attention, as the pistol-bearing sailor emerged. He held the fabric back as another man of imposing height ducked through the doorway.

Before they'd reached the island, Daniel had expected to find the filthy, primitive surroundings, the gritty, degraded men, but he hadn't expected the sight that stood before him now.

Halo Jones topped six feet, his lean, hardened body clothed in a crimson damask waistcoat and breeches. He'd added a matching velvet hat, tilting the brim low over one eye. A black feather plumed from the crown. Gold chains draped his neck; the longest had a thumb-size diamond dangling from its length. Rings with an assortment of gemstones adorned all of his fingers. Blond hair, streaked white from the sun, framed his Danish face. Against his bronzed skin, his eyes were gunmetal blue, and they were focused . . . intently . . . on Morgan.

Daniel glanced at her and felt his insides twist into knots as her gaze roamed appreciatively over Halo's body.

"You never could pass up a chance to flaunt your riches," she said, her mouth curving with a teasing grin. "It's good to see some things haven't changed."

"When learning you were the one foolish enough, or should I say, brave enough, to sail into my domain, how could I resist dressing for the occasion?'' He lifted her hand, bringing it to his lips, but he didn't kiss it.

Daniel clenched his jaw until he feared his teeth might crack.

"It's been a long time, Morgan," Halo rasped, holding her gaze over her outstretched hand.

"Yes, it has," she murmured back.

"I've missed you." With a raucous laugh, he jerked her into his arms and closed his mouth over hers, ravishing her with a thorough kiss. A deep, forceful kiss that Morgan didn't fight.

Halo's pirates gathered close, laughing and exchanging jokes. Daniel barely heard them. Blood roared like a firing cannon through his head. He fisted his hands and willed himself not to move, not to rip Halo's groping hands from Morgan's back, or smash his head against the planks of his hut. He was outnumbered, and knew he'd be stopped before he took the first step.

"Sweet Jesus, love us," Tobitt choked. "We're dead men."

Every muscle along Daniel's spine twisted. Emotions tore through him, slicing with the lethal precision of a steel blade. He felt as if blood had been drawn, only his ran cold. He'd been a fool, a witless fool. He'd offered to protect her! How she must have wanted to laugh at him. But he'd offered because he'd begun to care . . .

He stopped the thought before he could finish it. He didn't care about her. She was a woman, and in his mind, women needed to be defended. He simply kept forgetting that Morgan didn't belong in the same category as every other female on earth. Should he live another day, he swore he'd never forget again.

Halo broke the kiss. Grinning down at her, he ushered her inside. She paused in the doorway. "Daniel, Mr. Tobitt, come along."

Halo slid his hand over Morgan's arm. "You're all the company I need, love. They can sleep outside."

She rested her palm against the pirate's chest. "I'm here on business, Halo. They come inside or I leave."

"Don't play your games with me, Morgan," he warned with a cutting edge to his voice, though his grin remained. He wrapped his arms around her waist, bending to nuzzle her neck. "I'm not one of your decrepit followers who'll do your bidding."

Calling himself an idiot of the highest order, Daniel leapt forward. The tip of a sword pierced his shoulder, nearly breaking skin, stopping him. A pirate with a grimy face and a toothless smirk urged him back.

Daniel's breath pumped in his chest; blood raced like ice through his veins. Halo grinned at Daniel while Morgan struggled to escape his hold. Damn it, regardless that she'd led him into a trap, he couldn't stand by and allow her to be molested. He clenched his hands and scanned the ground for a weapon. Anything, a board, a bottle; then he remembered the whiskey in the case Tobitt still held. He reached for the lid, but hearing a man's gasp made him pause.

Halo released Morgan, raising his hands slowly into the air. He stepped back, his mouth lifting with a dangerous leer. "I see you haven't changed."

"When a lady says no"—she shifted to the left, allowing Daniel to see the knife she pressed to Halo's stomach—"she means it."

"Ah, but Morgan, my love, you're no lady. Which makes us a perfect match."

Color flushed her face, but she merely smiled. "This isn't the time."

He ran the back of his fingers down her cheek, along the side of her neck, moving lower to the swell of her breasts. He sucked in a breath and jerked his hand away. "Careful, love. I'm still in my prime."

"Not for long if you don't keep your hands to yourself."

Daniel saw she'd lowered the knife several inches. Fury still churned inside him, but he couldn't help feeling a flicker of awe at her daring. He knew for a certainty that there wasn't another woman like her. And was glad that for once, her skills were focused on someone besides him.

She nodded to Daniel and Tobitt. "Come inside, and bring the whiskey."

Glaring at the man who held him at sword's point, Daniel pushed the blade aside and followed her. Tapestries and silk fabric draped every inch of wall space. A gilt settee with matching velvet chairs fought for space among trunks filled with gold cups and jewel-encrusted plates—a testament of Halo's skill as a thief. Piles of elaborate garments littered the massive four-poster canopy bed. Daniel glanced at the furnishings, and wondered how many lives it had cost to decorate the squalid shack. His muscles tightened with anger and renewed determination to bring Halo to trial.

The pirate poured himself a tumbler of brandy, then reclined on the settee. He took a lengthy sip, studying first Morgan, then Daniel. His attention slid over Tobitt with disinterest. "Morgan, love, what happened to your knife? The one you just tried to carve me with isn't befitting to your reputation."

She fingered the plain wooden hilt, a sorry comparison to the jeweled dagger she'd tried to stab Daniel with when they'd met aboard the *Sea Queen*. "It was lost when I raided the *Intrepid*."

Halo threw his head back and laughed. His coppery eyes glittered with appreciation. "Ah, yes, I heard rumors about that poor ship being stripped of sail and cannon. The witless crew had been set adrift, but only after you boiled the captain alive and ate him for dinner."

Morgan sliced Tobitt a suspicious glance. "Really? Only the captain?"

Tobitt muttered a curse. His complexion went from pale to ruddy.

"I knew that was your work, love, because you did the unthinkable. You left people alive to tell the story. Morgan the Scylla!" Halo raised his glass in a one-sided toast. "When are you ever going to learn from my example? You never leave witnesses behind. You either kill the crew or recruit them."

"I keep forgetting that part." She poured a brandy for herself, claimed a chair and propped her feet on the marble table.

"So tell me." Halo took a cigar from a box beside Morgan's boots. He offered her one, but she declined. Biting the tip, he spit it out, then lit the end from the flame of a candle. "Where have you been? I also heard you'd given up pirating."

"Only keeping out of sight until King George finds another country to invade and conquer." She sent Daniel a cursory glance, which somehow pulled him to her side. He didn't like hovering in the background, with the situation out of his control, especially when he had no idea what to expect when two cunning pirates gathered together.

Halo eyed Daniel's protective move with disdain. "Is that why you've come to me? Because you need a safe place to hide?"

"Perhaps." She studied the coppery liquor in her glass. "We're also in need of supplies."

He leaned forward, bracing his forearms on his thighs, and gave Daniel a territorial look meant to provoke his temper. "It'll cost you, Morgan." He glanced at her, and his mouth twitched with a knowing grin. "Far more than that case of whiskey your lackey's holding."

"Your protection isn't really what I'm after," Morgan said in a smoky voice that made Daniel tense. "I was thinking of something more permanent."

What was she saying? This wasn't part of the plan they'd

discussed. Daniel gripped her shoulder and squeezed, but she acted as if she didn't notice.

"I'm intrigued," Halo said arching a blond brow.

"I hope so." Morgan glanced over her shoulder at Daniel. A cat-and-cream smile softened her lips before she turned away. Lifting her glass to Halo, she said, "Because I want to become your partner."

Daniel's fingers dug into Morgan's shoulders. She held her breath and endured the pain. And kept her eyes forward. She'd seen him angry often enough to know the veins along his neck would be extended, throbbing with the racing of his blood. His eyes would be pinpoints of steel, sharp and deadly. The scar at his temple bleached white from strain. No, there was no need to turn around. The air trembled with the heat of his fury. He thought she intended to betray him. For that she was sorry, but it couldn't be helped.

She blamed it on her female intuition, the creeping sensation at the back of her neck. She imagined a snake was slithering around her throat, preparing to squeeze until the life drained out of her. Perhaps it was the cunning lift of Halo's mouth, or the calculated glint in his tawny eyes, whatever, she knew he'd contrived a plan of his own before she'd ever dropped anchor. He was only toying with her now. He wanted something. Her ship, her cargo. *Her.* Which meant the plan she and Daniel had devised wouldn't work.

"A partner," Halo mused, leaning against the settee. "What makes you think I need one? I have everything a man could want. A seaworthy ship, a crew who have no qualms about stealing or killing, enough riches to spend in two lifetimes."

"Surely there's something you're lacking?" she said, knowing she was teetering on the edge of a cliff. She wanted to bait her hook and lure Halo in. But she knew catching him could prove a huge mistake if she didn't have the means to escape.

"Well, now that you mention it. There is a something of value I've had my eye on."

Morgan tensed, knowing what was coming, and knowing she was the one who'd started them all down this dangerous path.

"You would make an excellent addition to my treasure chest," Halo mused.

"No." Daniel's snarl vibrated the room.

Morgan tightened her grip on her glass as Halo's gaze snapped to him. "You'll have to excuse my first officer," she said. "He doesn't agree with my plans for the future."

"How uncharacteristic of one of your crewmen." Halo rose and poured another portion of brandy. When he turned back, he leveled Daniel with a challenging glare. "I thought they all suffered from the malady of spineless followers."

"They're loyal." Heaven help her, the two men were ready to circle each other like wolves, each intent on staking his claim. Considering they were in Halo's camp, she had no doubts as to who would win if they came to blows.

Halo crossed to Daniel, stopping within a foot of him. Each man sized the other up, staring, sneering, refusing to back down. Morgan wanted to sigh in disgust. Though she didn't entirely blame Daniel for his aggressive stance. He was, after all, unarmed, and at the mercy of a notorious killer—and a woman he didn't trust.

"Where did you find this one, Morgan?" Halo's brow raised in a critical arch as he walked around Daniel. "He's at least a score younger than the rest of your crew. And correct me if I'm wrong, but he doesn't seem the type to follow orders. Especially from a woman."

"I'm not here to discuss my crew." Placing her drink

on the table, Morgan rose. "But I would like to know your thoughts on a partnership."

Moving to her side, Halo slipped his arm around her waist. She gritted her teeth, hating the feel of his hand against her hip, his fingers groping her flesh. She didn't dare look at Daniel, knowing she'd see murderous fury in his eyes.

"Order your men to leave, and I'll be happy to *discuss* doing business together."

"Tobitt," Morgan said. "Leave the whiskey by the door."

"I knew you'd see it my way." Halo downed the rest of his drink and sighed with satisfaction.

"Morgan . . ." Daniel growled. He didn't need to say more. She understood his meaning perfectly. He wouldn't allow her to remain behind—not that she intended to. She'd surprised Halo once with her knife. She wouldn't be so lucky again.

"It's late." She pulled away and stepped around Halo. "I'll return in the morning. Then we can continue our discussion."

He grabbed her arm. "You'll—"

"Release her," Daniel warned.

Morgan wanted to close her eyes and groan. Why couldn't he stay out of this? She knew what she was doing. But knowing Daniel, she should feel fortunate that he'd remained quiet this long.

"You'd better tell your boy to keep his jaw shut or he'll lose it."

"We'll return in the morning, Halo," she insisted, not wanting to "tell" Daniel anything.

"If you leave now, there'll be no partnership."

She winced as his fingers dug into her skin. She jerked her arm free. "Don't threaten me, Halo. I came here offering you a chance to combine forces. If you're not interested, then say so and we'll leave."

He considered her a moment. Stepping back, he ran

his hand over his mouth and jaw. A slow smile twisted his lips. "Maybe you're right. Maybe you should return in the morning."

A shiver jarred her shoulders as if cold dead fingers had touched her back. *He's giving up too easily,* she silently worried. *He doesn't intend to let us live until tomorrow morning.*

He pulled a pocket watch from his vest. "Say, before breakfast?"

Daniel tensed beside her. She looked up in time to see his brow furrow as he stared at the watch Halo cradled in his hand. A muscle pulsed in Daniel's jaw; a breath hissed from between his clenched teeth. Not sure what caused his reaction, but certain he was at the end of his tolerance, she gripped his arm and urged him toward the door.

Once Daniel and Tobitt were outside, she paused at the threshold and faced Halo. "Until morning, then."

He raised his empty glass in salute, a shrewd glimmer in his coppery eyes. "I look forward to when next we meet."

She nodded and walked out the door, feeling a shiver of doom chase after her.

Chapter 14

"What the hell do you think you're doing?" Daniel demanded the moment they stepped on board the *Pursuit*, taking pride in having restrained himself this long. Never in his life had he been so vulnerable, so powerless . . . He stopped the thought, admitting that Morgan had repeatedly stripped him of any sense of control since the moment they'd met.

"Keep your voice down," she whispered, turning away to face the crew, now gathered on deck. "Tobitt, extinguish all but a few of the lanterns. Roscoe, bring up every available keg of gunpowder from below."

"No one move," Daniel ordered.

"Unless it's to get some rope so we can hang her," Thomas said dryly as he came through a hatchway. "She betrayed you, didn't she, Daniel?"

She threw Thomas a reproachful glare. "We don't have much time."

"That's right, Morgan," Thomas said. "If we're all to die, I want to make sure you go first."

She shoved her way past the men to the binnacle box

and struggled to lift a mound of coiled rope. "Fine, I'll tie this to the stern myself."

Daniel took her by the arm and forced her to drop the rope. "No one's doing anything until you explain what the hell you're about. You asked me to trust you, Morgan. Then you betrayed me and every man on this ship."

"I did no such thing."

"Your sudden desire to join forces with Halo Jones leads me to believe otherwise."

"I'll explain everything, Daniel, later. But right now, we must hurry."

In a barely civil tone, Thomas chided, "Did I not tell you she'd turn on you, *partner*?"

Morgan went still, her eyes frosting in the lantern light. Her chest heaved with each breath she took. Yet she didn't say a word in her defense. But what more was there to say? Daniel released her. She'd made her choice, and Halo seemed to be it. That didn't explain why she'd made another mistake by returning to the *Pursuit*. But that was a question he'd save for later. If they survived.

"Roscoe," Daniel said. "Have the cannons loaded and ready to fire. Tobitt, see that every man has a musket and powder. Now that we've found Halo, we're not leaving without him."

"You can't attack him like this," Morgan argued.

"You don't have a say in this, *love*," Daniel ground out.

"There's a better way," she insisted.

Taking her arm, he pulled her toward the hatchway. He was going to lock her in the hold with the rats and rotting food, as he should have done the moment he'd captured her. Without a word, the crewmen, who'd listened to every word, parted a path for them. He needed her out of the way. He needed a clear head and time to think. About Morgan and her betrayal, and about Halo and his gold pocket watch. How in God's name had he come into possession of it?

"Daniel, listen to me!" She fought his grip, but he'd be damned before he'd let her go. "We have to get off this ship."

"I've already heard what you have to say. We're doing things my way now, Morgan."

At the hatchway, she spun to face him, blocking the opening. Daniel felt a sharp, familiar jab at the base of his throat. His stomach muscles clenched and his breath locked in his lungs. The knife's steel blade dug into his skin.

"You'll have to kill me this time, Morgan, because I'll not release you. I've made that mistake one too many times."

Her brows narrowed with determination. "Telling Halo I wanted to be his partner was a ruse."

"Is that so?"

"I lied, Daniel—"

"Something you do so well," he interrupted. He eased back from the knife, but she adjusted the pressure, keeping the tip taut without breaking the skin.

She drew a steadying breath. "He's planning to attack us."

"Kill me, Morgan, because I'm not falling for any more of your tricks."

Her chin came up and her eyes glimmered with flashes of temper. She stepped back as far as he'd allow, then tossed her knife aside. The crew heaved an audible sigh of relief.

"When I saw Halo," she said, "I realized we needed another plan. A better one."

"Which you've come up with, of course." Daniel wanted to curse his own stupidity. He was listening to her lies when he was determined not to. "Why didn't you tell me about this change?"

Her hands came to her hips, her fingers flexing with agitation. "I'm not used to discussing my decisions.

Besides, what would you have had me do? Tell Halo, 'Excuse us, but I need to discuss this partnership with my first officer'?"

"You're not on the *Sea Queen* any longer, Morgan. This is my ship, my men. Your error has put their lives at great risk."

"I do what I believe is right, Daniel," she argued, filling the words with a wealth of emotion.

"What makes you think you're right this time?"

"Because every pirating trick I know I learned from Halo. He wants something, and he's going to come here to get it."

"How do you know?" He was afraid to listen, wanting to believe her when that was the last thing any sane man would do.

"He let us leave," she said simply.

To his frustration he saw the logic behind her words. Halo had been angry with Morgan for shunning his advances. He'd wanted her, yet he'd conceded, and much too easily for a pirate used to having his way.

"*If* you're telling the truth—"

"I am."

"You should have discussed it with me."

"I would have, had there been time." She squared her shoulders, lifting her fortitude as high as he'd ever seen it. "I'm sorry."

Daniel felt something tighten inside him. He'd expected another argument, not acquiescence from someone as proud and stubborn as she. "It's too late for apologies now. And I don't have the patience to pursue this further. It's time I caught a killer."

"You already have one killer, Daniel," Thomas said with disgust. "And you haven't done the rational thing with her. What does it matter if you catch Halo?"

"Halo's going to board this ship," Morgan said, her jaw clenched with frustration.

"He's not going to live long enough to do anything."
Daniel urged her to descend the ladder, but she refused.

"He's on his way," she asserted.

"How do you know?"

She briefly closed her eyes. "I never learned how to kill,
much to Halo's disappointment. But I learned how to be
devious. And I learned it from him."

Tobitt came up on Daniel's right. "I had a queer feeling
in Halo's shack, Capt'n. Maybe she's right. After all, she
knows 'im better'n we do."

"Tobitt!" Thomas cried. "You deserve to hang with her
for making such an appalling suggestion."

"If she was working with them pirates," Tobitt reasoned,
"do you think she'd return tae the *Pursuit* with us? That
don't make sense. She'd stay on the island where it was
safe."

As she heard Tobitt's defense of her, Morgan's mouth
dropped open for a split second. A smile threatened to
appear, but she cut it off. "Daniel, I promise you, he's
gathering his men right now. They'll wait until we're
asleep; then they'll board. They'll take this ship and kill
anyone who resists."

"Then we'll blow their skiffs out of the water before
they get 'ere," Tobitt suggested.

"We'll still be vulnerable to the half-dozen cannons he
has trained on the *Pursuit*," Daniel reasoned.

Morgan nodded in agreement.

"Witnessing the two of you together," Daniel said, his
tone hard and clipped, "I can't believe Halo would attack
you."

"Then you don't know a thing about Halo Jones. He'd
murder his own mother for a handful of gold."

"What do ye suggest?" Roscoe asked, coming close to
Daniel's left.

Daniel glanced around him and realized that all the
crewmen had gathered while he and Morgan were arguing.

Only Thomas stood apart, his arms crossed over his chest, a disapproving scowl on his face.

Daniel met Morgan's clear gaze. Her brow was knitted in a frown, her gray eyes issuing a silent plea for agreement. "The decision is yours, Daniel. Do we stay and fight?"

"We." We meant he had to trust her—one more time. "As I see it, there's only one choice to be made," he said, never taking his eyes from hers. "We have to abandon ship."

The lanterns had been doused.

A hush descended over the deck, as dark and mysterious as the silent cove three stories below. Moments before, Morgan had listened to Daniel devise a plan of attack. She'd offered her advice, which he'd taken, combining it with his scheme. He'd been shrewd, daring, a true pirate, though she'd kept that to herself.

The men moved quietly about their assigned duties, creeping like the mice that forever inhabited a ship, knowing that speed and care meant the difference between success and failure. She'd explained the layout of the island as best she remembered it. Once Daniel gave the signal, they would abandon ship. Everyone would swim ashore, except for Tobitt and his men, who would strike out for Halo's vessel, *Devil's Luck*, moored on the other side of the cove.

On shore, another handful of men would encircle the camp and subdue anyone remaining there, taking care not to harm the children. Morgan was to be stationed on the beach, away from any conflict. That part she'd objected to, but Daniel had been adamant. She didn't know if he was worried about her safety, or if he feared she'd try to change the plan once again. It didn't matter. He'd believed her about Halo attacking. He was afraid to trust her, but he was beginning to, a little at a time.

The crucial part of the plan lay in Daniel's hands. His group had to reach the cliff and capture the cannons. Once Halo boarded the *Pursuit*, Daniel would fire them on his own vessel, repeating the volleys until his ship sank in a fiery blaze. The crew had protested attacking their own ship, but once again, Daniel had stayed firm. Ships could be replaced, he'd told them, unlike the lives Halo had taken.

From her position at the forecastle, Morgan could hear Tobitt whisper orders to empty the kegs of gunpowder onto the deck. The black, deadly pile rose like a shadow, promising death and destruction. She shuddered, wanting to be off the ship as soon as possible.

The few articles the crew deemed too valuable to leave behind were shoved into knapsacks and strapped to their backs. Every knife and sword available had been claimed. Morgan had fastened a cutlass to her waist, tucking her borrowed knife into the waistband of her pants. She'd ordered the pistols and muskets left behind, certain the weapons wouldn't make it ashore without being rendered useless. Gunfire would ruin their surprise, anyway. And more than anything, she wanted Halo to be surprised.

The muscles along her spine tingled, and she knew that Daniel stood behind her. She turned and searched his face, barely able to discern the strong lines of his jaw or his disturbing eyes in the darkness.

"Everything's ready," she said, keeping her voice low.

"The men have begun descending the ropes." He touched her lower back and urged her to the stairs. "It's time to go."

She placed her hand on his chest to stop him—and touched heated skin, crisp swirls of hair. She felt the strong beat of his heart, the sureness of each breath he drew. If things went wrong, this might be the last time she saw him. There was so much she wanted to say, so much he made her feel that she needed to understand. But where Daniel was concerned, she seemed doomed to never have enough time.

"This will work," she said, needing to convince herself as much as him.

He shook his head. "Blowing up my ship seems as sane as anything else I've done since meeting you."

He covered her hand with his, pressing her palm tight against his skin. His heartbeat quickened. Hers joined in, vibrating until she heard nothing but the roar of blood in her ears.

"Promise me you'll stay out of the way."

She sighed. "I can take care of myself."

"Aye, you've proved that often enough."

"Then let me come with you," she insisted softly.

He wrapped his arm around her waist, drawing her flush against him. "For once, Morgan, do as I say."

"I'm the eldest child. Following orders goes against my nature." She rubbed her hand over his taut muscles, breathed in his musky scent.

"Morgan," he began, then hesitated as if reluctant to say whatever was on his mind. "You understand Halo may not survive."

She frowned at the thought, hating that anyone, even someone as heartless as Halo Jones, had to face such a violent end. "Either he dies here in battle or in London, after a humiliating trial and a painful hanging. I think he'd prefer everything to end here."

"Capt'n," Tobitt whispered. "Everyone's in the water, wait'n' for ye."

"We'll be right there."

"Daniel," she said when he pulled away. "You'll be careful?"

In a deep, gravelly voice, he said, "You haven't seen the last of me."

"And afterward? Once we've captured Halo?" Every

nerve inside her twisted. "You'll keep your promise and let me go?"

His hands moved to her shoulders, flexed almost painfully. She thought he wanted to shake her. Instead, he cursed, pulled her to him—and kissed her. A deep, possessive grind of lips against lips that lasted only seconds.

Releasing her, he swore in a rough voice, "We're going to survive tonight, Morgan. As our reward, I'll finish this kiss. Then I'll let you go."

Daniel crept through the brush, holding his breath in anticipation of snapping a twig or surprising a luckless pirate. His wet clothes clung to his hot body, cooling the adrenaline pumping through his veins. Thomas was behind him. He'd asked to remain on the beach, but Daniel had refused. Morgan might be able to defend herself, but Thomas hated her, and had made it clear he'd take any opportunity to mete out his own justice.

Thinking of Morgan made him miss his footing. A thin branch cracked beneath his boot. Daniel and the ten men accompanying him all froze. He strained his ears, listening for any sound that might signal he'd alerted the enemy.

Hearing nothing but croaking tree frogs and the whine of mosquitoes, he breathed a sigh of relief and continued. He couldn't think about Morgan without feeling a tightening in his chest, a yearning for something more.

Nor could he escape the twisting in his stomach, the fear that he was destined to lose her. *"You'll keep your promise and let me go?"* As a man of his word, he'd have to free her, abandon her to an unknown fate. *But she'll be alive.* It shouldn't matter that he'd never see her again. But it did. God help him, it did.

Someone tapped his shoulder and drew him up short, saving him from his disturbing thoughts. He turned to find Roscoe behind him. "They're up ahead, Capt'n," he whispered. "I can smell smoke from their fire."

Not one to argue with a gunner's instincts, Daniel signaled for half the men to circle back to the left. Morgan had said the cannons were stationed close together.

He eased forward, knowing they had to hurry. If Morgan was right, Halo should be climbing aboard Daniel's ship at any moment, only to discover it abandoned. Or if Morgan had been mistaken, or, worse, she had lied about Halo's intent and the pirate was still in his camp, then Daniel had possibly sent a dozen of his own men to their deaths. He shook the dire thought away. She hadn't lied. Every instinct, every impulse inside him said to believe her.

As if hearing his doubts, Thomas venomously whispered, "This is insanity."

Daniel held up a hand for his partner to be silent. He pointed ahead of him. In the shadows beneath a cluster of swaying palms, a pair of sleek, black swivel cannons were mounted on sturdy carriages. Exactly where Morgan said they would be. Daniel smiled into the dark, wishing she were here so he could kiss her for telling him the truth.

A small, banked fire burned between the cannons. Beside it two men slept. Another stood near the edge of the cliff, watching the cove.

Daniel waited a few minutes to give his crew time to get in position; then he crept forward, into the open. Behind him, he heard Thomas and the other men fan out. The willowy grass crunched beneath their feet, twigs snapped, clothes rustled as they increased their pace. The pirate on watch turned, spotting them. Daniel charged forward, past the two men on the ground who'd begun to stir, and caught the watchman around the waist. The man flew backwards in Daniel's grasp, landing with a thud, his upper torso hanging over the cliff.

Daniel rose to his feet and hauled the man up by his shirt. The pirate opened his mouth to shout a warning.

Daniel landed a blow to the man's jaw, producing a sickening crunch. Unconscious, the pirate sagged to the ground. Behind him, Daniel heard sounds of struggling. Then all was quiet.

"Thomas? Roscoe?"

"Aye, Capt'n," Roscoe chuckled. "We're 'ere and in possession of two fine cannons."

"Bind the pirates while I check on the others." Daniel hurried along the cliff's edge, praying as he went.

When he reached the section where the next pair of cannons were supposed to be, he slowed, searching the area before he stepped into the opening. A knife at his back made him suck in his breath and raise his hands.

"Move," the voice demanded. "And don't try noth'n'."

"Willie?" Daniel asked, recognizing the voice as one of his crewmen.

"Capt'n?" The knife disappeared, and his young carpenter rushed in front of him. "Sorry, Capt'n. I thought you was a pirate."

Daniel rested one hand on Willie's shoulder and nodded toward the clearing. "Are the cannons secure?"

"Aye, all of 'em. You just give the signal when to fire."

Nodding, Daniel headed back to Thomas and Roscoe. "Now we have to wait." He drew the spypiece from inside his shirt and searched the cove for signs of life. Morgan was down there somewhere, hopefully tucked into a safe hiding place. Though he doubted it. Unease crept over the nape of his neck. He should have brought her with him. But he hadn't trusted her enough. He should have known better. She'd given him signs all along. She'd never harmed him or his men when she could have. Yes, she'd lied to him, but only to protect her family.

Damn it, he thought, feeling his skin tighten with dread. He should have brought her with him.

* * *

Morgan kept behind the line of trees and brush, waiting, when every instinct in her body insisted she climb the cliff to be with Daniel. He could capture the cannons without her help, but any number of things could go wrong. She knew these pirates, how they thought, the underhanded tricks they played. Instead of being of some use, she hovered in the shadows with her stomach in knots and her imagination soaring with every horrible possibility.

"He has to be all right," she whispered to the dark. She couldn't bear to think about him hurt, possibly dying. He was too strong, too vital. Too much of everything she needed. How Jo would laugh if she could see her sister hiding in the dark, worrying over Daniel, while the threat and thrill of battle loomed ahead of her.

Jo wouldn't have taken orders from a man. But then Jo had never cared about a man so much she'd willingly sacrifice her freedom to ensure his safety. Morgan closed her eyes as the truth settled in, squeezing the breath from her lungs. She wanted to deny her feelings; everything would be so much easier if she didn't care about Daniel. If she didn't love him. But she did. God help her, she did. She tucked the truth away, because it hurt too much to think about it now. Later, she thought; later she could feel her love for him, dream about what could have been. But not now. His survival was what mattered most.

Wind rustled the long, leafy palms overhead, stirring sounds like chattering voices. She tensed, glancing at the pier, but all remained quiet. The *Pursuit* rested in the cove like a towering shadow, a dark sea monster waiting to spring its trap. She prayed that Tobitt and his men were aboard the *Devil's Luck*, securing it for their escape. She smiled, thinking how the giant sailor had encouraged Daniel to listen to her. Perhaps her horrid reputation was finally wearing off.

A prickling sensation lifted the hairs at the base of her neck. She held her breath and listened. Someone was behind her. She felt stares on her back. She tried to reassure herself that it was one of the crewmen assigned to guard the beach with her.

She turned and glimpsed Halo's chilling grin seconds before his fist struck her face. Lightning exploded behind her eyes. She felt herself falling.

And then she felt nothing at all.

"I see them," Thomas said with a surprised laugh. "They're in skiffs, rowing toward the *Pursuit.*"

"So she guessed right," Daniel said from beside him.

Thomas glanced over his shoulder. Daniel couldn't read his partner's expression in the dark, but from the sudden spike in tension, he assumed he'd been given a look of reproach. Thomas's next words proved it.

"That doesn't give you the right to release her."

Daniel felt the now familiar jolt of dread in his stomach. "I gave her my word, Thomas."

"Which is meaningless to a pirate."

Daniel raised the spypiece and focused on the *Pursuit's* main deck. He spotted several shadowy figures scurrying toward the hatchways, where they disappeared into the decks below.

"It won't be long now," Roscoe chuckled, "before they realize she's as empty as last year's bird's nest."

"Prepare to fire, Roscoe. And remember, our target is the *Pursuit,* not the *Devil's Luck.* If we sink both vessels, we'll never get off this island."

"Aye, Capt'n."

"Damn you, Halo," Daniel whispered, adjusting the telescope, searching the shapes hurrying from one end of the ship to the other. "Where are you?"

Someone on board ship lit a torch. Daniel spotted a man taller than the rest, with white-blond hair, black coat and breeches. Grinning, Daniel said, "There he is, in all his pirate glory."

"Now, Capt'n?" Roscoe asked.

"Now." Daniel kept his scope focused on Halo's towering form.

The cannon roared to life, billowing smoke and flame. A flash of light illuminated the deck . . . and the dark-haired woman trapped in Halo's arms.

"God, no!" Daniel choked. *"Morgan!"* His shout was lost as another cannon fired, then another and another.

Chapter 15

"Where the bloody hell are they?" Halo demanded, taking Morgan by the arms and shaking her. "The ship's empty!"

Her head jerked back. Pain flared in a jagged streak down her spine. Her stomach lurched until she feared she'd throw up. She swallowed back the nausea, focused on breathing. She touched her throbbing temple with her fingers. Blood trickled warm down the side of her face where Halo's ring had left a gash when he'd hit her.

He shook her again, and she forced herself to say, "They're gone."

"Gone!"

The rest of his tirade was lost in the blast of a cannon. Halo spun toward the cliff. He let out a murderous roar. Men around her shouted, dropped the food they'd begun to pillage and ran for the sides. She had to escape. *Now.*

Her knife had been stripped from her, the cutlass as well. Bending her arm, she rammed her elbow hard into Halo's ribs. He grunted, loosening his hold on her. Spinning away, she stumbled for the railing. Leaping onto it, she dove into open air. She held her breath. Wind buffeted her face, pulled her hair. Black water rushed up to her. The world exploded behind her in sound and color. Screams and cries, fiery reds and blinding yellows.

She hit the water and plummeted into its cool, slippery grip. She went deeper, sliding further into the dark, her body as limp as a doll's. *She was still too close to the ship*. The gunpowder stored in the *Pursuit*'s belly was about to ignite.

She kicked her feet and used her arms to swim away. She felt sluggish, weak, dizzy. Pressure tightened her chest; her lungs burned. Her head pounded, felt as if it would explode. She forced herself to swim, reach the surface. Her head broke through the rippling waves. She gulped in a lungful of air. Wood splintered and crackled behind her. Billowing heat buffeted the back of her head. She turned. Flames rose like a dancing devil in the sky, shooting higher in swirls of gold and bloody reds. She heard men shouting, but not from the ship. Pirates were in the water, swimming toward her. She turned away. The shore—she had to make the shore. Daniel would be there.

Finally her feet touched the sandy bottom. She stood, then fell back to her knees. Everything spun out of control. She clasped her head between her hands. Someone grabbed her arms. Panic tightened her throat. *Not Halo*, she wanted to scream, but couldn't.

"We got ye, Morgan." Daniel's crewmen helped her to her feet and toward shore. She wanted to cry with relief.

Her wet clothes clung to her skin; she could barely lift her sodden boots. She felt as if she were trudging through knee-deep mud. Stumbling, she collapsed on the beach and rolled onto her back. Staring at the sky alight with flames, she fought to catch her breath.

An explosion shook the land. A blast of heat blazed over her skin. Daniel's men fell to the ground beside her. Trees bent and swayed. Wood and shredded debris shot past her, littering the beach. Someone screamed. The fiery rumble echoed through her chest, through the air, rolling over and over until it faded altogether.

"Morgan," one of the crewmen said, rising to his knees beside her. "Are ye all right?"

" 'Course she ain't all right, you idiot," another man chided. "Look, she's bleed'n'."

Morgan knew she should get up, help capture the pirates swimming for shore. She couldn't move. *Daniel—I need to see Daniel.* She heard shouts, men arguing. Why they argued she didn't know, though she should. She tried to think, focus, but it was no use. Ash rained down on her in flakes of gray snow. She closed her eyes. *Daniel . . .*

Daniel skidded down the base of the cliff, sending rocks and debris scattering. The *Pursuit* burned like a massive funeral pyre, but he no longer cared. He'd seen Morgan leap from the ship moments before cannonballs ripped through the hull, igniting the gunpowder. He'd lost sight of her once she hit the water. She could be drowning even now.

His skin iced, and a shiver of dread swept through his limbs, pushing him to move faster. She should have been safe, hiding near the beach. What the hell had gone wrong?

He jumped the last few feet, his boots hitting packed sand just as the ship erupted into a ball of flame and flying wreckage. The worst of it landed where Morgan had been. His heart stopped in midbeat. But he kept running, pushed by fear, by hot terror that bled through his veins like acid. He searched the water for some glimpse of her. The surface trembled as if a giant had slapped it in anger. Nothing— he could see nothing but shattered wood burning on top of water, pirates struggling for shore. "Please, Morgan, please . . ."

A shout down the beach drew his attention. Patrick, one of his men, was waving his arms, yelling something Daniel couldn't hear.

When Daniel reached him, Patrick gripped his arm and pulled him along. "She's 'ere, Capt'n."

"Morgan?"

"Aye. We didn't know he'd caught her until—"

Daniel didn't wait to hear more. He set off at a dead run for the cluster of men fifty yards away. Slowing enough to push them aside, he ordered, "Let me through."

They parted, and the sight they revealed stopped Daniel cold. Morgan lay lifeless, her eyes closed, her arms limp by her sides. Her wet hair was matted against her shoulders and pale face. Blood ran in a black trail from her temple into her hairline. He knelt beside her, afraid to touch her, afraid she wouldn't open her eyes and berate him for leaving her on shore.

Afraid her skin would be cold with death. A shudder jerked him, and denial screamed through his mind. Her anger he could deal with, but never her death. Not that. Not after all they'd been through.

He cupped one side of her face in his hand, felt the cool softness of her skin. "Morgan! Wake up!"

She didn't respond.

Unable to tell if she was breathing, he placed his ear against her chest—and heard the rhythm of her heart, beating faint and slow. The fear shaking him to the core eased, but only slightly. "Find a torch. I need more light."

He heard someone take off at a run. Beyond the circle of men, he registered the sounds of pirates reaching shore and being taken prisoner. He should help, but he couldn't—not now.

"Morgan." He lightly slapped her cheek. "Answer me."

Her head lolled to the side.

"Damn it, Morgan." He lifted her by the shoulders and cradled her body against his. Torches were found and lit. "I'm giving you an order. Open your eyes!"

Her brows pinched with a frown.

"That's it. Wake up." He ran his hand over her face,

brushing back hair and sand. Ripping the hem of her shirt, he wiped blood from her cheek and jaw, and revealed an inch-long cut above her temple. The skin had begun to purple and bruise. He kissed her brow. "Talk to me, Morgan. For God's sake, say something."

"Stop giving me orders." She turned her face into his chest. "You're hurting my head."

Daniel closed his eyes and held her to him. Never in his life had he been as frightened as when he'd seen her on the *Pursuit*. Yet somehow she'd survived. The relief draining through him now ran deep, overwhelming him with its strength.

When had she come to mean so much to him? How had a woman who equally annoyed and amazed him burrowed into his heart without his realizing it? It didn't matter, he thought. He had her in his arms now, and he'd be damned if he would let her go.

"She's gonna be all right then, Capt'n?" Roscoe asked as he pushed through the crowd and knelt beside him.

"Aye, I think so."

"Oh, she's alive." Thomas heaved an annoyed sigh. "Too bad."

Daniel shot a warning glare at Thomas. He'd had enough of his partner's derision. If he'd ever doubted Morgan's innocence before, he didn't now. Not after what he'd discovered in Halo's possession.

"Look what we got 'ere, Capt'n. None other than Halo Jones." The sailor released a heckling laugh as two of his companions hauled the bound pirate forward. "There's more of 'em pirates that jumped ship. We're pickin' 'em off the beach as easy as cherries off a tree."

Blond strings of hair hung in Halo's face. His wool coat and breeches pooled water at his booted feet. Fury darkened his jaw and hardened his eyes, but otherwise he seemed unharmed.

"Excellent," Thomas said, pointing to a crewman.

"Return to the camp and bring some rope. Make sure it's strong. Now that we have both Morgan and Halo, I say we have a double hanging."

"Then you better get a rope for yourself, Thomas," Halo said in a voice chilled with warning.

"Shut up!" Thomas struck out, landing a solid blow to Halo's jaw, forcing him to his knees.

"Enough," Daniel ordered. "There won't be any hangings. We're taking Halo and his men to London."

"What about her?" Thomas demanded, pointing to Morgan, who was struggling to sit up on her own. "Are you going to release her, or keep her? If you want a whore, I know plenty who have far more to offer."

"Morgan is none of your concern," Daniel said in a voice that shook with warning. He rose, coming eye to eye with the partner he realized he never really knew.

"She was with Halo. You saw her on the *Pursuit*—which was my ship as much as yours, by the way," Thomas argued. "I say I have plenty of reason to be concerned about your *interest* in her. It's clear to me now. They planned this together."

"Did they?" Daniel asked. "Morgan knew I'd capture her? She knew I'd meet you in a damaged ship and that I'd insist on finding Halo? Yes, I can see how she planned this entire thing. She's quite cunning." He crossed to Halo and took the gold pocket watch from his vest pocket.

He opened the case and read the engraved words out loud. " 'To Captain William Egham, the finest friend and captain I've known. Forever in your debt. Daniel Tremayne. 3 September, 1757.' "

He snapped the lid closed and clenched the watch in his fist. "How did you come by this, Halo?"

"It's obvious," Thomas interrupted, his body trembling with anger. "After Morgan killed Egham, she gave the watch to Halo. Perhaps as a gift for her lover."

"Daniel, I didn't . . ." Morgan interjected. With Roscoe's help, she struggled to stand.

Daniel raised a hand to stop her from interfering. "Did she give this to you, Halo?"

The pirate grinned, and his eyes hardened to coppery spears. "Well, now, I might be willing to tell you how that came to be in my possession—if you're open to a little negotiation."

"You're going to London, regardless of what you tell me."

"Aye, that I don't doubt." Halo narrowed his gaze on Thomas, promising retribution. "But there are any number of ways to die. I'd like to choose my end."

Daniel nodded in agreement. "Explain the watch."

Halo's jaw hardened into a dangerous line. "It was too nice a piece to pass up, seeing how your captain didn't need it any longer."

A tremor erupted in Daniel's soul. He hissed out a breath, fighting the overwhelming need to take his revenge for Egham's death here and now. "You killed Captain Egham?"

"Egham learned about my . . . association . . . with Thomas."

"Shut up!" Thomas pulled his cutlass free and lurched forward, steel flashing in the torchlight. Daniel caught his arm, twisting it, wrenching the sword free. He shoved Thomas back.

"He's lying," Thomas yelled, turning in a frantic circle, searching the sailors' closed faces. "Don't listen to him. He's a pirate, a murderer."

Daniel stuck the steel tip in the sand. "Go on, Halo."

"Thomas, here"—a leering smile twitched the corner of Halo's mouth—"offered Egham part of the gold as hush money, but he refused. What were we to do?" Halo shrugged with indifference. "The man had to die."

"And the rest of the crew you killed had to die, too?"

"Wherever did you find such a sorry, loyal bunch?" Halo muttered.

Daniel's vision blurred; his heart slammed against his chest at a frantic pace. He clenched and unclenched his fingers around the watch, wanting to deny everything Halo said. But he couldn't. It made too much sense.

"What did you do with the cargo?" Daniel asked.

Halo chuckled. "Thomas and I split it, of course."

A red haze bled over Daniel's mind. His own partner had betrayed him, murdered their friend and the crew. He'd blamed Morgan for their deaths, labeling her as a murderess, dooming her to an execution of the worst kind.

Rage shook through Daniel, tempting him like a slithering asp to end Halo's miserable life. No one would blame him. He wrapped his free hand around the hilt of Morgan's knife, tucked in a sheath at his waist, felt the gems mold against his palm. The weight would balance perfectly between his fingers, making the final act so easy. He released the knife and took a step back, forcing a breath through his teeth. He couldn't do it, not without making him as low and filthy as the two men before him.

He nodded to Roscoe. "Take them and the others you've captured to the *Devil's Luck* and lock them below."

"You can't do this!" Thomas pulled and kicked, fighting the men dragging him toward the skiff tied to the pier. "You can't believe him. He's a cutthroat. A pirate. Damn you, Daniel! Listen to me."

Something hard and unforgiving settled over Daniel. He turned away, unable to bear the sight of his partner any longer. His gaze collided with Morgan's. Her clear eyes were wide, solemn, sympathetic. When they should have been condemning.

He'd ripped her life apart. Because of him, she'd always be a hunted woman. And nothing he did from this moment on would change that.

* * *

Night lifted from the beach in gradual layers. The quiet blacks that cloaked every corner gave way to a swirl of gray blues, shades of lavender and pink. Birds rose from their nests, soaring over sand and rock, circling to inspect the dying remains of a once fine ship.

Morgan sat near the shore, watching the lap of water reach for her boots. She was reluctant to leave. The pirates' women and children were already safely on board the *Devil's Luck*. She didn't know what would happen to them, but anything had to be better than their squalid island life. She told herself she wanted the pirates chained below before she boarded. But wanting to avoid Halo and Thomas wasn't what really kept her on land. During Halo's confession and the hours since, she'd watched Daniel withdraw like a storm pulling inward instead of bursting out, holding on to its rage instead of unleashing it. She understood the hurt he must be feeling; she felt it for him. Everything he'd believed in—his partner's trustworthiness, his reasons for hunting her down—had been a lie.

How did a man as virtuous and noble as Daniel Tremayne accept that someone he'd valued and trusted had used him?

She pushed herself to her feet and paused, swaying as her head spun. She closed her eyes and waited for the dizziness to pass. The bleeding had stopped long ago, leaving behind a steady throb that was more annoying than painful. Feeling steadier, she walked into the cove, clothes and all, until she was waist deep. Inhaling a deep breath, she sank into the water, hearing Daniel shout her name as her head went under.

Cool, liquid fingers washed over her, carrying sand away from her face, the crevices of her clothes, cleaning blood from her matted hair.

Two hands gripped her under her arms and hauled her up.

"What do you think you're doing?" Daniel demanded.

Gasping with surprise, she pushed dripping strands of hair out of her face—and saw fear darkening his tired eyes. "I was rinsing off."

"You . . . damn it, Morgan. You should have warned me. Seeing you disappear beneath the surface . . ." He swiped a hand through his hair in frustration.

She couldn't help but smile at his disgruntled tone. "Did you think I'd planned to make my escape by swimming away?"

An amused glimmer flashed in his blue eyes, but quickly faded. "I wouldn't put it past you." He put an arm around her waist, drawing her into the crook of his body. "Let's go. We're the last to leave."

She let him lead her out of the water, but stopped him once on shore. "Daniel, about Thomas—"

A muscle leapt in his jaw. "I don't wish to speak about him."

"I understand. He hurt you. I'm sorry for that."

"You're . . ." He closed his eyes and bent his head. "You have nothing to be sorry for, Morgan. It's I who needs to apologize. If not for his lies, I never would have come after you, kidnapped you from your home . . ."

His voice trailed off, but when he looked up, she knew what he had left unsaid. He wouldn't have been determined to see her punished for a murder she'd had no part of.

She cupped his cheek in her hand. "You did what you thought was right, just as I've done these four years past."

His hand closed over hers. "You should hate me for what I've done, not make excuses for me."

Hate him? She could no more hate him than she could stop breathing. Yet she couldn't tell him that; now wasn't the time. She curled her fingers around his neck and urged him to her. His eyes focused on hers, darkening with instant need. Their lips touched, pulled away, touched again. Soft, unsure. His breath washed her face, warm and moist, as he whispered her name. He gathered her fully in his arms, holding her with a care that made her tremble.

Earlier, while hiding on the beach, she'd realized she loved him. The truth had filled her with apprehension and fear. Wasted emotions—she understood that now. Their time together might be short, but it was real and powerful, creating memories she would keep her entire life. Yes, she loved him, with her life and breath, with all her heart.

Daniel deepened the kiss, took it over, molding their mouths into one. His hands moved over her back, her waist, her buttocks, lifting her against his hardening ridge. His moan fed hers. He stirred desire to life inside her, embers that rose in a luscious heat throughout her limbs. Liquid smoke rushed through her veins. She breathed in his scent on the cool morning breeze.

His hand came around her side, cupped her breast without warning. She gasped in surprise; her body tightened. Curling her hands in his hair, she closed her eyes and focused on his fingers kneading her full mound, his thumb flicking the pearled nipple again and again. Her breath shivered from her lungs.

"Daniel . . ." She couldn't say more. He had to understand how much she wanted him.

He reached beneath her loose shirt. His hand closed over her bare flesh. She tensed, her head dropping back. Lightning struck from his fingers, sizzling where he touched. Skin against skin, his heat bled into hers. The sensations were too much, too bold and overwhelming, yet she wanted more. Had to have more.

"Morgan," he said, his voice tight with strain. "I want you. God, how much I want you." He kissed a path down her neck to her breast. His mouth was hot through her shirt, warming her skin, laving the nipple until the tip pebbled beneath his touch. Lightly he bit her with his teeth. Morgan shuddered, felt her knees tremble, threaten to collapse.

She reached for his shirt, wanting it gone. Urging him upright, Daniel stiffened as he looked over her head.

"Capt'n!"

She heard the faint shout. *No, no, not now.* She pressed her forehead against Daniel's chest. Frustrated tears filled her eyes. Would she never feel all of him? Touch him, know him?

"Capt'n, we're ready tae set sail," Tobitt called from twenty feet away.

"Very well." Daniel ran his hand over her wet hair, then kissed it. "First *your* men won't leave us be, now it's mine." He tilted her chin so she had to look at him. "Are you all right?"

When she nodded that she was, he took her hand and led her to the pier, where they boarded the skiff and rowed to the *Devil's Luck.* Morgan scaled the rope ladder, feeling Daniel's presence behind her. Once she gained the deck, she froze and stared speechless. She heard Daniel climb aboard and pause.

"What's this?" he asked.

The entire crew of seventy men crowded the deck, each one lifting a cup in a silent toast. A crewman, Willie, stepped up and shoved a goblet of wine into each of their hands.

"We want tae thank ye, Morgan," Tobitt said from his position in front of the group. "For helping us capture Halo Jones and seeing our crewmates' deaths avenged."

A sailor beside him nudged him in the ribs. Tobitt cleared his throat and added, "And for not scorching the flesh off our bones when we tried to hang you."

A shouted cheer roared past the tip of the masts. Morgan smiled, taken aback, unsure of what to say. Tears tingled the backs of her eyes. If she didn't escape to a private room now, the entire crew would see the fearless Morgan the Scylla dissolve into tears.

Laughter broke out among the sailors as toasts were made to her health and long life. Tobitt spread his large hands out to his sides. "Tell us how we can repay ye."

"A hot bath would be a wonderful start."

"A bath it is, then." Tobitt turned and started issuing orders. Men scurried, arguing over who would cart the buckets to her cabin.

She blinked back the need to cry, pressing the glass of wine to her chest. She had to get below. The tears were welling, threatening to roll down her hot cheeks. She didn't want anyone to see her like this. Daniel must have sensed her wavering emotions, because he placed a hand at her waist and urged her toward the hatchway on their left, leading to the stern of the ship where Halo Jones's cabin would be.

At the end of the companionway, he opened the door and allowed her to enter the chamber first. Barely into the room, she came to an abrupt stop. A startled, choking sound erupted from her throat.

Daniel muttered an oath behind her.

Heavy brocade fabric in vivid purple draped the walls, partially concealing bookshelves and a length of paned windows. Silver candelabras were fastened to each end of a massive oak table. The candles were an elaborate, if not outrageously dangerous, method of lighting for a ship, Morgan thought. Her wet boots sank into the Turkish rug that ran from one length of the room to the other. Gold plates and cups were haphazardly stacked on a shelf above a trunk that contained heaven knew what. But the most impressive piece that drew her eye—actually there were two things—was the heavy four-poster bed, draped with netting, the mattress piled high with satin coverlets and down pillows.

The second item, one she'd never seen before but thought she could grow to love, was a tiled bathtub trimmed in gold, large enough to hold every inch of her body with room to spare. The marvel was tucked at the rear of the cabin beneath the bank of windows. She crossed the room, setting her wine aside, and reverently ran her fingers over the smooth surface. Whoever was lucky enough to enjoy such a luxury would be able to soak at their leisure with only a view of the horizon to intrude. Or perhaps a bath at sunset would be best, she mused. Or beneath a blanket of stars.

She shook her head, wondering at her whimsical thoughts. She turned, not surprised to find Daniel watching her, his emotions as volatile as a restless sea. She shifted, unsure of what to do. "Halo's taste in decor leaves something to be desired."

"I'll have whatever you don't like removed."

She nodded and glanced down at the tub. "Except this. I do believe I could become attached to something as fine as a private bath."

His eyes darkened, the pinpoints swirling with need, with lust, with emotions she could only guess at. She ought to kiss him, she thought. She stepped forward, but he straightened, his shoulders going rigid with sudden tension. There was an internal battle going on inside him. She saw it in his eyes, his iron jaw and clenched fists. But why? What had caused the sudden change?

He'd kissed her with care and tenderness only a short time ago. Why didn't he take her in his arms again? They had so little time before he released her at some distant port—a thought she didn't want to dwell on.

Why had he changed? What was happening?

Daniel broke the awkward moment by reaching for the knife sheathed at his waist. Holding it by the steel-honed tip, he held the hilt out to her. The *Sea Queen* blade.

Hesitantly, she reached out and gripped the handle,

almost sighing as her fingers wrapped around cool metal. The gemstones nestled against her palm like a familiar friend. She looked at him inquisitively.

"It's yours. I thought you'd want it back."

"To sever loose ends when I leave?" He tensed still further. She wished the words back. Obviously, he didn't want to think about the new path her life would take a few days hence any more than she did. Because he didn't want to let her go, or because releasing her went against his duty? She wished she knew the answer.

The clearing of a throat brought their attention to a line of men waiting in the hall with buckets of steaming water. Daniel moved aside as pail after pail of precious water was poured into the expansive tub. She could already imagine the warmth sinking into her skin, easing her muscles, soothing her overtired mind. It was an indulgence she truly meant to savor.

She turned to thank Daniel, but he was already gone.

Chapter 16

"Hands to the braces!" Tobitt called to the crewmen midship.

"Ready about," Daniel ordered. The helmsman spun the wheel to the left. Wind whipped over the stern, snapping the sails taut. The *Devil's Luck* groaned as she picked up speed and sliced through foaming swells.

"With the wind at our back, we'll reach England in four days' time, Capt'n." Tobitt rubbed his hand over his leathery jaw, his big body shifting in tune with the ship. His brow furrowed as he studied the crewmen working below. "Unless ye're plannin' on makin' a stop somewhere first."

Daniel followed his first officer's gaze. The pressure that had clasped hold of his chest when he'd left Morgan to her bath tightened like an unmerciful fist, squeezing for all it was worth. Morgan had emerged from below, and was smiling as the rough, sea-toughened men gathered around her. Her hair glimmered down her back, a drape of wet mink in the afternoon sun. God save him, the woman was beautiful. But not even the tanned, healthy glow of her skin could disguise the ugly bruise above her temple, a reminder that she wasn't as invincible as she liked to pretend.

She should be resting, he thought. She'd come closer to death than he cared to remember. The sailors parted, allowing him to fully see her and the gown she wore. Every nerve along his spine twisted into a row of knots. Was she out of her mind, dressing in a whirl of fabric that seemed fashioned from clouds and air? The white gown pearled against her skin, the scooped neckline revealing far more of her breasts than he cared for anyone besides himself to see. Full sleeves draped her arms. The material flowed down her body, clinging to her narrow waist, molding to her long legs. With every sway of the ship and gust of breeze, the gown moved like a whispered caress.

"She's going to cause a bloody riot," Daniel said between his teeth. "Where did she find such a dress?" He started down the stairs leading to midship, but halted when she broke away from his men and came toward him.

"This is a pirate ship, Capt'n," Tobitt said with wonder. "Ye wouldn't believe the things we've found hidden in the hold so far."

She paused on the lower deck, looking up at him, giving him a clear view of her slender neck, the slope of her breasts, and a décolletage that could make a man blind with need. Her smile faltered. "Daniel—"

"Go below, Morgan," he ordered more brusquely than he'd intended. But, Sweet Jesus, he'd just come to terms with her dressing in tight breeches like a man. Seeing her covered with a slip of nothing was more than he could bear.

She straightened and took a step back, her eyes going wide and dark with hurt. "Am I to be locked away as a prisoner then?"

Daniel bit back a curse and descended the stairs. Reaching her, he placed a hand at her back, urging her toward the hatchway. She refused to budge.

"Am I your prisoner?"

"Of course not."

"Then why—"

"Where did you get this gown?" he asked, clasping his hands behind his back. He'd made a second mistake by touching her. His first had been to kiss her on the island. He couldn't give in to his need for her, not until he had his emotions under control. Which seemed impossible. His fingers had felt her firm skin through the gossamer fabric, confirming what the play of the wind had already made clear. She wore nothing beneath.

"It was in a trunk in Halo's cabin." She gripped a handful of cloth and lifted the too-long skirt off the deck, revealing her bare feet. "It was the only thing I dared wear in public."

If this was the most respectable garment she could find, he knew he wouldn't survive seeing her in whatever she'd rejected. He cleared his throat in order to soften his tone. "Perhaps we can find you something else to wear."

She stared at him a moment, her eyes rife with questions. "Daniel, we need to talk."

"Later." Aye, they needed to talk, but she would ask questions he didn't want to answer—like where did he plan to release her?

She nodded, her chin jutting with pride. Her shoulders squared in a way he'd come to admire as she turned to make her way back to the captain's cabin. Daniel held his ground when every part of him wanted to follow her. He needed more time to find the words that would undoubtedly shatter what remained of her world.

He didn't plan to stop before reaching England. Because Thomas had been right. He couldn't let her go.

Morgan had used hundreds of outrageous tricks during her life as a pirate, she admitted as she navigated the companionway, a task made difficult since her arms were full of supplies, but this trick was the most scandalous of them all. For the last hour, she'd put a few of the crewmen to work in secret. They hadn't balked when she'd made her wishes known, but had grinned like conspiring thieves.

Something was troubling Daniel, and he refused to discuss it with her. She refused to be put off any longer. And she knew just how to break through the sullen barrier he'd erected between them.

Reaching her cabin, she kicked the door closed behind her and unloaded her arms of the smoked beef, pitcher of wine, and bowls of figs and nuts she'd pilfered from the kitchen. She arranged them on the table so they'd look somewhat appealing. She wished the cook had prepared a hot meal, but he'd only growled as he showed her the food stores he had to work with.

She'd speak to Tobitt about setting out lines for fish on the morrow. They didn't need to live on . . . She stopped herself. This wasn't her ship, and she wasn't going to remain on board for long. They were sailing for England, but first they had to stop somewhere along the way. But where? That was but one of the things she had to discuss with Daniel. At Le Havre in France? she wondered. She'd heard of a village south of there, Bayeux, that might resemble her home. She closed her eyes and tightened her hand around the pitcher's brass neck.

It didn't really matter what village she ended up in. She'd never see her family again. Or Daniel. Wherever she went, she'd be alone, for as long as she lived. She pressed her other hand to her shaking stomach.

Drawing a deep breath, she pushed the distressing thoughts aside. She had two, maybe three days left; she intended to make the most of them.

Hearing a knock at the door, she sighed and whispered a prayer of thanks for the interruption. "Come in."

The door creaked, and Roscoe poked his graying head inside. "We're all ready, Morgan. Capt'n's still on deck."

"Excellent. Bring them in."

Shouldering the oak panel open, he carted in two buckets brimming with near-boiling water. A half-dozen men followed, each taking turns emptying their pails into the tub. As the men filed out, Roscoe lingered to say, "If ye be need'n' anything else, ye just let me know."

"Thank you, Roscoe."

On his way out, he added, chuckling, "It's too bad ye don't have the *Sea Queen* no more. A few of us just might 'ave joined up with ye."

Smiling, she closed the door, then crossed the room to pull the drapes aside, fully revealing the sun's final descent. Fiery amber merged with blue. The colors rolled together, creating shadows that chased each other across the expanse of rippling water. She lit tapers in the candelabras, praying that the seas, which had settled considerably, would remain calm.

As she surveyed the room, her stomach tingled with nerves. She didn't want to consider the food, the tempting bathwater and seductive lighting as a trick, but that was what they were. A trick of the most desperate kind. She blew out a breath. "All right, Daniel Tremayne. Let's see if you can escape this."

Daniel spotted her the instant she came on deck. The skin at the back of his neck had prickled, alerting him that she was near. She walked through the graying dusk, bypassing crewmen without a glance, and headed up the stairs to the forecastle deck and to his side. She stopped so close her breasts were in danger of brushing his chest. His skin tightened in anticipation.

She tilted her head back, meeting his gaze with seductive resolve. A new and startling combination, and one almost impossible to resist. She needed to be kissed, he thought; wanted to be kissed. Her gaze flickered to his mouth, where it lingered before making a slow trail back up to his eyes. She swayed toward him, an alluring pull that had nothing to do with the roll of the ship.

"I need to talk to you," she said in a smoky whisper.

His blood heated at just the sound of her voice. He should kiss her now, he thought, before she learned he wasn't going to release her. Once she knew the truth, she'd never look at him this way again. But he couldn't take her to his bed, love her the way every muscle and sinew in his body demanded, knowing he was deceiving her. They'd been through enough deception and trickery already. He would tell her of his plans for her in due time, but he wasn't ready yet.

"I'm busy, Morgan. It will have to wait until later."

She considered him a moment, then glanced down the length of the ship. "You can't put me off forever."

"I don't have time now." He didn't want to snap at her, but, God save him, he had only so much self-restraint.

Her brows narrowed with a cunning look. "Make time for me now, Daniel, or I'll change my gown." In a tone that sounded suspiciously like a purr, she added, "I'm sure your crew would love to see what else Halo kept in his cabin."

A jealous haze spiked through his veins. "Feminine wiles? I thought that form of trickery would be beneath you."

She shrugged, and for an instant he thought guilt shadowed her face.

But she was right; he couldn't avoid or postpone the truth forever. She deserved to know his change in plans, however much she would hate to hear it. The sooner she knew of his decision, the more time she'd have to adjust. "Very well." He held out his hand. "After you."

He followed her to her cabin wondering if, after they'd

had their "talk," she would throw him out or allow him
to stay and share the cabin with her during their first night
back out to sea. If by some miracle she did allow him to
stay, he damn well wouldn't be sleeping on the window
seat.

Ducking through the portal, he came to a complete and
numbing stop. She continued inside. At the table, she
turned to him, allowing candlelight to flow over her hair
and down her body, illuminating her as if she were a vision
and not a woman made of flesh and blood.

"I see I spoke too soon," he managed to say. "You're
quite apt at using feminine wiles."

She glanced behind her at the laden table. When she
faced him, her cheeks were flushed and her lashes were
lowered. "You have to eat. And you smell of sweat and
smoke. I thought you'd like to bathe."

Heat and blood pulsed through his groin. Need tightened into a coiled rope in his gut. He forced himself to
draw a breath. Did she know what she was doing? Where
this would lead?

"Morgan—" he began.

She shook her head, stopping him. She crossed the
narrow space and proceeded to unfasten the empty leather
sheath at his waist. "First a bath and food; then we'll talk."

As she untucked his shirt from his pants and lifted it
over his head, his vision narrowed on the woman before
him. Diamond-clear eyes sparkled in a face molded by
strength and wisdom. Her hair could make a man weep
for the chance to touch it. A musky, sun-filled scent that
was hers alone surrounded her.

She was unlike any woman who'd passed through his
life. She lacked social graces and milk white skin. She could
wield a sword or blow up a ship or trick a man into falling
in love.

God help him, he had to find a way to save her—save

them both—because he couldn't release her any more than he could live without her.

Morgan reached over the tub and opened the panel of windows, allowing the music of the sea inside. But her ears were focused on the sounds behind her—Daniel removing his boots, letting them drop with a thump to the floor; the rustle of his pants as he stripped those off next. Her plan had been to help him with his clothes, but once she'd had his shirt off, her modesty and trembling nerves had overruled. Mumbling an excuse about the wine, she'd left him to his own devices.

She wanted to turn around, see him the way she'd only imagined. But she didn't dare for fear of touching him. She'd told him a bath and food first; then they'd talk. Considering the way her breath tingled through her lungs and her hands flexed with the need to feel his skin, she thought perhaps the talking should wait. *Indefinitely.*

She heard splashing as he stepped into the tub. Still facing the sea, she closed her eyes the same instant he sighed. He must be fully settled, she thought, submerged in the water and safely out of sight.

"I'll have that wine now," he said, his voice soft; she couldn't read his mood.

She poured a goblet of red wine and turned to hand it to him. He was reclined in the steaming water, his eyelids half lowered, his gaze lazily focused on her. A breeze swept in, attempting to cool her overly warm skin. She shook her head, trying to clear her mind, but it didn't work.

Handing him the goblet, she moved to a chair between the bed and table, allowing a view of his upper body and nothing more. But that was enough to make heat swirl like invisible smoke beneath her skin.

She'd seen men in every state of dress . . . or undress . . . while living aboard ship. She'd learned to turn a blind eye and ignore bare chests and legs, or, worse, whenever they anchored in a secluded cove and the men would bathe. She hadn't forsaken her modesty; she'd simply accepted the occasional exposed derriere as a fact of life.

But then, none of the men on her ship had looked like Daniel Tremayne.

With his jaw set in a rigid line, he lathered a cloth and began soaping his arms and chest. The only sound in the room was the hush of wind and the dripping of water. She tried desperately not to watch, but, heaven help her, in all her life and during all her travels, she'd never seen anything so erotic as Daniel relaxing in a tub, with steam curling in vaporous waves, dampening his skin, the dark tips of his hair.

She furrowed her brow. Perhaps *relax* wasn't the right word.

There wasn't anything peaceful about the way his eyes narrowed on her, their hard blue centers flashing like chips of steel. The muscles in his broad shoulders were bunched beneath tight, sun-darkened skin. Her gaze skimmed down his arms, her attention focusing on his hands—hands that had held her in both passion and fury.

His long fingers gripped the cloth, dragging it up to his chest, through swirls of crisp black hair and over mounds of muscle. She clenched her hands and drew her feet up into the chair, securing her gown around her.

"You've never attended a man with his bath, have you?" he asked in a deep, baiting tone.

"Of course," she retorted. "So many I've lost count." She looked away, wondering what had come over her. She was totally out of her element. She knew about ships and currents and reading the stars. She knew nothing about men—at least not men like Daniel.

Except that he wanted her—that she knew. She also knew he was fighting it. Why would he do so when they only had a few days to spend together? She knew she risked leaving her heart behind, undoubtedly shattered into tiny pieces. But she was willing to take that risk. All they had was now, and she wanted every second she could steal.

But what was stopping Daniel? Was he afraid he might care for her too much? Was he protecting his heart? Perhaps he'd been hurt before. She wished she knew more about his past. Or maybe he didn't care for her at all and wanted to part ways as friends. Or perhaps he was married! She almost came out of her chair. Why hadn't she considered that before?

"Do you have a wife?" she heard herself blurt.

He arched a dark brow. "No. Why do you ask?"

She shrugged to conceal her relief. "I just realized that you know everything about me, but I know almost nothing about you."

"There's not much to tell."

She scoffed so loudly Jo would have been proud of the unladylike sound. "You've *earned* a reputation far worse than mine, Daniel."

"That was war," he said, and she thought she saw regret in his eyes.

"But why take the risk? You're an earl, with wealth beyond a common man's dream. You could have lost everything."

"But I gained much more."

"Wealth, you mean." She'd almost forgotten that he was motivated like any other man.

"No. My name."

"Excuse me?"

He sighed and continued in a detached voice. "My father had a weakness for the gaming tables. That wouldn't have been so bad had he not also had a poor mind for investments. He nearly bankrupted us. By the time I'd learned how dire our situation was, my father was ill. From guilt and regret, I suspect."

Daniel stared out the window, and for a moment Morgan

didn't think he'd continue, but he finally said, "When he died, the creditors demanded payment. They encouraged me to sell my home, the belongings that had passed through five generations."

She listened, stunned. She'd assumed he'd lived a privileged life of ease, and that the war had merely presented a diversion and an opportunity to add to his wealth. Her face heated with shame. She should have known better.

"That's when I started World Quest Shipping."

"With Thomas as your partner."

He nodded. "We were more successful than I'd ever hoped. I paid my father's debts, restored my home."

"You never answered why you joined the war."

"To restore honor to my father's name," he said simply, but she knew how much it meant to him. She may not have known him long, but she knew that duty and honor were the things Daniel valued.

"What of your mother?"

"She never knew how desperate our situation was."

"How could she not?" Morgan asked.

"My father never told her, nor did I."

Morgan crossed her arms over her chest and frowned at him. "She had a right to know, Daniel. Women aren't as weak as you seem to think."

"You don't know my mother." He regarded her with something close to respect. "She isn't like you."

His words sent a tingle throughout her body. She didn't know what to say, so she folded her hands in her lap and stared at them.

She heard Daniel say something. Frowning, she looked at him. "Excuse me?"

"My back."

"Your back what?"

A grin tweaked the corner of his mouth. "I thought you've assisted with men's baths before. Dozens of them."

"I have," she lied.

"Then wash my back." He held out the dripping cloth.

She stared at his hand, the length of his arm, her gaze lifting to the challenge in his demon-blue eyes. Perhaps she'd overreacted earlier. Daniel's withdrawal might be nothing more than his preoccupation with his past, with Halo's capture. Or with his friend's betrayal.

She prayed that was the case, because she needed Daniel as she'd never needed anyone in her life. Kneeling beside the tub, she took the lathered cloth from him. He leaned forward, propping his forearms on his bent knees. She stared at the solid plane of his shoulders and back, and felt her skin tighten in response. She squeezed the cloth in her fist.

"Why couldn't you be fat and ugly?" she said, not realizing she'd spoken out loud until Daniel glanced over his shoulder at her, a devilish gleam in his eyes.

"Would it help if I blindfolded you?"

Heat flooded from her roots down to the tips of her breasts. He knew how he affected her, and was enjoying it. But did he plan to do anything about it? She slapped the washcloth against his back and scrubbed. She put her weight into it, imagining that the sculpted muscles were the hull of her ship and in desperate need of scraping. Barnacles and seaweed collected after long months at sea. No doubt Daniel had a few traits he needed scoured from his character. She heard him grunt, and continued working until her arm ached from strain and his skin glowed vivid red.

"If you're trying to skin me alive, a knife might work better."

My knife. She sat back, and returned his questioning gaze. Water dripped down her arms, soaking her thin gown, but she barely noticed. Her heart pumped hard against her ribs.

"Why did you return my knife to me?" She thought she'd known the answer. He trusted her and was setting her free. But days from now, not today. Had returning her blade been his way of saying good-bye, of severing the ties between them? Their time together didn't have to end now. Didn't he see that?

But it will end, Morgan, her mind whispered. She closed her eyes for an instant. Aye, it would end. It had to, because it couldn't be any other way. She knew he cared for her, but what more could he give to a commoner wanted for piracy? His love? His vow of marriage? A future with Daniel was impossible; she'd known that from the beginning.

"The knife is yours," he replied.

"You don't think I'll use it on you?"

"No." The certainty in the set of his mouth, the resolve in his eyes, made her throat go dry. "No."

She pressed the back of her wrist to her forehead. Sweet Mary, she didn't know what to feel or do. How he must think her insane. She'd never felt so insecure, so unsure of her future. For so long, her goal had been to save her village. That she'd done. She had only her own life to consider now, but whenever she thought about it, it seemed bleak and empty. That was why she had to have this time with Daniel. She needed more than the memories of their few kisses—she wanted to remember more, so much more.

He leaned back in the tub. The water rippled, blurring the flat of his stomach, the length of his legs, the dark shadows in between.

"What's wrong, Morgan?" He took the washcloth and reapplied the soap. "Something is distressing you."

Why have you grown so distant? she wanted to ask, but decided he had to first realize how important the next few days were to them both. "As a matter of fact, there is something I need to know." She wiped her hands on a towel. "Where do you plan to release me?"

He looked out the window. "I haven't yet decided."

"You haven't decided?" She frowned. A muscle pulsed in his jaw, a sure sign he was angry. She pushed up on her knees and shoved his shoulder to gain his attention. "We're three days out from England. I need to know."

"I'll tell you," he said between clenched teeth. "Soon."

What did he mean, soon? Her chest constricted, squeezing her heart until it beat slow and hard against her ribs. She shook her head in denial, pressed her fingers to her mouth. She didn't want to say the words pushing to the forefront of her mind, but they were there for her to see in the vivid blue of Daniel's eyes. "You aren't going to let me go."

"Morgan . . ."

She rose to her feet, stumbling back as the horror sank in. He was taking her to London; that was why he was so reluctant to talk to her. Returning her knife had been a ploy to gain her trust. And the kiss on the beach—why had he done it if he'd never intended to set her free? He'd lied . . . tricked . . . She backed to the door, turning, her eyes blurring with tears.

"Morgan, damn it!"

She heard splashing behind her, knew she had only seconds to escape. She had the door open and had reached the hall before his arm locked around her waist, lifting her off the ground and against his soaked body.

Several sailors in the companionway stopped to gawk, then chuckled as Daniel carried her kicking and fighting back inside the cabin. He slammed the door behind him.

"Put me down," she demanded.

"No."

"I can't breathe." She wedged her fingers between his arm and her stomach, but he wouldn't budge.

"Will you stop struggling and listen?"

"Why?" she asked, feeling a sob push through her chest. "So you can tell me how you'll be in the front row at my hanging? That was your promise when we first met. And you always keep your promises, don't you, Daniel?"

"Sweet bloody Jesus." He set her on her feet.

She whipped around, her arm flying. He caught her wrist inches before it connected with his face. Pinning her arm behind her back, he caught her other one and secured it, too.

"Now listen to me."

"Go to hell."

He tightened his hold, locking her chest to chest, hip to hip. He gritted his teeth and sucked in a breath. Heat flared between them. Her nipples hardened, shocking her with intense pleasure-pain. She wouldn't let her body betray her. Not now. She pulled back, but he cupped her buttocks, lifting her, pressing his solid shaft into her core. She gasped, horrified by the raw, sensuous heat spearing through her veins.

"Stop," she choked on a sob. "Don't do this to me."

"Nothing's going to stop us this time, Morgan."

She twisted against his grip, refusing to give in. "Then you'll have to rape me."

He froze, his grip easing. He cupped her head and forced her to look at him when she turned aside. "Trust me."

She started to scald him with her retort, but his mouth took hers in a startling, merciless kiss. He filled her, raking her tongue with his, taking and demanding, stopping the cries that tore up her throat.

He bent his head, pressing his lips to the curve of her neck, sending tingling waves of sensations beneath her skin. She had to fight him; God help her, she had to.

"Blast you, Morgan. I don't like what I've done—"

"Then let me go."

"I can't."

She didn't know if he meant now or three days hence, or both. But she felt the pull of regret weighting his shoulders and his words. She wouldn't care. She refused to care. He'd betrayed her.

"I've cost you everything."

"So you're going to take the last thing I have left? My life?"

He pulled back to look at her. In the flickering candle-light, his eyes were turbulent, his jaw taut. Edginess infused his shoulders. "I judged and condemned you, then hunted you down, determined to claim revenge and punish you for a crime you had no part of."

His words broke through her anger. She stilled, her chest heaving with panic and fear, so much fear that he was lying to her again.

"You believed Thomas," she said, not fully understanding how she could utter a single word that would defend Daniel's actions. "He was your friend." *And I am nothing but a pirate you used to gain a bigger prize.* She swallowed, trembling with the effort to hold back her tears.

"Aye. I believed him, even when I began to have doubts. I refused to consider that he might have betrayed me. Instead I focused on capturing you, bringing you to trial. To every sailor alive, Morgan the Scylla was a name to be feared. To me, you were a murdering thief that deserved to be hanged."

"Apparently, nothing's changed." She strained against his hold, but his arms tightened like possessive clamps around her back. His heat seeped through her wet, cling-ing gown, swimming through her limbs. Only moments before, she'd been ready to beg for him to hold her, now all she wanted was to escape.

"Everything changed the moment I saw you."

"What are you saying, Daniel?" Looking at him now, hearing his voice tremble with suppressed emotions, she realized he was heartbreakingly human. That made her want to hate him all the more. He could deceive her, use her, and yet she still loved him. She knew then that God had never created a bigger fool than her.

"I want your forgiveness."

"Forgive you?" She choked on the words. "For what?

For kidnapping me from my home? Or for breaking your promise to set me free?"

He ignored the latter part of her question, saying, "You wouldn't have been happy being married to your farmer."

"You think I'd be happier being hanged?" she demanded.

"I know you, Morgan." He released her hands to cradle her body against his. His low, possessive words pushed tears into her eyes. He'd hit too close to the truth about Peter. She wouldn't have been content being married to him. There was only one man who could possibly make her happy. And he was still determined to see his duty through to the end.

Yet Daniel couldn't know how she felt about him. How deeply she cared for him despite all her efforts not to.

"Trust me," he whispered, resting his forehead against hers.

"How can you ask that of me?" She balled her hands against his chest, but lacked the will to push him away. She wanted to believe that she could trust him, but how could she when he refused to set her free? "You're taking me to London."

"Not as my prisoner, Morgan."

She felt hope shiver through her. "You . . . you . . ."

"I'm not taking you to Marshalsea Prison."

"You aren't breaking your promise to release me?"

He shook his head, his eyes filling with tenderness. "Never to you."

She drew a steadying breath as his unexpected answer sank in. "I don't understand. If you don't intend to take me to the prison, why take me to London at all?"

"I have to deliver Halo and Thomas."

"You can do so after you've released me."

"You want to be dropped off on some shore where you'll have no one to protect you?"

"It's the way it has to be!"

"I'm not abandoning you like a worthless piece of baggage."

He was speaking nonsense. Didn't he understand that in some distant village she would be able to take care of herself, but if he took her to London, he'd be risking her life? "I can't set foot in the city, Daniel. If I do, I'll be arrested and sentenced to hang."

"I'll protect you. I swear I will."

"You can't," she cried.

He gripped her head between his hands, forcing her to meet his gaze. "You asked me to trust you. Now it's my turn."

"You ask too much."

He brushed a kiss across her lips, a teasing caress that promised more if only she would agree. "I thought I could free you, Morgan, as I promised, but I can't. I need you, in my life. Today, tomorrow. I can't let you go."

Didn't he know a life together was just as impossible as her traveling to London without being found out? But, Sweet Mary, she wanted to believe him.

"Trust me," he urged again. "I have a plan that will clear your name."

"A plan?" She clenched her fists against his bare chest as hope took hold of her heart.

"It's risky." He grazed his thumbs across her cheeks.

"Those are usually the best," she murmured as she looked into the blue of his eyes. They were intense, determined. Longing, fear and fervent desire swirled deep in their core. She made an instant decision, praying that neither of them would live to regret it. "All right, Daniel. You have my trust."

Chapter 17

Daniel briefly closed his eyes, feeling a huge weight lift from his shoulders. Receiving Morgan's trust was a gift he'd never thought he'd receive. He wouldn't take it for granted. Nor would he betray her. He'd given his vow to protect her, and he would.

She didn't know the details of his plan, though he knew that question would soon be rolling off her lips. Yet she'd put her life in his hands, trusting him to save it. He tried closing his mind to the doubts that forced their way in. Keeping her safe in London would be the riskiest task he'd ever faced. Yet she had to stand before the king, face him, ask for mercy, or forever be a criminal.

He wouldn't let her down, he vowed. Life had done that to her enough already.

"Tell me of your plan," she said, taking a step back. He pulled her closer against him, hugging her scantly clad body to his.

He drew a deep breath, aware of the breeze blowing through the window, brushing loose strands of hair about her cheeks. He felt the tension in her spine, felt his own body shift to better fit against hers. He'd been hard since the moment he'd stepped into the cabin; holding her, feeling the curves of her thighs, the flat of her stomach, the pointed tips of her breasts, only intensified the ache in his loins. But he ignored his needs. Now wasn't the time. He had to consider the best way to explain what he had in mind. She had no love for England's wealthy, believing they cared nothing for people like her. Yet those same people were the ones who could set her free.

"I have friends," he explained. "Very influential friends, who have the king's ear."

She looked at him, her gray eyes smoky with doubt. With more than a little sarcasm, she asked, "You think these friends of yours will whisper some powerful words and the king will grant me amnesty?"

"In a word, yes."

"Why would they bother?" she challenged.

"Because I'll ask them to."

"It doesn't make sense for you to align yourself with me. You should release me, Daniel. Now, before it's too late."

"Morgan—"

"No, listen. What if your friends fail?"

"They won't."

"How can you be so sure?" she asked.

The doubt he'd been fighting, along with his fear, made him pause before answering. "You'll remain on the *Devil's Luck* until everything's settled. Once I'm assured I have their support, I'll arrange for all of us to meet with the king. Until then, no one except my men will know you're here. You've won their loyalty. They won't let your whereabouts be known."

"But Thomas and Halo would."

Daniel ground his teeth. "You'll be set free long before they see sunlight again."

"Why are you being so stubborn?" She splayed her fingers across his chest as if she meant to push him away. She didn't. "I'm a danger to you. Why can't you see that?"

He ran his hands up her back, feeling the curve of her waist, the toned muscles over her ribs. "Don't you know?"

She rolled her eyes in exasperation. "Because you want to make love to me? That's fine for now, but you'll eventually grow tired of me. Then what?"

Grow tired of her? He didn't think it possible. She continually amazed him, surprised him, challenged him to question everything he *thought* he'd believed in.

"I have to consider my future," she continued. "I do have one, don't I?" A formidable look darkened her eyes. When he nodded, she added, "And I don't know that I care to be your mistress."

He didn't care for the idea, either. But what alternative was there? Marriage? Once the charges against her were cleared, could she possibly fit into his world of blue bloods? He ran his thumb across her tanned cheek, wondering what society would think of the healthy color. The work-scarred fingers and callused palms she rubbed against his skin made him achingly aware that she would stand out among a group of ladies, a vibrant wildflower lost among a crowd of greenhouse roses. She could captain a ship, outmaneuver the Royal Navy, but could she run his household staff, plan a ball, entertain his select group of friends?

Did he care?

"Morgan," he said, hardly knowing how to continue. "When I came to Dunmore I wanted—"

"You wanted to fulfill your need for revenge," she said, but without any strength behind the words.

He shook his head, admitting what he'd known all along but had refused to accept. "I wanted you."

She sucked in a tiny breath, her silver eyes searching his. "For how long, Daniel? A day, a week, a year? I know it can't be forever."

He wanted to deny her claim. He wanted forever with

her. But a woman like Morgan went against his duty to his country, his family. He had to marry within his class to preserve his heritage; it was a fact that had been drilled into him from the time he could walk. For all of his adult life, he'd put his personal needs aside to protect the home and values he believed in. Correct the mistakes his own father had made. Yet, he wanted Morgan, whose social status and notorious past went against the very values he'd vowed to protect!

He'd devised a plan to keep her with him, but he'd never answered his own question: keep her as what? Wife or mistress? It was one or the other. He had to make a choice.

Promise her forever, a voice urged from the back of his mind. He wanted to; God help him, he did. But the words wouldn't come.

As if she sensed the battle he fought, she cupped his face with both hands. "If you do the impossible and win my freedom, you will have given me more than I could have hoped for."

"Morgan . . ." he whispered, pressing his lips to her hair. Regret unlike anything he'd ever known squeezed his chest. *Give her forever!*

"We don't know what will happen, Daniel. All we have is now. I want *now,*" she said. "When we were on the *Pursuit,* you made a promise to finish our kiss. I believe it's time you kept it."

A hesitant smile pulled the corner of his mouth. He ran his hand down her face, almost afraid to touch her, feeling as if his heart were being ripped from his chest. "I kissed you before we left Halo's island."

"That doesn't count. We were interrupted again. Remember?"

Remember? He hadn't been able to forget. He bent his head and kissed her, shuddering when she leaned into him, opening her mouth to accept the deep thrust of his tongue. She was moist and hot, her sweet taste filling his senses. He slanted his head, deepening the kiss, absorbing the moan that rose from the back of her throat. She burrowed her hands in his hair, holding him tight as if she were afraid he'd let her go. He swore that would never happen, nor would they be interrupted.

Nothing, and no one, would stop them from making love this time. From the instant they'd met on the deck of her ship, fate had been leading them to this moment. The rush of desire, the instinctual need to become a part of her couldn't be ignored or held at bay. He'd fought his feelings for her for too long. He didn't intend to repeat that mistake again. She belonged with him.

Her hands shook as she ran them down his neck, across his shoulders. "I've wanted to touch you since the day we first met."

She skimmed kisses over the column of his throat to his chest, stopping here and there to taste his skin. Her warm breath fanned out, lighting sensual fires in his blood. He watched her brush her lips across him, testing, teasing, searing the sensitive surface with her touch.

He drew in a breath, expanding his lungs, dropping his head back as her fingers dusted his upper body, stroking, kneading, trembling in a desperate search. His hands tightened involuntarily around her waist. Heat tumbled through his body, winding down to his core. He wanted to hold still, relish in the feel of her hands, but, God help him, he wanted more. He had to fill his arms with her, mold the length of her body against his, release the desire that brewed like a tempest beneath his skin.

For too long, he'd imagined lying above her, breathing in their mingled scents as he pushed through her core, sank into her heat. He knew she'd be tight and velvety. With her, he'd find a pleasure so intense it would border on sin.

Her hands skimmed down, over his buttocks and around

to the front of his thighs, close; she was so close to touching him.

Daniel's control snapped. A growl rumbled from his chest, bringing Morgan's startled gaze up to his. "I'm going to make love to you."

Her eyes glazed with need, her cheeks flushed. A soundless "Yes" escaped her pink lips.

"I'm not going to stop."

She answered by raking her nails up his sides. Sparks spiraled through his chest to his belly, igniting flames in his groin. Without clothes to hinder him, his erection burrowed into the warm, damp satin of her gown. Lush and seductive, his eyes closed as he savored the feel of her silken grip.

But more . . . he wanted more. He wanted all of her.

Morgan shook with a need that was edged with fear. This was all so new, so overwhelming. She felt exposed, raw, her nerves so tightly wound she could scarcely breathe. The tremors had started near her heart when Daniel had said he'd wanted her. *He wanted her.* For now that would be enough. It had to be. She could still hear his voice, gentle, yearning, filling with pain he hadn't bothered to hide. His words opened a door to her soul, revealing an emptiness that had been there all along. It expanded, growing wider, deeper, a mysterious, aching void that only he could fill.

Daniel kissed her, his mouth hard and demanding, forcing her to leave her thoughts behind. She let herself go, content to drown in the circle of his arms, spin with the reality that this wasn't a dream. He was here, alive and whole, and he wanted her with a sureness that matched her own.

She breathed in his scent of soap and lust. He tasted of honey left in the sun, warm and rich, melting across her tongue. Sensations blazed through her veins like a trail of falling stars. Heat burned in their wake, singeing her gown, her blood, the center of her being. This couldn't continue, she thought. She'd never survive. He was too much, too overwhelming. There would be nothing left of her but smoke and ash.

But if she were to die now, she wouldn't care. If tomorrow never came, it wouldn't matter. She was in Daniel's arms—a place she never thought she'd be.

He tore his mouth from hers. His chest heaved as he said, "One of us is overdressed."

Without a qualm, knowing that shyness had no place between them, Morgan started to lift her gown. He stopped her, laying both of his hands above her bodice. Pushing her straps down her shoulders, he flattened his palms against the swells of her breasts. Her skin rippled, drawing tight and full. Her nipples pebbled to aching peaks. Her eyes slipped shut as her lips parted on a breath.

Seconds ticked by as she waited for him to move. She listened to the strained sounds of their breathing, the hush of the sea. *Please* . . . she wanted to beg, but her throat was too tight for words. Frustration swirled like a whirlpool through her mind, tunneling down to her stomach and lower, where the heat and flames had gathered, burning her from the inside out. She couldn't take much more. Yet she didn't know what to do. She needed . . . she needed . . . Daniel. He'd know how to turn her impatience into ultimate pleasure. So why did he wait?

Slowly, reverently, he drew his hands down, pulling the fabric lower, exposing more of her breasts to his touch. She sucked air into her lungs and held it. Her head fell back. She released her breath in a sigh that became his name. She swayed, but miraculously didn't fall.

Her gown slipped to her waist, over her hips, pooling at her feet. Warm air swept in from the window, whispered around her legs and up in between, tingling like an erotic touch. Her hair draped her back, the cool tendrils grazing her skin, tickling, heightening her already sensitized nerves.

"My God, you're beautiful."

Hearing the reverence in his voice, she opened her eyes. Daniel released her and stepped back. With his face taut, and beautiful with need, he gazed at her breasts, his eyes narrowing with a hunger she'd never before seen. This wasn't the look of a man who wanted to satisfy his need. She saw adoration and respect. She closed her eyes. *Don't see more than is there.* They had this moment, she reminded herself. Nothing more. She couldn't let herself believe they had anything more.

"Daniel . . ."

As if knowing her thoughts, he gripped her neck and brought her to him, kissing her hard and fast. He broke away, trailing his lips down her chest, loving the slope of her breast, finding his way to her nipple. He took her into his mouth. Morgan gasped, and gripped his shoulders. Lightning ripped through her. She couldn't breathe.

He sucked hard, rolling the knotted peak with his tongue, sending stabs of pleasure down her middle, adding to the inferno ready to explode.

"Daniel, please . . ."

As if deaf to her plea, he switched to her other breast and laved the dark circle with his tongue. His large, rough hands skimmed over her flesh, down her thighs, then up and over her bottom, building the urgency that burned in her veins. Her legs trembled, giving way. Daniel caught her up in his arms. She clung to him, grateful that he was taking her to bed. Finally she'd know the weight of his body, the feel of his legs against hers. At her leisure she could explore and taste and feel. Those were things she longed for, things that would make her complete.

He laid her down. Instead of a soft mattress and satin covers, hard wood pressed into her back. The table was cool, firm and unyielding. Twin candelabras spilt light over

Daniel's dark waves, now loose and wild about his face. Beads of sweat beaded his brow. Strain etched lines into the corners of his eyes, around the harsh set of his mouth. A mouth she wanted to enjoy again and again. She licked her bruised and swollen lips, and tasted the desire he'd left behind.

Standing above her, he moved between her thighs, a brazen position that shocked her. She felt opened, exposed, throbbing with a need she couldn't foresee how he would fulfill. Yet somehow, it felt that this was where he belonged. She hooked her legs on his hips and wrapped her calves behind him, nudging him closer, bringing the solid length of his erection into view. She wanted to touch him, learn his shape and texture. Daniel distracted her by trailing his fingers over her body, from her collarbone to her breasts, where he made lazy, agonizing circles, then lower, over her ribcage and stomach, to the dark curl of hair where their bodies almost met.

She couldn't see what he was doing. But she felt the instant his fingertips grazed her feminine place. She arched her back and gasped in surprise. Light splintered behind her closed lids.

"Do you like that?" he asked, his voice husky with passion.

She gripped the edge of the table near her head. He continued his play over her flesh, burrowing deep, then lifting away to trail an invisible path, shocking her with sensation after sensation.

She opened her mouth to answer, she worked her jaw, but no sound would emerge. It didn't matter. She didn't know if she liked what he was doing to her or not. The feelings were too intense, maddening. Her hips moved of their own accord, pushing, straining against the pressure of his hand. The new, agonizing need twisted and tightened, stealing her breath. God help her, what was he doing to her?

He was leading her toward something, taking her close, but not close enough. Something was missing. She felt it in every drop of blood that pulsed in a hot, urgent stream through her veins. He continued touching her body, sending her through fire and ice, hot and cold, hard and soft. Pleasure and pain. They had to merge, become one.

A sob burned her throat. "Daniel, now . . ."

With his hand still nestled at her core, he leaned over her, kissed her lips in the same teasing manner. "Do you know what's about to happen, Morgan?"

"Yes." She nodded, unable to say more.

"Tell me," he insisted with a sensual lure that was too calm, too controlled when she was unraveling like broken thread.

"I'm going to murder you if you don't make love to me. That's what's going to happen."

He chuckled, his breath warm and welcome against her neck. "I am making love to you."

She shook her head and started to object. Daniel's thumb skimmed over her center, circled, then came back, finding the nub that held every nerve, every sensation, making her blind with need. She sucked in a lungful of air, arched her back.

"That's it," he whispered into her ear. "You told me you'd never been with a man."

"If you doubt me now—"

"Have you ever felt anything like this, Morgan?"

She would have slapped him if she'd been able to loosen her grip on the table. She settled for shaking her head.

"I hadn't thought so. I want you to enjoy it so—"

She lifted her head and took his mouth. Her arms came around his neck, locking him to her. Her hips bucked against his hand, lighting spark after spark, bringing her to the edge of pleasure.

"Daniel," she said against his lips. "Please, help me."

He shuddered, a growl tearing from his throat. "I don't want to hurt you."

She felt the tip of his erection press into her opening slightly, easing a path.

"Not yet, damn it," he said as if to himself.

"Now!" She tightened her legs around his waist and lifted her hips, drawing him in. Her skin stretched, the narrow entry filling with his thickness.

"No, Morgan," he said furiously. "Come for me first."

She held on to his shoulders. "I don't know how."

"Yes, you do." He massaged her outer core while he rocked against the one inside, slipping deeper and deeper until sensations fused, spiraling higher, lifting her to a dangerous height.

Her body tensed, tightening around him and for him. Splinters of her soul began breaking off, flying free, taking her breath and her heartbeat. Lightning crackled with an explosive rush. She opened her mouth to cry out, but no sound made it past her throat.

Heat spasmed through her limbs, numbing her mind. It went on and on, rolling through her, sweeping her up and setting her down, tossing her like a rag doll cast to the sea. Daniel plunged inside her. She felt something give, tear, but there wasn't any pain. He gripped her shoulders. His head dropped back, his neck cording as he released a pained, guttural sound.

He pumped into her, straining one final, furious time.

Morgan lay on the table, her body tingling with aftershocks, her mind floating and languid, a foolish smile on her lips as she turned her head and kissed Daniel's temple. He'd collapsed on her moments after reaching his release. Supporting himself on his elbows, he fought for calm as his breath rushed through his lungs. She could feel his heartbeat against her chest, a stronger, more force-ful beat than her own.

Strong enough to turn to, to lean on, if only . . . She squeezed her eyes closed, refusing to let regret of any kind ruin this moment. Opening her eyes, she trailed her fingers through the dark waves of his hair, letting candlelight weave a path through the rich strands. It amazed her that simply touching him could make her so deliriously happy. There was so much she now knew about Daniel, yet there was much more she still had to learn. Was he ticklish? Where was his favorite place to be kissed? How deep did his feelings for her go?

She skimmed her hand over his sweat-slick shoulder and turned her head away. She didn't want him to look at her and possibly read that question in her eyes.

The *Sea Queen* blade lay within her reach, sparkling like a star from her past. She picked it up, balancing the com-fortable weight in her palm. The gemstones winked in the light before she closed her fingers around them, pressing their shape into her skin. Strong, dependable, the tooled dagger had guided her through the darkest part of her life. The darkest so far, she silently amended. Where would it take her in the future?

"If you're thinking of stabbing me with that, let me first say that lovemaking improves the second time around."

With a calculated smile, she held up the knife, angling it so light speared off the deadly tip. "So you say, but how can I be sure?"

Still coupled with her, he tilted his hips and gave her a devilish grin. "Give me a moment and I'll show you." He nibbled the line of her jaw. "But first, why don't you put that down? You don't need it any longer."

She felt a glimmer of passion come to life deep in her soul. He shifted his weight to a more comfortable position, allowing his hand to slide down her side, then up to her breast, where he cupped, lifted, massaged the weight until she moaned with pleasure. His thumb grazed her soft nipple, causing it to tighten. He kissed his way down her neck, and she knew she had only seconds before his mouth would close over her pebbling tip. She tensed, anticipating the unraveling sensation.

The metal hilt warmed in her hand, sending a vibrating hum along her arm. *You don't need it any longer.* His words rolled over and over in her mind. She heard herself say, "I found this aboard the *Sea Queen,* impaled in the captain's desk."

He stopped his explorations to look at her. The purpose in his dusky eyes was now threaded with concern. "Go on."

"It was what gave me the idea to become a pirate."

Taking the knife from her grip, he thrust it down, burying the blade in wood. His body tensed with sudden anger. "You aren't a pirate any longer, Morgan. And you don't have to bear the responsibilities for your village alone. Not any longer."

"You intend to bear them along with me?" she asked, dreading his answer to the question because no matter what he said, she knew it was impossible.

He ran the backs of his fingers over her cheek, brushing stray tendrils from her face. The anger faded from his eyes. "Aye, I'll be with you."

Her chest constricted with futile hope, and tears burned her throat. He was deluding himself. She loved him all the more for it, but she couldn't let it continue.

"I know you think your plan will work, Daniel. Even if it does, I'll always be a pirate, wanted for crimes I did and did not commit. You can't change that, or protect me if I'm caught."

"Can't I?" He gathered her in his arms and effortlessly swept her off the table. She clung to his shoulders, but she needn't have bothered. He held her tight against him, almost making her believe that nothing could tear them apart.

Forcing a grin that didn't touch the disquiet in his gaze, he chided, "You have little faith in me."

"It's not you I doubt," she said. "But the courts."

He shook his head as if pushing away her doubts. Lifting the waterfall of netting that draped the bed, he laid her on the satin-covered mattress and followed her down. Turning onto his back, he pulled her on top of him. Morgan took the initiative and straddled his hips. Daniel growled low in his chest as skin met skin. She leaned over him, just enough so the tips of her breasts brushed the coarse hair dusting his chest. She shivered with pleasure, loving the sensation.

He watched her, his eyes burning with heat and desire. His hands raked up her thighs to her waist, holding her tight. He wanted to be inside her. Making love may be new to her, but she understood the reckless tension she felt trapped in his limbs, his broad shoulders, the line of his jaw.

She wanted him, too. Desperately, with every breath she took. But this was all they had, she admitted, lifting slightly, guiding him to her. She clenched her jaw as her flesh stretched and gave, burning with a soreness that, to her amazement, soon faded. She moved slowly, building the warmth, feeling the friction. Tingles danced up through her body like a thousand fireflies caught on a breeze.

She wanted him, loved him, gloried in the way he made her feel, and in the possibilities those feelings created. She had three short days to drown in his scent, memorize the taste of his skin, learn his curves and textures. Three days. It was more than she'd ever hoped to have. She didn't share Daniel's faith in his friends. When he failed to gain the king's agreement, Daniel would realize he had to take her away, free her to make her own way. Tears pooled and dropped from the corners of her eyes.

They had three days. She could be satisfied with that, she told herself. *Yes, I will be satisfied with that—when ships take flight like birds in the sky.*

A vague shout and a change in the lull of the ship brought Daniel awake. He lay still, gathering his bearings, but it only took seconds for him to recall where he was and whom he was with.

Morgan lay on her back beside him, her auburn hair a tangle across her pillow and his arm. With her face turned toward him, the morning's milky light softened the curve of her jaw, the slender tip of her nose, even the bruise at her temple. Silken lashes shadowed her cheekbones. But he knew the dark circles beneath her eyes were more than a play of light. She was exhausted, physically drained from her ordeal over the past few days.

Waking her every few hours during the night to make love to her hadn't helped, he mused. Not that she'd complained. In fact, she had been the one to initiate their last round of love play. She'd thought he'd been asleep as she'd run her hands over his stomach and down his legs, around his sex, drawing close, but never touching. Over and over she'd teased and tormented with the barest brush of her fingers. Just when he'd decided to grab hold of her hand and show her what he needed, she'd cupped him in her palm, her cool fingers caressing his heated skin. She'd explored and fondled, bringing him to an erection that had bordered on pain.

His groin tightened with the memory, coming to life against his belly. Daniel stifled a groan. As much as he wanted to make love to Morgan again, he didn't think he could do it. Not yet, anyway.

Besides, she needed to rest and heal, and regardless that she might fight him every step of the way, he intended to take care of her. Rising up on his elbow, he looked down at her and brushed wispy curls from her brow, pausing to rub the satiny strands between his fingers. Her breasts, barely covered by rumpled bed sheets, rose and fell with each soft breath. One arm was draped across her stomach; the other touched his thigh. He'd never seen her so relaxed, without the wariness that always stiffened her spine, the alertness that shaded her eyes.

Protect her.

The possessive, overwhelming thought rose up from his soul. *Protect her.* His hand trembled against her hair. Pulling away, he rose from the bed to keep from waking her. He crossed to the window, welcoming the dawn's crisp breeze over his heated skin. He drew in one breath after another, clearing the sensual haze from his mind. He had to focus on his plan, something he couldn't do when Morgan was within arm's reach.

Lord Tennyson, Lords Ashcroft, Chapman and Riley had been close friends with Daniel's father, and later with Daniel, by helping him finance World Quest Shipping. If not for them, he would have lost Leighton Castle. Combined, they controlled half of England's wealth and lands. With their support, King George would listen to Daniel's plea and free Morgan.

And if they refuse to help me? He clenched his jaw against the thought. What would he do? Find a remote village somewhere in Europe, where she could live in secret under a different name. And then what? He scowled as the sun crested over the horizon, splashing golden light over the sleeping sea. Would he visit her on occasion? Or sail away and forget she even existed? Both options were as feasible as his walking away from his duties as Earl of Leighton.

Another possibility brewed in the back of his mind, but he rejected it before it fully took shape. He refused to consider keeping her as his mistress. The mere idea sullied what he felt for her.

There was only one option that remotely appealed to him, and that was to marry her.

Hearing Morgan stir, he glanced at the bed. With her body veiled by netting, she seemed surreal, a vision from a dream. She'd turned onto her side, extending her arm to the place where he should be. He rubbed his chest, imagining the feel of her hand warming his skin, her tapered fingers arousing him without intent. Following the length of her arm to the curve of her bare shoulder, he drew in a tight breath. As always, the sight of her started a fire in his soul.

He didn't have to wonder if she felt the same for him. He'd witnessed her emotions last night in the silver of her eyes, the reverence of her touch. She loved him. She may not know it yet, but she loved him as much as he loved her.

An ache seized his chest, squeezing with equal amounts of fear and awe. He hadn't realized that caring so deeply could bring as much pain as it did joy. But he wouldn't change what he felt. He loved her. Loved her with every beat of his heart.

Then marry her.

He tried to envision his mother accepting a baseborn daughter-in-law. Instead he imagined her fainting from shock. Would his peers accept Morgan or turn their backs? All his adult life he'd been driven with one goal in mind— to protect and restore his family name. Only now did he realize that his heritage didn't mean a damn if Morgan wasn't there to share it. As his wife. Daniel smiled, thinking about the things he would be able to show her, give her. But his smile faded.

First he had to convince King George to free a pirate he'd ordered the Royal Navy to capture, then sanction a marriage between a commoner and an English lord. Any sane man would tell him he stood a better chance of walking on water.

But sanity had nothing to do with his decision.

He loved Morgan, and he would marry her or he'd die trying.

Chapter 18

"Ye wouldn't believe the torturing devices Halo has below," Tobitt said uneasily, glancing everywhere except at Morgan and Daniel.

After a leisurely, and unappetizing, breakfast of dried beef and warm ale, she'd accompanied Daniel on deck to check their course and face the knowing grins of every sailor on board ship. Only Tobitt tried to disguise the fact that he knew exactly what had transpired in their cabin all night. She was grateful for his tact, not needing any additional reminders. The blissful memory still had her walking slowly and with great care.

"It's a bloom'n' medieval dungeon down there," Tobitt complained as he glared at a crewman who'd stopped mending a sheet of sail to grin at them as they passed. Scowling at the first officer, the man turned back to his task.

"He's got chains and metal cages," Tobitt said as they strolled from one end of the ship to the other. "Whips and cat-'o-nines hang on the walls like bloom'n' pictures. Rocks that would crush a man's chest are stacked in a corner. And the rack—God save me, there are still blood stains from the last poor bloke they stretched."

"That's horrible," she said, and she meant it, but a mischievous part of her couldn't help teasing the old sailor. Struggling to keep a straight face, she asked, "Does he have a stove and branding irons?"

"Not that I saw," Tobitt said, drawing his thick brows into a frown.

"What about a pillory?" she asked. "From my experience, gathering information from prisoners is much easier if they're forced to stand bent over with their neck and wrists locked in a wooden frame. It's a far worse punishment than mere chaining."

Tobitt stopped walking to gape at her. "Are ye saying ye had a room like Halo's? That ye tortured . . ." He ran a scarred hand over his mouth. "And 'ere I was almost convinced the rumors about ye eat'n' your prisoners was a lie."

She didn't know why she teased the poor man, only that for the first time in her life she was truly happy and desperately in love. Besides, it had been a lifetime since she'd even thought to tease anyone. She was surprised she still remembered how. "Well, I've given up my bad ways, Tobitt. I'm a reformed pirate."

"Capt'n." Tobitt propped his huge hands on his hips, his green eyes taking on a shrewd gleam, making him look for all his seriousness like a giant leprechaun. "Tell me our Morgan is makin' fun of me."

"I wouldn't know, Tobitt," Daniel admitted, slipping his arm around her waist. She grinned foolishly at his possessive touch. "I didn't see any chains or a pillory. But she did tie me to the mast."

"During a storm," Morgan couldn't help adding with impish delight.

A knowing grin spread over the sailor's ruddy mouth. "Ye are a wicked pirate, then."

Chuckling and shaking his head, the first officer left to see to his duties.

"I suppose I should consider myself lucky the *Sea Queen,* wasn't fitted like the *Devil's Luck,*" Daniel whispered against her ear.

She looked at him, and realized she risked becoming lost in the blue depth of his eyes. "I don't know . . . the thought of you in chains, at my mercy . . ."

When a group of sailors came by to settle down and eat their rations, he urged her to the bow. Once out of hearing range, he said, "You don't need chains to have me at your mercy, Morgan."

His words lacked their earlier lighthearted banter. His gaze narrowed, focusing on her. The stiff breeze whipped his hair about his face, making him seem wild and dangerous, a cunning warrior of old. He could be all those things, she admitted, but he was also kind and protective, loyal to a fault. And passionate. Her heart hammered as her emotions swelled, becoming too large for her to grasp.

"I love you, Daniel."

He stiffened; a muscle in his jaw pulsed as he started to speak.

She held up her hand and shook her head. "No, don't say anything, please. I know what you're thinking."

"So you can read my mind now?"

She shook her head. "I don't expect anything in return. I just wanted you to know."

He cupped her face in one of his hands, drawing her close with the other. "That's your problem, Morgan. You never expect anything in return."

She started to object, but the words caught in her throat. For her entire life it seemed, she'd *thought* only about others, *done* only for others. Caring for her family had come as naturally as breathing. Accepting those responsibilities was something she had to do.

She'd always wanted more from life, but she'd never

guessed how incredible that "more" could be. But now she knew.

God help her, now she knew.

"Ease down the helm, Mr. Tobitt," Morgan called, forgetting it wasn't her ship or her duty to give orders, but old habits were hard to break, especially now that she controlled so little in her life.

She gripped the railing as the *Devil's Luck* eased closer to the distant shore. They were passing Sea Reach, a broad stretch of river they had to pass before entering the heart of the Thames. Wind caught the forward sails, drawing them dead ahead, closer to Tilbury Point. Her skin chilled as they maneuvered past the desolate stretch of craggy rock and sand. Her gaze locked on the gibbet, and the rusted iron body cage dangling from its wooden arm.

Empty, but for how long?

A shudder racked her shoulders. *His plan might work,* she silently reaffirmed. *Please, God, let his plan work.* This time tomorrow she might be free to go wherever she wanted, live however she wanted. She tightened her grip on the balustrade, her nails digging into the polished wood. Daniel's arm came around the front of her waist, as if he knew she needed his support. He pulled her back against his chest, pressed his mouth into her hair.

She closed her eyes for an instant, letting his strength flow into her mind, down her neck and through her body. How many times had she dreamed of leaning against a man she loved, and sharing the fear that weighted her soul? She placed her hand over his. She had to cherish every moment they shared. She'd finally found her dream, but only fate knew if it would last.

She opened her eyes just as they sailed past a notorious landmark. With a revealing quiver in her voice, she said, "That's where they displayed Captain Kidd after they hanged him nearly sixty years ago. I wonder who will be next."

"Come below," he said.

"And hide?"

He sighed, his warm breath a caress along the side of her face. "For once, I wish you'd behave as a regular female."

"For once, I wish I were a regular female."

He took her shoulders and turned her around. The certainty in his eyes made the tremors in her stomach ease just a little. "I'm not going to let anything happen to you."

Looking at him, nearly drowning in the heat of his eyes, she knew he meant the words, just as she knew he couldn't protect her. Not forever. Perhaps she would evade capture while in London, but what about afterwards? Staying with him put *him* in danger. She couldn't allow him to take such risks, ruin his life, possibly give up everything he valued. No, she had to leave him, and the sooner the better.

"I trust you, and I love you." Then against his lips she whispered, "No matter what happens."

After days at sea with nothing but the sound of waves, the occasional laughter between men, and the cry from hungry seagulls, the noise and bustle from the shores of London set Daniel's teeth on edge. Or perhaps it was sailing past the waterfront at Wapping, with its narrow streets of row houses, timber yards and wooden cranes that had him pacing and snarling orders. Smells of rotting wood, weeds and sewage drifted on the breeze like rancid smoke, lodging in his lungs.

He thanked God he'd convinced Morgan to stay below after seeing Tilbury Point that morning. She knew enough about Executioner's Dock; she didn't need to see the gallows, set up near the shore at the low-tide mark. As he drifted past the simple pillars held upright by a thick over-head beam, he imagined a faceless pirate still dangling by a rope as the tide swirled in, slowly and mercilessly swallowing everything in its path.

He closed his eyes, fighting to push the image from his mind, but it sharpened, defining not into a man but a woman with dark, tangled hair and silver eyes.

"No!" He snapped his eyes open.

"Capt'n?" Tobitt asked, coming to a stop beside him.

Just ahead, Daniel spotted the forest of masts belonging to ships moored four and five deep near the Custom House Quay. They'd arrived. There was no turning back now. His plan had to work. Lord Tennyson had to support him. Because if he didn't, Daniel would lose Morgan, and she was the only thing that mattered.

"Once we anchor, Tobitt," Daniel said, motioning for his first officer to follow him while he gathered the few items he'd need ashore, "you're to remain here and protect Morgan."

"Ye can count on me, Capt'n."

"I want her to stay below. Out of sight. Do you understand?"

"Aye. Not even the mice will know she's on board."

"Excellent." Daniel shielded his eyes from the sun's glare, then called to a group of men near the forecastle. "Back tops'l! Let's bring her to a stop."

He had put Roscoe in charge of taking the women and children to a boardinghouse. Daniel would see to them later. For now, he had to focus on taking Halo Jones, his crew, and Thomas to Marshalsea Prison. But first he had one more order for his first officer.

"And, Tobitt, if Morgan gives you any trouble, be firm with her."

"Firm, sir?"

"Is that a problem?"

"Ah . . . no, sir."

Daniel sighed when Tobitt cast a squeamish look toward the stern of the ship where—hopefully—Morgan was resting in the captain's cabin. Pulling a key from his pants pocket, he handed it over, advising, "Lock her in if you must."

A few more hours and it would all be over. Morgan would be free ... and his. Ready to put his plan into motion, he turned away—and ignored the foreboding chill that snaked down his spine.

"You're going to regret this, Daniel." Thomas whispered his threat in a harsh, unrecognizable tone. Three days in the hold had removed any pretense of innocence. The man who'd emerged was an angry, depraved criminal. A man Daniel didn't know.

"I already do, Thomas." Hearing the guards talking to the magistrate in a nearby office in Marshalsea Prison, Daniel started to join them, but his partner caught his sleeve with his chained hands.

Thomas pulled him aside to the stone walls slick with decay and age. In a voice fevered and slightly mad, he demanded, "Unchain me. Tell them you made a mistake."

The pain of betrayal that had weighed on Daniel's soul since the moment he'd learned of Thomas's deception now turned cold with contempt. "You stole from me, Thomas. That I could forgive, though I still don't understand why you did it. You were a rich man. We were both more successful than either of us dreamed. You'd saved your estate, had everything you wanted. Money, position, women."

"You know nothing about what I wanted." His onetime friend pierced him with crazed brown eyes.

Daniel searched Thomas's hostile gaze. "You're right, I don't know anything about you or what drove you. But I do know you're going to pay for what you've done. You murdered Captain Egham and Captain Williams," Daniel said, barely restraining the urge to beat his fists into Thomas's face. "You slaughtered their crew!"

"*I* didn't kill them. Halo did."

"You let it happen," Daniel seethed. "You arranged it, decided they should die, then stood by and watched."

Thomas rolled his eyes and muttered to himself, "I knew going into business with you would be a mistake. I should have chosen someone more . . . open-minded."

"You obviously did when you began dealing with Halo."

Making a tsking sound, Thomas grinned. "Halo was merely a means to an end. No, I should have started World Quest Shipping with someone else, someone with vision."

"I'm sure you'll have time to contemplate your mistakes before your trial begins," Daniel said dryly.

"My *mistake* was not letting Halo attack your ship and . . . well . . ." Thomas raked a calculated look over Daniel.

Daniel didn't need to hear the rest of what Thomas had to say. If Halo had managed to kill him, Thomas would have had free rein of the company and control of all its profits. *And he would have been the executor of my estate! Leaving my mother at his mercy.*

"Everything had been running perfectly until the blasted war ended," Thomas complained. "Then you had to return and get involved again. I had to come up with a way to sell *my* cargo without running it through your books."

Daniel stared at the man beside him, wondering who he was. He'd known Thomas all his life. They'd been friends who'd both faced losing their homes and titles. That common bond had united them as partners. How was it possible that Daniel had never seen Thomas's true nature? How had he been so blind?

"Well, Thomas," Daniel said, wanting to escape the dim building, the rank smells of mold and sewage. "Fortunately, I did return to discover your scheme. You're going to pay for the lives you took, and for casting suspicion on an innocent woman."

"Innocent? Morgan?" His derisive laugh thinned, turning cruel and threatening. "She's far from innocent, *partner*. She's as guilty as the rest of us."

Daniel cursed himself for bringing any mention of Morgan into the conversation.

Thomas threw a glance at the pirates chained and guarded by Daniel's crew. "She's not going to get away with her crimes any more than you are."

Laughing, Thomas turned away, but quickly sobered, his demeanor becoming stoic and refined when the magistrate entered the room. Daniel started to ask Thomas what he'd meant, but his onetime friend refused to even look at him.

Daniel crossed to the large desk where prisoners were admitted. He had to hurry. He wanted the process of filing charges and listing names over with. He wanted out of the dreary building with its endless chambers filled with countless men who awaited trial and possible death. But mostly, he had to escape Thomas's threat. *"She's not going to get away with her crimes any more than you are."*

The words echoed in Daniel's mind like the warning they were meant to be.

Light flickered from a dozen sconces along the burgundy painted walls, spilling over polished furniture that gleamed like wooden gems. Light pooled on the marble floor, glimmering with the fire of emerald stars tossed to earth. Voices and murmuring laughter floated from a room to Daniel's left, a front parlor where he'd undoubtedly find Pall Mall's newest members, their chests and egos puffed with pride for being admitted to the elite club. Someone smoked a pipe, adding its sweet, velvety scent to the other familiar sights and smells.

After spending months at sea, being both hunter and

hunted, after discovering a woman he loved and a friend he couldn't trust, Daniel felt he'd stepped into the one place in the world where sanity still ruled. Nothing ever changed in London's most austere club. Ever. Only the rich were allowed, and only if one's heritage and title gleamed like polished gold.

"Lord Leighton," the butler droned when he spotted Daniel.

"Billings, it's good to see you again." He handed his hat to the butler, grateful that he'd had the time to stop by his town house to bathe and change. If he'd dared enter the private club wearing britches and a shirt that smelled of sweat and the sea, he'd have been tossed out on his backside, regardless of his standing.

"We haven't seen you for some time," the butler said, leading Daniel down a hall, knowing from years of service who Daniel would most likely want to see. "Will you be in town for long?"

"That's a good question, Billings. One I hope to have an answer to soon." Coming to a closed door, he asked, "Is Lord Tennyson here today?"

"Yes, sir. They're all here." Billings opened the door, admitting Daniel into a room in which few were allowed, regardless of whether they possessed the wealth and title required to be a member of Pall Mall. This room was a club within a club. A place where the true power of England reigned. A place where Daniel's father had belonged before his near ruin and death.

"Gentlemen," Daniel said, stepping inside and tugging on the cuff of his forest green coat, feeling strangely confined in the garment.

"Tremayne, where the blazes have you been?" Lord Tennyson barked, his graying brow arching with surprise. He, along with Lord Riley, Lord Ashcroft and Lord Chapman, rose from their velvet high-backed chairs to greet him. "It's been damn quiet since you left."

Daniel stepped into the group, shaking each of their hands. "It's good to be back." He smiled, because it *was* good to see his friends again.

"We'd begun to think you'd been lost at sea," Ashcroft said around the Spanish cigar clamped between his teeth.

"Chapman thought it was time to auction your chair. But he's the practical one," Riley chuckled, reclaiming his own seat. "I voted to wait awhile longer, see if you'd swim ashore. Which, apparently, you have."

"You have my thanks for not discounting me quite so fast, gentlemen." Daniel accepted a crystal glass of brandy from a passing servant, half wishing the man would bring him the entire bottle. Resisting the urge to down the bittersweet liquor, he took a sip, then said, "But then you might regret not acting once you've heard what I've come to ask of you."

Lord Tennyson, the oldest and most respected man in London, narrowed his shrewd gaze on Daniel, his pale gray eyes already probing between the lines. Daniel endured the older man's speculative stare. Before Thomas's deception, he wouldn't have hesitated asking these men for help, certain he could count on them. Trust them. Now he wondered if he could trust anyone except himself . . . *and Morgan.*

"Daniel, you look about as comfortable as a duck in the desert," Lord Chapman said. "Why don't we all get settled before you tell us what's on your mind?"

Taking his seat, Daniel rested his forearms on his thighs and stared at the tumbler he cupped in one hand. Listening to the quiet descend over the room, feeling his friends' gazes cutting him with their keen assessment, imagining the questions rolling through their minds, he took a deep breath and prayed he wasn't making a mistake.

Grasping on to Morgan's logic, he asked himself, *What other choice do I have?*

"I took Thomas Burke to Marshalsea Prison today," he announced.

"Thomas is back? Excellent." Riley took a rare and expensive cigar from a teak box on the side table. Rolling the cigar between his lips, he asked, "Why didn't he come with you?"

"I believe the question we should ask, Riley, is why did Daniel take Thomas to the prison?" Lord Tennyson cut in with his usual calm perception that was legendary in Parliament and society alike.

Daniel ran his hand over his mouth, feeling tired and worn and furious all at once. "Thomas is the one responsible for Captain Egham's death."

He held the elders' gaze as the men alternately voiced their denials and demanded an explanation. Receiving Lord Tennyson's barely discernible nod, he continued, "It all started with the end of the Seven Years War."

Daniel told them about the attack on the *Intrepid*, Captain Egham's death, and his relentless hunt for Morgan because of Thomas's lies. He described Morgan and her crew, his capture and ultimate release. Then his success at finding her in her village. The only details he omitted were his personal feelings for her.

The men seated around him remained silent, not asking questions or interrupting, making it impossible for Daniel to gauge their thoughts. After relating the events following Halo's capture that revealed Thomas's guilt, Daniel paused, unsure how to proceed.

The grandfather clock against the far wall chimed the hour of four. He had to hurry, he realized. He'd been away from the ship too long. No one besides his crew knew Morgan was on board, and they wouldn't tell. But still, he wanted to be with her. She'd be nervous, frightened.

Because Thomas knows. But he was locked away in prison where he couldn't reach her. That fact didn't stop the dread from tightening Daniel's skin. *Morgan.* He had to see her, make sure she was all right. He pushed to his feet and was halfway to the door when Lord Tennyson's voice stopped him.

"Why did you come to us, Daniel?"

He stopped. What was he thinking? He couldn't leave yet. Morgan was safe, he reassured himself. Tobitt would protect her. He faced the men who were his last hope of freeing the woman for whom he'd willingly sacrifice his name, the heritage he'd once valued, his very life, if it would free Morgan. "Gentlemen, there's something I need you to do for me."

"What do you mean, he left?" Morgan propped her hands on her hips and gave the towering sailor her best glare. She felt the sun's last rays at her back, their warmth fading as the shadows drew near. Her time was coming to an end, slipping away like sand through an hourglass. She shivered in her silk gown and hugged her arms to her waist, afraid of what she had to do, but knowing she had no choice.

Tobitt crossed his arms over his barreled chest, pursed his lips and stared at the planked floor of the forward deck. " 'E went ashore near three hours ago tae hand over the prisoners."

Morgan ran her fingers through her tousled hair. How could she have fallen asleep, now of all times? Daniel had wanted her to rest, but she'd only laughed at him. Rest when her life and his were at stake? Yet, in spite of her frazzled nerves, she'd fallen into a fitful sleep.

Daniel left without saying good-bye. He'd thought she'd be here upon his return. He had no way of knowing that Morgan had a plan of her own—one that would ensure his safety.

If only she could see him once more. She clamped her jaw tight to cut off the tears building behind her eyes.

They'd said all they needed to. He'd promised to protect her, and she'd told him she loved him. What more was there to say? No, it was better this way, she decided, feeling as if her heart were twisting in half.

"Did he say when he'd return?"

The first officer shook his head, rustling his shaggy red hair against his shoulders. " 'E didn't. Only that you was tae stay out of sight. And that's what you're gonna do."

She didn't argue as Tobitt led her down the familiar companionway to her cabin.

This was her chance to escape, she thought. She should have left hours ago . . . She stopped berating herself. She had to sneak off the ship and reach town. If there wasn't a dinghy available, she'd have to swim, which wasn't an option she cared for, but one she'd take if she couldn't find another way. The docks weren't too far, and she was a strong swimmer.

Once she reached shore, she'd disappear in the crowded streets, blend in with the countless people in the countless alleyways and hidey-holes. She had no money, but there were plenty of valuables in Halo's cabin she could take and later sell to gain passage to any port. Any port, that is, except the one she was in.

Entering her cabin like a docile lamb, she turned just as Tobitt gave her a jubilant smile and closed the door.

She bit down on her lip. The most important thing was to get away before Daniel returned. For his sake, she had to run. Where she went didn't matter, as long as it was out of England, and away from Daniel. But time was running out.

"I have to hurry." She opened the enormous chest to rummage through the mound of clothes and jewels when she heard a sound. She paused, her eyes going wide when she recognized the noise as the grating of a key—turning in a lock.

* * *

Daniel clenched his hands into fists and forced a calming breath. It was anticipation racing through his bloodstream, he reassured himself, not panic. Still, he gritted his teeth, wanting to take the oars away from the hired boatsman and row the skiff toward the *Devil's Luck* himself. He couldn't wait to tell Morgan the good news. He needed to hear himself say the words as well, hardly believing there were still people he could trust and count on. Tennyson, Riley, Ashcroft and Chapman had all supported him, vowing to do all they could to convince the king to grant Morgan amnesty. With their support, he couldn't fail.

Yet wariness tightened the back of his neck in a cold, relentless grip. The dinghy he'd left at the dock had been nowhere in sight. It was nothing, he chided himself. Roscoe and the rest of his men had undoubtedly purchased the list of supplies Daniel had ordered and had returned to the ship. Which meant they'd be prepared to leave London all the sooner. That is, as soon as Lord Tennyson arranged a meeting with King George III.

As the distance closed between the ship and the dinghy, Daniel's anticipation grew, nearly bursting in his chest when he finally gripped the rope ladder dangling over the hull's side. He heaved himself up one rung at a time, climbing to the light glowing above. She'd be there to greet him with a smile on her face and worry in her eyes. Or perhaps she was locked in her cabin, he thought with a grin, furious that he'd taken such an extreme precaution.

It didn't matter what mood she was in. He intended to kiss her, fill his arms with her warmth; then he'd tell her what he'd accomplished.

When he reached the balustrade, the skin at the base of his nape rippled in warning. Why hadn't someone called out? Considering the gentle breeze, he should be able to hear voices, men moving about. Likewise, the man on watch should have spotted him. But the night was calm, eerily so, like a bottled storm, building, surging, ready to erupt. He climbed over the railing, turned, and froze, at once understanding his premonition.

Morgan stood near the base of the main mast wearing an ivory gown more suited for bed than for a public viewing. Her bare arms were pinned to her sides by chains that crisscrossed her waist and locked at her wrists. Soldiers with bayonets had forced his crew against the opposite railing.

"What the hell is going on?" he demanded, stepping forward to rip Morgan free.

"Stay where you are, Lord Leighton." An officer from the King's Navy came into Daniel's line of sight, aiming a pistol at him.

Daniel fisted his hands. Fury pounded through his veins like a sea at war. "What is this about, Lieutenant?"

"I've orders to bring you and Morgan the Scylla to King George immediately."

"For what reason?" he asked, though he needn't have bothered. He already knew. *Thomas.*

"You're both to be charged with piracy against the Crown."

Two soldiers took his arms and tied his wrists together in front of him. Anger blurred his vision, singed his skin. He'd promised to protect her; he'd given his word that she wouldn't be harmed. There was no guessing what Thomas had said to poison the king's mind.

He'd been an arrogant fool! How Morgan must loathe him. Why hadn't he released her when he'd had the chance? He'd been selfish, wanting to keep her for himself when he should have let her fly, free, the way she was meant to be.

Daniel met her gaze, though it nearly killed him to do so. Her expression was solemn, and pain-filled. A guard forced her to cross the deck. Reaching his side, she hesitated, raising her clear, fearless eyes to his.

Her voice quivered as she whispered, "I'm sorry."

As she was led away, he dropped his head back, saw the night's first star blink into view, and wondered if that was fate laughing at him. *She* was sorry. Fury swept through him in violent waves. This wasn't her fault; it was his, and his alone.

He'd be damned if he'd let her suffer for it.

But he'd be equally damned if he knew how to stop it, because now the tide was tumbling over them both.

Chapter 19

Morgan's horse, a docile bay, followed the band of guards through the dark, misty streets of London. Damp air swirled around the mare's hooves, floating up to coat Morgan's skin. After the guards had hauled her from her cabin, her thin gown had become soaked within minutes. The fabric clung to her body, making her feel all the more vulnerable and exposed. Chilled to the bone, she clenched her jaw to keep her teeth from chattering. What she wouldn't give for a pair of pants and a heavy wool shirt. And her knife, she added, though it would do little good against chains. She kept her chin tilted up and her gaze forward, fighting the humiliation and fear that had pushed tears into her eyes.

Daniel was somewhere ahead of her on the dark, quiet street, undoubtedly seething with fury. For as long as she lived, she'd never forget the disbelief in his eyes when he'd climbed aboard the *Devil's Luck* and seen her chained like a slave. Then the flash of blinding anger had hardened his features to stone. He hadn't said a word after his brief encounter with the lieutenant. She hoped never to hear the furious words that had to be overwhelming his mind.

He was to be charged with piracy because of her. How he must regret the day he'd met her.

Who could possibly believe he'd broken the law? Or perhaps the question she should ask was who would accuse him of doing so? She suspected she knew the answer.

Apprehension constricted her chest like a steel band. She'd told Daniel to release her. Damn him, why had he refused? He could be free now, safe at Leighton Castle far to the north. Instead they would both pay for her crimes.

She heard a guard announce that they'd arrived. Where they'd arrived, she had no clue. Dread swept down her spine like a final breath. Pulled from her pensiveness, she glanced up and felt her jaw drop. A towering stone wall, the color of burnt ash, stretched out on both sides of her, disappearing far into the night. Gothic windows gleamed like clever eyes in the flickering light, watching, accusing her as she drew near. Directly before her, the torches lighting the mouth of an archway failed to reach inside the dark, menacing cavern, creating an abyss that no one except her seemed reluctant to enter. She gripped her horse's mane, cringing when the chains binding her rattled like a hovering ghost, reminding her that she was trapped.

"Sweet Mary," she whispered. "This is Marshalsea Prison?"

A guard snorted beside her. "This ain't no prison, wench. This is King Henry VIII's gate. Beyond that is Windsor Castle."

Morgan gaped at him, unable to utter the words ringing in her mind.

"Ye don't think the king is gonna cart hisself to a prison in the dead of night for the likes of ye, do ye?"

"No, I just . . ." She hadn't thought she'd see the king at all, despite what the lieutenant said, imagining instead that she'd be locked away in a cell until the day of her trial.

They rode through the archway, emerged at a well-

tended lawn and continued to a building far more imposing than the "gate" she'd just passed. Made of ivory-col-
ored stone, the four-story St. George's Chapel inspired awe
and fear with a single glance. Life-size marble statues of
robed men and women were imbedded in stone pillars
fifty feet above her. On a higher ledge, gargoyles glared
at her with black, slanted eyes. Wind whipped down the
wall, sounding strangely like laughter. Additional columns
lined the gabled roof like spears stabbing the blackened
sky.

The guards came to a stop and helped her dismount
before a pair of foreboding oak doors. Torches hissed and
burned from their brackets on the walls, throwing shadows
across the ground. The solid panels were closed, creating
a barrier between the sinful world outside and the sanctity
within.

For the first time in her life, Morgan wanted to turn and
run. Only there was no escape, she realized, no way to win
this fight. Her cunning and well-honed skills wouldn't help
her here. This time, her monstrous reputation had sealed
her fate.

She felt a tug on her arm and gratefully looked away
from the ominous building. Daniel's troubled gaze met
hers.

"Stay with me," he warned. With his hands bound in
front of him, and purpose chiseling the lines in his face,
he led her up the steps and into the entryway. The guards
flanked their sides.

They passed through the nave, a richly paneled room
with a stone vaulted ceiling, cracked from years of wear.
Banners, helmets and swords belonging to the Knights of
the Garter, the highest Order of Chivalry, lined the
immense chamber. She'd heard stories about the royal
shrine, but never imagined that a day would come when
she would see it. At the far end of the majestic room, she

saw at least a half-dozen stately tombs, the final resting places of past sovereigns.

Why would King George want to see them here, where the very air was intimidating, imposing? For those very reasons, she assumed. Who could lie while in such austere surroundings? If she weren't already trembling with cold, she'd shudder with trepidation.

They stopped before the altar just as a side door opened. A gaunt man entered, his powdered wig and black unadorned suit making his sharp features and knife-thin body seem all the more severe. A much younger man appeared next, richly dressed in a sapphire blue robe trimmed with gold thread. His tumble of black hair fell around boyish features and kind eyes. She spotted a third man, freshly bathed and dressed in clothes fit for a king, though she thought a devil better described Thomas Burke.

Her suspicions came crashing into her mind. She swayed, suddenly dizzy. She felt waves of anger rolling off Daniel in a dangerous tide. He tensed beside her, every line in his body hardening with suppressed rage.

"Your Majesty," Daniel said in a voice that echoed through the chamber. He bowed to the man in the blue robe.

Morgan stared at the young king who'd worn the crown for little more than a year. Should she curtsey? Bow? Spit on his satin slippers for continuing the war his grandfather had begun, forcing her down a desperate path of survival? If Jo were here, the latter would have been the most likely course of action. But King George III was little more than a boy, hardly older than Jo, certainly not old enough to shoulder the responsibilities of a country in turmoil. Nor would he understand the dire circumstances that had led her to pirating.

"Lord Leighton," King George said with a reluctant

nod. "After everything you've done for England, it pains me to see you cast so low."

"I can imagine the story you've been told," Daniel said, barely concealing his bitterness. "But I assure you, the charges of piracy aren't true."

"Do you deny the identity of this woman?" He pointed a slender finger at her. "Is she not the infamous Morgan the Scylla?"

"She is."

"The same pirate who plundered our ships, murdered innocent men?"

"She—" Daniel began.

"Were you not harboring a wanted criminal aboard your vessel?" the king interrupted.

"There are partial truths to what you charge me with, Your Majesty. If you'd but hear me out."

The king glared at Morgan. "Is it true that you are a cannibal?"

Morgan opened her mouth to answer, but having the king's attention focused on her stole her breath.

He stepped behind the altar as if his question brought the need for a protective barrier. "Can you truly scorch the flesh off a man's bones? You seem a skinny, pitiful thing to have earned such a vile reputation."

"The rumors are exaggerations, nothing more," Daniel said in her defense.

"Hmmm." He looked at Daniel, then nodded to Thomas. "What about your partner's grievances, Lord Leighton?" Clasping his hands behind his back, he bent his head, seemingly on the verge of making a final, and dire, decision.

Shivering, Morgan cast an anxious glance at Thomas, who looked down at her from the pulpit. His disdainful smile promised retribution.

"Mr. Burke claims you have betrayed him in the worst way. He says you have twisted the events, laying the guilt at his door. His allegations are highly upsetting. They can't go unpunished. Not now that the truth is in the open.''

"But it isn't," Morgan said, unable to keep quiet any longer. Her fate may be to die as a criminal, but that didn't mean Daniel had to join her in the gallows. And he wouldn't, not if she could help it. She'd admit to anything if it meant saving his life.

"Morgan," Daniel warned between clenched teeth.

"I gave you no leave to speak," the king snapped.

"Would you condemn an innocent man, then?" she asked, shaking with equal amounts of fear, anger and cold.

"Are *you,* a known pirate, going to attest to Lord Leighton's innocence?" the king mocked.

"I may be a pirate, Your Majesty, but that doesn't make Lord Leighton guilty of the same."

"You were on his ship, were you not?"

She nodded.

"Yet he failed to bring you to Marshalsea Prison with the other prisoners. Why is that, do you think?"

What could she say? He'd kept her hidden because he had a foolish notion that they could stay together, that her past wouldn't catch up to her, ruin her life and his. Because he was a wonderful man who'd wanted to make a few incredible days last forever?

"I told you, did I not?" Thomas crowed, drawing up beside King George. "She's working for Daniel. He'd hoped to get her out of the city before she was discovered. If you hadn't shown compassion and rescued me from prison, I would have been sentenced to hang while these two carried out their crimes against you."

"Your Majesty." Daniel took a step forward, but a guard forced him back with the tip of his bayonet. "He's lying. I made a full report of Thomas's involvement with Halo Jones."

"Yes, I read the report. I found it strange that you'd failed to mention this woman."

"I hadn't realized an incomplete account of the past week's events were cause for imprisonment."

"Beware, Lord Leighton," the king warned. "I've shown you a great deal of leniency by bringing you here instead of hearing you out before all of court."

Daniel made a slight bow of concession. "Then I'll plead my case and allow you to judge my fate."

"I believe we've heard all we need to," Thomas said.

"I wasn't aware you spoke for the king," Daniel returned.

The older man who'd hovered in the corner like a shadow, watching the exchange, now whispered in King George's ear. The young sovereign pursed his lips, then looked to his advisor for reassurance.

"Very well," the king said. "Lord Leighton, I shall hear your claims."

Daniel sent Morgan a reassuring glance. "Thomas Burke and I started World Quest Shipping at the beginning of the Seven Years War. My hopes had been to save my estate from financial ruin. I'd thought Thomas's goals had been the same, since his family home had been in a state similar to my own. Because I trusted him, I gave him control of the company while I took several of my ships to fight in the war."

The king raised a brow. "Yes, I recall the sacrifice you made. My grandfather spoke of it often."

"The raids on my ships didn't start until the end of the war, Your Majesty, when I left my post in the Navy and returned to World Quest."

"A coincidence," Thomas said.

"Yes," Daniel agreed. "One that should have alerted my suspicions. But I didn't see the connection. And why should I? My *partner* was on both ships that were attacked. He and a handful of crewmen were lucky enough to survive while both captains were murdered. The cargo had been a complete loss, the ships ripped apart."

"You aren't telling me anything I don't already know, Lord Leighton," the king said with a wave of his hand. "If you have something new to add, do so. And quickly."

"Thomas claimed Morgan attacked the *Intrepid* and killed Captain Egham. His story was what drove me to hunt her down."

"If you'll recall, I told you not to go," Thomas said. "Like a fool, I'd feared for your life, when all along she was raiding ships by your order, dividing the cargo with you."

"I ordered her to raid my own ship?" Daniel challenged. "Steal my own cargo?"

"How do I know what your agreement was with her? For all I know, she disobeyed you, acted on her own," Thomas sneered. "She is a pirate, after all. Hardly someone to trust."

"I trust her with my life."

"Which was your mistake."

Daniel drew a strangled breath. Morgan wanted to reach out to him, but she kept her chained hands at her waist. She didn't want the king to know how deep her feelings ran, certain that Thomas would use that against Daniel, as well.

"She led me to Halo Jones's hideout," Daniel continued. "And helped capture him."

"For a price," Thomas said in an aside to the king. "She demanded that Daniel release her if she helped capture one of her own kind."

"Is this true, Lord Leighton?"

Regardless of the chains and guards, Morgan didn't know what kept her from backing away and running from the building. She felt as if a vortex swirled around her, pulling her down, miring her in misconstrued facts that would send her and Daniel to their deaths. Nothing he said would make what he'd done seem right. Thomas would twist it around, mold it like clay in his hands until it suited him.

"Yes, I'd agreed to release her," Daniel said. "I'd begun to doubt that Morgan was responsible for attacking the *Intrepid*."

The king raised his hand to stop Thomas from speaking. "And what caused this doubt?"

Daniel looked at her for a moment. She held her breath as he revealed emotions better left hidden. Didn't he know he couldn't save her? The less he made of their relationship, the better his odds of being set free.

"I set a trap for Morgan's ship, the *Sea Queen*, only she trapped me, instead. I spent time with her, and learned she wasn't the vicious monster that legend reputes her to be. She could have killed me any number of times, but she didn't. She treated me fairly, setting me ashore with enough provisions to survive. That wasn't the behavior of a ruthless killer."

"Do you have proof of this?" the king asked.

"Only my word, Your Majesty," Daniel replied in a tone that said that should be enough.

But it wasn't. "I need evidence, Lord Leighton."

Daniel tensed, futilely twisting the ropes binding his wrists. "There were other signs that everything wasn't as it seemed. Thomas had been adamant that she hang before we reach London."

"Because she's an outlaw, Daniel," Thomas shouted, swiping a hand through his blond hair. "Why do you continually forget that point? She's a criminal, a pirate who steals and murders. She deserves to die. And so do you for being in league with her."

He was losing, Daniel thought, feeling the ground slipping out from under him. Nothing he said would prove Morgan innocent. It was Thomas's word against his, and apparently King George preferred to believe the lies that slipped from Thomas's tongue like oil off velvet.

Morgan shivered beside him, fighting the cold, fighting the fear that he knew had to be icing her veins. Yet she stood as tall and proud as the first time he'd seen her on the deck of the *Sea Queen*. Only now her only protection was a damp, gauzy gown and a veil of tangled satin hair. And eyes that possessed the courage of ten men.

"Unless you can come up with something more substantial, I'll be forced to end this now and let it proceed to trial in the courts." King George sighed and turned away.

"I found this with Halo Jones," Daniel said, desperate to delay the inevitable. In an awkward movement because of his bound wrists, he took the gold watch from his pocket and handed it to the nearest guard, who gave it to the king. "This was Captain Egham's; a gift from me. Halo admitted taking it from the captain before killing him. This proves Morgan wasn't responsible for his death."

Thomas snickered. "It only proves she gave it to Halo after she murdered Egham."

With every lie Thomas uttered, violent, blinding fury pushed deeper into Daniel's mind. This injustice couldn't happen, but nothing he did or said was going to stop it. Eyeing the bayonet the guard beside him held, he decided that if he couldn't save Morgan, he'd be damn sure Thomas didn't survive, either.

"If it's proof of guilt you need, King George, I have it right here." The baritone voice rolled like thunder from the back of the nave.

Turning, Daniel felt relief rush through his limbs, nearly sending him to his knees.

"Lord Tennyson, what are you doing here?" King George reprimanded, though in a tone far softer than he'd used with Daniel. "This is a private meeting."

"Coming to the aid of a friend." Lord Tennyson stepped from the shadowy entryway, and was followed by Lords Chapman, Ashcroft and Riley. "It was sheer luck that I learned of this meeting."

"This doesn't concern you, gentlemen," Thomas said.

"Oh, but it does. As the original backers of World Quest Shipping, I believe we have a stake in Daniel's future—and yours, Thomas."

"If you know what this is about, then I'm sure you know it has nothing to do with World Quest." Thomas ran his palm down the front of his coat, amplifying the tension stiffening his shoulders. "Perhaps I can meet with you tomorrow."

"Now suits me better, Thomas." Lord Tennyson reached Daniel's side, glanced down at the rope knotted at his wrists, and shook his head. He withdrew a folder from beneath his arm and held it out to the king's advisor, the Earl of Bute. "I believe you'll want to take a look at these before continuing this interrogation."

"What is it?" Daniel asked, unable to believe the pendulum might be swinging back in his favor.

"A few records we found. Not at the World Quest office as you might expect, but at Thomas's home."

"You broke into my town house?" Thomas demanded, paling visibly.

"Of course not. Your butler admitted us." Lord Riley smiled without humor. "The bills and receipts we found in your study offered quite a surprise."

"Those records have nothing to do with Daniel's association with pirates." Thomas eyed the open file in Lord Bute's hands. "If you found some discrepancies, I'll be glad to discuss them later."

"Let's discuss them now." Lord Tennyson raised a graying brow, silently asking the king's permission. "Shall we?"

King George nodded to Lord Bute. "What does it say?"

The advisor's brows pinched together as he flipped through page after page. "A list of gambling and assorted investment debts incurred and paid off, Your Majesty. The amounts of which would allow us to finance a small war."

"Thomas has been embezzling from World Quest for

years. Beginning, I believe, when Daniel joined the Seven Years War." Lord Tennyson strode past Daniel, pausing to glance at Morgan. A faint smile pulled the corner of his mouth when she didn't drop her gaze.

"When Daniel returned, Thomas was desperate to replace the money before anyone noticed. From what I can gather, he thought the best way to go about it was to steal his own cargo, sell it, and funnel the money back into the company."

"You have no proof."

"Yes, we do," Morgan said. "Halo's testimony."

"What?" Thomas laughed. "The testimony of a pirate?"

She nodded. "A pirate, and your partner, who isn't going to let you get away with using him as a scapegoat."

The next few minutes happened in a blur for Daniel. King George ordered his guards to cut him free and arrest Thomas, deciding that Thomas would stand trial beside Halo Jones. From the expression on Lord Bute's face, both men would undoubtedly be sentenced to hang.

Despite what his onetime friend had done, Daniel felt a pang of grief that was interrupted by pats on his back as Lord Tennyson and the rest of his colleagues offered him congratulations.

Through it all, the only thing Daniel could focus on was the shine of hope in Morgan's eyes as she watched him.

Pulling the ropes from his wrists, he tore off his jacket, putting it around her shoulders. He rubbed her arms, desperate to bring color back into her lips and pale cheeks.

"Lieutenant." Daniel motioned to the soldier. "Unlock the chains. Free her."

"Wait!" King George commanded.

Daniel turned to the altar, pulling her to his side as he did.

"Morgan may have been cleared of the crimes against the *Intrepid*, but she's still a pirate, Lord Leighton," the king said. "An outlaw wanted by the courts of England. She must stand trial for her offenses."

Daniel shook his head, not believing he'd come so close to freeing her, only to be shoved back down to defeat.

"No." The single word pushed through his body, shaking his lungs, his limbs, the very air around him. "No."

"Daniel," Lord Tennyson urged. "You can hire the best legal counsel for her. Perhaps . . ."

Daniel knew how that sentence would end. Perhaps they would be lenient and make her death quick and painless. That would be the most he could hope for. She couldn't stand trial; she couldn't. He wouldn't allow it.

He felt his bones go rigid, his muscles strain with the need for action. Blood pulsed through his body like acid, burning him with fury. "It's your fault she's a pirate, Your Majesty! You're the one responsible for the crimes you believe she committed!"

"Daniel, please," Morgan whispered, her eyes going wide with horror.

"You go too far, Daniel," Lord Tennyson warned.

He ignored them both. "You failed her, Your Grace, as your grandfather did before you."

"You're testing my patience, Lord Leighton," King George said, his young features sharpening. "I listened to your claims about Thomas Burke, but you can't convince me that this woman is innocent. Or that I am to blame for her crimes."

"I wouldn't even try, Your Majesty, because she is guilty." Daniel faced her, saw the surprise in her eyes. He slowly circled behind her as a solicitor would a witness on trial. "She's guilty of shouldering the sole responsibility for her family and the people of her village. A task made nearly impossible because of the Crown's heavy taxation, and the pillaging of her village. Her people were starving, dying before her eyes, and she had no way to help them and no one to turn to. There were no young men left in her village; you'd taken them to fight your war.

"She's guilty of trying to survive," Daniel said, laying his hands on her shoulders. He felt her tremors through the weight of his coat, and each one tore through him. "What she did may have been wrong, but she did what she had to. Men like you and I gave her no other choice. *We* should be the ones on trial for the crimes we forced on her."

"Is this true?" King George glanced at his advisor. "People were starving?"

Lord Bute lifted his shoulders in a shrug that said, *What did you expect?*

"She raided ships for food and nothing more?" the king asked Daniel, a troubled frown marring his youthful face.

"Nothing more."

"And you believe she's killed no one?"

"I know she hasn't."

"What about her vicious reputation?" King George demanded.

"Rumors, tall stories passed from one sailor to another."

King George glanced doubtfully at Lord Bute, then back to Daniel. "What's to keep her from returning to her criminal life?"

"Not what, Your Majesty, but who."

"The time grows late, Lord Leighton," the king complained in a tired voice. "Don't speak to me in riddles."

"*I* intend to keep her out of trouble."

"And how do you intend to accomplish this?"

"By marrying her."

Morgan spun in his arms. "You can't!"

"I must agree with her," Lord Tennyson said. "A marriage between the Earl of Leighton and a pirate would be highly irregular."

"To put it mildly." King George signaled that he'd had enough of the meeting. "In payment for doubting you and having you arrested, Lord Leighton, I'll offer this. Find another way to guarantee she won't return to her criminal life, and I'll grant her amnesty. But I can't agree to your marrying a commoner. It's out of the question."

Thomas was back in jail where he belonged, and Morgan was almost free; Daniel refused to give up now. "She might be a commoner, Your Majesty, but she's also the strongest woman I've ever known. How many women—or men— do you know who would sacrifice their life for someone they loved? Morgan has done so, willingly. Time and again."

Sighing with exasperation, King George hesitated as if unsure whether he should leave or order them all thrown in jail. Lord Bute whispered something in the king's ear. Daniel waited, anxiety tightening every nerve until he thought his spine would snap. He couldn't imagine the fear Morgan must be feeling. He wanted to gather her in his arms, reassure her, but he couldn't. Not yet.

"Oh, I see. That could possibly work," King George muttered to his advisor. Straightening, he faced his audience. "You say Morgan is willing to sacrifice everything for others, Lord Leighton. You seem prepared to do the same for her."

"I am."

"You realize your peers will ostracize you if you take her as a wife."

"My peers will change their minds when they come to know her," Daniel assured him.

"And if they don't?"

"I love her, Your Majesty," Daniel said, watching her, relieved to finally say the words he should have told her before now. Her eyes filled with tears. "It wouldn't matter."

"Yes," the king mused in a thoughtful tone. "I can see that you do. If I release her to your care, she'll be your responsibility. By that, I mean if she ever, *ever*," the King stressed, "sails the *Sea Queen* again, or if anyone related to her, you included, has anything whatsoever to do with pirating from this day forward, you will all suffer for it. I'll not show you mercy again."

King George focused his pale blue eyes on Morgan. "Do you understand? I will have you hunted down and hanged on the spot if I hear even a whisper that Morgan the Scylla is pirating my seas."

Morgan drew a shuddering breath. "You have my word."

Daniel took the key from the lieutenant and unlocked the chains weighing her wrists, a task made difficult because his hands were shaking. He dropped the chains to the floor with a clank that resonated throughout the room.

He lifted Morgan in his arms, crushed her against his chest and carried her from the chapel—and never looked back.

Chapter 20

The wind blew hot through Morgan's hair, lifting the strands, tangling them behind her as the *Devil's Luck* cut through the North Sea, heading for home. The brush of heat seeping through her pores and curling through her blood wasn't enough. She needed more. Remnants of bone-cold fear still trembled through her heart, beneath her skin. Her fingers were stiff where they gripped her arms through the wool of Daniel's coat. She still wore the wispy gown she'd donned the night before. The gauzy material, now dry and whisper soft, molded to her legs. She should go below, find something of the crew's to wear, but she couldn't bring herself to move.

She needed to smell the salty open air, see the glare of morning light where it washed the unfurled sails before splashing across the polished deck. They'd sailed past Harwich. Dunmore was little more than an hour away. She tilted her face to the sun, begging it to warm her, pour its strength into her limbs.

After the unbelievable meeting with King George, Daniel had carried her from the chapel, refusing to let her walk. He hadn't allowed her to ride her own horse to the ship,

but had placed her before him. His arms had been a vise
around her waist, his chest a wall at her back. She'd welcomed the feel of him, his warmth and strength of will.
She needed more of that now, she thought, before they
reached Dunmore and she was forced to say good-bye.

He'd offered to marry her, but she knew he'd said it
only as a last resort to save her life. He hadn't meant it,
and she wouldn't hold him to it.

"I love her, Your Majesty." Tears brimmed her eyes, just
as they had when he'd made his vow. If only it were possible.
She rubbed the nape of her neck and called herself a fool.
She was alive, and free. She would see her family again.
That should be enough, but the ache in her heart told
her it wasn't. *"I intend to keep her out of trouble,"* Daniel had
told the king. *"By marrying her."*

She pressed her fingers to her lips, blinking to help the
wind dry her tears before they fell. Her thoughts tumbled
through her mind, and she was powerless to stop them. If
only it weren't impossible for them to marry; if only it
wouldn't ruin his name, his reputation, the very life he'd
built. But marrying Daniel was as feasible as catching falling
stars.

Turning, she spotted him at the stern of the ship, speaking to Mr. Tobitt. She assumed they were discussing their
heading, because Daniel pointed to the sails and spoke.
Probably ordering a change in direction. They would need
to reduce their speed before sailing into Dunmore's cove.
There was no need to keep her village a secret any longer,
she reasoned, not now that the king knew her real identity.

A gust of wind caught Daniel's shirt, flattening it against
his muscled chest and tapered waist. He'd rolled the white
linen sleeves halfway up his forearms, revealing taut muscles. His hair was pulled back into a queue; a beard shadowed his jaw. He smiled at something Mr. Tobitt said, and
Morgan found herself smiling as well.

He needed an earring, she thought, maybe a rapier

sheathed at his side; then he'd look like a true pirate. She glanced down at her tattered gown and realized she looked like a helpless maiden, kidnapped from her bed for some scandalous purpose. Ransom, perhaps, or maybe she was his lost love?

"Sail away with me, Daniel," she whispered to herself. Then she closed her eyes and turned to face the wind, shutting the impossible wish away.

A warm shiver ran over her back, and she knew Daniel had crossed the deck and now stood behind her. She opened her eyes, but she couldn't face him. "The tides around Dunmore can be dangerous. Perhaps I should pilot the ship in."

She felt his eyes on her, questioning, assessing. "We aren't stopping at Dunmore. Leighton Castle is further north."

She steeled herself against the lure those words possessed. She couldn't believe them. She couldn't let *him* believe them, either. Turning, she said, "You told the king you'd marry me to save my life. I'm grateful you offered, but I'll not hold you to it."

Daniel braced his arms on either side of the railing, trapping her. "Is that so?"

"Don't smile at me, Daniel," she ordered, furious that he could behave with such lightheartedness when she felt as if she were breaking in two. "I won't marry you."

His grin vanished. "Aye, you will, the moment we reach my home."

"And what of your mother?" she demanded. "Will you shame her by marrying a commoner?"

"Don't worry about my mother. I'll take care of everything."

"You'll take care of everything, all right. If you tie yourself to me, you'll bring your home and name and wealth down around your ears. I come from a different world,

Daniel. I won't fit in," she declared, when what she really meant was she'd never be accepted.

She could tolerate criticism, even disapproval, but Daniel deserved a wife he could be proud of. A woman who'd bring honor to his family, not shame.

No, she had to end this now, or he'd try to fight the world for her. He'd gain nothing but his own destruction. No matter how much she loved him, needed him, she would never allow that to happen.

"Sail ho!" a sailor called down from the masthead.

Morgan crossed the deck and saw a three-mast vessel approaching on their port side. The ship cut through four-foot swells with ease. Morgan gripped the railing as the other ship's sails were adjusted, bringing her on an intercept course with the *Devil's Luck*. The pulse in her throat began to pound, the rushing sound blocking the call of the wind, the creak of the hull, the curious questions passing from man to man.

She recognized the vessel. How could she not? She knew it as well as she knew her own name.

"Oh, God," she said, though the word barely made it past her throat.

"Well, that's a ship I never wanted tae lay eyes on again," Mr. Tobitt said, coming up beside them. "Pardon me for saying so, Morgan."

"What the hell are they doing?" Daniel demanded, taking the spyglass from Tobitt.

She pressed both hands over her mouth, too stunned to answer. How . . . ? Why . . . ? From the *Sea Queen's* mainmast, a Jolly Roger snapped in the breeze like a challenge. Seconds rushed by, the ships closing their distance like two enemies in a deadly dance. She spotted her crew hurrying over the decks preparing . . . preparing to do what? That she didn't know, couldn't even attempt to guess.

Why had they left the village? She'd told them they could never return to sea. But they didn't know how imperative that order now was. King George's warning still burned in her ears. *"I will have you hunted down and hanged on the spot if I ever hear Morgan the Scylla is pirating my seas."* That warning had extended to Daniel, as well. And Jo and Grace.

"Tobitt," Daniel said, looking through the telescope. "Have the gunner man the cannons."

She gripped his arm. "You can't attack them."

"I don't know their intent, or who they are, for that matter."

"I'm sure it's Jo."

"It could be, unless *she* was captured."

"Don't fire, Daniel, please."

"I don't plan to unless they force me." Looking through the spyglass again, he gritted his teeth and growled, "Bloody hell. Jo *is* captaining the *Sea Queen.* Any idea what she's up to?"

Morgan took the telescope and searched the other ship, holding her breath when she found her sister standing midship, her legs firmly planted on the swaying deck. Jo pointed to several crewmen and issued an order, sending them hurrying to complete some task. Even from this distance, Morgan could tell that the blood of adventure ran hot in her sister's veins. She'd always thought pirating was a game. Had she decided to ignore the dangers of roving the sea? Apparently she had, not caring if she risked everyone's life.

Morgan closed the telescope with a furious snap. "I've been gone barely two weeks, and already she's playing captain. How can she be so irresponsible?"

"Would she recognize this ship as Halo's?" Daniel asked, his voice grated with irritation.

"Probably, which means she *should* turn her vessel and sail in the opposite direction."

"But Jo won't."

"No, she won't. My sister does love a challenge. She still hasn't forgiven me for not allowing her to kill anyone."

Daniel looked down at her, his eyes glittering with humor. "You are heartless, aren't you?"

Brushing her forehead with a kiss, he turned away, ordering the sails lowered and an anchor to be dropped, which would slow the ship. Within minutes, the ship glided over the ocean's surface. The *Sea Queen* had done the same, gradually moving within a narrow distance of the *Devil's Luck*. Jo ordered grappling lines thrown over. As restless as the seas were, a warning pushed up the back of Morgan's throat. This was insanity. They couldn't bring the ships close enough to board. Someone could fall while crossing and be crushed or drown.

No one else seemed of the same mind. Soon, the ships were moored together, and a sturdy plank was laid across the railings.

Jo crossed to the *Devil's Luck* first, her steps bold and confident. Grace was right behind her, then Uncle Simon, Jackson, Henry and a dozen others, all landing on deck and fanning out in a circle around Daniel. When the last man gained the wooden plank, Morgan tensed, recognizing him. Peter.

Moving to Daniel's side, she watched in dismay as each man from the *Sea Queen* drew a sword or dagger.

Daniel tensed, and she knew he was prepared to order his men to draw their weapons. Morgan placed a hand on his forearm, stopping him.

Not wanting to meet Peter's closed expression, she frowned at her sister. "Why have you brought the *Sea Queen* out? I told you it was too risky."

"I didn't like the idea of you dying and becoming a martyr," Jo said with a smirk. She lifted her sword, holding the tip two feet from Daniel's chest. "We decided to rescue you."

"How did you find me?" Morgan moved in front of him, not trusting that her sister wouldn't do something foolish.

"We were lucky," Peter said uneasily, glancing from her to Daniel. He was obviously confused; she didn't blame him, because she knew just how he felt. "We set sail to search for you the day you vanished."

The day of her wedding. The unspoken reminder vibrated between them. She frantically wondered if he'd challenge Daniel—Peter had every right to—but his eyes were flat, unreadable, his jaw tight. She didn't know him well enough any longer to know what his expression meant, what he might be thinking or feeling.

Jo's gaze narrowed. "Move out of my way, sister. You aren't the target. He is."

Morgan turned her attention to her sister. "Put the sword down, Jo."

Jo ignored her order and instead glanced down Morgan's body, noting her revealing dress. Her mouth thinned with anger. "What have you been doing to my sister, Captain Tremayne?"

Gripping Morgan's waist, he lifted her aside as if she weighed no more than air. In a warning tone that trembled her bones, he answered, "Saving her life."

"Isn't that an oxymoron, Captain?" Jo arched a russet brow and laughed. "You *kidnapped* her so you could *save* her?"

"Morgan!" Grace called, running forward and wrapping her arms around her waist. "We've been so worried about you."

Morgan ran her hands over her sister's silver blond hair. She had to get everyone back to their village and hide the ship. But she had no idea how to break the volatile moment. Jo made the decision for her.

"Board the *Sea Queen*, Morgan," Jo ordered. "We're taking you home. If the captain knows what's good for him, he'll forget where we live."

"No," Daniel said.

"Morgan," Peter said hesitantly. "You don't have to be afraid of him. He can't stop you from leaving."

Grace pursed her mouth in a frown as she glared at Peter. "She's not afraid of the captain. She loves him."

"She's coming with us." A cunning smile curved Jo's full mouth as she cut her sword through the air in warning.

Daniel turned just as Mr. Tobitt tossed him a rapier. Assuming a stance that matched Jo's, he said, "She's staying with me."

Morgan pushed Grace toward Jackson. "Stop this, both of you!" She gripped Daniel's arm, tried to lower it, but it was no use. "Let me go with her, Daniel. This is for the best."

"So you can marry a man you don't love?" he demanded, his eyes never leaving Jo's. "I don't believe so."

Morgan risked a quick glance at Peter, and realized he wasn't surprised or enraged by Daniel's declaration.

"What do you say?" Jo purred to Daniel. "Do we fight for her?"

"No, you will not." Morgan moved between the pair, the tips of both weapons inches from her body. "Jo, I command you to drop your sword."

"I'm afraid I can't do that, sister."

"Move aside, Morgan. You're not leaving."

She faced Daniel, tears pushing to the surface. "Why are you doing this?"

"I faced the king to earn your freedom. I'm certainly not going to give you up now because your sister and crew want you back."

"I told you I won't marry you."

"You're going to be my wife, Morgan. And you're going to live at Leighton Castle. Accept it."

"Your wife?" Grace repeated on a gasp.

"But she's to marry me," Peter added in a tone far from insistent.

"Perhaps once, but no more." Daniel straightened to his full height and tossed his sword to the deck.

Peter lifted his hands in an unsure gesture. "Morgan, what is it you want? I don't pretend to know what has happened, but it's obvious to me that there is something between the two of you."

Gripping Morgan's hips and stopping her from answering, Daniel pulled her to him. "She wants to be my wife."

She numbly shook her head. "I can't."

"Yes, you can, Morgan," Grace insisted with a disgruntled sigh.

"You said you loved me," Daniel said. "Were you lying?"

"Of course not."

"Then there's no reason we can't marry."

She pushed against his chest, furious that he was teasing her, tempting her with an impossible dream. "There's every reason. I'm a pirate."

"Who's been granted amnesty."

"Amnesty?" Jo blurted.

"She'll tell you about it later," Daniel said.

"I'm still engaged to Peter. I'd be his wife if you hadn't kidnapped me."

"Then it's a good thing Captain Tremayne escaped that horrible island and found us," Grace piped in. "You don't love Peter, Morgan, and Peter doesn't love you. Isn't that so?" Grace asked, turning to the other man.

Peter opened his mouth to answer, but shrugged instead. "I would have done my best by you, Morgan. You must know that."

"Oh, Peter . . ." Morgan didn't know what else to say. He was a good man, but regardless of what happened once she left Daniel's ship, she couldn't marry him.

"I take that to mean your engagement is at an end." Daniel gave her a smug grin.

"That changes nothing," she said, scowling because he had the gall to smile. "I'm a commoner. Your peers will never accept me and they'll ostracize you."

"My peers will accept you, just as my crew has."

She glanced at Mr. Tobitt, who'd once fainted at her feet, and Roscoe and the other crewmen who'd routinely made the sign of the cross when she passed. Each man smiled and nodded, supporting Daniel's claim.

Did she dare believe them? They had accepted her, but they were as common as she was. England's wealthy wouldn't be so tolerant. Or forgiving.

"I love you, Daniel," she said, fisting her hands in his shirt. "And I would be proud to be your wife, but I won't do that to you."

"You are the most stubborn . . ." Daniel released a frustrated breath; the muscles in his jaw clenched. "Were you always a pirate, Morgan?"

She frowned. "No."

"You taught yourself how to be one."

She nodded hesitantly, not understanding what he was trying to say.

"So you *learned* how to be a pirate."

"What does that have to do with anything?"

"It has everything to do with our future. I have no doubt you can learn how to be a lady. My lady."

Tears blurred her vision. She shook her head. "Not the kind you deserve."

"Before we met, do you know the kind of woman I thought I deserved?"

She closed her eyes, certain she didn't want to hear him list qualities she'd never possess.

"I wanted a woman who was meek, who would never voice her opinion because my wife wouldn't have the audacity to have one."

"Then I would never make you happy." She glanced to the side, achingly aware that both crews were listening to Daniel, knowing his list would grow longer and more painful to hear.

He continued as if she hadn't spoken. "I *thought* I wanted a woman who needed to be cared for, one who wouldn't concern herself with anything more troublesome than which gown to wear and which ball to attend. She would have nannies to tend to her children and servants to keep her home. If she was pretty, I'd consider that a bonus."

"I'm sure you know any number of women who would love to fill that challenging role," Morgan snapped with sarcasm. Meek and witless? Was that truly the kind of woman he wanted? She would never, ever be the wife he described.

"Yes, Morgan, I could have had my pick." He nodded, straightening, staring at her with such longing that her throat went dry. "Then I met you."

She held up her hand to stop him, but he grabbed hold of her hand and pressed it to where his heart beat firm and sure. "For the first time in my life I met a woman— a pirate, of all things—who loved with all her heart, who had enough courage to risk her life to save the people who relied on *her*. She should have been taken care of, yet she was the strength and backbone of her family."

"Daniel, please stop."

"That is the woman I fell in love with, Morgan," he said in a quiet voice that made her want to believe. "That's the woman I intend to marry."

He kissed her brow, then gathered both her hands and brought them to his lips. "You didn't have a choice before, but you have one now. Morgan, you've done your job, you've sacrificed your happiness, you've saved your village. It's time to make a new choice. You can return to your quiet life in Dunmore. Or . . ."

He kissed her hands, making it difficult for her to breathe.

"You can sail away with me," he whispered, repeating the prayer she'd voiced only a short time ago.

Tears fell from her eyes.

"Share a life with me."

Her heart and mind swirled with confusion. She tasted salty tears in her mouth, felt the heat of Daniel's body pressed to hers—a sensation she wished could go on forever. She wanted to say yes, shout to the sky that she'd marry him, but how could she? He would sacrifice everything. Why didn't he see that his friends would turn their backs on him? His business would suffer. The home he'd fought to save would be in jeopardy once again. His world would change into something he despised, causing him to hate her in the end.

"I can't marry you," she said resolutely, though she loathed each word.

"I'm willing to risk sharing my life with a stubborn pirate." Pressing her hands to his chest, he added, "You're courageous, Morgan. And willful and determined. It's time you took a risk for yourself."

"Daniel—"

"Marry me," he said in a furious whisper.

"Say yes, Morgan," Grace pleaded from behind her.

Morgan glanced at both her sisters, then at Peter, who, smiling, nodded his approval.

"Marry me," Daniel urged again, touching his brow to hers.

"Bloody hell, Morgan," Jo scoffed. "Say yes."

She felt her resistance breaking. She tried to put it back together, but her dreams slipped through, making her want to grasp Daniel to her and keep him forever. Her heart pounded against her chest, hurting with the amount of love she felt for him. She gave him a watery, trembling smile. "I love you."

"Then be my wife."

"You're going to regret this someday."

"Never," he vowed. "Now tell me yes."

Smiling through her tears, she repeated, "Yes."

Cheers roared around the deck, lifting toward the sky. Daniel wrapped her in his arms. Smiling, he bent to kiss her, a tender, sweeping kiss that promised a lifetime of joy. Each touch of his lips melted away her doubts and fears, yet one thought remained, circling her mind like a familiar voice.

Life was made of choices. This time she'd made the right one.

Epilogue

"If you're going to do it," Jo said, glaring at the torch in Morgan's hand, "then let's get it over with."

"Are you sure this is the only way?" Grace worried her bottom lip. Her blue eyes reflected like crystals in the receding dusk.

"Aye, it has to be done." Holding the torch aloft, Morgan wished it wasn't so, because carrying out her last duty as captain of the *Sea Queen* was breaking her heart.

Daniel and a skeleton crew had helped sail the vessel into deep water a league off Dunmore's coast, where she was now anchored. The men had disembarked and were waiting below in a dinghy for Morgan and her sisters to join them. They had to hurry. Night approached in a blanket of mist.

"But—" Grace started to object.

"Morgan's made up her mind," Jo huffed. "Nothing we say will change it." Turning away, she softened her voice. "She's right, Grace. The *Sea Queen* will only put us in danger if we keep her."

"But do we have to burn her?" Grace propped her fists on her slender hips, giving Morgan a glimpse of the headstrong woman she would become. It stunned her to realize her baby sister wasn't a baby any longer. "Can't we keep her in the cove at Dunmore? She could be our very own museum."

"It's too risky," Morgan said, though her tone lacked conviction.

"Maybe not." A glimmer of mischief warmed Jo's eyes. "You're married. *He* certainly won't allow you to sail her again."

Morgan didn't bristle as she might have two months before, because she knew Jo had softened toward Daniel, forgiving him for his aristocratic ties. He'd done more than marry Morgan. He'd taken her sisters into his home and brought work to her village for those who wanted it.

The flame snapped with the breeze, hissing at the damp night air, reminding her that it was time to act. Yet she hesitated in raising the fire to the sails bound to the yard above her.

Her heart belonged to Daniel—that she couldn't deny—but a part of her would always belong to the sea— and her ship. The *Sea Queen* had saved their lives, kept their small village from disappearing into obscurity. It had brought her to the love of her life.

How could she destroy it?

"Maybe Grace is right," Morgan said, more to herself but her sisters heard her.

"What do you mean?" Jo asked, mimicking Grace's stance.

Morgan reached for the knife at her waist and withdrew it from its leather sheath. She held the polished dagger balanced in her palm; the large ruby, sapphire and emerald sparkled like colored glass. The metal warmed against her skin, as if the carved hilt were slowly awakening, waiting for her command.

"What are you doing?" Jo asked.

Morgan extended her arm, holding the *Sea Queen* blade out to her middle sister. "Take it."

Jo shook her head and took a step back. "It's yours. It always has been."

"That was because I captained the ship. Take it."

Hesitantly, Jo reached for the blade. When her hand was within inches from touching the knife, Morgan closed her fingers around the hilt. "It's yours on one condition."

Jo narrowed her gaze. "Say it."

"Give me your word you'll never take the *Sea Queen* from our cove."

"What are you talking about? You're going to burn her."

"No, she isn't," Grace whispered with an angelic smile.

Jo's eyes rounded with dismay and hope. A smile threatened, but she kept it from taking full bloom.

"Give me your word, Jo." Morgan's arm trembled with her conflicting needs. She wanted to keep the knife that had become the symbol of their survival close to her heart, yet she knew she had to pass it on. It wasn't her burden to carry any longer. "You know the king's warning. I must have your word."

Jo nodded solemnly. "You have it."

Morgan opened her fingers, letting Jo take the knife. As the weight lifted away, she realized she'd made another choice that would affect their lives. Would Daniel think her insane for keeping the *Sea Queen?* Would he understand that she acted out of love for the ship that had changed their lives? She decided he would. But there was another, more compelling reason she couldn't destroy the vessel.

The well-sanded deck, the curved hull that groaned like a familiar song, the sails that had been mended time and again were a reminder that even when choices were difficult, anything was possible when you acted out of love. It was a lesson she didn't want to forget.

Smiling at her sisters, she said, "Let's take her home."

We hope you've enjoyed ONCE A PIRATE. Now look for Tammy Hilz's next installment of the Jewels of the Sea series, ONCE A REBEL, available February 2001 in stores everywhere!

A burning hatred for the pampered aristocracy leads Joanna Fisk into the heart of glittering London society, where she meets Nathan Alcott. To raise money for a shelter, hot-tempered Jo decides to rename the *Sea Queeen* and take it back to the seas as the *Sea Witch*. When she learns Nathan's secretly taking a cache of gold to France, she attacks his ship. Taking the gold . . . and Nathan as her prisoner . . . leads Jo into a dangerous adventure as they race to save his kidnapped sister. As passion rises between them, Jo is stunned to realize that she's fallen in love with the very man she's supposed to hate.

ABOUT THE AUTHOR

After selling the computer resale business she owned with her husband, Tammy Hilz left the corporate world to answer the creative voice that had been whispering to her for years. Thus began her new career in writing, a challenge she hasn't once regretted. Winner of the prestigious RWA Golden Heart award, she lives in McKinney, Texas with her husband, Steve, her three children, John, Christi and Trevor and two obstinate cats, Bonnie and Clyde. You can write to her at: *hilz_tammy@msn.com*

COMING IN NOVEMBER FROM
ZEBRA BALLAD ROMANCES

__EMILY'S WISH, Wishing Well #2
by Joy Reed   0-8217-6713-5 $5.50US/$7.50CAN

Intent upon escaping her troubled past, Miss Emily Pearce flees into the night, only to come upon Honeywell House. Rescued from uncertainty by celebrated author, Sir Terrence O'Reilly, Emily becomes the heroine of the greatest love story of all—their own.

__A KNIGHT'S PASSION, The Kinsmen #2
by Candice Kohl   0-8217-6714-3 $5.50US/$7.50CAN

Ordered by the King to wed two cousins from the borderlands of Wales, Raven and Peter met their match in Lady Pamela and Roxanne. Thrown into marriage by royal decree, the brothers soon find that what began as punishment can end in love.

__ADDIE AND THE LAIRD, Bogus Brides
by Linda Lea Castle   0-8217-6715-1 $5.50US/$7.50CAN

Seeking a fresh start in a virgin territory, the Green sisters leave for the charter town of MacTavish. There is only one thing that stands between the sisters and a new life ... they have one month to wed if they are to remain in MacTavish. Will the necessity to leave lead to the discovery of love?

__ROSE, The Acadians #2
by Cherie Claire   0-8217-6716-X $5.50US/$7.50CAN

Warm, vibrant, and exceedingly lovely, Rose Gallant vowed to keep alive her family's dream of finding her long-lost father, but her heart dreams of finding true love. Amid the untamed forests and moss-strewn swamps of Louisiana Territory, Rose discovers the fulfillment of love.

Call toll free **1-888-345-BOOK** to order by phone or use this coupon to order by mail. ALL BOOKS AVAILABLE NOVEMBER 1, 2000.

Name _____

Address _____

City _____ State _____ Zip _____

Please send me the books I have checked above.

I am enclosing	$ _____
Plus postage and handling*	$ _____
Sales tax (in NY and TN)	$ _____
Total amount enclosed	$ _____

*Add $2.50 for the first book and $.50 for each additional book.

Send check or money order (no cash or CODS) to:

Kensington Publishing Corp., Dept. C.O., 850 Third Avenue, New York, NY 10022

Prices and numbers subject to change without notice. Valid only in the U.S. All orders subject to availabilty. **NO ADVANCE ORDERS.**

Visit our website at **www.kensingtonbooks.com.**